"Good evening, madam. M...

Diarmid lounged nonchalantl... ...aming length of fat pine held in... ...his granite jaw. The ...ickering light cast demonic shadows on the planes and angles of his lean face, and Lucy froze, stunned. It was as if the gut-tering flame had transformed the Highlander from an arrogant, flesh-and-blood man to a rakish, cruelly handsome demon.

He cast her a searing aquamarine gaze, then bent to light his pipe. The fat pine had burned down to an ember, leaving only Diarmid's wide, sensual mouth and gleaming white teeth illu-minated by its glow. He held the spark to the bowl and puffed. The rich, spicy scent of Orinoco tobacco drifted to her nostrils.

Lucy's heart thundered to life. She had to bolt, run, escape, but her feet were leaden blocks welded to the floor. Before she could force her stunned extremities to life, Diarmid's hand shot out and gripped her upper arm in a firm but painless clasp. He drew closer, and there was no mistaking the menace beneath his velvet touch.

They stood thus for what seemed like eternity. Slowly, Lucy's numbed senses thawed. She could hear the slow rhythm of Diarmid's breathing and for one mad instant, she fancied she could hear the steady beat of his heart. His breath caressed her cheek, soft and intoxicatingly scented with cherry and tobacco and fine French brandy. He chuckled, in-exorably drawing her into the predatory challenge of his eyes.

Her heart raced beneath her confining stays, fast, faster, until she thought it would burst from her throat. Desperate to still her maddened pulse, she clutched her free hand to her bodice. It touched the outline of the candlestick she had thrust between her breasts. Blank horror swept over her, and all coherent thought vanished from her mind.

Diarmid's lips brushed her ear. "I would like to think, madam, that passion for your husband has driven you here, helpless before your desires."

Dear Romance Reader,

In July, we launched the Ballad line with four new series, and each month we'll present both new and continuing stories set everywhere from medieval England to the American West—the kind of passionate, romantic stories you love best, written by the most gifted authors. At the back of each book, we'll tell you when you can find subsequent books in the series that have captured your heart.

This month talented Cindy Harris introduces the charming new *Dublin Dreams* series. When an anonymous benefactor brings together four penniless women in one stately Dublin square, none of them expect to find love. Yet in the first book, the widow of a dissolute gambler meets her romantic match when she has **A Bright Idea.** Next, rising star Linda Lea Castle presents the second of a trio of spirited *Bogus Brides.* In **Mattie and the Blacksmith,** a schoolteacher who longs to be properly courted discovers that the most unlikely suitor may be the one who steals her heart.

Fabulous new author Lynne Hayworth is also back with the second installment of the *Clan Maclean* series, **Autumn Flame.** Will a spirited pickpocket make a proper wife for the overseer of a Virginia plantation? Finally, Cherie Claire concludes the atmospheric *Acadians* trilogy with the story of **Gabrielle,** a woman who will risk anything to save the bold privateer who had claimed her, body and soul. Enjoy!

Kate Duffy
Editorial Director

The Clan Maclean

AUTUMN FLAME

Lynne Hayworth

ZEBRA BOOKS

Kensington Publishing Corp.

http://www.zebrabooks.com

ZEBRA BOOKS are published by

Kensington Publishing Corp.
850 Third Avenue
New York, NY 10022

All Kensington Titles, Imprints and Distributed Lines are available at special quantity discounts for bulk purchases for sales promotion premiums, fund-raising, educational or institutional use.

Special book excerpts or customized printings can also be created to fit specific needs. For details, write or phone the office of the Kensington special sales manager: Kensington Publishing Corp., 850 Third Avenue, New York, NY 10022, attn: Special Sales Department, Phone: 1-800-221-2647.

Zebra and the Z logo Reg. U.S. Pat. & TM Off.

First Printing: April, 2001
10 9 8 7 6 5 4 3 2 1

Printed in the United States of America

One

Lucy Graves gnawed her lip and peered at the cracked fragment of mirror hanging on the alehouse wall. Six centuries of smoke had blackened the chamber's crumbling plaster and bare timbers, and ghostly white fingers of fog crept in through the open window. The Mermaid Tavern made a prime spot for her capers, for 'twas popular with seamen both exotic and common, and it lay but a short stagger from the muddy, reeking waters of the Thames, where barques and brigs and men-o'-war floated silently at anchor.

She sighed, then slanted a defiant glance at her reflection. She could avoid it no longer, curse it all. But when it came down to a choice between prostitution and thievery, she would pick stealing every time.

She jerked up her chin. Aye, she was a thief, and no denying it. That lone, dismal fact had assumed the heft and breadth and height of the most unscaleable prison walls over the last ten years—years in which the rigors of survival had far outweighed her dreams of respectability. She doubted not at all that prison would be her end, but at least she had a reason for her deeds: No matter what, she would *not* follow in her mother's footsteps. That road led to ruin as surely as the Thames led to the sea.

Suddenly, like a creature from the blackest depths of that sea, Lucy's stepfather loomed up behind her. She scowled at his reflection in the mirror's wavy glass, but before she could recite a silent Romany curse, Jock O'Donohue lurched forward and caught her around the waist. He reeked of stale piss, rotten teeth, and ha'penny ale.

"'Ere. No time to primp, me fine wench. Get yer arse in that there chair and thank the devil yer Gypsy da left ye some tricks along with that bonnie face. Not that ye got the sense to profit from them—without me firm hand to guide ye, that is." Jocko turned, snatched up Lucy's scarlet wool shawl—a prize her brother Mick had begged from a flogging school bawd—and tossed it over the rickety table in the center of the chamber.

Lucy knotted a frayed kerchief over her rippling black hair. 'Twas useless to argue. Fighting with Jocko merely brought a vicious slap from his filthy, callused hand; or worse, the threat of forcing her onto the streets as a strumpet, a doxy— oh God's bones, as a whore. There; she'd said it. Best to call a spade a spade. She shivered, although the low-ceilinged chamber was hot this early June evening. Jocko—blast his putrid soul to the eternal pits of hell—had forced her mother onto the streets and into an early grave dug by clap and starvation. She wouldn't let him do the same to her—or to Mick.

Jocko stumped through the chamber door and shambled downstairs. The wail of a fiddle and the off-key strains of a bawdy song drifted up from the taproom, where Jocko had lined up their first customers of the evening: a young pair of lovers fresh from the country, eager to taste the thrills of London's East End. The cove was drunk, Jocko had told her, and the wench was itching to hear her fortune from the famous Madame Zora—better known to Alsatia's rufflers, vagrants, pickpockets and bawds as Mistress Lucy Graves.

Mick popped from his hiding place behind the moth-eaten curtain that covered the back wall of the chamber. He waggled his brows and flashed her a gap-toothed grin. "'Tis just one last time, Loose. Ye can do it. And we be desperate for the chink, aye?"

"I know we need the money." Lucy flounced down on a stool, then caught up her grandmother's tarot cards. They were the last gift she had received from her real father, Nikolas Gravesceu. She shuffled the deck and closed her eyes. If Da were alive, she'd never have sunk so low. And if it weren't for Jocko's vile ways, she wouldn't be here tonight.

In the ten years since her father's death, Lucy had saved every brass farthing—precious coins earned by dancing in the streets, serving ale in the taprooms, and *dukkering* fortunes to louts with more money than sense. She'd ferreted away every shilling that hadn't gone to fatten poor Mick's scrawny bones, and month by month and year by year, her leather bag of coins had grown larger. So had her dreams.

Lucy opened her eyes and glanced down. She clutched the tarot cards in a death grip, and stark white bands stood out across her fingernails. She had sworn she would get Mick away from here. Away from the rats and the shit in the streets, away from the consumption and scrofula and fleas. Away from the gangs of cutthroats and cutpurses who were more than anxious to recruit a spry, small lad like Mick into their perfidious ranks. But most of all, she had sworn to get them both away from Jocko.

She released her grip on the cards and sighed. Last week she had come home to find Jocko dead drunk in their fetid rookery near the stable on Half Moon street. Eager to add a threepence to her hoard, she had pried up the loose floorboard beneath her pallet, pulled out the leather sack, and gasped. It was empty.

Oh, Jocko had denied lifting it, and had beaten her black and blue for daring to hide money in the first place. But she knew the truth. His weeklong drunk and the bottles of old French brandy rolling about under his bed were all the proof she needed. Her money had vanished and so had her hopes.

Mick's piping voice caught her attention. "We ain't got no choice, Loose. Either I joins up with Black Jack's gang, or we cozen the yokels, or we starves." He snatched the cards from her hand and slapped them on the table. "Quick. They be comin'."

He darted across the chamber and blew out the candles, leaving just the whale oil lamp to light the room. Its guttering flame cast mysterious shadows on Lucy's tiny crystal ball, and she smiled. 'Twas a most effective touch. Mick scooted behind the curtain.

A tall young man dressed in a leather jerkin and rusty homespun breeches ducked into the room. He blinked, obviously disoriented by the eerie, still darkness after the glare and riot of the tavern below. His ladylove crowded in behind him, her rabbity eyes bright in a wide, freckled face.

Lucy shook back her waist-length black hair, then turned so the lamplight flashed on her gold hoop earrings. Fake gold, they were, but they added to the illusion. So far no bumpkins had noticed the difference.

"Good evening," she intoned. "Please shut the door." She fixed the cove with a penetrating gaze, then smiled enigmatically. Her slanted black eyes never failed to unnerve. She motioned toward two chairs, strategically placed with their blackened, carved backs just inches from Mick's hiding place. "Be seated and tell me, why do ye seek Madame Zora?"

The pair gulped and exchanged nervous glances.

"Ye have a question, no?" Lucy thickened her Romany accent. Thanks to the perfect mimic's ear she had inherited from her father, she could turn the exotic lilt off and on as needed. "A question of grave importance, mayhap?" She gazed meditatively at a spot just above the wench's head, then picked up her crystal ball and rolled it in her hand. "I start with your palm, madame. Your beautiful face tells much, but the palm tells all."

The girl blushed, then thrust out her hand. Lucy took it, paused a moment, then widened her eyes. "Ah, madame, ye have no ordinary palm! Ye have a palm of greatness, of destiny. There is much I can tell ye." She leaned forward, voice husky as a man's. "There's luck in your palm, madame. Much luck. Ye'll call to rememberment all your long life what Madame Zora tells you this night." She released the hand and sat back.

The wench looked dazed. "What do you see?"

"I can tell much more for half a bull. Half a crown to ye," Lucy added.

The girl pouted, then poked her lover in the ribs. "Pay her, Ned."

Ned groped sheepishly for his pocketbook, then slapped a coin on the table. Lucy palmed it, then darted a glance toward the curtain. Mick best be heads up. With the lamp guttering so low, it was darker than usual in here—but better too dark than too light. It never would do for this gangling oaf to catch her little brother's daddles in his pockets.

She smoothed her red-and-yellow striped skirts, then picked up her cards. The wench sounded as if she were from Yorkshire. Lucy's mother had been from those parts, and Lucy recognized the accent.

"Ye've undertaken a long journey," she declared, shuffling the deck with the blurred speed of lifelong practice. "A journey from the north." Smiles and astonished nods all around. "Ye've still a long way to go, and much be at stake. . . ." She stole a glance at the wench's waist, which bulged discreetly beneath her cloak. Much at stake, indeed. "But a promising—a *fruitful* outcome is sure."

The curtain gave a faint ripple, and Mick's muddy, gaptoed boot slid forward. Time to step things up. She held the tarot deck toward her customer. "The cards reveal all, madame. Please cut."

As the wench cut the deck, Lucy hypnotically waved her crystal ball inches above the lamp's blue flame. Then she began a low Romany chant. Ned stared, jaw sagging. In truth, so much of her art was illusion and misdirection—a vital skill, since Mick's scabby little paw was now creeping into Ned's pocket.

"Ahhhh!" she keened. Her stooges jumped, and Mick slipped back behind the curtain. Success. She brandished the deck over her head. Oh, she hated stealing, and she hated cadging poor innocent louts. But there was no other way. She had to get Mick out of London and away from Jocko once and for all. Mick loved and trusted her with all his oversized heart, and she couldn't fail him.

Quickly, she laid three cards on the table: the Wheel of Fortune, the Knight of Swords, and the Sun. Interesting.

"A great change be coming, and a grave hardship." She fixed the pair with a burning gaze. "And a man lies at the heart of it"—she winked at the girl—"as they always do, madame. But there be a promising outcome. Aye, right promising indeed."

The wench's eyes grew wide. "What kind of outcome?"

Lucy deftly swiped the cards back into the deck. " 'Tis impossible to tell. The cards keep their counsel." Now, if she could just get the lackwits out the door, she and Mick would be home free.

"But I got to know!" The girl clutched a hand over her belly. " 'Ere, Ned. Pay her more—"

Lucy froze. "No, madame, I prithee. 'Tis not a matter of money. The cards . . ."

Ned groped for his nicked pocketbook. He looked confused at its absence, then his brows lowered.

Lucy jumped up. "Pray excuse me—"

"Wait roight there." Ned lumbered to his feet like a bull ready to charge. "Me pocketbook's gone. Ye stole me money."

The wench gasped, then shrieked, "Thief! Thief! Help— we've been robbed!"

Lucy whirled and darted toward the door. She must draw them off Mick. Before she could reach it, the door burst open and the publican lurched into the room.

" 'Ere—wot's all this?"

Ned grabbed Lucy's arm and shook her until her teeth rattled. "This Gypsy bawd stole me pocketbook."

"Listen to me," Lucy gasped. "Ye're mistaken. Me hands never left your sight—"

A stumbling, thrashing, ripping sound interrupted her protest. The tall curtain tore from its rod and Mick tumbled into the melee. Lucy's heart contracted. Poor, brave, foolish Mick. How many times had he tried to save her from Jocko's beatings? He was her knight in shining armor; the only one she'd ever have.

"Stop it!" Mick kicked Ned in the shins. "Don't ye dare touch me sister!"

The publican grabbed Mick's birdlike arm and yanked him

toward the stairs. "I'll have no Gypsy tricks in my establishment. 'Tis Newgate for ye, me lad."

The crowd from the tavern surged up the stairs, slavering for diversion and reeking of smoke and vomit and cheap rotgut gin. "Thief, thief, thief!" they bellowed. " 'Tis Tyburn tree for thee!"

Then a voice—a slurred, sibilant Cockney voice—rose above the din: "Oi saw 'em nip his purse. They be in it together. Check the brat's pockets."

Lucy's shoulders slumped. There was no use fighting; she knew that voice. 'Twas Jocko, giving them up.

The magistrate hammered his gavel and Lucy stepped forward. The Old Bailey courtroom was just as Jocko had described it—and the vile sod should know, since he'd set an East End record for the number of times he'd been hauled up on drunkenness and rioting. The narrow, grimy windows admitted little light and no breeze, and flies buzzed through the somnolent air, adding their drone to the whispers, rustles, farts, and coughs of the restless crowd. Lucy shuddered at the nauseating stench of sour sweat and rotten teeth. God's nose, did she smell that bad? More than likely, for Newgate Prison had been even filthier than she had imagined.

She and Mick had spent a week in the notorious jail, dumped in a vast subterranean labyrinth of fetid cells along with streetwalkers, highwaymen, debtors, murderers, and thieves. To her astonishment, the inmates had wandered about freely, and they fought, flirted, and coupled in dank corners against the slimy stone walls.

Lucy's exotic beauty instantly had attracted a gang of leering coves, and she had spent her first night in Newgate with her mind racing and her arms wrapped around Mick. Earlier in the day she had given the turnkey her fake gold earrings in exchange for a stale bun and a putrid tankard of water for her brother. Now her tarot deck was her remaining object of value. She couldn't bear to part with it, but she knew the rules of Newgate: Food, clothes, and most of all, protection, must be purchased. If, come morning, she didn't have chink or goods to barter, she would be at the mercy of a gang of louts raring to dance the blanket jig.

The magistrate banged his gavel and the Old Bailey courtroom quieted. Lucy gripped Mick's hand and stepped before the judge, spine straight, chin up, head high. She fought the urge to cross her fingers. God's knees, would Old Dame Luck be with her? Her da had always said the Rom were the luckiest folk on earth, and in truth, it seemed his declaration was prophetic, for she had awakened that first morning in Newgate to familiar words.

"San to Rom? Come now, wake, lovely sister. *Tacho rat?"*

She sat up. Was someone speaking Romany? Here?

She twisted and faced the ugliest man she had ever seen. His pox-pitted skin gleamed like greased mahogany in the flaring torchlight. One eye was black and slanted and handsome, like hers; the other oozed a dull yellow crust that reminded her of dried egg. He all but bristled with wild black hair, a long, matted beard, and two dangling gold earrings. Real gold, this time. She'd stake her life on it.

"Mandi Rom," she whispered. "I am Gypsy."

The giant laughed, revealing teeth sharpened to points. He lifted her to her feet, then bent and shook Mick. "Up, *pralo.* Time to eat." He bowed to Lucy. "I am Ardaix, known to these *gorgios* as the Egyptian." He winked, then escorted them to a large cell containing a fresh straw pallet, an oak table and chairs, beeswax candles, and a whole roast chicken.

Lucy gasped, "God's ribs—roast fowl!"

Ardaix laughed and tossed a drumstick to Mick. "Here *chavo,* eat. I see that yer *bokhalo*—hungry," he added, noting Mick's puzzled gaze. He jerked his chin at Lucy. "The boy— he's not *tacho rat?"*

She shook her head. "Nay, not true blood. Mick's me halfbrother. He's eight. His proper name be Malachy O'Donohue, and I'm Lucy Graves . . . er, Gravesceu. We had the same mother but different fathers."

"Had?"

"Aye. Both my parents be dead."

And so their alliance began. Ardaix took them under his protection and made it clear to Newgate's scum that she was his distant kinswoman. As such, her virtue was unassailable, and any cove who pawed her would pay with his life.

" 'Tis a matter of *Rom* honor, no?" Ardaix had said the night before her trial. "These *jakals* see not that ye be a *rawnie*—a very great lady. But I see, and I help, eh?" With that, Ardaix had explained what she must do to save Mick and herself from dancing the gallow's jig—for stealing a purse containing five pounds was a hanging offense.

Now Lucy discreetly picked a louse from her forearm and squashed it between her fingernails. She wished Ardaix's pull with the Newgate jailers had extended to procuring her a bath. She must look like a filthy thief. The magistrate glared down from his high bench and Lucy raised her chin. What cared she for the elderly man's funereal black robes and long, full-bottomed wig? She refused to quail.

"Bailiff, what is the crime against these two?"

A rat-faced little man in a black frockcoat scuttled forward. "Theft, your worship. Five pounds pilfered in a tavern." He curled his lip at Lucy's red-and-yellow striped skirt and ragged, green-muslin bodice. "During some dubious manner of Gypsy fortune telling, your worship. 'Tis clear the pair are but knaves, pickpockets and thieves."

The magistrate's falcon eyes narrowed over his gold-wire spectacles. "What say you to this charge, madam?"

" 'Twas a misunderstanding, milord—"

"Nonsense, woman." He glanced down at a sheet of paper. "The charge says the lad was apprehended with the purse in question in his pocket. And there's mention of a witness against you."

The magistrate scanned the packed courtroom, and Lucy's heart sank. If Jocko turned his Irish gift of gab against them, she and Mick were well and truly hung.

"Bailiff, where is the witness?" the magistrate queried.

"Seems he's not present, your worship."

The magistrate flung himself back in his black leather chair. "Madam, you have been charged with theft. Although

the witness against you is not present, 'tis well known that
Gypsies are unrepentant tricksters and thieves. Therefore, I
sentence you both to be returned to Newgate until such time
as arrangements may be made for your execution on Tyburn
gallows." He reached for his gavel.

Lucy shot forward. "My Lord, wait." He stopped in mid-
hammer. She offered him an innocent smile, then slanted her
eyes just a bit. "Is not English justice the most famous in
all the world?"

"Aye, madam." The magistrate's voice made it clear that
he was exercising the utmost patience. "That's why I'm sen-
tencing you—"

"Have not our fair Parliament and noble King made pro-
vision to protect those citizens who have the esteemed privi-
lege to serve the Church of England?"

The magistrate rolled his eyes. "Madam, do not have the
temerity to claim benefit of clergy."

"I do, my lord." Lucy lowered her eyes penitently and took
another step forward. Here was her chance—if she could pull
it off. "England's law puts forth that those in the service of
the Church are not subject to punishment by hanging. My
brother and I must be given the chance to prove that we have
been educated by the Church, my lord, and are thus under
its protection."

The courtroom quieted and the ragged crowd leaned forward,
astonished at Lucy's speech. She knew what they saw: a grimy
Gypsy wench from the gutters of Alsatia, London's notorious
crime district. They hadn't expected this sudden upper-class
accent issuing from a trollop's lips. She bit back a smile. Neither, it seemed, had the judge.

He eyed her with uncertainty. "Madam, I must admit you
have not the speech of a Cockney wench—nor of a Gypsy."

Lucy smiled and slanted her eyes a bit more. Thank God
her da had passed on his flair for acting and mimicry—and
that her mother had been an educated woman. "As I said, my
lord, I have been educated in the service of the Church of
England. My mother—God rest her saintly soul—was daugh-

ter to the vicar of St. Botolph's, near York." Lucy omitted the fact that her grandfather had left the Church of England to become a radical Methodist who roamed the byways of England, preaching to farmers in the fields.

The magistrate took off his spectacles, bowed his head, and rubbed two fingers over the bridge of his nose. Lucy thought she detected a wisp of a smile. The man sighed. "Bailiff, bring forward the Bible." He dropped his hand and pinned Lucy with a glare. "Madam, at least thrice a day tuppeny cutpurses traipse through my court. These deluded wastrels think that if they can read the Neck Verse, I am required to let them off. They memorize the verse practically at birth, trusting it will prove their ability to read, and thus establish that they are members of the clergy. Of course, they are no more able to read than my left boot. I assure you, madam, such ruses do not fly in my court."

He twitched his robes into a more flattering drape. Lucy detected a self-satisfied gleam in his eyes. "No indeed, madam. If 'tis benefit of clergy you claim, you shall not read the Neck Verse." The hawk brought forward a large, leather Bible, then thrust it at Lucy. "Now, madam"—the magistrate grinned almost maliciously—"open the Book at random and read me a passage."

Lucy smiled demurely. She closed her eyes and waited for inspiration, then deftly flipped to the passage she sought. The courtroom went deathly still as she began to read in a low, husky voice:

" *I will sing of mercy and of judgment. Unto thee, O Lord, will I sing. I will behave myself wisely.*" She paused and glanced at the judge, fluttering her lashes just a touch. *"I will walk within my house with a perfect heart. I will set no wicked thing before mine eyes. I will not know a wicked person.'* "

She glanced up. A smile twitched the magistrate's lips. "Shall I go on, my lord?"

The magistrate leaned on his elbows and rubbed a hand over his mouth. "Please do," he said in a strangled voice.

Lucy warmed to her task. With great brio she read, " *'He*

*hath looked down from the height of his sanctuary. To hear
the groaning of the prisoner; to* loose *those that are appointed
to death'—"*

The crowd began to chortle and poke one another in the
ribs. Mick caught her eye and winked. She shook her head
sternly, then smothered a grin.

The magistrate made recourse to the gavel. "Enough. You
have more than made your point, madam." He cocked his
head and his wig tilted askew. By now his fierce gray eyes
sparkled. "Merely to humor my curiosity, madam, does the
boy read as well?"

"Aye, my lord." She bent and whispered in Mick's ear,
then handed him the Bible. He flipped pages, then threw back
his bony shoulders and theatrically turned toward the rustling
crowd.

" *'Be ye m . . . merciful, as your F-father is also merciful.'* "
Mick's Cockney accent added a delicious lilt to Christ's words.
" *'Judge not and ye shall not be judged; c . . . condemn not
and ye shall not be condemned; forgive and ye shall be f . . .
forgiven.'* " He blushed to the tips of his filthy, peaked little ears
and tugged at Lucy's skirt. She bent and he whispered, "Did Oi
do okay, Loose? Wicked hard, some of them words be."

The courtroom rippled with laughter. A man called, "Aye
to that, lad. Well said."

"Let 'em go," a one-eyed prostitute shouted. "They be
clergy, all roight."

The magistrate banged his gavel. "Silence in the court."
Lucy caught his eye and felt an odd clutch in the pit of her
stomach. Suddenly the elderly gentleman wasn't smiling.
"Madam, you have proved most efficaciously your ability to
read, thus establishing your claim for benefit of clergy. The
sentence of execution is hereby commuted.

"However, madam, benefit of clergy does not extend to a
judgment of innocence. You and your brother have been found
guilty, and you must atone for your crime." He glanced down
at his papers, then gripped the gavel. "Thus be it ordered by
the court. You will be branded on the arm for thievery, then

transported in indentured servitude to the American colonies to be sold at custom of the country for a term of seven years."

The gavel fell.

Lucy's head nodded forward. She was so tired, so tired, and the ship rocked so soothingly, back and forth, back and forth, side to side, side to side. Soothing as Mother's arms—

She jerked awake. God's eyeballs, what was the matter with her? She couldn't fall asleep, not with Mick so ill. She glanced at her little brother, then pressed her hand to his forehead. He burned with fever. She slouched back against the weeping ribs of the *Eliza Pratt*'s hull and pounded her thighs with both fists. Oh, sweet Jesus, this couldn't be happening! She was supposed to protect Mick. She couldn't allow him to die.

Already a dozen of the transported convicts had succumbed to the Black Assizes—ship's fever. It took less than a week for each victim to waste away, first with cries of delirium, then with a frightening silence. Once a day, the third mate opened the vented hatch cover and descended the ladder into the putrid confines of the *Eliza Pratt*'s hold. Two sailors scuttled after him to ladle weevily pea soup or rancid porridge into the convicts' boiled-leather cups. Then they dragged out the dead.

Lucy had thought the sailors buried the corpses at sea, with a proper service and words from the prayer book said over them.

"Don't be daft," an Irish horse thief named Rory Quinn had snorted when she confided this belief. "They trow 'em overboard for the sharks to take."

Lucy stared at the pale, checkerboard pattern of sunlight leaching through the hatch cover. When Mick had taken ill, their fellow convicts had driven them into the darkest corner of the hold, near the overflowing buckets used as the jakes. The stench of urine, shit, vomit, tar, and whale oil nearly had felled Lucy, and bile clogged her throat each time she inhaled. It seemed she spent every waking hour batting away the hordes of bloated flies that feasted on the jakes, then crawled on her and Mick.

Despair made her long to bury her head in her hands, but they were too filthy. The sailors allowed the convicts only three cups of fetid water each day—barely enough to stay alive, and certainly not enough to stay clean. No wonder fever rolled through the ship like flood tide.

"Oy, Lucy. 'Ow's me old pal Malachy?" Rory Quinn ambled up, his gate exhibiting the roll peculiar to those long aboard ship. Had they truly been at sea for a month?

Lucy raked a coarse, straggling curl from her eyes. God's elbows, her hair had once been so beautiful, lustrous and black as raven's wings. She tossed the greasy hank over her shoulder. "Not well," she rasped, unable to offer Rory the tiniest smile. He had been so kind to them, and had stoutly declared that any lad with the fine Irish name of Malachy deserved respect. Mick had adored Rory, until the fever had laid him low.

Rory thrust out his cup. " 'Ere. Drink me water. Ye'll be down sick yerself if ye don't. And then who'd be nursin' Malachy?"

"Ta, but I'll let Mick have it, if ye mind not." She dribbled water over her brother's cracked lips. "Here, luv. Drink for yer old sister Loose." Mick murmured and turned his head away. Deep purplish hollows ringed his eyes, and one grimy cheek was swollen and covered with pus, courtesy of a rat bite. She turned to Rory.

"I've got to do something. When the sailors bring the food, will ye help me? Mayhap if we beg—"

Rory gave a bark of laughter. "Jaysus, Mary and Joseph— what fancy world are ye livin' in? Those coves don't care for the likes of us. We're scum to them, we are. And who's to weep or wail or give a shite for a lad dyin' o' the fayver?" He crouched down next to her. "There's but one thing ye can do. I've told ye before—"

"Shut yer gob, ye nag nipper. I can't do it."

She knew what Rory meant, for they'd discussed it often over the last two days. Despite her layers of grime, Rory had made it clear she was still a tempting beauty, and when she'd confided her desperation to save Mick, he'd hit on the bright idea of her dancing the blanket jig with the ship's sawbones in exchange for proper food and medicine.

"Oi, ye can right enough. Don't be so squeamish." He winked. "If my prime charms tempt not yer virtue, at least let yer prized maidenhead do some good for Malachy."

Lucy stared through the stifling gloom and gnawed at her lip. She had sworn she would never become a whore like her mother, but she also had sworn to protect Mick. Perhaps Rory was right. If she truly meant to help her poor little brother, she should stop at nothing.

The hatch cover thunked open, and Mick whimpered in his sleep. Lucy glanced at his pinched and ashen face, then leaped up and sped toward the sailors.

Two

Williamsburg, Virginia, 1763

Diarmid Maclean swung down from his stallion, then slapped the reins over an iron hitching post. Sunlight danced through the maples lining Duke of Gloucester Street, and cast dappled shadows on the Raleigh Tavern's wooden steps. Normally, Diarmid would have reveled in the sun's warmth on his shoulders, but on this crisp, late-September morning, raw, blinding anger blocked all finer sensation.

As he bolted up the steps to the ordinary, a group of white freedmen caught his attention. He halted and turned. The men lounged outside the blacksmith's forge, cursing and calling lewd remarks at a young slave girl hurrying by. One burly laborer caught Diarmid's icy gaze, then thrust up a middle finger and spat in the dirt. Diarmid sucked in a lungful of air and plunged down the steps. Saint Iona—after the morning he'd had, he'd love nothing more than to vent his rage on a crude, lackwitted lout.

Carriage wheels shrieked, a horse neighed, and galloping hooves thundered to a halt inches from Diarmid's riding boots.

" 'Ods bodkins, Maclean! Is this how you play the hero—diving 'neath my shay? Lud, there are better ways of defending a lady's honor, sir. Bleeding to death in the street softens not a maiden's heart—nor parts her thighs."

Harry Cheney, Diarmid's closest friend, jumped down from the shay. Diarmid bowed and wryly noted that Harry looked more than resplendent this morning. His coat was the latest style of peacock-blue tabby—a watered silk more often reserved for ladies' ball gowns—and red plush breeches encased his thighs.

Diarmid cast a pointed look at the lumpy musculature enhancing Harry's thin legs. "I see Rathall has upped your quota of padding," he dryly remarked.

"Horsehair and muslin. 'Tis a miracle what that tailor does for one's figure." Harry bowed and his black eyes sparkled. "What he does for my purse is quite another matter." Diarmid arched a sardonic brow, and Harry's impish face took on a wounded air. "Mock me not, Maclean. Not all gentlemen are blessed with your formidable physique. If the rest of us are forced to pad, 'tis merely to even the playing field with you."

The corners of Diarmid's mouth twitched into an involuntary smile. As always, Harry's jests contrived to banish his dark moods—if only for a moment.

Harry tossed the reins to one of the boys who loitered outside the tavern and begged for pence to hold a gentleman's horse. "Why the black glare, Maclean? Surely the overseer of Stanton's Grove has better things to do this fine morning than chastise a bevy of sots for their bawdy humor."

Diarmid spun on his heel and stalked up the tavern steps. "Aye, I've better things to do, and gettin' stark, starin' drunk is on top o' me list." As always when he was furious, his aristocratic accent took on the burr of the Scottish Highlands—a most irksome tendency. He was fiercely proud of his birth and breeding, but he had no desire to remind the Virginia gentry why he had come to their colony.

He stooped and entered the ordinary, then instantly regretted the decision. The low-beamed, paneled taproom overflowed with men, most well into their cups despite the early hour. Tavernkeeper Joshua Haimes sloshed ale into great pewter tankards, and a high-stakes game of whist occupied several planters near the bar. A group of fat, prosperous-looking merchants argued loudly over the inferiority of their competitors' wares, and a gaggle of wealthy young bucks smoked and diced and congratulated themselves on playing truant from the College of William and Mary.

Diarmid and Harry elbowed their way to the bar. The tavernkeeper greeted them with a hearty smile.

"A dram of whiskey, Mr. Maclean? Or, if ye prefer, I've in a fine French brandy."

"Whiskey," Diarmid said. "Why so crowded this morning, Haimes?"

Joshua Haimes wiped his hands on his leather apron, then set a small green glass before Diarmid. "The *Eliza Pratt*'s anchored downriver. Captain Pratt's decided to sell his jailbirds here in Williamsburg, for it fetches a better price. The planters mislike going aboard ship to buy indentures, ye know." Haimes reached for the bottle containing Harry's favorite: Virginia peach brandy. "Your neighbor Isaiah Ludlow was here earlier." He shot Diarmid a sour look. "To take the pick o' the litter before the public auction, I doubt not."

Diarmid clenched his whiskey glass, then slammed the glass back on the bar. The mere mention of transported convicts sent his pulse thundering to his ears. "So, you've a crowd of vultures come to prey on the misfortunes of others, eh? By Saint Iona—"

Harry laid a manicured hand on Diarmid's tense arm. "Perhaps we should go. I know this practice troubles you—"

"Nay." Diarmid thrust his empty glass toward Haimes. "I've come to drink away my sorrows, and drink them away I shall." He smiled coldly, pleased that he had forced his accent back into its usual patrician drawl.

Harry tossed a coin on the scarred and blackened bar, then waved Haimes away. "Lud, Maclean, I know well your tendency to moodiness, but you're downright surly today. Has Ludlow been up to some mischief?"

Diarmid shrugged. "For once 'tis not Ludlow making me grit my teeth—at least not directly. 'Tis Celia."

"Celia? Are you at it again? 'Ods bodkins, our good Lord exhibited a rare sense of humor when He paired the two of you." Harry chuckled, revealing a white-toothed overbite. "Remember when Celia didn't want you to sail to Charleston?

You argued for days, then she had Royal put buckthorn and castor oil in your corn pudding. You couldn't get off the chamber pot and missed the boat!" Harry guffawed and slapped his thigh. Diarmid noted that his friend's padding shifted to a most unflattering spot.

He cast Harry a quelling glare, then stalked to the small, diamond-paned window overlooking the tavern's backyard. A low wooden platform had been hastily constructed at one end of the packed-dirt expanse, and a large canvas tent sagged behind it. The men from the taproom slowly drifted outside, where no doubt the auction of indentured servants would take place in a few minutes' time.

Diarmid turned to leave, but Harry blocked his way, mischievous eyes dancing. "Forgive me, Maclean. But if you didn't want me repeating the tale, you shouldn't have told me." He leaned against the window's deep sill and smoothed his pointed French mustaches. "Now, tell. What's Celia up to this time?"

Diarmid stared dolefully into his empty glass. There was no hope of another drink now, for Haimes had gone outside to watch the auction. "The demanding old shrew gave me an ultimatum. Either I marry Venetia, or she'll sell Stanton's Grove to Isaiah Ludlow." He gritted his teeth and attempted to cool his feverish thoughts. By Saint Iona, he couldn't make a misstep now. There was too much at stake.

Since his arrival in Virginia sixteen years earlier, Diarmid had devoted his life to Stanton's Grove. With carte blanche from his imperious employer, Celia Stanton Lee, he had turned Stanton's Grove into the greatest tobacco plantation on the James. Over the years, his aristocratic manners, exceptional education, and—no sense in denying it—intense personal charm had won the old lady's heart—if a dragon like Celia could be said to have a heart. And three years ago, to his great joy—

"She promised," he snapped. "For years she's said she'd leave Stanton's Grove to me. 'Tis always been an understanding between us. No one loves that place the way I do. No one can keep it running like I can. By all that's right and holy, Stanton's Grove should belong to me. Now the old bitch has the temerity to change her—" He spun and hurled his glass into the fireplace. It exploded into a thousand emerald shards.

Harry grabbed his arm. "Lud! Calm yourself, Maclean. Do you want tongues wagging more than usual? You know 'tis whispered that you've bewitched Madam Lee. There's many about who resent a mere overseer having such power. . . ."

Harry's voice faltered, but Diarmid knew what he had been about to say: Although Diarmid's noble bloodlines had earned him entrée into Virginia society, many planters deemed it unsuitable for a mere overseer to have control over the colony's finest plantation. After all, they whispered, Diarmid Maclean might have been a powerful laird back in Scotland, but he was in Scotland no longer. He was in Virginia. And he had come here as an indentured servant—a transported convict guilty of treason.

Diarmid slumped against the smoke-stained wall and gazed out the window. "I know what you're thinking, Harry. That I was a vile convict, banished for treason." He shook his head and snorted in disgust. "Treason. So they called it. But I ask you, by what right is it treason to support England's true king? Prince Charles Edward Stuart—"

Harry held up a hand, then fluffed the lace ruffles at his cuff. "Lud, Maclean, not another Jacobite rant."

Diarmid touched his fingers together, then bent them into a steeple. "Jacobite, from the Latin *Jacobus,* meaning James. Prince Charles Edward Stuart—son of James the Third, grandson of James the Second, great-grandson of Charles the First, and great-great grandson of James the First—Queen Elizabeth's chosen heir. The Stuarts are England's rightful kings."

Harry gave an elaborate yawn. "Aye, and all those 'greats' and 'grands' are giving me a royal headache." He leaned his silk-clad elbows on the windowsill and watched as Captain Obediah Pratt climbed the rickety wooden platform. "You said Celia gave you an ultimatum. That sounds *much* more interesting than your dusty old Stuarts."

Diarmid considered throttling his foppish friend, then ruefully shook his head. Harry was interested in nothing more serious than the latest London fashions. Expecting him to appreciate the politics of monarchy was a fool's errand. "She told me she would leave Stanton's Grove entirely and legally to me if I would marry Venetia."

Harry shot up, languid pose abandoned. "Marry Celia's niece? My dear fellow, where is the difficulty in that? You've courted Venetia for years. Lud, we all expected to hear the banns—"

"The hell ye have." Diarmid folded his arms and glared down his nose. "I told ye weeks ago, 'tis all off between us. I caught Venetia takin' a whip to Mercury when he dared to bathe and poultice the gashes on her horse—gashes she'd made with those wicked spurs o' hers." He halted, appalled by the abrupt return of his Highland burr.

All at once, memories of Scotland washed over him—bitter memories of war and betrayal, and of a woman more beautiful and more heartless than Venetia. He raked a hand through his hair. How had he ever been daft enough to desire such a lass? Och, there must be some flaw in him, for why else should he ever be drawn to selfish, calculating females?

Harry turned his hands palms up in a Frenchified shrug. "But to lose a plantation over a sick horse and an uppity slave—"

Diarmid whirled, grabbed Harry by his stock, and shoved him against the wall. "Dinna ever say that. Mercury may be a slave, but he's still a human being."

He released Harry and slumped into a chair opposite the window. 'Twas no use trying to make his friend, or anyone, see. No one understood Diarmid's friendship with the slaves under his care. No one understood his abhorrence of slavery itself. And no one understood his dilemma: He—Diarmid Niall Altan Maclean, a warrior who had sacrificed everything for the cause of freedom—might one day own two hundred souls.

With wintry eyes and a frozen heart, he watched as the first bondservant hobbled up the steps to the wooden platform. Och, what was he to do? If he didn't play his cards right, Stanton's Grove and its slaves would pass into Isaiah Ludlow's sadistic hands.

Harry, too, stared out the window. "My apologies, Maclean. Lud, my wife told me you were too smart to ever marry a harpy like Venetia. I should have paid Patsy more heed." He strolled forward, distracted by the scene unfolding on the stage outside.

A thin young lass stood at the center of the platform. She was scrawny, filthy, and pathetic, but as Diarmid's gaze swept over her, a grudging admiration warmed his cold eyes. Despite a barrage of lewd remarks from the drunken students, she held herself like a queen: chin high, spine straight. Her hair rippled to her waist like a midnight river, and Diarmid easily detected a rare, exotic beauty beneath her layers of grime. At Captain Pratt's order, the wench stepped forward, and Diarmid caught the flash of sunlight on her fetters. A blade of memory stabbed his heart. He dropped his gaze.

"Let me get this straight." Harry turned, impish eyes gleaming. "You don't want to marry Venetia, but you do want to inherit Stanton's Grove."

Diarmid nodded distractedly, then looked out the window. His gaze seemed bent on returning to the wench.

Harry clapped his hands together, then briskly rubbed them in a circle. "My dear Maclean, I've hit on the perfect solution. You can avoid marrying Venetia, pay Celia back for the dreaded chamber pot incident, and perhaps, if you're as brilliant as you like to put forth, you can inherit Stanton's Grove as well."

Diarmid dragged his gaze from the wench, who now jested with the students, saucily trading jibe for jibe. Could she be Scottish? 'Twas rare to see such braw spirit in an English lass. He leaned his chair back on two legs and graced Harry with a look of elaborate patience. "My dear Cheney, what are you babbling on about?"

Harry flung his arms wide. "You can't marry Venetia if you're already married!"

The chair crashed down. "Are you mad? You know I've no desire to wed."

"Think about it," Harry said. "You know what a bully Celia is. Like all bullies, if she sees she's beaten, she'll back down. And if you've truly got her wrapped around your little finger, she'll change her will sooner or later, especially if she likes your new bride. Then Stanton's Grove will be yours, sans the vile Venetia." He paced back and forth, and a smile curled his mouth. "Now we must find the right woman. . . ."

Diarmid set his jaw. "I'm *not* getting married." He'd learned the hard way that women were nothing but scheming jades, and he'd certainly never tie himself to one, not when there were plenty of lonely widows eager to kindle his passion and warm his bed.

"What about Martha Giles?" Harry named a buxom widow with three children and a hundred acres. "She'd be overjoyed to take you to husband, even if you didn't love her." He rolled his eyes and grimaced. "Lud, listen to me. Since when did marriage have anything to do with love?"

Diarmid ignored Harry and stared at the raven-haired bond-servant. More like she was a Gypsy, for now she teased young Randolph Byrd with words he recognized as cant—the lingo of London's guttersnipes, Gypsies, and thieves.

"Give us a dance!" Byrd called.

Much to Diarmid's astonishment, the wench broke into a jig. She was lithe and graceful as a cat despite the fetters on her delicate ankles, and her pert breasts joggled enticingly beneath her ragged bodice. Quick, urgent heat suffused Diarmid's groin. Och, indeed, women were shameless jades—although this particular jade promised wild, exotic pleasures along with her schemes. The aching heat in his loins migrated to his cheeks. Harry noted his discomfiture and winked.

"Enough of this foolery." Diarmid jumped up and paced to the bar. "I'd as soon marry that Gypsy bawd as Martha Giles, or Venetia, or any other woman in the colony."

"To quote the Avon bard, 'The gentleman doth protest too much, methinks.' " Harry tapped a finger against his Van Dyke beard and studied Diarmid's face. Diarmid poured himself another glass of whisky, then drained it in one gulp. Raucous laugher erupted from the backyard and his gaze flew to the window.

"That was from *Twelfth Night,* was it not?" Harry asked.

" 'Twas *Hamlet,* lackwit. And 'twas the lady who protested."

Harry's brows fluttered up. "Ah, we mustn't forget what a scholar you are." He studied Diarmid a moment longer, then strolled to the bar. "Did I tell you that Nimbus just foaled?" Nimbus was Harry's most prized possession: a chestnut mare that had beaten Diarmid's thoroughbred stallion at every race in the colony.

Diarmid poured another drink, gulped it, and shot his friend a dark glare. Horses were his passion, and he wanted Nimbus almost as much as he wanted Stanton's Grove. "When are you going to sell me that nag? You know you can't afford to keep her."

"On the contrary, I can't afford to sell her—not when she wins five hundred barrels of tobacco off you each and every race day. But . . ." Harry picked up Diarmid's empty glass and tossed it nonchalantly in the air. "What say we bet for her?"

"What's the wager?"

"It will serve both our ends. If you win, you get Nimbus and, perhaps . . . just perhaps . . . Stanton's Grove?"

Diarmid grabbed the glass in midair. "What's the wager?"

"My dear Maclean, don't glower so. It quite distorts that handsome face of yours." Harry flicked imaginary dust from his peacock-blue coat. "If I win, I get one thousand barrels of tobacco, I keep Nimbus, *and* I get the satisfaction of forever reminding you that you're not as brilliant and finely educated as you think."

Diarmid towered over his preening friend. "What's the wager?"

"Simply this. That in three weeks' time, you can't take that Gypsy trollop you're so lecherously drooling over and transform her into a lady fine enough to win over Celia Stanton Lee."

Diarmid whirled and stalked to the door. Harry's voice called after him.

"Oh, and Maclean? You must marry the wench."

Three

A cool breeze brushed Lucy's burning cheeks and sent a shiver down her spine. She closed her eyes and prayed to the saints that her nipples—erected by the chill air—didn't show through the ragged tow-linen of her chemise. 'Twas bad enough standing with matted hair and filthy feet in front of this crowd of coves. That they should ogle her body and exchange sniggering remarks was beyond endurance.

She raised her chin and took a deep breath. She had to endure—and somehow she had to turn this wretched situation to her advantage. She had to cajole this rowdy throng into recognizing her worth. If she must be sold at custom of the country, she would call on every ounce of Rom wit and brains and talent to ensure that her purchaser was a man of honor and kindness, a man who would be happy to help her find Mick.

Oh, Mick.

Captain Pratt ordered her to step forward and Lucy swallowed her tears. How could she have let this happen? She was all Mick had left in the world. Just last night—their last night in the *Eliza Pratt*'s fetid, vermin-ridden hold—she had vowed to give him a fine new life here in the colonies.

"Virginia," she had whispered, clutching his frail little hand. " 'Tis a lovely word, aye? It rolls off the tongue like almond comfits. We'll be merry here, luv, I warrant it. We'll have a great manor where we'll eat roast beef and hot cross buns and plum pudding every night of the week. We'll never be cold and we'll always wear smooth linen and Brussels lace and the softest silks from faraway China."

"We don't need no prime victuals or fancy garb, Loose." Mick's face was smudged, and hunger hollows ringed his enormous blue eyes. But he was alive. No Black Assizes had drained his soul and left his scrawny, precious little body to the sharks. She hadn't let it.

"We got each other," he whispered. "An' that's better'n anything ol' Virginny can dish up." Suddenly his eyes clouded with pain and she crouched over him, panic jolting her stomach and speeding her heart.

"Shhhhh," she said, touching her finger to his blistered, feverish lips. "Don't try to talk. You're still very sick."

"Ye still got yer *dukkerin'* cards, Loose?"

"Aye." Her tarot deck was wedged safely under a loose plank behind the jakes, for the stench from the brimming piss buckets was a better guard than the king himself could boast. "But ye don't believe in that tripe. Ye know 'tis only to gull country louts and lovesick scullions."

With the unreasoning vehemence of the very ill, Mick had insisted on having his fortune told. She fetched the cards and shuffled, then let him cut and select a single leather rectangle. 'Twas the Ace of Swords.

Mick's gaunt face turned pale as a maggot's belly, and fear uncoiled itself in Lucy's heart—smooth and cold and stealthy as a viper. The Swords meant loss, upheaval, sorrow, separation—a terrible fortune, the worst possible, considering her poor brother's dreadful illness and the uncertainty of what lay ahead.

Mick's eyes widened with horror. " 'Tis a sign, Loose."

Lucy snatched the card from his hand. "God's knees, no one can know the future. How many times have I told ye that, ye silly goose? It all depends on how we live here and now. We make our own destiny." That really was the truth; she knew it. But a serpent of doubt began to slither through her veins.

Suddenly the ship heeled to port and a piece of rope shot from under Mick's raised pallet. Inspiration struck and she

snatched it up. "I know. Me da taught me this." She looped
one end of the rope around Mick's bony wrist. " 'Tis like the
cord they use in the Rom wedding ceremony."

Mick's brow wrinkled. "Will we take a vow, then?"

"Aye." She tossed him a brave smile and winked broadly.
"In a Rom wedding, the couple promises to stay together as
long as they love, then go their separate ways. But we're
brother and sister and we'll always love each other, so we'll
vow to stay together always, no matter what. Nothing will
separate us, ever." She smiled into his enormous blue eyes.
"Now, do you promise?"

"Aye, Loose."

She wrapped the other end of the rope around her own
wrist, pulled it taut and tied it tightly. "Now we're bound in
body as well as in soul. Nothing will ever come between us,
and if it does, neither one of us will ever rest 'til things are
set right."

"Now there's a choice piece."

Lucy snapped from her reverie and stared at the crowd
spilling from the back of the Raleigh Tavern. Quickly, she
picked out several respectable-looking older men dressed in
tailored coats, broadcloth breeches, glossy leather shoes, silver
knee-buckles, and tricorn hats. They looked a prosperous lot,
withal. Planters, mayhap, for Captain Pratt had told her that
Virginia was the greatest land in the world for growing tobacco. Lucy lowered her gaze and looked demure. If she
wished one of these gentlemen to buy up her indenture and
help her find Mick, she must seem sweet and biddable.

"Come now, wench. Show us your assets."

Lucy's gaze flew to a group of dandies milling about near
the platform. None could have been over the age of eighteen,
and they dipped snuff, patted their powdered wigs, smoked
elaborately carved pipes, and swigged from silver flasks. The
young fop who had spoken strutted forward, then lounged
against the wooden stage. Bits of dried food clung to his

waistcoat, and pockmarks riddled his freckled face, creating an odd illusion of spots floating before one's eyes. He winked lewdly.

Captain Pratt hustled forward and waved his hand as if to shoo the dandy away. "Off with you, sir. You are drunk, most disgracefully drunk. This is a respectable sale of England's finest indentured servants. We'll have no blackguards here."

The young man drew out a bulging pocketbook, then flourished it grandly. "Sir, you overstep yourself. I am Randolph Byrd of Tazewell Hall, and I come in search of a maidservant for my mother." He leered at Lucy and attempted to shove the purse back into his waistcoat. It flew open and coins rained onto the dirt. Byrd didn't notice.

He lifted the hem of Lucy's petticoat. "Come now, my beauty. What say you to a little *private* inspection?"

His companions roared and Lucy suppressed a sigh. A glance at the back of the crowd confirmed her fears: the respectable planters no longer seemed interested, for they clearly had pegged her as a doxy unfit for proper service. She clenched her fists in the folds of her skirts. God's ears! She couldn't let Old Dame Luck desert her now. She appraised Byrd's spotty face. Despite being the worse for drink, his hazel eyes seemed kind and his beribboned garb was of finest paduasoy. She could do worse.

She slanted her eyes and skipped just out of reach. "Ye be a wag, sir. My privates are my assets, and my assets be private."

Young Byrd blushed and looked pleased with himself. His companions hooted and pounded his spindly back. "You have the look of a Gypsy," one of them called. "Can you give us a Gypsy dance?"

Byrd's leering eyes fastened on her breasts. "Aye, give us a dance."

Lucy inhaled sharply. She was not a piece of meat to be poked and prodded and haggled over like mutton in the market. Why couldn't these dolts see that she was respectable? Straw in her hair and grime on her cheeks didn't make her a drab. A coarse, ripped chemise and bold, red-and-yellow skirts didn't make her a trollop. She ought to spit in their eyes.

Then she remembered Mick, still weak and puny from the fever. She loved him more than life—and she had to find him, no matter what. There was no telling what disaster the future would hold if she didn't. Aye, if saving him meant dancing like a carnival bear, then dance she would. Gathering her skirts, she closed her eyes and broke into a jig. The crowd hooted and catcalled its approval.

Lucy hopped and swayed until dizziness swept across her brain. Her fetters clanked and bit into her raw ankles, and arrows of pain shot up her calves. She smelled her own sweat in the crystalline air, heard the song of a mockingbird through the bright morning light, felt the cool breeze caress her hot cheeks. Oh, Virginia, Virginia—such a lovely name. Could she be free here? Would she and Mick ever get their fine new life? Or would the Ace of Swords bring them poverty, disease, despair—perhaps even death?

"Stop that ridiculous dancing!"

Lucy's eyes flew open. A man had bellowed at her, but his voice belonged to no limp-wristed fop. It had been deep and strong and resonant, the voice of an aristocrat, or of a powerful warrior. Her startled gaze scanned the crowd, then fixed on a man striding toward her. There could be no doubt he was the speaker, for he exuded a nonchalant air of command that brooked no opposition. Dandies gave way all around.

He was lean, long legged, and very tall, and he moved with the predatory grace of a jungle cat. His hair—black and glossy as Yorkshire coal—swept back from a widow's peak and was tied with a leather thong at the nape of his neck. Perfectly proportioned muscles weighted his broad shoulders, and he wore his clothes with casual flare. A wealthy planter, mayhap. Yet those clothes—severe white linen shirt, impeccably tailored breeches, and ebony coat unrelieved by any ornament save plain silver buttons—those clothes bespoke a clergyman or a scholar.

He climbed the platform's rickety steps and Lucy scanned his face. A handsome devil, indeed—with high cheekbones and a granite jaw warranted to make a lady swoon. His nose was long and severely straight, with the tiniest droop to the chiseled tip, and his austere features reminded her of the saints on the stained-glass windows of Westminster Abbey. In all, 'twas a pensive face—stern, refined, and . . . cold.

He swept past her without a glance, then spoke to the captain. His deep voice was pitched low enough that the crowd couldn't hear, but Lucy clearly discerned his words.

"Good morning, Pratt. I wish to buy this wench but have no wish to do so in this public manner. Shall we step inside? I assure you I shall top any offer an auction could bring." Without waiting for an answer, he strode toward the tent.

Captain Pratt nearly split a gut agreeing to the man's request. He bustled forward, grasped Lucy's elbow, and pushed her toward the sagging flap of canvas that covered the tent's entrance. She stumbled to the edge of the platform, then tried to step down. Suddenly her fetters snagged and she pitched forward.

"Do watch your step, madam." The tall stranger caught her upper arms, then lifted her down into the tent's intimate gloom. "I shall have those shackles off in a moment. In truth, they are a barbarity no person should be forced to endure."

Lucy opened her mouth to thank him, but he released her and sharply turned away. He and Captain Pratt conferred in hushed tones for several minutes, then the captain left the tent. The tall stranger turned, and his gaze swept lazily over her figure. His eyes were cool, yet a hot flush seared Lucy's skin.

"Madam, you dance with much grace," he said. "May I assume that you indeed are a Gypsy?" For the first time, his eyes met hers. Lucy bit back a gasp.

His eyes were wide set and black lashed, but 'twas their color that startled her so: They were pure, clear aquamarine— the brilliant blue-green of Caribbean seas—warm, seductive seas that her da had described in many a dashing tale of pirates and mermaids and perilous reefs.

She lowered her gaze and gave herself a stern mental shake. God's heart, what a fascinating color, and dazzling against his dark skin. But she couldn't lose her wits over a handsome pair of eyes, even if they were the hue of heaven itself. If he and Captain Pratt were about to strike a bargain, she had to step in.

She curtsied. "A Gypsy I am, sir, and proud of it."

He cocked his head and studied her face with lazy nonchalance. "How so?"

Unaccountably annoyed, she planted her hands on her hips. "The Rom are an ancient race, my lord. Kings and queens we are. We're prouder, smarter, luckier, and cleaner than you *gorgios*—Englishmen."

"I'm Scots, actually." The man arched a brow at her reeking garments. "Cleaner, you say?"

"Aye, cleaner—if given half the chance. The *Eliza Pratt's* hold wasn't a palace garden, your worship. 'Twas crawling with rats the size of pigs, lice the size of rats—" She halted, appalled at her idiocy. What was the matter with her? If the man thought her crawling with disease and vermin, he'd never buy up her indenture.

As if to confirm her fears, he turned away. There was no mistaking the tension in his broad shoulders, and his jaw hardened perceptibly. Lucy straightened her spine. If this raven-clothed scholar was too saintly to countenance a bit of muck, then she would do better elsewhere. She gathered up her skirts, raised her chin, and swept around to face him. "If ye have no wish to buy me bond, your grace, then waste not me time."

He stepped close and grasped her wrist, and his chill aquamarine gaze seared to her very bones. "Madam, I have absolutely no wish to buy you. I wish to marry you."

Lucy slumped against Captain Pratt's walnut traveling desk. Dizziness swept over her and she pressed a hand to her roiling stomach, where hunger gnawed like a plague-ridden rat. Hunger—aye, that was it. She could have sworn this towering black lord had said he wanted to marry her.

"Please forgive my abruptness, madam. I had no wish to upset you. I am Diarmid Niall Altan Maclean, of Stanton's Grove." He bowed elegantly and with surprising grace for

such a large man. "For reasons of my own—reasons I wish
to keep private—I find myself in immediate need of a wife.
It was, ah . . ." He glanced at his silver-buckled shoes, and
the faintest wry smile quirked his lips. "Pointed out to me
that you might make a suitable bride."

"Are ye stark, starin', screamin' barmy?" Lucy leaped up
and shot across the tent floor as fast as swirling skirt and
clanking chains would allow. "Captain Pratt? Captain Pratt!
Get me out of here right now. This cove's as mad as a March
hare."

Diarmid chuckled. "Mad? Aye, perhaps I am, but there's
no use shrieking. I asked the good captain to give us a few
minutes alone so we could . . . get acquainted."

Lucy whirled. She didn't like the insinuating tone lacing
that odd drawl of his. What was he, anyway—Scottish or a
colonial? Who cared? Whoever this Diarmid Maclean was,
he *wasn't* going to take advantage of her.

"Get acquainted, is it? I'm no doxy, ye daft sod. Just 'cause
I look like a ruffler, it doesn't mean I am one. If ye come
looking for a flourish, ye've come to the wrong place. I'd
never dance a blanket jig with the likes of ye. Now shove
off or bite me arse."

Fast as thought, he caught her chin in his hand, then
pressed a long, tanned finger to her lips. "Hush, lassie. Gypsy
queens dinna swear."

Then he smiled, as quick and brilliant as candle flame.
Laugh lines crinkled the corners of his eyes, and two deep,
masculine dimples appeared at the corners of his mouth.
Stunned, Lucy found herself staring at his sensual lower lip.
It had the tiniest dent in the center, as if God had touched
him there and left a mark of special favor.

He released her, serious once more. "Madam, my offer of
marriage is entirely proper. For reasons of my own, I need a
wife for a certain period of time. If you consent to fill that
role, I give you my solemn oath as a gentleman that the marriage will be entirely chaste. I assure you, I have absolutely
no designs on your, ah . . . virtue." His arch gaze lingered

on her breasts and a teasing smile curled the corners of his mouth.

Lucy skittered back a few paces, then scanned Diarmid's face. His chin had a slight cleft, and a tiny scar marked one side of his upper lip, thin and white against his tanned skin. Her da had had such a face—deliciously savage and full of character.

"Where'd ye get the scar?" she asked.

"The scar?"

She raised a hand as if to touch it. "On your lip."

He abstractedly brushed a knuckle across his mouth. " 'Tis nothing. Now, madam, will ye agree to me proposal or no'?"

She lifted her eyebrows. So the black lord was Scottish after all. There was no mistaking those wicked rolling *r*s. "But why are ye proposin' to the likes of me? A toff like ye could have his pick of ladies."

"Let's just say in this situation I dinna need a lady—I need a queen." Again he smiled, slightly mocking, quick, dazzling—like the sun playing hide-and-seek among the clouds. Lucy felt her wariness vanish like dew from the morning grass.

"Ye know bond servants can't marry, don't ye? Captain Pratt told us 'tis against the law 'til the indenture's served."

"Aye, I know. But if you consent to my terms, I will free you before we wed. In return, you must agree to act as my wife—a *proper* wife—for a certain period. After you've fulfilled our bargain, I'll give you your freedom paper."

"How long will ye want me?"

"At least a month. Perhaps as long as a year. Until I inherit Stanton's Grove."

"That's your plantation?"

"Aye, the finest on the James River. The finest in the colony."

Lucy studied the man before her—a man with a warrior's shoulders and a devilishly disarming accent, a man with shimmering aquamarine eyes, by turns ice and fire. Surely he had some mad plan afoot, some scam likely to run them afoul of hawks and catchpoles. Oddly, instead of putting Lucy off, this thought lit a spark of excitement in her belly. The voyage from England had been the closest to death—and hell—she'd ever come. Now she was primed for life and a bit of rum sport. Besides, there was Mick.

She slanted her eyes. "I might agree to your terms, your highness, but I have a condition."

"You are in no position to bargain, madam." He flashed her a stern, aquamarine-eyed glare, but the corners of his mouth twitched.

"I think I am. I'm scratchin' your arse. Ye can scratch mine."

He winced. "This condition?"

"Will ye buy me little brother? He's just eight years old and sick to boot—but a spry, game lad all the same. A man came by this morning. Captain Pratt dragged Mick away from me and sold him. I don't know who to. I caught a glimpse of the cove, but Captain Pratt won't tell me his name—a pox on his flea-bitten yard."

Diarmid frowned. "You try my patience, madam. I said you are in no position to bargain, and I meant it. I have no need for a runny-nose, light-fingered brat."

"But—"

"No buts, madam. I hold all the cards here—a term a thieving Gypsy like you should understand. You either agree to my stipulations, resulting in freedom and a brief, chaste marriage in the lap of luxury, or you will be taken back aboard Captain Pratt's ship with the other . . . ah, *undesirable* bondservants. From there you will be shipped to Barbados, where you will be sold into ten years' hard labor in the sugarcane fields."

He caught her arm, then lowered his mouth until his lips were inches from hers. His whiskey-scented whisper caressed her cheek. "Let me assure you, madam, the planters of Barbados are not like we gentlemen here in Virginia. 'Tis rare for a servant to live out his—or her—indenture."

Lucy wrenched free. Her hands shook and she knotted them in her skirts. How could she have thought him handsome? He was nothing but a black-hearted devil, for only a devil would turn his back on a poor, sick boy lost somewhere in the wilds of Virginia. Suddenly, the thought of Mick steadied her. She would be no help to him in Barbados—wherever that was. She had to stay here. She had to grasp this chance at freedom, this chance to find Mick, this chance to *escape*.

She glared up at Diarmid's austere face, then swept into a deep curtsey. "My lord, I agree to your terms."

She would use this black devil, just as he was using her. She would dance to his tune and make a fine wife. And at the first possible moment she would find Mick and rescue him and they would flee this damnable place—far, far away, into the fine new life she had promised.

Four

"Welcome to my home, Mistress Graves." Harry Cheney made a leg and bowed, then ushered Lucy over the threshold. Lucy slanted him a smile. At least Harry Cheney was a gentleman, which was more than could be said for that black-hearted devil who would soon be her husband.

She suppressed a derisive snort at the thought. Clearly, Diarmid Maclean was no gentleman. After she had agreed to his terms that morning, he had left her in Captain Pratt's musty tent for hours, without so much as a crust of bread or a noggin of small beer to fill her empty belly. Only when it was dark had he returned. Silently, he had bundled her into Harry Cheney's shay and they had rattled through the empty streets of Williamsburg to a large frame house on the edge of the town. It had been clear that milord Maclean had no wish for his friends and neighbors to see him sporting about with a filthy transported convict.

Lucy stepped into Harry Cheney's front hall and gasped. Never in her life had she seen such splendor. The wide central hall stretched the length of the house, and a gleaming mahogany staircase with carved and turned balusters rose gracefully into the shadows. Fragrant beeswax candles flickered in shiny brass sconces, and a crystal chandelier cast a flattering glow on her host's mischievous face.

" 'Tis lovely," she gasped, avidly admiring the hand-blocked wallpaper.

"Lud, 'tis nothing," Harry replied. "You should see Stanton's Grove. Maclean's the luckiest man in the colony to live in such a showplace—and even luckier to be wedding you, madam." He caught her grimy hand and gallantly raised it to his lips, stopping just short of kissing it.

"Fie, sir. Ye be a wag and a liar, though a most kind one." Lucy drew back her hand and sternly reminded herself to speak like a lady. Thank God she had inherited her da's talent for mimicry. She might look like a guttersnipe, but she could ape the accent of Queen Charlotte herself. Turning, she caught her reflection in a graceful gilt-framed mirror. She froze, mortified to the very depths of her soul. Black grime caked her fingernails, dried porridge and spilled beer stained her torn bodice, and moldy straw nested in her hair—along with other, livelier things, no doubt. Worst of all, she smelled like a London sewer on the hottest day in August.

Diarmid stepped in front of her. "Perhaps you should call Madam Cheney," he said to Harry. "The preacher arrives soon, and Mistress Graves is sorely in need of a bath." His nostrils flared and Lucy's temper flared along with them.

"You needn't remind me of my condition," she snapped, exhaustion and embarrassment getting the better of her tongue. "I know I'm disgusting—" Tears welled in her eyes and she stumbled to a halt. No. She couldn't show weakness, couldn't let this arrogant knave get the upper hand. "You should try rotting for two months in a verminous transport ship," she muttered, desperately blinking back tears. "Then perhaps you won't be so high and mighty!"

Diarmid's penetrating gaze raked her flushed cheeks. Then he leaned down, jade eyes suddenly soft with understanding. "I beg your pardon, madam. I had no wish to offend you." He caught her hand and bowed over it just as Harry had. Then, to her utter astonishment, his lips brushed the surface of her skin.

Her mortification increased a thousandfold. After the rigors of the day, pride was the only thing keeping her going—pride and her determination to escape this sly varlet as soon as possible. She couldn't afford to let him charm her, or pity her. She snatched her hand away.

A sturdy young woman descended the stairs. Her sandy

curls nestled beneath a neat muslin cap and a green-and-white sprigged apron covered her overskirt and petticoat of quilted yellow chintz. Freckles dusted her snub nose and her blue eyes danced with lively interest.

"Lord love us, Harry," she exclaimed. "What have we here?"

"My dear, please allow me to present Mistress Lucy Graves." Harry beckoned Lucy forward. "Mistress Graves, my wife Patsy."

Lucy curtsied. "H-how do you do, Madam Cheney."

"Mistress Graves is recently arrived from London," Harry said. "She met with misfortune on the journey. Her bags were stolen—"

"There's no need for fabrications," Diarmid snapped. He took Patsy's hand and bowed, then broke into that quick, dimpled smile.

Lucy caught her breath. She would never get used to that smile. In repose, Diarmid's lean face was invariably grave, cold, aloof, but those dimples could melt marble. Again and again during their brief time together she had caught herself watching him, anxiously awaiting his dazzling smile. It always took her by surprise. Always.

Diarmid drew Patsy Cheney into the front parlor and they conferred for several long minutes. When they emerged, Patsy took Lucy's hand and smiled.

"My dear, please accept my felicitations! Now let us hurry, for we must make you ravishing. Diarmid tells me the preacher will be here anon and we mustn't keep the anxious bridegroom waiting!" Patsy waved Lucy toward the stairs. Lucy gathered her skirts and hurried up.

Patsy led her to a guest chamber beautifully and simply furnished with blue-and-white-striped wallpaper, a tall maple chest, a Windsor chair, and a mahogany four-poster bed topped with a hand-netted canopy. The air smelled of beeswax and lemon verbena.

Patsy pulled the bell cord and said, "Take off those things, my dear. I'll have my maid prepare a bath and we'll scrub you clean. I'm afraid you'll have to wear my clothes until Diarmid can obtain some of your own."

Overjoyed at the prospect of a bath, Lucy wriggled out of her grimy garments. Too late, she remembered the brand on her upper arm: a deep, blistered *T* marking her a thief. Patsy's eyes widened when she saw the brand; then she blushed and dropped her gaze to Lucy's tiny waist and curving hips. "Hmmmm. I'll have to pin the skirt," she said. "But you're ample in the bust, so we'll have no trouble there."

The door opened and a young black girl glided in carrying an enormous bucket of steaming water. Behind her, an older black woman struggled with a copper hip bath. Patsy gestured to the older woman.

"Mistress Graves, this is Garnet, my maid. She'll help you bathe."

Lucy and the black woman sized each other up. Garnet was lean and straight-backed, with high, prominent cheekbones and skin the color of coal dust. Her skirts were brown calico and her hair was wrapped in a white turban knotted in the front.

Lucy clutched a hand over the wretched scar on her arm. "I . . . I'd rather do it myself." Somehow, the thought that Garnet was a slave bothered Lucy immensely. She had brushed too close to slavery herself to enjoy another's subservience.

"Nonsense," Patsy said, shooing Lucy into the tub. "Poor Madam Lee is quite old and ill. I'm sure she'll wish you to assume the running of the household, and as Diarmid's wife, you soon may be mistress to some two hundred servants. You'd best get used to it." Lucy noted that Patsy didn't use the word *slave*. Gilding the lily, no doubt.

She squatted in the tub, mortified to be so skinny and dirty and naked. What would the slaves think, seeing her thief's brand? Suddenly, the import of Patsy's words sank in and her stomachache worsened. His highness had said nothing about her running a household.

Garnet poured steaming water over Lucy, and she gasped, "Who's Madam Lee?"

Patsy picked up a cake of clove-scented soap. "She owns Stanton's Grove. Diarmid is her overseer, though in truth he's more like a son—a recalcitrant son."

Garnet sluiced water over Lucy's waist-length hair, then scrubbed it vigorously with clove soap. Lucy inhaled the luscious scent and rested her shoulders against the warm copper tub. Diarmid had said nothing about an employer; she had assumed Stanton's Grove belonged to his family. She picked up a cloth and scrubbed at her ankle. "How old is Madam Lee?" she asked.

Patsy considered. "She must be nigh onto seventy-five—and a fierce old dragon, though a heart ailment has laid her low. Half the colony runs in fear of her whilst the other half dances attendance. Diarmid's the only person who has ever stood up to her."

Lucy ducked under the fragrant water and rinsed the soap from her hair. So that was it. Diarmid was scheming to wrest the plantation from the poor old bawd. Sly cove, indeed. She surfaced, feeling strangely unsettled. She couldn't decide if she admired Diarmid's tactics or not. The stews and alleys of Alsatia had taught her the importance of surviving at all costs, and she had no disagreement with the strong clawing their way to the top. But somehow it bothered her that Diarmid should be so underhanded.

"You and Mr. Cheney seem to know Diarmid well," Lucy stated nonchalantly.

"Aye. He and Harry have been the best of friends for years. At first 'twas a bit awkward, with Diarmid's history—" Patsy halted, pink suffusing her freckled cheeks.

"What history?"

Patsy motioned Lucy to stand, then squeezed a towel down the length of her sopping-wet hair. "Never mind my prattling. Diarmid will soon be your husband. He'll tell you all about himself as he sees fit."

Lucy stamped a foot, sending a slosh of water onto the wood floor. "God's eyebrows! I scarce know the man and we're soon to wed. Can you not tell me more about him?"

"I'm sorry, my dear," Patsy murmured, dropping her gaze

along with the wet towel. "But Diarmid must reveal his own secrets."

Suddenly, reality clenched its icy hand around Lucy's belly. She was about to commit her future—and Mick's—into the care of an elusive stranger with an unspeakable past and an unfathomable heart. Could she do it? Nay, surely not. She couldn't tie herself to any man cruel enough to turn his back on a sick child. Such a man would be a rakehell, a rogue without honor.

A shiver rippled over her damp skin. Diarmid had promised their marriage would be chaste, but only a fool believed a rogue. A startling image of his massive shoulders and chiseled features flashed through her mind. Clearly Diarmid was a man of intense physical appetites, for he exuded alarming virility and a blatant masculinity that turned her bones to water. His severe garb and scholarly air couldn't mask the taunting heat of his aquamarine gaze. Swallowing, she envisioned the power of his muscled thighs, then imagined herself helpless beneath him, those thighs hot and demanding against hers.

Patsy wrapped Lucy in a towel, then took a tortoiseshell comb to her snarled hair. The comb snagged and tears sprang to Lucy's eyes. She bit her lip. She had to get hold of herself. No matter how alluring he might be, no matter how he tried to charm her, she wouldn't sacrifice her virtue to a black-hearted knave like Diarmid Maclean. The day her mother had died, Lucy had sworn never to follow in her mother's footsteps, and she wouldn't break her promise now. She would not become a whore.

She took a small, ragged breath. Married or not, it was whoredom to lie with a man she didn't love. She would not trade her body for favors and consideration.

A tiny smile curled her lips. Back aboard the *Eliza Pratt*, Captain Pratt had tried to test her virtue. Secure in his power, he had offered to send the sawbones to Mick in exchange for her maidenhead. Lucy had made a counteroffer.

"The sailors cant that ye set a great store by the devil's books." She had nodded at the cards on the round oak table in Captain Pratt's cabin. The third mate had taken her there in response to her strident demands to see the master of the leaking piss-bucket they called a ship.

"Aye, and what's it to the likes of ye?"

"Any betting men would rather win a prize than take it. So deal a hand of ombre, and I'll wager ye the sawbone's services against me maidenhead."

Lucy grinned, recalling the scene. Captain Pratt might love the cards, but he held no favor with Old Dame Luck. Thanks to quick fingers and quicker wits, Lucy had beaten him royally. When the captain had threatened to horsewhip her for cheating, she taught him a few of her Gypsy tricks. After that night, the captain's winnings had risen miraculously, and Mick had received the most solicitous attention from the ship's doctor.

Patsy nodded at Lucy's smile. "I can see you have a fondness for Diarmid, so I will tell you this. Your betrothed is the finest man in the colony—my dear Harry excepted, of course. Governor Fauquier calls on him often, for Diarmid is most exceptionally learned. Bookkeeping, trade, law, surveying, planting, politics—why, none in the House of Burgesses can compare. And he breeds the most magnificent racehorses." She motioned to Garnet, then moved toward the door. "Garnet will pin your hair while I fetch some clothes."

Lucy sat at the tiny dressing table. Silently, Garnet began plaiting, twisting and curling Lucy's hair into an elaborate upsweep; then their eyes met in the dressing-table mirror. Lucy straightened her shoulders and raised her chin.

After a long moment, the slave smiled. "This hair of yours be thick an' coarse as a horse's tail. An' your eyes so black and wild. Whoooeeee." She gave a long, low whistle. "I think Master Maclean done met his match."

Lucy grabbed the slave's hand. "Garnet, tell about Mr. Maclean. What's his true character?"

Garnet tied a ribbon of cherry silk around Lucy's hair. "Chile, Miz Patsy's right. They ain't none finer than Master Maclean. Why, that man just loves hosses, and I always says a gentleman who's kind to hosses is kind to people. An' he sure is popular with the ladies." Her grin broadened and she chuckled. "They fight over him like hogs over slop, 'specially Miz Venetia Lee."

"Who's that?"

"That be Miz Celia's niece. Her daddy's head magistrate, but she ain't no lady. You watch yourself with that one." Garnet bent and mopped spilled water from the floor. "Folk gossip that Master Maclean and Miz Venetia be special friends, if you take my meanin', but Master Maclean ain't never offered to marry her. He just goes his own way, cool as creek water." She considered for a moment. "If'n you ask me, I'd say that man's got a powerful heart. He just lost it somewhere and don't even know it. I say all his cold manners and fancy book learnin' be a mask, so's he can survive."

Lucy picked up a towel and knelt beside Garnet, then mopped at a soapy puddle. They worked in silence for a moment; then Garnet took the cloth from Lucy's hand. "An' chile? You an' me knows somethin' about survivin', don't we?"

Diarmid paced the length of Harry's paneled dining room, then turned and strode back. At Diarmid's request a few minutes earlier, Patsy had placed a bottle of the finest amontillado sherry on the serving board against the wall. Now she, Harry, and the preacher waited in the front parlor, no doubt as anxious as he to begin the marriage ceremony. The only thing missing was the bride.

He snorted. Bride, indeed! Never in his wildest nightmares had he imagined himself marrying a Gypsy thief snatched from Tyburn tree. Captain Pratt had been more than happy to inform Diarmid of Lucy's crime—and of her unholy talent for cheating at cards. Diarmid rubbed his jaw and smiled mirthlessly. Och, the joy of marrying a wench he'd have to watch at every turn.

He ceased his pacing, then snatched up the sherry. To his intense surprise, the prospect of watching Lucy didn't bother him nearly as much as it should have. In truth, he rather fancied the idea of keeping an eye on the little trollop, though he'd be damned if he'd let her realize it. Like a fine racehorse, Lucy clearly possessed courage in abundance and a lithe grace that was stunning to behold. Besides, his life had been empty of late. It would do him good to bestir himself and tame the unruly wench.

He swallowed a mouthful of sherry, then tilted the glass of amber liquid toward the firelight. He found it odd that London's gutters should have spawned a lass with such spirit. And Lucy's accent was as changeable as his own: one minute she sounded the whore, the next a fine lady. He frowned, intrigued. There was a desperate valiance about Lucy, a gritty determination to win at all costs. He found it admirable. In truth, that was why he had taken Harry's absurd bet.

He held a hand out to the crackling fire. It annoyed him to admit that his friend's harebrained scheme made a bizarre sense of sorts. Diarmid couldn't marry Venetia if he was already wed, and he hadn't the slightest doubt that he could turn Lucy into a lady so elegant that even Celia would welcome her with open arms. Aye, the odds were good that he would come out of this with Stanton's Grove, and with Nimbus—glorious, light-footed Nimbus. His lips quirked into a sardonic smile. A light-footed racehorse and a light-fingered thief. Och, he was a lucky man.

The door clicked open. He turned and Lucy entered, then swept him a graceful curtsy. Somehow he managed to swallow his sherry without choking. For a long moment he stood utterly still, then he deposited the glass on the table.

Lucy slanted her eyes and cast him a killing smile. "I beg your pardon, your excellency, but a lady at her toilette operates on a wholly different standard of time. Do I meet with your approval?"

Diarmid could not believe that the stunning creature standing before him was the filthy, scrawny, foul-mouthed wench he had dragged from the auction block earlier in the day. Saint Iona—he'd never seen such an exotic beauty. Her raven hair gleamed in the firelight. Tantalizing little ringlets rested below the fragile perfection of her ears and a single lock curled down over her shoulder to caress the lush mounds of her breasts.

He bowed and kissed her hand, savoring for an instant its velvety texture and spicy scent. "Madam, you leave me speechless. Harry will apprise you of the full magnitude of that compliment—no doubt averring that this is the first time such an event has ever occurred." He flashed her a wry smile.

She blushed deliciously. "Thank you. I . . . I've never seen such fancy garb in my life. The East End whores—" She halted. "I mean the, um, ladies of the evening had rum duds, but never the likes of this."

She held out her skirts and twirled, blissfully unaware of the stir she was creating in his breeches. He reached for the sherry and poured two glasses. "Indeed, madam, Patsy has lent you a bonny frock." 'Twas a deep cherry-red silk cut low to the point of sending a man into heart failure, with tight, elbow-length sleeves and a split skirt tucked up over a cherry-and-gold-striped petticoat. Wisely, Patsy hadn't risked any of her jewels on her jailbird charge, and a single cherry-silk ribbon adorned Lucy's slender throat. Diarmid noticed a tiny pulse beating there, just above the ribbon. His fingers twitched.

"Tell me more about London's ladies of the evening," he said dryly. "Did you often look to them for fashion advice?"

She tapped his wrist with her ebony fan, then took the glass he proffered. "You're a tease, milord, as well as a trick-ster."

Such exotic eyes. Diarmid had never seen the like. Really, they weren't black at all, but a very deep brown, with amber flecks sparkling in their depths. They were wide-set and bewitchingly slanted, with thick, black lashes.

She blushed under his bold scrutiny, then gulped her drink and glided closer to the fire. " 'Tis prime sherry, your grace. At the Cat and Mutton, Mistress Hyde only gave ale to the serving wenches. Of course, that didn't stop us from draining the dregs when the old bawd wasn't looking." Lucy appeared fragile and delicate in the dancing firelight—until she thrust out her glass and demanded a refill. He reminded himself that appearances could be deceiving.

"Although drink is beloved in the colonies, madam, you would do well to mind your intake," he warned. "Ladies don't indulge to excess in public."

She tossed back the second glass. "Then do they in private?"

She had a wee mole just above her left eyebrow. The piquant little beauty mark added spice to her exotic air, and to his dismay, he found himself captivated. He spun on his heel and strode to the relative safety of the window. Harry, Patsy, and the preacher waited, and Diarmid couldn't waste time lusting after a woman he could never touch.

Lusting. The word brought him up sharp. Och, the sherry must have gone to his head. He was Diarmid Niall Altan Maclean, Highland warrior and laird's son, confidant of Prince Charles Edward Stuart, trusted friend to the royal governor of the Colony of Virginia, powerful overseer of Stanton's Grove. He had been educated in Paris, Florence, Edinburgh, and Rome, and he wouldn't lose his reason over a draggle-tailed thief from the stews of Alsatia. Besides, he had promised Lucy a chaste marriage and, as yet, he had never broken a promise.

But how could he have known what seductive beauty lurked beneath all that grime? She quite astounded him: cheeks like tawny silk, eyes like midnight fire, and breasts high and lush and round enough to drive a man to drink. He tightened his jaw. No one in Williamsburg would question his sudden marriage; one glance at Lucy's beauty would explain all. A cold smile thinned his lips. In truth, her looks and grace would make his task all the easier. He would have the wee trollop fit for the royal governor in no time—indeed, for George III himself, blast his vile German heart.

He stalked back to the sherry bottle. Lucy had reached it first. She cast him a taunting smile, then poured a shot and gulped it as if she were a starving dog. By Saint Iona, this was all he needed: a Gypsy thief who was a tosspot to boot.

"Madam, that will be enough." She flinched at the harshness of his voice, but he forged on. "We have little time, and you will spend that time listening to exactly what I expect of you." He snatched the bottle from her hand and slammed it down on the table. "You will spend the next three weeks under my tutelage. When I have determined that you are fit for polite society, we shall take you to an entertainment. If you succeed in fooling my fellow planters and their lady wives, you will be ready for the real test—Madam Lee."

He clenched his hands behind his back and paced to the window. "Celia must be completely convinced that you and I are man and wife in every way." She squawked in protest and he held up a hand. "As I stated earlier, I haven't the slightest intention of touching you—ever. Though why a tart should so protect her virtue is quite beyond me."

Lucy darted across the room and snatched up the sherry bottle. "You know nothing about me, so don't turn up that elegant nose of yours. I may have been a thief, but you're a—"

He reached her with one long stride. He tried to wrest the bottle from her, but she skittered out of reach. She tossed him a taunting smile, waved the bottle under his nose, then upended it and drank. He snatched it away and slammed it down so furiously it almost shattered.

"Dinna test me, woman!" he bellowed, furious Scots accent flaring. He dragged her against him. The weight of her breasts crushed against his chest and desire flared in his cock. "Nothing would please me more than to turn ye over me knee, bare your bonny arse, and give ye the beatin' ye deserve."

Her head lolled back and her curls tumbled loose. "Ye'll have a rum time tryin'," she slurred. Her knees buckled and she collapsed, unconscious in his arms.

Diarmid swept her up and rushed from the room. Saint Iona! He hadn't meant to frighten her, but her haughty temper drove him to distraction. He glanced down at her beautiful, hollow-cheeked face. 'Twas pale and drawn in the hall's dim light, and she felt as light and frail as a wee sparrow in his arms. For one mad instant he longed to crush her to his heart and never let her go.

He kicked open the parlor door. It hit the wall with a crash. Harry, Patsy, and the preacher leaped up.

"Strike me blue, Maclean! What have you done?" Harry rushed forward, Patsy close on his clattering, three-inch red heels.

Diarmid gently placed Lucy on the settee. "Not a bloody thing. One minute we were talking, the next she fainted. Dinna give me that look, Harry. I'd never hurt her."

Harry assumed a wounded air. "We heard you bellowing from here."

"Stop it, both of you." Patsy knelt, then chafed Lucy's hands. Lucy's eyes fluttered open. "There, sweeting, 'tis all right. You fainted. Are you well now?"

"I beg pardon," Lucy murmured. "I haven't eaten all d-day and the food on my, er, voyage . . . well, 'twas scanty. The sherry went to my head—"

Patsy jumped up, mortification evident in every freckle. "Oh, my dear! What you must think of me! 'Tis I who must beg your pardon. In all the excitement I forgot to offer you refreshment. Oh, how rude you must think me. . . ." She rushed toward the bell pull, chattering like a monkey.

Lucy glanced at Diarmid. Her amber-flecked eyes were enormous and their despairing expression struck him like a fist. He scowled. How could he possibly marry the lass, then turn her off once Stanton's Grove was his? Och, he would supply her with money enough to live in gracious comfort anywhere outside Virginia—but those sad, frightened eyes weren't starving for money. They were starving for love.

He stormed into the candlelit hall, then strode into the shadows. Och, Saint Iona help him. Love was the one thing he couldn't give.

Five

Lucy slipped into the dark upstairs corridor, then stealthily shut the bedchamber door. By her best reckoning, it must be one o' the clock in the morning—her wedding morning. A wry smile straightened one corner of her mouth. 'Twas a shame she wouldn't be around to see the surprised expression on milord Maclean's face when he discovered his bride had flown the gilded cage he had so arrogantly wrought.

She crept down the stairs, carefully testing each step before settling her full weight on it. The third step from the bottom creaked loudly and she froze. What would she say if her new husband caught her? She pressed her back against the wall and gazed up at the door to his chamber, just visible over the carved balustrade. Patsy Cheney hadn't turned a hair when Diarmid coldly had requested sleeping quarters separate from Lucy's. No doubt poor Patsy was used to his high-handed ways.

All was silent upstairs. Lucy drew a wavering breath and resumed her furtive progress, with each step regretting what she was about to do. Harry and Patsy had been so kind to her. They had fed her, fortified her with brandy, then stood up with her while the vicar of Bruton Parish had read the lines of the marriage service. Lucy could scare remember how she had behaved throughout the tense service. Badly, no doubt, for when it came time for her to speak her vows, milord Maclean had gripped her elbow with steely fingers and given her a tiny shake. She had considered bolting, but he had glared down his severe nose with such ferocity that she had quickly reconsidered.

Her stocking feet touched the polished boards of the downstairs hall, then she glided toward the dining room, as silent as the darkness around her. Earlier, she had noted Harry and Patsy's excellent silver plate and had quickly assessed its worth. Now guilt assailed her. Never before had she stolen from people who didn't deserve it, from folk she knew and liked. She paused at the dining room door. Was there any other way?

Diarmid had made it clear she couldn't escape him. When Captain Pratt had drawn up the document certifying that Diarmid had freed her, her aloof husband had folded it and hidden it in his coat pocket, scowling at her all the while. His aquamarine eyes had glinted like seawater as he informed her that the document would be locked away until such time as he decided that she had fulfilled her end of the bargain.

"Make no mistake," he said, more remote and austere than she had ever seen him. "Freedmen are forbidden to travel or even walk the streets without their freedom paper. If you're caught without it, you'll be arrested and thrown in gaol." He had flashed her a wolfish smile. "And rest assured, my gallows bride, I won't rescue you a second time."

The mere thought of the degrading scene made Lucy jerk her chin and slip resolutely into the dining room. As much as she hated to hurt Harry and Patsy, she had to rescue Mick, and to do so she needed money.

Her stomach knotted and she gnawed at a fingernail. It seemed guilt was to be her constant companion in this wretched colony. If she hadn't been sleeping so soundly yesterday morning, Captain Pratt would never have been able to sell Mick away from her. Lucy rolled her neck from side to side, trying to release the coiled bands of tension aching down over her shoulders. How could she have been so careless? Mick was all she had, and it was her fault he was gone.

For an instant she imagined she heard his piping voice: "Rattle yer pins, Loose! 'Tis almost cockshut. The droll will be shut if ye don't bestir."

Her lips curved into a smile. Her mischievous little brother had loved the theater—the droll, he called it—especially when there were plays about pirates. She and Mick had sneaked into the pit most afternoons, their pockets bulging with sweet-meats they had filched from the orange girls, who were always too busy flirting with the fops to notice. Then they had hooted and laughed and tossed orange peels and witticisms at the grease-painted actors. It had been rum sport.

Lucy's hand closed around a silver candlestick, and Mick's fortune card—the terrible Ace of Swords—flashed across her mind. She had to do this. She had to rescue her little brother, wherever he was and whatever the cost. To do otherwise would seal his awful destiny.

She smiled tremulously and stuffed the candlestick down her bodice. Of the pair of them, Mick always had been the rescuer. He desperately had wanted a puppy, and forever had been dragging home stray curs—pitiful creatures with worms and fleas and pus-filled scabs riddling their gaunt ribs. Aye, poor, lonely Mick had longed for a dog, but he'd loved horses most of all. Whenever he managed to slip Jocko's grasp, he had bolted to the livery stable. There he'd spend hours currying the spavined old dray horses or watering the filthy nags whose misfortune it was to haul the heavy coal wagons. She could almost hear those carts now, lumbering and rattling over the cobblestones.

Lucy shuddered. There had been another cart that sounded like that, a cart no Londoner could bear to hear. It, too, had been drawn by a derelict nag whose head bowed low in the traces and whose worn hooves clopped with hopeless fatigue. 'Twas the Raker's cart, come to drag away the dead.

Panic shot through Lucy's veins. She dashed forward, blindly yanked open a sideboard drawer, then grabbed a handful of silver spoons. God's teeth! She wouldn't think of it, wouldn't torture herself with memories of her mother's death.

She bit her lip. On the day Agnes Graves had died, Lucy had sworn to save Mick from the abuse they had suffered at Jocko's hands. She had vowed to repair all the damage her weak and foolish mother had wrought. She had thought success was within her grasp when she and Mick had sailed for Virginia, but Mick had fallen ill, then disappeared. And now the Ace of Swords haunted her sleep, along with another, much older nightmare.

Lucy thrust the handful of spoons under her skirt, into a hidden pocket hanging from a string at her waist. God's teeth, why had Agnes always been too drunk and weak and servile to watch over them? A good mother looked after her children, but Agnes had never even tried. She merely had cowered beneath Jocko's slaps, then slunk back and kissed his hand the way a cur grovels to a cruel master.

God's knees, she would never let a man have such power over her. Loving Jocko had ruined Agnes Graves O'Donohue. It had forced her to turn her back on Lucy and poor, hungry, frightened little Mick. It had sent her to the raker—and, perhaps, to hell.

Lucy glanced around the gracefully proportioned dining room one last time, then squared her shoulders and hardened her resolve. She would never follow in Agnes's footsteps. She would fix things instead. She would save Mick and give him a fine new life, just as she had promised. If doing so meant thieving from friends, then so be it.

She returned to the hall, then crept toward the front parlor. She'd purloin the two candlesticks on Patsy's tilt-top table, then be on her way. Taking a deep breath, she slipped into the darkened parlor, then tiptoed across the thick Turkey carpet. The fire had been banked, but a few embers still winked on the hearth, like foxes' eyes in a lanthorn's light. She could feel the coal's warmth on her bare forearms. She took another step, and the spoons clinked, unnaturally loud in the close stillness. She muttered a silent curse and flattened her hand against her inner thigh.

If she could escape the house without waking anyone, she could dash into the woods and hide until a passing wagon could take her into town. Dressed as she was, in Patsy's cherry-red gown, no one would take her for anything but an impoverished gentlewoman. She should have no trouble pawning the silver when the shops opened. She had no idea of the name of the man who had purchased Mick, but if she could make it to the Raleigh Tavern, she would question the serving wenches there. Surely one of them would know the man.

She eased forward, one hand groping blindly for the edge of the damask armchair. The table with the candlesticks lay just beyond, on the other side of the fireplace. Her hand touched the chair's back and she edged around it. Suddenly the chair creaked. Something moved in the inky blackness. There was a flaring sound, then guttering yellow light blazed from hearth to mantel. Lucy gasped.

"Good evening, madam. May I offer you a pipe?"

Diarmid lounged nonchalantly against the mantel, a thin, flaming length of fat pine held inches from his granite jaw. The flickering light cast demonic shadows on the planes and angles of his lean face, and Lucy froze, stunned. It was as if the guttering flame had transformed the Highlander from an arrogant, flesh-and-blood man to a rakish, cruelly handsome demon.

He cast her a searing aquamarine gaze, then bent to light his pipe. The fat pine had burned down to an ember, leaving only Diarmid's wide, sensual mouth and gleaming white teeth illuminated by its glow. He held the spark to the bowl and puffed. The rich, spicy scent of Orinoco tobacco drifted to her nostrils.

Lucy's heart thundered to life. She had to bolt, run, escape, but her feet were leaden blocks welded to the floor. Before she could force her stunned extremities to life, Diarmid's hand shot out and gripped her upper arm in a firm but painless clasp. He drew closer, and there was no mistaking the menace beneath his velvet touch.

They stood thus for what seemed like eternity. Slowly, Lucy's numbed senses thawed. She could hear the slow rhythm of Diarmid's breathing and for one mad instant, she fancied she could hear the steady beat of his heart. His breath caressed her cheek, soft and intoxicatingly scented with cherry and tobacco and fine French brandy. He chuckled, inexorably drawing her into the predatory challenge of his eyes.

Her heart raced beneath her confining stays, fast, faster, until she thought it would burst from her throat. Desperate to still her maddened pulse, she clutched her free hand to her bodice. It touched the outline of the candlestick she had thrust between her breasts. Blank horror swept over her, and all coherent thought vanished from her mind.

Diarmid's lips brushed her ear. "I would like to think, madam, that passion for your husband has driven you here, helpless before your desires." He chuckled again, a low, wolfish sound that pricked the hair on the back of her neck. "But somehow I doubt it."

He set the pipe on the mantel, then stirred up the fire, never releasing her arm from his steely grasp. The firelight burnished his tanned skin and limned the austere perfection of his profile with gleaming gold. He turned back to her, then raised a hand. She flinched and he stopped, surprised. Then a quick understanding softened his gaze.

"I'd never hit you, madam, no matter the provocation. But you've been hit before, aye?" His voice was dangerously kind.

She jerked up her chin, furious that she had shown any weakness. He might hold her captive, but she still had her pride. "Cease lording your pity," she snapped. " 'Twas merely reflex at the pawing of a brute."

He frowned quizzically, then pulled her closer. " 'Tis strange. I was sitting here in the dark musing on the trouble you're bound to cause me, then suddenly you appear. Are you real or are you a dream?" His husky voice was ever so slightly slurred.

Lucy's gaze darted to the tilt-top table, where a half-empty bottle of French brandy reposed. God's toes, her cool, refined husband was well into his cups. And he had the gall to call her a tosspot.

He traced his long, callused finger down over her cheek, leaving a delicious shiver in its wake. "Truly, ye are a Gypsy queen, or mayhap a witch, for cannot such creatures befuddle their adversaries? Cloud their minds and addle their reason?" He dragged his thumb over the tender flesh of her lower lip, and drugging warmth coursed through her. "Ah! Those wild black eyes soften." He arched a brow in mock surprise. "I'd begun to think they flashed only with anger. Or with accusation."

"I accuse ye of nothing, milord. But then, mayhap ye have a guilty conscience."

His grip tightened and he lowered his head until a mere ribbon of darkness separated their lips. "Dinna trifle with me, woman. Was wedding me such torture? Ye acted as if ye were bein' hanged, not married. 'Twill be about the town in no time—Maclean's wife is afeared of her own husband." A hoarse Scottish burr laced his words, and he shook her, jade eyes stormy. "Am I so cruel to save ye from slavery? To give ye your freedom and a life of luxury? Am I such a beast that ye willna touch me? Och, wench—touch me, and touch me now."

His wide, sensual mouth closed over hers. At first the kiss was a mere caress, a warm, tantalizing tease. Then he grasped her hair, ground his mouth to hers, and thrust his tongue between her lips. She gasped, shocked by the thrill that seared through her veins. His tongue plunged into her mouth, hot and urgent and searching, each stroke a rhythmic seduction, a relentless demand. Desire blazed like molten flame through her blood and she trembled, melted, yielded.

As if sensing her surrender, Diarmid bent her back and crushed her to him. His body pressed into hers and flattened her breasts against the sculpted hardness of his chest. The silver candlestick she had thrust down her bodice bit into her flesh. She caught her breath. God's bones—Diarmid couldn't mistake its unwieldy jut.

He released her, then grabbed her shoulders with frightening ferocity. "Ye vile, conniving, wretched little thief! Is this how you repay Harry and Patsy's kindness?"

She tried to wrench free. She had to escape before he found the spoons—

Ignoring her helpless squirm, he plunged a hand down her bodice. His fingers thrust between the firm curves of her breasts and closed around the candlestick. He cursed softly and yanked out the silver column, scratching her skin and popping one ripe mound from its confines.

"How dare you?" she gasped. She righted her bodice, then hurled herself backward, breaking his steely grasp. A spoon slipped from its pouch beneath her skirt and clattered to the floor.

"How dare I? How dare you!" Diarmid shot forward and pinned her arms behind her, catching her tight against the muscles of his chest and thighs. "How dare ye steal from my friends, ye lyin' trollop! Ye gave me your word ye'd honor our bargain, but honor's a mockery to whores, aye? 'Tis nothing for the likes o' ye to betray a trust, to steal what's valuable, to slink away into the night." Diarmid's brows knit in the indignant scowl of an avenging angel—or of an enraged demon. "Ye must be amused that I fell for your Gypsy wiles. Och, but how could I let myself feel anything for ye? Those sad black eyes are a ruse, a Gypsy trick to lull my suspicions."

Without warning, he thrust his hand down over her hip, then groped among her thick silk petticoats until he felt the outline of the hidden pocket. Lightning-fast, he grabbed the hem of her petticoat and flung it up. She squealed, kicked him in the shin, and skittered away. He grunted in pain; then his booted foot shot out and caught her around the ankle. She lost her balance and plunged backward. Her shoulders thudded against the thick Turkey rug and the breath rushed from her lungs.

Diarmid mounted her in an instant. His powerful thighs straddled her hips and pressed her into the rug, and he held her shoulder with one hand, then thrust the other beneath her skirts.

Lucy gasped, desperately trying to drag air into her paralyzed lungs. Then she felt Diarmid's strong fingers groping against the bare flesh of her thigh. Panic spiraled through her. Oh, God's bones, she was naked down there—

Diarmid's warm fingers seared across the curve of her inner thigh, then lit on the hidden drawstring pocket. With a growl of triumph, he grasped it and yanked, snapping the thin string. As he did so, the back of his hand brushed the crisp private curls at the juncture of her thighs. Lucy froze, fear and mortification numbing her completely. This couldn't be happening. She hadn't protected her virtue all these years to lose it to the arrogant lust of this Scottish colonial rogue.

Diarmid chuckled. "Och, at last I find your treasure, my queen. Does this mean I get to plunder?" His tongue flicked out and traced the curve of her ear, then he playfully nipped her lobe. Gooseflesh tore across Lucy's skin and she bit back a moan.

He arched a taunting brow, then his lips—moist and slightly swollen from the passion of their kisses—curled into a secret smile. He straightened his long legs, then lowered his full weight over her body. His fingers brushed across her womanhood, then he cupped his hand over her, sealing her and claiming her.

Lucy went limp, awash with embarrassment and despair. His touch intoxicated her, drugged her with a deep, burning need that ached to be met. He lowered his lips to hers, then rubbed his palm against her pubic bone in an expert, massaging motion. Wild desire flared through her, enflaming her flesh and sending her hips bucking against his hand. A delicious wetness welled up inside her, moistening her swollen tissues and dampening his fingers.

He chuckled, a low, wolfish sound of possession. "Ye're mine now, me wee Gypsy queen." His Highland burr was musical, magical, maddening. "And ye'll release me from my promise, aye? Why should we torture each other with this foolish chastity when we both want to—"

Lucy stiffened. Summoning all her strength, she wrenched her arm free and slapped his handsome, taunting face.

"Ahhhh." He reared back and his hand flew to the reddening patch where her blow had landed.

Lucy scrambled up and the pocketful of spoons jangled to the floor. "Don't you ever touch me!" she shrieked, no longer caring who heard. "I'm not your slave and I'm not your whore. You may be my husband, but you don't own me and you never shall."

She staggered back, shivering with anger and fear and self-disgust. How could she have been so weak? How had she let him touch her so intimately, so wantonly? Worst of all, how could she have enjoyed it? She was no better than her mother. Nay, she *was* her mother—a panting bitch in heat, eager to turn tail for any cur to mount.

Diarmid stood and moved toward her, hands outstretched in a calming gesture. "Shhhhh, lass. Ye'll wake the dead. I didna mean to scare ye. Ye must know I'd never force ye, but I thought ye wanted me." His aquamarine gaze scanned her flushed face and an almost boyish puzzlement knit his brows.

"Stop it!" She pressed both hands to her ears, desperate to escape the seductive intimacy of his voice. She wanted his anger, not this calm concern.

He flashed her a beguiling smile, then beckoned her closer. "Come here, me bonnie lass, and hush your fashin'. 'Tis not as if ye're a maiden—"

"Ohhhhh! How can ye be so vile? Ye know nothing about me, ye pox-ridden knave. I've kept me virtue—" To her intense dismay, Diarmid threw back his head and laughed. She thrust her hands on her hips and stamped her foot. "I'm telling ye the truth, varlet. Why persist ye in believing that I'm a bawd? Ye're rotten and mean and . . . and inconceivably patronizing!"

He bent and retrieved the stolen spoons, laughing heartily the while. Then he straightened and brushed the back of his hand across his mouth in an attempt to smooth his face into seriousness. "Och, I begin to believe you are a Gypsy queen—or at least a verra fine actress. Where else would a trollop learn such big words?"

"Don't dare tease me, you black-hearted swine. Compared to the likes of you, I am a queen. At least I have some warmth in me veins."

Diarmid's lips curled at the corners, like tiny devil's horns. "Have I no warmth?" He arched a rakish brow. "Och, at the moment I feel verra hot—"

"Ye turned your back on me poor sick little brother. I

begged ye to find him and buy back his bond so we could be together—"

"I don't remember begging. Demanding, perhaps."

"Don't interrupt. Mick's the only family I've got. I've sworn to protect him. I . . . I love him." Tears clogged Lucy's throat, then welled into her eyes and raced down her cheeks. She dashed them away.

"Shhhhh, lass. I beg pardon for upsetting ye so. I had no idea ye truly loved the lad. 'Tis a horrible thing to lose a brother ye love, aye?"

Diarmid's voice sounded hollow, and Lucy's gaze flew to his face. It was no longer teasing, but taut and strained. He noticed her scrutiny and their eyes held for a long moment, then he broke into that beguiling, dimpled smile. Lucy's heart did an odd little flip.

"Come here, lass." He tenderly took her hand, then sat in the armchair and drew her onto his knee. "How about striking another deal?"

"A deal with the likes of ye? When cats bark."

He grinned. "Ye should see the wary look on your face. Ye act as if I were the devil himself." He produced a cambric handkerchief from his waistcoat pocket, then gently mopped her cheeks. "The deal is this—swear to abide by my wishes and play the perfect wife, to never steal, and to never try to escape again, and I'll look into finding your little brother."

"Oh, Diarmid—do ye mean it?"

"Madam, I believe that's the first time you've used my Christian name. It sounds uncommonly fine on your lips, although I do rather like being called 'your highness.' " He tossed her an elven smile, and once again she noticed the tiny dent in his lower lip. For an instant, she contemplated kissing it. "Do we have a deal, Madam Maclean?"

She slanted her eyes. "Aye, my lord and master."

Suddenly the parlor door flew open and Harry Cheney entered. An absurd tasseled nightcap covered his shaved head. "Lud, Maclean. I heard a shriek. Is something amiss?"

Lucy's startled gaze flew around the room. What had Diarmid done with the spoons? Oh, she couldn't be caught now, not when Diarmid had promised to find Mick.

Diarmid winked lecherously and flashed his friend a smile. "Everything is in perfect order. I was merely showing my wife how a Virginia gentleman likes to spend his wedding night." As he pulled her close and naughtily slapped her bottom, she heard the faint clink of silver spoons in his waistcoat pocket.

Six

"Stab my vitals, Maclean. This is your maddest scheme yet." Harry Cheney flipped open a small gold box, took a pinch of snuff, and inhaled. Three loud sneezes followed. "I said, this is your maddest—"

"I heard," Diarmid snapped. Sighing wearily, he leaned back against the stone wall that fenced Patsy Cheney's flower garden. All around him the rolling fields and forests of Sugarplum, the Cheney plantation, glowed with the promise of a splendid autumn. The apple trees in the orchard bowed under their load of fruit, hints of orange and gold tinged the maples ringing the plantation great house, and the tobacco barns here and at Stanton's Grove were filled with the withering brown stalks of drying Orinoco.

He and Harry had slipped away to this serene spot in a desperate attempt to escape the noise and chaos inside the house. Diarmid's mouth eased into a rueful smile. Somehow, noise and chaos followed Lucy like lightning followed rain.

"You needn't bite my head off," Harry sniffed. "I'm merely telling you this for your own good. Even if Lucy fools everyone and even if Celia leaves you Stanton's Grove, *someone* must work the fields."

Diarmid reached for his pocket flask. Even though it was midafternoon, he was already on his fifth shot of whiskey. Or was it his sixth? He took a long pull of the smoky, aromatic liquor, then closed his eyes. Och, 'twas good, and it never failed to remind him of home—of Loch Linnhe and the Isle of Mull and *Taig Samhraidh,* the Maclean estate. Lost now, curse the bloody Sassenach army to the vilest pits of hell! Gone to pay the price for his, and his brother Jamie's, Jacobite treason.

Something black and lithe and venomous coiled in Diarmid's belly. At least Jamie had been loyal to their clan and to Bonnie Prince Charlie, unlike their eldest brother, Lachlan. Diarmid twisted his jaw, then clenched it tight. Nay, Lachlan was their brother no more. He was dead to them, as dead as their beloved Uncle Alexander and nigh onto two hundred Maclean clansmen. Dead, all of them, on Culloden's blood-soaked battlefield. The field of honor, they'd called it, but it had been a slaughterhouse for the Jacobites and a death sentence for Diarmid's kin.

And it had been his fault.

"Demme, Maclean! Has your new bride so tired you that you can't attend to our conversation?" Harry waggled his brows and languidly fanned himself with a perfumed, lace-trimmed handkerchief.

Diarmid's gaze snapped back to his friend. Slowly, painfully, he forced himself to numb the despairing ache in his heart. Too many years and lives had been lost to the mistakes of the past. He had to make reparation, and he knew only one way to do it.

He rubbed a hand down over his face. "Lucy tires everyone, as you well know." Harry also damn well knew that Diarmid and Lucy slept in separate chambers, at Lucy's strident insistence. His lips thinned in a sardonic smile. If he was weary, it was from a grueling tobacco harvest, not bed sport.

Meditatively, he rubbed his cool silver flask against his cheek. Och, but Lucy was an infuriating wench. Proud, haughty, demanding—but also witty and delightfully charming. She could be sweet and waiflike one moment, then maddeningly mischievous the next. Suddenly he ached to turn her over his knee and tan her bonnie wee backside. His manhood stirred at the mere thought.

He squirmed into a more comfortable position, then yawned. "Harry, this wee talk of yours sounds more like a lecture, and I'm too tired to listen. As to my mad scheme, I've never been more serious in my life. There will be difficulties—"

"Difficulties! You have no idea. Do you truly believe your fellow planters will countenance you freeing two hundred slaves? Why, the very thought is absurd. They would starve, run wild—"

"Enough." Diarmid kept his voice low, with just a touch of steely menace. He had the pleasure of watching Harry's brows flutter up. "You refer to people, not animals. No human should have to endure a life in chains, enslaved to an oppressor." He inhaled sharply, nostrils pinching with strain. He had served out his indenture twelve years ago, yet he still felt enslaved. He doubted the chains of his past would ever fall away.

"But my dear friend, the colony simply will not allow it," Harry argued. "The mere hint that you might free your slaves will send people to the courts, to the governor, and more than likely to arms."

"Cease this litany of doubt." Diarmid shot to his feet and strode toward the vegetable gardens. Although it bitterly taxed his pride to do so, he had to concede Harry's point. Diarmid couldn't free the plantation slaves once Stanton's Grove was his. The colony couldn't absorb them. Jobs were nonexistent for freed Africans, and in truth, most of the Stanton's Grove workers were field hands skilled only in hard labor. There was nowhere for them to learn a trade, and no white person in Virginia would give them custom even if they did.

He passed through the light wooden gate into the vegetable garden, then strode between the broad leaves and twining runners of Patsy's pumpkin plants. There was only one solution to this mad scheme of his: If he could get Celia to leave Stanton's Grove to him, he could free the Stanton's Grove slaves upon her death, then hire them back as sharecroppers. But he still would need a special waiver from the chief magistrate, and the magistrate was Barnabas Lee, Venetia's drunken father.

Diarmid reached down, ripped off a pumpkin leaf, and

crushed it in his hand. Why did he persist in fashin' over a dream? The slaves might never be his, so there was no point in gnawing himself into a frazzle. He hurled the crushed leaf to the ground. Och, but it galled him that all his hopes rested on that thieving Gypsy he'd taken to wife. If she failed to win Celia's approval, Stanton's Grove and its slaves would never be free.

"Maclean! Maclean, where are you?"

Diarmid turned to see Harry descending the steep slope of lawn toward the vegetable garden. At his heels trotted the Chevalier de Peyronny, the French dancing master from Williamsburg. Diarmid had hired the Chevalier to teach Lucy something other than the jig. So far, the trollop had proved as intractable and unteachable as a mule, and Diarmid had been too busy overseeing the Stanton's Grove tobacco harvest to discipline her properly.

The dancing master bustled forward, grizzled periwig askew, pockmarked face flushed. He halted in front of Diarmid, then planted his fists on his narrow hips. His bloodshot eyes looked ready to pop from their sockets.

"Monsieur, I 'ave 'ad enough! Madame Maclean, she is ze vixen, ze *demoiselle sans merci!* I try to teach, I beg, I plead, but *non,* she will not learn."

Diarmid bit his lower lip and quelled the urge to laugh at the Chevalier's banty-rooster pose. He bowed gravely. "Pardon, Chevalier. How rude you must think me to so neglect your exceptional pedagogical efforts. I quite agree that Madame Maclean is, ahem"—he adroitly disguised a chuckle with a cough—"a bit high-spirited. Perhaps things would go more smoothly if you thought of her as an unruly filly in need of a firm hand."

Suddenly his blood gave a predatory surge. What an alluring prospect: bringing his headstrong wife to heel once and for all. He clasped the dancing master's scrawny elbow and escorted him up the lawn. "Come, monsieur. Let us go teach your pupil some manners."

* * *

The sight of Patsy should have warned Diarmid. He found her in the front hall, collapsed on a Chippendale side chair, dabbing perspiration from her brow. He strode up, Harry and the Chevalier in tow.

"Where's Lucy? She should be in the parlor practicing her dancing."

"Diarmid, I've had enough." Patsy sighed. "My nerves can't take any more. All day long she's been at it—teasing and taunting the Chevalier, telling bawdy jokes to Jupiter, even getting up on the dining table and dancing some outrageous Gypsy thing called *flamenco*. The Chevalier says the dance is banned in all the polite capitals of Europe." Patsy blushed. "He says it . . . it incites unseemly passions."

Diarmid arched a brow at the dancing master. "And did it?"

The Chevalier drew himself up to his full height—just under Diarmid's armpit. "Monsieur, I am outraged!"

Patsy held up a limp hand. "No more arguing, please, Chevalier." She turned pleading eyes to Diarmid. "That's not all. After dinner she sneaked down to the kennel and released the foxhounds. She brought them into the kitchen, fed them the leftover ham, then raced them through the house. 'Twas awful. Baying, barking, jumping on chairs—"

"Who was barking and jumping on the chairs? The dogs or Lucy?" Diarmid forced his face into the gravest lines but couldn't keep a smile from quirking the corners of his mouth. Leave it to Lucy to come up with such an outrageous scheme. Truly, he had to take a firm hand with her. A very firm hand. Right on her bonnie wee arse. His manhood stirred in anticipation.

"Diarmid Maclean, don't you dare grin at me." Patsy stood and snapped her skirts back into their customary neat lines.

"I always smile when confronted with such beauty." He bowed and winked rakishly. "Now tell me, where's the shameful imp now?"

Patsy dimpled, then waved him toward the stairs. "Be off with that Scottish charm of yours. Lucy's in her bedchamber with Mistress Rathall, the mantua maker. She brought out the gowns and hats you ordered."

Diarmid kissed Patsy's hand, then bolted up the stairs two at a time. As he strode down the hall, Lucy's husky laughter drifted through her chamber door.

"A prime jest, Mistress Rathall. God's lungs, you'll never be able to lace me if you make me laugh so. Here, wait—I've got one. Why are a bawd's privates like a gentleman's hat?" There was a pause, then Lucy's laughter pealed through the doorway. " 'Cause they be so frequently felt!"

Diarmid entered the chamber and found Mistress Rathall doubled over with laughter, a white lawn chemise clutched to her waist. Hats, cloaks, stockings, petticoats, overskirts, bodices, ribbons, and gloves of every imaginable color and fabric littered the room. The windows were open, the curtains billowed in the breeze, and a foxhound reposed on the silk-covered bed. Diarmid noted the beast was gnawing a ham bone.

For a moment, he didn't see Lucy amid the chaos. Then her laughing voice issued from the far side of the bed: "Oh, if only Mr. Maclean could see this. I vow 'twould give him heart failure—and do I so fancy being a widow."

Diarmid froze Mistress Rathall with a baleful glare. Then he rounded the corner of the bed and halted.

Lucy was bent over, slipping on a shoe and offering him a startling view of her enticing backside. She wore a diaphanous gauze chemise, impossibly tight stays and a wide-brimmed straw hat trimmed with pheasant feathers.

"What do you think, Mistress Rathall? Is this too much?" She straightened and pirouetted. Her cheeks paled and her jaw dropped at the sight of him. "D-Diarmid."

"Leave us," Diarmid snapped. The dressmaker scuttled out behind him. He bowed nonchalantly, then lifted the hat from Lucy's head, tossed it to the floor, and boldly appraised her breasts. "Too much, my dear? On the contrary. From where I stand 'tis far too little." Color rushed to her cheeks, a luscious pink blush that suffused her slender throat and enticing cleavage. He caught her hand and pulled her toward him.

"Madam, if you wish to give me heart failure—widowhood being so devilishly attractive to you—you're succeeding admirably."

Och, and indeed she was. Her tight stays molded her breasts into ripe mounds, offered up to his ravenous gaze like plump peaches on a tray. Her gauze chemise made no pretense of hiding the dark triangle between her thighs, or the rich, dusky rose of her nipples. A shudder of pure lust surged through him, threatening to sweep away all reason.

Lucy's imperious black eyes met his. "Take your hands—and your eyes—off me, you lecher." He flashed his most raffish smile and she twisted in his grasp. "Let me go. You're hurting my arm."

Anger flared through him and he fought the urge to throw her on the bed and suckle her sweet flesh until she begged him to ravish her. By Saint Iona, why did the little doxy insist on protecting her nonexistent virtue? Talk about bolting the barn door once the horse was fled!

"Aye," he snapped, "and I intend to do much worse if you don't straighten out."

"Oh? And do you always force women into accepting your embraces?"

"I've never forced a woman in my life."

Lucy cast him a scathing glance. "Spare me, your grace. You own two hundred slaves. Don't tell me you haven't done terrible things to them many times over."

Diarmid whirled and whisked the foxhound off the bed. "Madam, you would fare better if you talked less. Don't presume to judge things you know nothing about."

His acid tone didn't slow Lucy one whit. "Oh, I know the likes of you well enough. Liars, cheats, knaves—I've dealt with plenty in my day. But you—you heartless blackguard—you're the worst of all."

Diarmid folded his arms over his chest and dug his fingers into his palms. She would *not* make him snap. He arched a wry brow, knowing the gesture vexed her. "Madam, is it your monthly flux that makes you so peevish, or is it something I've done?"

Lucy snatched up a silk dressing gown, threw it on, and belted it with sharp little yanks. "You know bloody damn well why I'm vexed. We've been here a week and never once have you rattled your pins to find Mick. Day in and day out I've begged you to start looking, but you won't even discuss the matter! Why on earth should I play the dutiful wife and learn to dance and talk and say 'Yes, sir' and 'No, madam,' and use the right fork when I can't even trust you?" She flounced down on the bed and pouted deliciously. "You promised."

"Madam, I never promised. I merely said I would look into it. I've spent the entire week riding back and forth to Stanton's Grove, keeping the largest plantation on the James in smooth running order. I've had no time for incidentals—"

"Incidentals! Mick's me brother—"

"Calm yourself, madam. I understand your feelings—"

"Like hell! Does a block of ice understand a candle flame? All you care about is Stanton's Grove and your fancy Greek books. You never talk to me—maybe because I don't speak five languages the way you do, milord High and Mighty—and you never notice me. I've tried all week to please you—"

Diarmid threw his head back and roared with laughter. "Please me? *Please* me? Madam, since the moment you arrived you've done nothing but disrupt this house and turn its inhabitants into raving lunatics."

Lucy rammed her tiny feet into a new pair of green calamanco shoes. With infuriating nonchalance, she tilted them this way and that until she found an angle she admired. Diarmid fought the urge to strangle her. Och, the haughty wretch didn't even have enough manners to attend to her husband. He leaned over and snatched the shoes from her feet.

"Name one thing you've managed to learn this week"—he waved a shoe under the foxhound's nose—"and I might spare your shoe from Kip's eager jaws." The dog whined and lunged for the dainty object.

"Don't, please." She grabbed for the shoe, eyes pleading. He dangled it over her head. "I've never had such prime duds in me life, Diarmid. *Please* don't take them."

Her piquant little face looked genuinely distraught, and he felt a pang of remorse. Really, he shouldn't tease her, but she rose to the bait so easily, he found it well nigh irresistible. He tossed her the shoe. Och, who was he fooling? He found *her* irresistible. Not that he would ever let her know it. She caught her prize and rewarded him with a dazzling smile. Long-forgotten warmth flooded his veins.

Nay. His muscles tensed and his jaw hardened. He would not give in to her cozening wiles. Her actions had proven her nothing but a thieving Gypsy—a charming, scheming jilt who could destroy a man on a selfish whim. He'd had bitter experience with such a woman, with disastrous consequences to himself—and to others.

He turned away and glazed the ice of reason over his heated emotions. Nay, he would never soften his heart again. In truth, he had frozen his feelings for so long, he doubted he *could* love again, even if he wanted to. And he most definitely did not.

He glanced back at Lucy. She had hidden her shoes safely under the bed and was now rolling a green silk stocking up her slender calf. She glanced up and offered him an uncertain little smile. Suddenly he longed to go to her, to pull her onto his lap and wrap her in his arms and reassure her that she would never again know abuse, hunger, and poverty. But he couldn't, no matter how much he desired this beautiful, infuriating creature. He took several slow, aching breaths and ordered himself to remain cool, aloof, unreachable, no matter how he desired her.

"Madam, I believe I asked you what you have learned this week," he said. "I remind you that we have fourteen days to turn you into a lady fit for polite society. Harry informs me that Governor Fauquier is planning an assembly at the Governor's Palace two weeks hence—"

Lucy's face lit up like royal fireworks. She clapped her hands and kicked her green-stockinged feet in the air. "A party at the Governor's Palace! Oh, Diarmid, 'twill be rum sport—and mayhap we can find out something about Mick."

He ignored that. "You won't get to attend if you persist in acting like a draggle-tailed gallows bird."

She stuck out her tongue, then rose with queenly grace. "Oh ye of little faith. In case I informed you not, my father, Nikolas Gravesceu, was a showman renowned throughout London and beyond. From Covent Garden to Whitehall, from Blackfriars to St. James' Palace, me da's talent was legend." She gave her flowered silk dressing gown a regal flourish, then swept around the room, chin up, head high. "He played Romeo, King Lear, and Hamlet, he played Othello, Macbeth, and Puck. He danced and sang and made ladies swoon with the poetry of love and sob with the laments of cruel, cruel death."

"That explains a lot," Diarmid remarked dryly. He cocked his head and studied the exotic perfection of Lucy's high cheekbones. "Gravesceu—'tis Hungarian, is it not?"

"Aye."

"And you Anglicized your name to Graves?"

"Aye. What of it?"

"Lucia Gravesceu," he murmured. "How delightful."

She blinked, eyes amber-flecked pools of fathomless mystery. "That's how Da used to say me name. Lu-*chee*-ah."

He took her hand and kissed it, silently marveling at its spun-silk softness, its spicy scent. What was that maddening aroma? Zanzibar cloves? Gilly flowers? Gypsy dust? " 'Tis the Italian pronunciation, for a *senora molto bella*," he said. "I'm afraid I don't know Hungarian, so Italian must suffice." He slanted her a rueful glance and she chuckled, an enthralling sound that curled his toes.

He drew her closer, turned her hand palm up, then kissed it again. "Then there's Lu-*see*-ah, the Spanish beauty who drives the toreadors to madness." He tucked an errant black curl behind her ear, fascinated by the drugging warmth of her skin, the tantalizing spice of her scent. "As for me, I prefer *Lu*-sha, who is, as the Chevalier says, *la belle dame sans merci*." He kissed her hand once more, this time succumbing to the urge to tease her by flicking his tongue across the surface of her palm.

She didn't react with the squawk of protest he had anticipated. Instead, her lips parted as she took an uneven little
breath. Then she slipped his grasp.

"That's enough," she said. "Tell me about the governor's
assembly."

" 'Tis no use telling you. You won't get to go."

She flounced down on the bed and snatched up a green-silk
garter. "Oh, yes I will. I just told you me da was an actor.
I've spent my whole life mimicking people, aping their accents, copying their mannerisms. I can speak as well as any
colonial bawd, no matter how grand she thinks she is." She
tied the garter with a defiant flourish.

Diarmid stood in front of her, spreading his legs a bit and
planting them firmly in her path, lest she decide to bolt. " 'Tis
no use, Lucia. No one's that great an actress. I've watched you
all week. Your manners are atrocious, you don't know which
fork or knife or spoon to use, you don't know how to address
ladies and gentlemen of title. There are members of the English
peerage living in Virginia, you know."

She straightened one stockinged leg, then tilted her head
to admire the effect of dark-green ribbon against pale-green
silk. "Don't call me Lucia. I like plain old Lucy. And I could
learn all those things in an hour, if I so chose. 'Tis no great
chore." She waved a hand at the foxhound. "Even Kip could
manage it."

"I doubt not that Kip could learn it. Foxhounds are most
intelligent." He caught her foot in one hand. " 'Tis your brain
that gives me pause. From what I've seen and heard, you've
not the wit to learn so much as a simple minuet." He smiled
with deliberate arrogance. "I dare not delve into more com-
plex matters, as I have no wish to shame you with your own
glaring shortcomings." She *tsk*'d in protest and tried to kick
him with her free foot. He caught that as well.

"Don't sneer at me, milord High and Mighty," she
snapped. "I can dance better than that simpering Gallic pigeon Peyronny ever dreamed of. I could gull even the gov-

ernor if I so chose. I could pass as a duchess at your piddling backwoods rout."

"Please, madam. Your tone deafens me and your assertions bore me." He clasped her ankles together with one hand and stifled a yawn with another.

"A pox on you, insufferable cove! You've insulted me quite enough for one day. I'll wager you I can fool everyone at your tawdry little carousal. By the time I'm through, they'll think they've had a visit from Queen Charlotte herself."

Diarmid arched a brow. "What do you wish to wager, madam? Think carefully, as you're bound to lose."

Lucy squared her shoulders and stared him straight in the eye. He got the distinct impression she'd rather spit. "I'll wager Mick," she declared. "If I win—which I shall—you'll find my little brother immediately, buy him back, and set him free, just as you promised. You'll also give him a home with me until such time as you deign to let me go. And when we *do* part, you'll give us enough chink to start a fine new life."

Diarmid frowned. Perhaps baiting her hadn't been such a good idea after all. He hadn't the time to track down a light-fingered brat who could be anywhere in the colony by now. Och, Saint Iona. How could a man of his intelligence and education have so grossly underestimated the trouble his convict bride would bring?

He glared down at her, determined to be severe and aloof—and was utterly undone. Her dressing gown had fallen open over her lush breasts and one delectable nipple peeped through the filmy gauze of her chemise. He still held both her delicate ankles. The action of lifting them had parted her dressing gown halfway up her long legs, revealing a luscious expanse of tawny flesh—an ambrosial banquet fit for the gods. With insolent laziness, he trailed his fingers up over the graceful line of her thigh. She gasped. The sound resonated through him, sending a potent throb deep into his swollen manhood.

"Believe me, madam, it is my very great pleasure to accept your terms," he murmured. He pinned her with a predatory gaze, then slowly untied her garter. "Now here are mine."

Seven

Lucy pressed her cheek against the cool windowpane and stared out over Williamsburg. The lavender-shadowed streets hummed with activity and the very air seemed alive with anticipation. Moments earlier a magnificent sunset had suffused the sky with a pink as soft and tender as rose petals, and as Lucy watched, the trees and the neat white clapboard houses had taken on the gentle light, until the whole world seemed to glow like the heart of heaven.

Lucy dug her fingers into the drapery fringe. That morning, she, Diarmid, Harry, and Patsy had returned from Sugarplum in a coach and four, complete with outriders and blue-and-gold liveried postilions. The road had been crowded with wealthy planters in similar equipages, all headed for the social event of the season: the governor's ball at the Governor's Palace in Williamsburg. Of course, Diarmid had insisted she stay out of sight during the journey. Heaven forefend that she should meet someone and give away her true identity.

She turned and stared into the cheval glass. God's bunions, the way his imperious highness treated her, you'd think she was a blithering fool. But she wouldn't let that arrogant Scot ruin her evening. She'd worked hard for tonight's triumph, and she doubted not at all that triumph she would.

A delicious shiver raced down her spine as she thought of the evening ahead. She couldn't wait until Diarmid saw her in her new ball gown. Mistress Rathall, the mantua maker, had taken Lucy on as her special pet when her salty, East London soul had recognized a kindred spirit. With a knowing

wink, she had waved away Lucy's tale that she was a distant
cousin of Harry's visiting from England.

" 'Tis high time this backwater hosts a beauty worthy of
my talents." She expertly appraised Lucy's face and figure.
Then she had launched into a creative frenzy that still left
Lucy breathless.

Her gown—like the evening to come—was sure to be a
triumph. For Lucy and Lucy alone, Katherine Rathall had
spurned the latest style, with its egrets and flounces and fur-
belows. "My dear, a tigress doesn't masquerade as a lapdog,"
the dressmaker had averred. Lucy grinned. No lapdogs here.
Her gown practically roared.

Mistress Rathall had selected a scarlet silk the shade of
leaping flames—a stunning choice that cast Lucy's tawny skin
and raven hair into bold relief. The gown's cut was elegantly
severe, with a split skirt artfully draped back over a black
taffeta petticoat. Jet beading shimmered across the underskirt
and gleamed on Lucy's elbow-length, black kid gloves. Sheer,
black silk stockings and black brocade slippers with ebony
buckles completed the ensemble.

Lucy stared into the mirror and gave the gown's neckline
an uneasy tug. The bodice dipped into a daring V between
her breasts. Diarmid would likely split a gut when he saw
her. With a little snort, she whirled and snatched up her
beaded ebony fan. If it took bold décolletage to garner attention from her elusive husband, then she'd rip her bodice to
the navel.

Patsy called from the staircase, "Lucy, dearest, please do
hurry. Diarmid wants to speak with you before we go."

Lucy straightened her spine and tightened her stomach
muscles. She wouldn't endure another lecture; not tonight of
all nights.

For the past weeks she had thrown herself into the role of
great lady. She was determined to win her bet with Diarmid,
and to acquire the style that would allow her to pass in polite
society and, ultimately, to escape and rescue Mick. For hours
on end she had glided about the parlor with books on her
head. She had curtsied until her back ached. She had studied

an endless litany of inane French phrases, practiced her table manners, memorized every title and manner of address known to the peerage. God's tongue—she even had learned to eat oysters! But she steadfastly had refused to dance.

She had thought this small defiance might goad Diarmid into abandoning his implacable coldness. She should have known better. Her aristocratic husband never once had deigned to notice her beyond his usual vague, polite inquiries into her health. When he wasn't overseeing the tobacco curing at Stanton's Grove, he was locked in Harry's library, that elegant, knife-straight nose of his buried in Plutarch or Plato or some P-christened scribbler's prose.

Lucy's brows contracted. A few days ago she boldly entered the library and inquired if he possessed a book she might read about the colonies. Diarmid had chuckled, then absently waved her away. "Madam, you needn't lie about your ability to read. Few in the colonies care for books. No one will note that you're illiterate."

God's teeth, the memory still stung!

Suddenly flustered, Lucy leaned over her dressing-table mirror and smoothed rouge onto her lips. How and when had Diarmid's attention become so crucial? She was the one who had spurned him. She had made it plain she scorned his advances. When he had bet entrée to her bed against finding and freeing Mick, she had laughed in his face. She was bound to win their little wager, so there was no danger in accepting his terms. Why, then—if Diarmid was so hot to bed her—had he so quickly lost interest in her?

With a despairing little groan, Lucy clenched her eyes tight. The field of her mind filled with a thousand fleeting images of her husband: sitting by the library fire, scholarly gold spectacles perched on his patrician nose; galloping his stallion through the fields of Sugarplum, his muscled thighs expertly controlling the animal's every movement; bending gracefully to pluck the last October rose from Patsy's garden, then handing it to Lucy with a courtly bow.

Then other memories piled in, memories of moody silence and closed doors and chilly avoidance. When was the last time she had seen Diarmid's sudden, dazzling, dimpled smile—that smile of a thousand suns?

"Lucy, are you coming?" Patsy's voice drifted up the stairs once more, her tone anxious this time.

Lucy caught up her black-and-scarlet silk shawl. God's ribs, she had to get herself in hand. What did she care for that insufferable Scot's kindness or lack thereof? In a few hours she would achieve her goal: She and Mick would be reunited. And Diarmid's alarmingly attractive virility could go hang. She hurried down the stairs, her black heels tapping on the wooden boards.

"Oh, my dear! You're breathtaking." Patsy swept Lucy into a rustling, lavender-scented embrace. "I've never seen such a gown."

"Strike me blue! At last a female whose splendor is worth the wait—my dear Patsy excepted, of course." Harry bowed and kissed Lucy's hand. "Are you ready to set them on their ears, little cuz?"

Lucy laughed, the sound low and nervous in her ears. "I believe I am. The question is"—she arched a brow toward the closed library door—"does his excellency find me so?"

Patsy fidgeted with her fan. "He's waiting. He sounded most put out with your tardiness."

Lucy rolled her eyes. "When has that autocratic Scot not been put out?" She sailed toward the library, then flung open the door and stepped inside. In her haughtiest tone she said, "Dearest husband, do forgive my laggard ways."

The last red beams of sunset slanted in through the tall windows and cast somber shadows across the book-lined room. Diarmid leaned on the fireplace mantel and stared into the flames, a pensive look on his face. Firelight, sunset, and shadow played across his dangerously handsome features in a dance both ancient and primitive and, for an instant, she thought her scholarly husband had transformed into a brooding satyr.

He turned and offered her an elegant bow, but there was no mistaking the anger in his glittering aquamarine eyes. Lucy skittered back, half expecting her dress to ignite. He closed the distance between them with one long stride.

"Madam, I find myself forgiving you constantly," he murmured. His challenging gaze seared down over her body, from the curling, high-piled perfection of her hair to the saucy, heart-shaped buckles on her shoes. "What do you do for me in return?"

"I will make you the envy of every man in the colony, milord."

Diarmid laughed, a harsh sound that sent tendrils of warning down her neck, and his blazing jade eyes caressed her bosom until she felt as if she had been burned. "I daresay your beauteous flesh will garner me every man's envy—a most gratifying asset indeed. Your headstrong airs are quite another matter. I find them an irritating liability."

With a flick of her wrist, Lucy spread her fan. "Assets, liabilities—you talk like a clerk, milord, and a tedious one at that."

"Tedium. Hmmm. Ah, yes, I remember such a thing—a quality in short supply when Madam Lucy Maclean is about." With the roguish insolence of an expert seducer, he lifted one of her long curls and trailed it across his cheek. "Tell me, madam, is this the night I banish your tedious chastity once and for all?"

Blatant desire flared in his eyes, and her breath caught in a startled gasp. He leaned close, grasped her chin in one powerful hand, then languidly dragged his thumb across the trembling curve of her lower lip. His mouth curled into a wicked smile, and her thoughts scattered like quail.

"Watch yourself, my queen. I tire of playing the gentleman." His eyes locked with hers, and he trailed his finger down the ripe curve of her cleavage. Giddiness seethed in her veins. "Keep enticing me this way and you'll find out just what a race of savages we Scots are." Then, for an instant, all taunting challenge vanished from his gaze. He lowered his mouth to hers, and his brandy-sweetened breath warmed her lips. She stood transfixed, heart jolting, suddenly wild to taste the passion that darkened his eyes from aquamarine to jade.

Then he chuckled, stepped back, and tapped her jaw closed. "Madam, I do believe this is the first time I've ever seen you speechless."

Lucy sprang away, appalled that she'd nearly given in to the sweet weakness coursing through her blood. She racked her brain for a suitable quip. Nothing came. Further mortified at her lack of wit, she cast him a scathing glance and was utterly undone.

God's knees, Diarmid was handsome enough to make a nun tear off her drawers and sprawl naked in the street. His coat was velvet, black and bold as a pirate's heart. He had abandoned his usual severe stock, and a cascade of Brussels' lace adorned his fine, white-linen shirt at throat and sleeves. Not even an audience with the king could get Diarmid to powder his hair, but Lucy preferred it as he wore it, clubbed back with a black-satin ribbon as glossy as the ebon waves it contained. Silver thread embroidered his jade-satin waistcoat and silver buckles adorned his shoes.

Lucy's gaze drifted down to his powerful thighs. His breeches were black paduasoy, elegant and startlingly snug, and to her astonishment, they strained over a sizeable bulge. Struggling for composure, she smiled and pointedly arched a brow at his masculine endowments. "I find that your . . . ah, *attire* leaves me quite without words, your grace. In truth, I find myself stunned. But *do* give my compliments to your tailor. I vow I can read the date on the crown in your pocket."

Diarmid's lips twitched and she felt a spurt of triumph. Let the blackguard tease. She could hold her own.

"And would you like to pick that pocket, my bonny, wee thief?" His voice, though teasing, was husky with sensual menace. "For a crime like that, I'd give you a lot more than a crown."

Lucy dropped her gaze, speechless once more. Why did she allow him to bait her? 'Twas like sparring with . . . God's ears, 'twas like sparring with a devilish, silver-tongued Gypsy king.

"Madam, our carriage awaits," Diarmid coolly remarked, clearly tiring of their game. "However, we'll not leave this house until you demonstrate your proficiency in the minuet. Dance is our dearest diversion here in Virginia, and I'll not have my new English bride disgracing me."

Lucy rolled her eyes. "When will you learn to trust me, your majesty? I've told you I can dance—"

He threw back his head and laughed, all glinting teeth and glittering eyes. "Trust you? Oh, madam, I'd sooner trust the Duke of Cumberland—the Sassenach dog who slaughtered my clan."

Lucy shivered. "Your grace, I find your sense of humor in rather poor taste—"

He grabbed her wrist, then pulled her against his chest and pinned her arms behind her. She squeaked in surprise, and for a horrifying moment, she feared her breasts might pop from her deep décolletage.

"I no longer tease," Diarmid hissed. "Tonight, madam, you shall prove yourself a lady or all will be lost. I've wagered more than you will ever know on this mad experiment of ours. Shame me, embarrass me, take so much as one misstep and you'll be in a Barbados sugarcane field so fast your lovely little head will spin." With stunning strength and speed, he whirled her into the minuet's opening stance: hand held high and clasped in his. "Now dance!"

A delicious heat shimmered through Lucy's flesh, leaving her wobbly and light-headed and very concerned that, despite all her haughty declarations, she wouldn't be able to dance a step. She couldn't drag her gaze from Diarmid's thunderous face but stared helplessly, entranced by the granite hardness of his jaw, the sensual curve of his lips, the chiseled perfection of his nose.

Then she raised her chin. She would *not* fall victim to his seductive power. Her pride was stronger than his dangerous allure.

Although there was no music, she swept into the steps of the minuet—turning, gliding, clasping his hand, swirling, bowing, lost in his eyes. Ha! She was the finer dancer after all. Romany blood always told true. There was no denying her grace, her flair. Then Diarmid's taunting gaze settled on her lips, and she stumbled.

"Madam, you disappoint me," he drawled, aquamarine eyes glinting with mock dismay. "You fill my head with wondrous tales of your Gypsy talents. I rush to your side, mad to partner such a goddess of the dance. And what is my reward? Crushed toes and scuffed shoes. I vow, a Clydesdale has more grace—"

"A pox on you. I'll give you crushed toes." Lucy aimed for his silver shoebuckle and slammed down her foot with all her strength. Diarmid deftly sidestepped.

"Tell me, madam, exactly what are those Gypsy talents of yours?" He flicked nonexistent dust from his sleeve. "Besides thieving silver spoons, that is."

Lucy aimed another kick at his shins. Then, noting the devilish curl at the corners of his mouth, she reconsidered. She'd pay the rogue back with his own coin.

"Wait and see, milord," she intoned in her best Madame Zora voice. "I promise you'll be astonished by what your future holds."

The Cheney coach turned off Duke of Gloucester Street and rumbled at a stately pace toward the tall, glowing windows of the Governor's Palace. Lucy felt a sickening surge of excitement and clutched a hand to her belly. God's heart, she'd never seen anything so lovely! She wished her da could see her now; and her thudding heart ached with longing to have poor Mick by her side. They'd scarce believe she'd risen from the gutters of Alsatia to the mansion of a royal governor.

She offered Patsy and Harry a valiant smile, then dug her fingers into her gloved palm. At last she had her chance to escape her wretched past. No matter how nervous she felt, she must take this first step—and she couldn't stumble. 'Twas the only way she could gain the respect and learn the information she needed to find Mick.

Tilting her chin, she quickly reviewed her London stage accent and new, painstakingly acquired manners. Then she muttered silent thanks for her da's early training. He had told her often that the Rom were the proudest race on earth, and if there was ever a time for pride, this was it. She might be a gallows' bird, a Gypsy thief, and a guttersnipe, but by God's knees, she could act!

The coach halted before the palace gates and a liveried footman helped Lucy descend. She clutched her fan and stared into the blue-velvet twilight, enchanted. The Governor's Palace was something straight from her da's fantastical tales of Cinderella.

An elaborate wrought-iron crest depicting the lion and unicorn of Great Britain surmounted the palace's towering brick-and-iron gates. Behind the gates, the mansion rose three graceful stories to a tall, narrow-windowed cupola that was silhouetted like a glittering topaz against the lapis-lazuli sky. Evenly spaced dormers broke the roof's elegant slant, and the light from a dozen flaring torches lent a warm reddish glow to the intricately patterned brick walls.

Diarmid stepped up beside her, offered his arm, and flashed her a smile of alarming brilliance. "Ready, my queen?" he murmured. The torches shone like blue heart flame in his glittering eyes.

They entered the great hall, and the swirling gaiety of Virginia society swept over them. The sound of a harpsichord and violins cascaded through the air and dueled for attention with the gentlemen's booming laughter and the bright, magpie chatter of the colony's loveliest belles. Hundreds of beeswax candles glittered from silver sconces and garlands of crimson autumn roses dripped from magnificent crystal chandeliers. Lucy felt her senses heighten, as if she were under the spell of some exotic drug. Obediently, she allowed Diarmid to escort her deeper into the crowd.

Polished mahogany side tables littered with crystal punch cups ringed the great hall's perimeter. Fragrant lavender potpourri filled blue-and-white Chinese porcelain bowls, and succulent aromas floated through the overheated rooms, promising coffee and chocolate and persimmon beer, roast beef and spoon bread and Virginia ham. Fresh pineapples towered from the silver etagere in the center of the twenty-foot supper table, and the sheer abundance of rare lemons, glossy olives, and pale, sugar-coated almonds made Lucy's mouth water.

And the clothes! She had never seen anything so colorful, so like drowning in a rippling, gossiping rainbow. Coral velvet vied with periwinkle satin and gold lace struggled to outshine an embroidered, jewel-encrusted dragon—and that all on a single gentleman's waistcoat.

"God's eyes," Lucy breathed. "And I thought *my* dress was gaudy. Lud, I don't stand out at all."

A smile of teasing gravity played across Diarmid's lips. "My queen, you would stand out in Paradise itself."

Lucy scrutinized his face, waiting uneasily for the scathing jibe to follow. None came. Instead her capricious husband bowed and kissed her hand.

She snatched it free. "A creditable imitation of tenderness, milord. I vow your acting skills rival my da's."

Diarmid's black brows slammed together. Before he could retort, a gentleman hobbled up beside them. A pair of keen blue eyes, wisps of powdered hair, and a profoundly hooked nose gave him the air of an inquisitive old falcon.

"Ah, my dear Maclean," the man said in a loud and resonant voice. " 'Tis a pleasure to see you, sir. And who is this lovely and charming creature?"

Diarmid bowed. "Good evening, Mr. Wythe. Allow me the honor of presenting you to my wife." Diarmid pinned Lucy with a warning gaze, then smiled stiffly. "My dear, may I introduce Mr. George Wythe, the ablest lawyer, finest teacher, and most brilliant scholar in Virginia—indeed, in all the colonies."

The older man gazed at Lucy in astonished delight. "Your wife! My dear Maclean, you quite take my breath away." With grave courtesy, he bowed and kissed Lucy's hand. "What an unexpected and truly felicitous honor this is, Madam Maclean. Your esteemed husband in one of my dearest friends, and I vow his new bride shall be, as well." Wythe's voice blared like a trumpet blast through the packed front hall. Several guests turned in obvious surprise, then strolled in their direction.

Lucy curtsied and slanted Wythe her most beguiling smile. "The honor is mine, sir." Acutely aware that a crowd was gathering around them, she raised her voice a notch. "You teach at the College of William and Mary, do you not? Even in England we have heard of that exemplary institution, and I rejoice to meet its finest scholar."

Wythe's sharp nose grew pink. "You are English, my dear? Ah, but of course you are, for few here in the colonies speak with such refinement." He patted her hand and drew her closer. "Are you a lover of books as well, Madam Maclean? There's not a man alive could stand proof against such exotic beauty as yours, but I know my dear friend Maclean. He would fain have wit along with loveliness."

The crowd around them grew larger, and Lucy heard several curious murmurs. She started to reply, then caught Diarmid's glare. Tightly restrained menace hardened the planes of his face, and there was no mistaking the chill in his eyes. He was sure she was going to embarrass him in front of this sweet old gentleman, curse his wary Scottish hide.

Her gaze flicked back to Wythe and her heart jolted. He, too, had intercepted Diarmid's threatening look. Now he watched her with the bright, steady eyes of a raptor on the hunt.

She tilted her chin. "La, Mr. Wythe, you know what a husband is like. He admires his wife not for how much she knows, but for how much she thinks *he* knows."

Wythe beamed at her quick retort, and the spectators roared with laughter.

Suddenly a woman's face swam into Lucy's field of vision; an icily beautiful face blessed with alabaster skin, a retrousse nose, and pouting, heavily rouged lips. She wore her powdered blonde hair in a towering confection of curls, puffs, and egrets, and a plunging bodice of lavender damask clung to her ample bosom. She was not laughing. Indeed, her pale, blue-marble eyes bulged and a furious flush mottled her cheeks.

"Oh ho, Maclean!" George Wythe called over the merriment. He beamed at Lucy. "I see you've met your match at last—a lady of wit and discernment as well as beauty. What say you to such spirit, eh?"

Diarmid pressed a hand to his chest and bowed his head in mock defeat. "Sir, Madam Maclean ever vanquishes me. Indeed, I declare that no man could ever get the better of her—except, perhaps, with pistols at twenty paces. And likely not even then."

"Maclean! Demme. Fine to see you."

The laughing crowd parted and a resplendent gentleman wearing a full-bottomed wig and a coat of scarlet tabby sailed toward them. From the abundance of ribbons and medals adorning his portly midsection, Lucy guessed he must be the governor. She swept into a deep curtsey.

The governor dismissed Diarmid's respectful bow and pounded him on the shoulder. "Thought to inquire where you'd been keeping. No need, now. No need." He pressed a gold monocle to his eye and ogled Lucy's bosom. "Did ears deceive? Your wife, you say?"

Diarmid reached down to help Lucy rise. "Aye, my lord. Please allow me to present Madam Lucy Maclean. She's a distant cousin of Harry Cheney's, from London."

"Pleasure, madam. Pleasure." Governor Fauquier kissed Lucy's hand, never lifting his monocled gaze from her cleavage. "Demme. Saw you not three weeks ago, Maclean. No talk of marriage then."

A rakish smiled toyed at the corners of Diarmid's sensuous mouth. Lucy stared in fascination, then her heart contracted with quick, exquisite pain. Dropping her gaze, she quelled a sudden wild urge to kiss the tiny, enticing dent in the center of his lip

"I married on impulse, my lord," Diarmid remarked dryly. "Rather as one shoots oneself."

The crowd roared, and Lucy stilled a swift jab of hurt. God's ribs, what ailed her? Why should she expect talk of love from her new husband, even here in front of people whom it was imperative to fool? Such words would only be lies. Diarmid had made clear the ruthless nature of their arrangement, and she had agreed with alacrity.

Diarmid's laughing gaze flicked to hers. Suddenly, a phantom of tenderness glimmered in the emerald depths of his eyes. Then he blinked, and all kindness vanished. Lucy's heart lurched. God's teeth! She knew what ailed her.

Diarmid had bewitched her. He enthralled her senses like the rarest perfume, the sweetest music, the softest silk. He intoxicated her like the richest wine and the strongest opium. Every night she dreamed of him, and every waking moment of the day she wondered: Did she please him? Could she best him? Would he help her? Would he spurn her?

His rare laugh—deep and husky and suggestive—sent quicksilver down her spine. The sound of his riding boots stomping across the hall sent her pulse bounding like a startled deer. The fleeting brush of his fingers—iron firm, yet astoundingly tender—threw her into a tumult of vague, liquid yearnings. And the scent of him, all tobacco and brandy and raw manhood—God's ankles! The scent of him dragged her down into wild, aching hunger, into a primal need so acute, she longed to strip naked and glory in his embrace. He was rich, dark, sweet. He was forbidden fruit, juicy and ripe, primed for the crush of her lips, the bite of her teeth, the thrust of her tongue.

She gripped her fan, and an ebony stick snapped beneath her fingers. Shock and fear and dismay ignited in her brain and shot across her mind like a burning fuse. This couldn't happen. She wouldn't let it. She had seen the devastation of so-called love: the easy cruelty and casual abuse of a man who held a woman in his power; the empty yearning and hopeless need of the woman who was his willing victim. God Almighty's right front tooth! It couldn't happen to her.

Then Diarmid tossed her an impish wink, and she knew it had. She had fallen in love with this autocratic, patronizing, taunting, and infuriating man.

She dragged her gaze from her handsome, beguiling captor and found George Wythe scrutinizing her face. A deep understanding warmed his keen eyes.

"Our dear Maclean styles me a great scholar," he said softly, "but in truth he surpasses me in all things. Perhaps most of all in the wisdom he has evidenced by marrying you, my dear lady."

Diarmid glanced down at her flushed cheeks, then studied her with amused, lazy hauteur, rather as a cat watches a trapped mouse. "I honor the compliment," he said to Wythe. "But I'm afraid you miscalculate the compatibility of wisdom and marriage. When one arrives, the other vanishes."

"I disagree with my husband, Mr. Wythe," Lucy retorted. "But I quite agree with you. Mr. Maclean *is* most wise. Indeed, I vow that he is nigh onto a genius, as are all husbands." She slanted Diarmid her most killing smile. Oh, no; she would not become his victim, not as long as she held breath in her lungs. "They must be, if they are to match wits with their wives."

Eight

Lucy slipped from the brilliantly lit ballroom into the silent, empty gardens behind the Governor's Palace. She inhaled the pungent scent of damp earth and shivered. The air held a chill—unusual for early October, or so Governor Fauquier had told her—and a mist-shrouded moon floated high overhead. It obscured the stars and cast a pale, lustrous glow across the flowerbeds. It transformed the terraces to pewter mirrors, limned the trees with pearl, and silvered the roses hidden among the canes of an English rambler.

With a sigh of contentment, she swept down the steps, then strolled between the raised flowerbeds. She scarce could believe this wondrous evening! From the moment she had arrived, the gentlemen of Virginia had vied earnestly and gallantly for her undivided attention, starting with Governor Fauquier himself. He had insisted on leading her into the first minuet, loudly declaring, "England's loss, our gain, eh?"

She pulled up a dried mullein stalk and idly trailed it behind her down the gravel path. Diarmid had glowered at her like a catchpole at a cutpurse, no doubt waiting for her to make some dreadful mistake. But she had shown him. The governor had stoutly declared her the finest dancer it had ever been his pleasure to partner, and from that moment her evening had become pure rum sport.

She danced with Byrds and Carters and Randolphs. She traded bon mots with a Colonel Tayloe and accepted an invitation to dine at Sabine Hall from Colonel Carter. She grinned. Did *all* these colonials have military titles? Most enjoyably of all, she had spent a good half hour in spirited discourse with a student of George Wythe's named Thomas Jefferson. It quickly had become clear that the tall, red-headed young man was smitten, and Diarmid had swept her away with a possessive, jade-eyed glare at her suitor.

Lucy tossed the mullein stalk over the garden's brick wall. The only blight on the evening had been the mysterious blonde woman in the vulgar purple dress. It seemed everywhere Lucy turned, the creature hovered, glowering at her with palpable dislike.

Lucy strode back toward the house. God's nose, who cared about some jealous colonial miss? 'Twas time to tackle her arrogant husband and demand her due as winner of their bet. An image of the Ace of Swords floated across her mind, and she shivered again. She *had* to find Mick.

"As far as I'm concerned, the little bitch can go hang."

Lucy halted, then ducked into the shadows of the enormous rambling rosebush. Two women stood on the terrace, heads together in intense discussion.

"Venetia, please—watch your language," the shorter woman said. "Someone might hear."

Lucy's heart accelerated beneath her confining stays. God's fingers—the purple-swathed harpy was Venetia Lee! Several times in the past two weeks Patsy and Harry had alluded to Celia Stanton Lee's niece, always in a most oblique manner. Garnet, Patsy's African maid, hadn't been so discreet. She'd made it clear that Lucy shouldn't trust Venetia in general, and with Diarmid in particular.

"How do you expect me to be calm?" Venetia snapped open her fan and waved it furiously. Even in the moonlight Lucy could see the angry flush on the woman's cheeks. "Diarmid is mine! He's been in love with me for years. He'd never marry anyone but me. You know it—so don't expect me to take this lying down."

"Are you certain?" the other woman queried. "He seems quite smitten with his bride. Why, his eyes never left Madam Maclean all evening—"

"Don't call that slut Madam Maclean!" Venetia whirled

and paced across the terrace. "Lud, this can't be happening. Why didn't I make him marry me sooner? He was happy enough to rut in my bed whenever the urge took him, but—"

"Venetia!"

Pain knifed at Lucy's belly. She caught a hand to her ribs and fought the impulse to double over. She had known that a man like Diarmid—so wickedly handsome, so blatantly virile—must have had dozens of lovers. But somehow she'd imagined them long ago and far away. Now to find his lover here, flaunting their passion, bragging about her claim on him!

" 'Tis true," Venetia said airily. "We've been lovers for years. And let me tell you, no one can match Diarmid Maclean's prodigious talents in the bedchamber. The man's positively brazen."

Rebecca gave a shocked squeak but scuttled closer, obviously eager to hear the scandalous details.

"The rogue's up to something," Venetia snapped. "And I'll get to the bottom of it if it kills me. He can't treat me like this. Everyone in the colony expected us to wed. Why, Aunt Celia all but demanded that he marry me three weeks ago." A sly smile curled Venetia's lips; then she patted a hand to her belly. "I managed to convince her that the Lee family would never survive the scandal of a bastard child."

Lucy's knees buckled. Without a sound, she slipped forward with a slow, frozen motion that seemed to last an eternity. She collapsed on the cold, damp grass, then sat and dragged her quaking knees up to her chin.

God's heart, she couldn't bear to hear this—not tonight of all nights. Just minutes before she had been sure of a joyous future. She had proven to Diarmid that she was a lady, despite her guttersnipe upbringing. She had been the toast of the party. She clearly had won their bet, and Mick was but a quick search away. She turned distraught eyes to the moon. How could she have believed it would be easy to change her fate? God's ears, she truly had believed that if she could pass as a lady, then she would win Diarmid's love.

Her heart gave an agonizing throb, and she flung her arms

around her knees, desperate to dull the pain. She couldn't *stand* to think of Diarmid in Venetia's arms—kissing her lips, pressing his lean, hard body to hers, murmuring words of love, of lust. . . .

God's eyes! Diarmid was no better than Jocko, no better than the hundreds of faceless coves who had spent their brutish passion on her mother's frail body, caring not a whit that the whore beneath them was a person—a sweet, bright girl from a Yorkshire vicarage.

Lucy struggled to her knees. How could she have thought she loved that vile, arrogant Scotsman? She ought to be horse-whipped for her foolishness. Hadn't years in the filthy, plague-ridden alleys of East London taught her that all men were dogs—scavengers who gobbled their fill, then skulked away? Love Diarmid! Ha! She could never love such a lying, scheming cad. Only a black-hearted knave would marry a woman for his own selfish ends, when another woman—a woman he loved—carried his child.

She stood; then her petticoat snagged on a branch and she stumbled forward, catching a rose cane to steady herself. A thorn raked her hand, bringing a welcome sting of reality. She pressed her finger to her lips to stem the blood.

She ought to thank Venetia for revealing Diarmid's vile ways. In truth, the dyed-blond doxy probably had saved Lucy from a life of misery—for love and misery were as inseparable as a rose and its thorns. Let Venetia be Diarmid's bawd. She, Lucy Graves, would rather die than be his whore.

Venetia and Rebecca turned to enter the palace ballroom. "I'll get him back," Venetia declared. "He'll never be able to turn his back on the passion we shared. And I'll get rid of that dark-skinned English slut, no matter what I have to do."

Lucy waited several cold, endless minutes, then stormed onto the terrace. Damn Diarmid Maclean to the blackest pit of hell! If he thought he was going to discard her in favor of Venetia once his precious Stanton's Grove was his, he had another thought coming. She would leave when and how she wanted, and entirely on her own terms, for she'd learned a

fascinating fact from young Thomas Jefferson: Divorce was
illegal in the colony of Virginia.

She slipped inside through the long French windows, then
stopped dead, shocked to her toes for the second time that
evening. "You!" she gasped.

Diarmid ducked into an alcove under the stairwell and
thanked Saint Iona for a convenient shelter. Venetia had just
swept in from the terrace, peevish jealousy practically shoot-
ing from her cold blue eyes. He heaved a sigh. Was dodging
her worth all this effort? Aye, it was, for at that moment a
private talk with Venetia was about as appealing as having
his limbs torn asunder by stampeding stallions.

Earlier in the evening he had bowed and greeted her, but
guests had surrounded them, and etiquette had prevented the
knock-down, drag-out fight he knew was brewing. Och, Saint
Iona, what a mess. Indeed, Venetia could wait.

Two young Byrd cousins strolled past, not noticing Diarmid in the shadows. "Stab my vitals!" the taller gentleman
said. "Is not Madam Maclean the most ravishing creature
one's eyes have ever had the pleasure of perusing?"

"Far too fine for Maclean," his companion averred.
"Demme, that Highland freedman has the devil's own luck—
first Stanton's Grove and now that divine, black-haired angel."

They sauntered past and Diarmid bit back a chuckle. Imagine describing Lucy as an angel! His smile faded, then jealousy and a grudging admiration twisted deep in the barren
reaches of his heart. Och, he had been unfair to the wee imp.
'Twas plain she was all she had claimed, and more. Governor
Fauquier had declared himself her slave in front of ninety
people, and Diarmid had thought he'd have to take a whip
to that gangling pup Jefferson. He could understand the gentlemen's reaction: Lucy's tiny waist and enticing bosom were
like cheese to hungry rats. But George Wythe's reaction puzzled him.

At the first opportunity, the old scholar had tracked Diarmid to the card room, then blithely cornered him beside the

punch bowl. "What's going on, Maclean?" he demanded. His voice was as mild as ever, but his eyes burned like quicklime.

Diarmid arched his brows disarmingly and contrived to look naive.

"None of your charming masks with me," Wythe said. "I've known you for sixteen years—ever since you came off a convict ship, indentured for Jacobite treason. 'Twas I who placed you at Stanton's Grove, was it not? I know what happened to you back in Scotland, and I know how it's scarred you. So tell me what game you're playing."

Diarmid cast his friend a wry smile. "I found myself wanting a bit of adventure, and marriage is the greatest adventure of all, aye? Rather like going off to war."

"I find it difficult to believe, sir, that you would risk hurting a sweet and sensitive young girl on a whim."

Diarmid threw back his head and laughed. "Sweet and sensitive? Och, that's the first time I've heard those words applied to Lucy."

Wythe scrutinized him closely. "I've seen how you've watched her this evening. I'm beginning to think you just might love her after all."

Diarmid snatched up his whisky glass, emptied it with one gulp, then slammed it back on the table with such force that it almost shattered. "You know my views on love," he snapped. "There's no such thing. Men and women come together because lust compels them. If they stay together, 'tis, at best, out of economic need or mutual lethargy or the realization that they won't find anything better. At worst, 'tis to control and torment and betray a person who cannot escape."

Wythe shook his head. "My dear Maclean, you've the wild, passionate soul of a Gael. Do you seriously mean to tell me you don't believe in love?"

Diarmid laughed, a harsh, razor-edged sound devoid of mirth. "To believe in something is to acknowledge that it exists. I don't believe in love because it does not exist."

"If something does not exist, has never existed, and will never exist, why should one deny belief in it so vehemently?"

Recalling the scene, Diarmid ran a hand over his mouth. Why, indeed? He had pondered the devilish question all evening. Wythe, the sly old fox, was never wrong. Did he see something Diarmid did not?

A burst of applause rippled from the ballroom, then feminine voices rose in giddy excitement, followed by low, masculine murmurs. Prompted by mild curiosity and a strong desire to halt his disturbing train of thought, Diarmid sauntered to the ballroom doorway.

The mahogany-paneled room was high-ceilinged, long, and rather narrow, with Chippendale chairs ringing the perimeter. Somehow, most of the governor's guests had crammed into its confines, pressed shoulder to shoulder and ranked several deep. A small orchestra, composed of violins, viola, cello, and harpsichord, filled one corner of the ballroom. The aroma of tobacco and lavender and sweat filled the air, and the gentle susurrus of silk skirts and feathered fans lulled Diarmid's senses. Then a quick flash of scarlet caught his attention. He stepped closer.

Lucy stood in animated discussion with an African fiddle player and two other black musicians. They nodded, then Lucy whirled and sailed to the center of the ballroom.

The glow from a thousand candles warmed her skin to the rich sheen of Egyptian amber, and Diarmid's heart slowed to a languorous throb. Time seemed to stop, and the restless crowd faded from his mind. The orchestra began to play, and a steady, syncopated rhythm filled the air. It seeped through his ears and eyes and skin, then roared through his blood to meld with his hammering heartbeat.

Lucy raised her chin, and her eyes blazed a regal challenge. With a dramatic flourish, she raised one hand high overhead and slowly turned in a circle, instantly commanding the crowd's rapt attention with the taut, sensual lines of her body. The room fell silent, except for the strange beat of the slave drum and maddening rattle of a primitive instrument Diarmid couldn't name.

A tantalizing flush suffused Lucy's slender throat, then washed across the lush swell of her cleavage. Her stays pinched her waist into a curve Diarmid ached to caress, and the scarlet silk of her gown shimmered in the flickering light, enticing him like a moth to a flame. Och, but she was a beguiling beauty. Her thick black hair gleamed like a midnight sky, and the long curl twining down over her shoulder made him long to wrap his hand around it and hold her down, hold her beneath him and—

Lust flared through his loins, hot and aching and potent. His fingers twitched with the need to caress the delicate curve of her breasts and trace the intoxicating angle where her jaw met her throat. He longed to cup his hands around her cheekbones and drown in the amber-flecked mystery of her eyes. He ached to suckle her pouting lips and lick the piquant black beauty mark just above her eye.

The slave's violin began a strange, exotic wail. The syncopated rhythm and minor key captured him. It conjured up images of wild, craggy mountains, of ruthless black-eyed bandits and glorious raven-haired women who danced around a leaping bonfire beneath the remote ice of a million merciless stars.

Lucy began to dance. With a lightning-quick flourish, she struck a dramatic pose—skirts in hand, one arm high overhead in a gesture of ancient defiance. Slowly, rhythmically, she tapped her feet and snapped her fingers. She swayed and whirled, stopping again and again to strike dramatic poses: head to the side and hands on hips; back arched and arms raised.

The music increased in tempo and intensity, and the crowd began to respond. They clapped in time to Lucy's stamping feet and swaying hips. Perspiration glowed across her high cheekbones. Her hair fell from its pins and streamed down her back like a river of night. In the dim light her slanted black eyes caught Diarmid's. She faltered for an instant. Then she jerked her chin and whirled away. The wild tempo increased and her gestures became more frenzied. She grew more daring, more savage, more desirable. Her eyes never left his, but blazed with fury and a centuries-old invitation.

Just then a man stepped from the crowd and strode toward

her. For an instant, Diarmid couldn't place him, as the man's back was turned. Lucy cast a disdainful glance at Diarmid; then she smiled at the stranger and sailed into his arms. As if on cue, the music changed from the wild syncopation of the forbidden flamenco to a sultry rhythm.

Recognition, then raw fury surged through Diarmid's gut. The man dancing with Lucy was that perverted, sadistic, grasping cur, Isaiah Ludlow.

Setting his jaw, Diarmid thrust his way through the crowd and onto the dance floor. By Saint Iona, Lucy had gone too far this time. He would tolerate much from his beautiful, thieving bride, but dancing with his bitterest rival was more than his Scottish pride—and temper—could stand.

Diarmid caught Ludlow's spindly shoulder in a steely grip. "Your pardon," he said through gritted teeth, struggling to keep his voice calm. "Madam Maclean forgets herself. She has promised this dance to her husband."

"It appears that you're the one who forgets himself," Ludlow replied. His low voice dripped resentment as he tried to shrug free. "Indeed, your luck is exceeded only by your arrogance. Who but you would believe both his wife and his position beyond the reach of others?"

Diarmid's muscles tensed. He would love nothing more than to grab Ludlow by the throat and shake the sneer off his face, but a flash of prudence prevented his violent impulse. He released his grip on Ludlow's shoulder, stepped back, and bowed rigidly.

"You remind me that I have been remiss in guarding my possessions," he said, voice smooth with velvety warning. "An error which shall not be repeated in future." Without waiting for a reply, Diarmid yanked Lucy to his side, then marched her off the dance floor and through the gawking crowd.

"Let go of me, you whoreson," Lucy hissed, teeth clenched. A livid blush stained her high cheekbones and outrage flashed in her eyes. Diarmid tightened his grip. If he weren't so intent on breaking her bonnie wee neck, he would find her high-spirited resistance quite tempting.

He thrust her through the French doors and out onto the brick terrace, then spun her around to face him. "Madam, you will shut your mouth. You are a disgrace to my name, to this town, and to the colony of Virginia. I will remind you that the Governor's Palace isn't Newgate Prison or some dockside whorehouse. Never have I seen such a wanton display—"

"Wanton display!" Lucy shrieked. She struggled in his grasp, squirming like a viper in a sack of eels. "I'm not the wanton here. I'm not the one who goes a-whoring about the countryside like a rutting bull. I'm not the one who lies and schemes—"

He shook her until her teeth clacked. "You are the queen of lies and schemes, madam—and the queen of thieves, for you've stolen the attentions of every man in the colony. Now control yourself. We shall leave at once."

"I'll go nowhere with you, you bloody sodding cove! And I'll not help you cozen an innocent old lady. Thief I may be, but at least I'm not a lust-addled knave who leaves doxies and bastards littering the hedgerows."

Diarmid caught her chin and forced her to look into his eyes. She glared at him, sparking defiance and haughty pride. What was the trollop carrying on about? Why this sudden fixation with his sexual prowess? A thought hit him, and his fingers tightened on her delicate jaw. She winced but refused to quail.

"Have you been speaking to Venetia?" he demanded.

"I wouldn't speak to that pox-raddled pisspot if my life depended on it. Now get your hands off me." Quick as the snake she was, she drew back her leg and smashed her knee into his groin.

Pain shot through Diarmid's vitals. It was a glancing blow, but he still flinched and lost his grip on the infuriating wench. Lucy skittered beyond his reach, then planted her fists on her hips.

"You can have your precious plantation and that painted harpy! I won our bet fair and square, and I'm lady enough not to stand in your way. Not as long as you honor our terms and agree to a few more of my own, that is."

He lunged and caught her around the waist. His momentum hurtled her backward, and they stumbled against the palace wall. Lucy's head snapped back and struck the brick with a sickening thud. She gasped.

"Och, me poor wee lass." Unaccustomed remorse deepened Diarmid's Highland burr. "I'm so sorry. I didna mean to hurt ye." He caught her head and ran his fingers through her hair, checking for injury with a tenderness that surprised him. The ebony strands felt like liquid silk to his touch. "I couldna stand to see ye with Ludlow, laughing and dancing in his arms. . . ."

"I despise you!" Tears glinted in Lucy's black eyes, yet still she struggled to defy him. "Why did you give me the chance to be a lady? Why did you trick me into believing I could be happy? We both know I'm doomed to the gutters." With a despairing cry, she pounded her fists against his shoulders.

Diarmid scooped her against him, then twined his fingers in the wild tangles of her hair. "Shhhhh, lass. Why do ye fash? Why do ye fight me and defy me so? Do ye no' see how I long for ye?"

Gently, he tugged her head back and kissed her full on the mouth. She gasped at his sudden invasion, then parted her lips with an innocence that almost duped him into believing her protests of virtue. Almost. Taking advantage of her momentary confusion, he molded his body to her soft flesh and deepened the kiss, reveling in the panicked flutters of her tongue against his. She tasted of spiced peaches and pure woman.

She pounded his shoulders, then moaned and squirmed beneath him, arousing him to the point of madness. He pressed her back against the rough brick wall, shielding her head from further bumps, his hand still twined in her hair. She tried to turn her face away, but he slanted his jaw against hers and urged her mouth wider.

"Och, lassie," he murmured against the slick curve of her

lower lip. "Can ye no' feel how I yearn for ye? Release me from me promise." She stiffened, and he groaned with frustration and sheer, aching desire; then plunged his tongue into her succulence again and again.

She gave a frantic wriggle, and her slender thigh slipped between his legs. Chuckling wickedly, he grasped the tantalizing curve of her buttocks through her billowing skirts, then lifted her until her toes barely brushed the ground. Desperate to keep her balance, she clamped her thighs around his leg. Slowly, languidly, his tongue still plunging and swirling around hers, he ran his hands up over the curve of her hips and up over her wickedly tight stays until he cupped the fullness of her breast. Its heaviness sent a shaft of lust straight to his manhood. He groaned against her mouth; his erection throbbed, stretched, ached to have her.

His fingers found the taut peak of her nipple, and he rolled the tempting point between thumb and forefinger, expertly coaxing it to diamond hardness. With both hands, he kneaded her lush breasts until she relaxed against him, limp and yielding, her weight a delicious feast he intended to savor right here and now—his promise of a chaste marriage be damned!

He released her mouth and trailed damp, nibbling kisses across her jaw and down her throat. Gooseflesh tore across her fevered skin, sending another dizzying shudder of lust to stiffen his cock. Murmuring reassurance, he eased the glorious weight of her breasts over her décolletage. Her stays plumped and pushed her mounds together like ripe, tempting fruit. He lowered his head and flicked his tongue across her nipple. She gasped and started; then she clutched at his shoulders and clamped his thigh between hers.

"That's it, lass," he whispered. "Let me love ye right here, beneath the stars." His hands encircled her waist, then pushed her hips down until the hard curve of her pubic bone ground against his thigh. He closed his lips around the ripe tip of her breast, then suckled gently and rhythmically, seducing her body into the wanton sexuality he knew she possessed—and doubtless had lavished on a host of fortunate men.

With a tiny moan, she tangled her hand in his hair and

pulled his mouth against her bosom. He deepened and hardened his suckling, then swirled his tongue around her nipple and teasingly bit the jutting flesh. Insistently, he rocked her hips and pressed her woman's core against the bone and muscle of his thigh, all the while imagining her naked and panting beneath him, legs spread wide in brazen invitation.

Lucy moaned, and her head dropped against the brick wall in an ancient gesture of surrender. Diarmid's erection clamored for release, and the ache in his loins keened with near-painful ecstasy. Cupping her buttocks in his hands, he nibbled her wet nipples, rocked her hips against his thigh, then renewed his deep, insistent sucking. She caught his rhythm, increased the tempo, intensified the pressure. The heat and friction of her body maddened him to the point of savagery; he dragged her hard against him and ground his cock against her womanhood.

"Diarmid," she rasped. "Please . . ."

Suddenly she arched her back and froze against him. She cried out in hoarse, passionate agony, and he barely had time to muffle the sound with a soul-stealing kiss. Then she collapsed, limp and helpless as a bairn in his arms.

Lucy slumped against the palace wall. The scratchy chill of the brick bit into her bare shoulders. Her breath came in desperate gasps. Passion crashed through her body and raged between her thighs in wet, shocking need. God's codpiece, what had just happened? One minute she had felt such acute, stunning pleasure, she had thought she would shatter and die. Then her mind and body had exploded into shudders of blinding ecstasy so intense she thought she *had* died.

"My queen," Diarmid murmured.

His breath was moist and whisky-scented against her cheek; his body was a furnace that consumed her. She closed her eyes and lost herself in his enthralling scent—all leather and tobacco and raw, male arousal. For several long moments, his heartbeat thundered against hers; then he eased her down the hard length of his body until her feet regained the terrace.

Her knees quavered. God's heart, she would dissolve into a puddle if he so much as glanced at her.

He did, of course. Heavy-lidded and passion-dark, his eyes seared through her panicked confusion. A wildfire of savage passion blazed in their emerald depths. Then, for a split second, she caught an aching vulnerability that frightened her to the very core of her being. She whimpered, loathe to surrender. He might have taken her body, but he would not take her heart.

Instantly, a cool, jade curtain whisked down over his gaze. He smiled, and his teeth glinted in the cold moonlight. "A pity I cannot take you right here," he drawled. "But, my dear madam, you're worth savoring in the comfort and privacy of my own bed, not the chill of the governor's garden." He swatted her bottom, then chuckled with the infuriating air of a rakish, taunting demon. "Let's go, Lucia. I cannot wait a moment longer to claim our wee bet's prize."

Burning with mortification, she clenched her eyes tight. Damn the man, and damn her own weak flesh. This is what had destroyed her mother—this pleasure, this yearning, this wild, terrible joy.

He leaned forward and tapped her chin with one long finger. "Och, lass, dinna look so regretful. I'm your husband, after all. And 'tis not as though ye havena had a man before." His Highland accent had returned, magical as a Romany blessing to her ears. Then his words filtered into her brain.

She flashed him a defiant gaze. "Sir, I am your wife in name only. As you will recall, you promised that our marriage would be chaste. I have no desire to warm your bed." He arched a wry brow and she blushed hotly. "That is, well . . . Oh, damn you! I may have the desire, but I'm not a whore. I've told you before—I'm a maiden."

Diarmid tossed her a smile of roguish amusement. "Madam, surely at this juncture your false modesty—"

"Be quiet!" To her horror, tears clogged her throat. She had to stop this before she made even more of a fool of herself. "You took advantage of me, as it seems your habit to do. As to *you* winning our bet—well, all I can say is, your arrogant attitude fits you like a sausage fits a casing. I won our bet. Everyone believes I'm an English lady of some rank and considerable wit."

"You won nothing, madam. Fooling Celia is the true test."

Sudden excitement bounded through her and she waved away Diarmid's stubbornness. He would abandon his ridiculous demands when he heard her news. "I just made your job easier," she said. She smoothed down her skirts and grinned with triumph. "I know who bought Mick."

She clapped her hands and twirled in a circle, ignoring the frown on Diarmid's handsome face. Handsome, ha! What cared she for fine looks and beguiling charm? In days she would be reunited with Mick—sweet, naughty, impish Mick!

"You spoke to the gentleman this evening," she continued. "Although by the rude way you acted, you may well have jeopardized our chance at buying Mick back. It seems Mr. Ludlow—"

"Ludlow? Do you mean to tell me Isaiah Ludlow is the man who bought your little brother?"

Lucy halted, startled by Diarmid's frigid tone. "Why, yes. That's why I agreed to dance with him. He's a strange cove, I'll grant you, but—"

Diarmid raked a hand through his hair, then stalked away across the terrace. Even in the moonlight she recognized the tense set of his broad shoulders and the tell-tale hardening of his angular jaw.

"What's the matter?" she asked. "Aren't you glad about Mick?"

"Och, my dear Lucy. Chaos follows you like a dog follows a bone." He turned, a weary half-smile on his lips. "Are you sure 'twas Ludlow bought Mick?"

"Of course. Don't you think I'd recognize him? Besides, he admitted it—at least in part. He said he'd purchased a young lad from Captain Pratt, but he wouldn't tell me where he was, or why he'd bought him. When he found out I was your wife, he grew even more strange." She gave a tiny shudder. "He looked at me like he could see me in just my shift!"

Diarmid's jaw twisted, then set in its usual granite lines. "Aye, I've no doubt. Did he agree to sell Mick?"

Lucy's pulse began to race. She had to succeed. Diarmid had to keep his promise. "Well . . . not in so many words. He said you had something he wanted, and perhaps you could come to terms. He asked me to tell you to call on him at Resolute, his plantation." She tilted her head, trying to read Diarmid's unfathomable expression. "Do you know what he might want?"

"Och, indeed I do. And 'tis quite impossible." Diarmid scowled blackly; then his lips twisted in a sardonic smile. "Nay, my queen. If Ludlow wants anything of mine, I'm afraid poor wee Mick must remain in his hands."

"Don't you dare say that!" Tears rushed from her throat into her eyes. He couldn't betray her like this. He had promised to find Mick and buy him back and free him so they could be together. "You're even worse than I thought. First you abandon your unborn babe, then you break your promise over another innocent child. Oh, you are vile!" She raised her hand to slap that black scowl right off his face.

He caught her arm and twisted it to her side as easily as if she were a sparrow. "What are you talking about? I have no children, born or unborn."

"You hateful, lying varlet!" She stumbled back, nearly blind with rage and heartbreak. He had taken her for a fool once, but no one took Lucy Graves for a fool twice. "You know Venetia carries your babe, and you've abandoned it the same way you've abandoned Mick. Thanks to you, we're all chained in misery, just like your slaves."

Quick, pained regret ghosted through his eyes, but she ignored it. Never again would she soften her heart to this scheming Scotsman. She lashed out and slapped his handsome, arrogant face with all her strength. Then she whirled and ran.

"Venetia, your lies begin to weary me," Diarmid said. He drew a slow, wavering breath, willing the anger and tension from his body. By Saint Iona, would this damnable night never end? First Lucy's appalling behavior with Ludlow on the dance floor, then that thrilling little interlude in the garden . . . His manhood gave an impertinent throb at the mere memory.

Och, but Lucy was a bewitching wench, Gypsy thief or no. He'd never felt such intense passion for any lass, and he'd had hundreds over the years. How had Lucy so charmingly put it? Aye—he surely had gone 'round the countryside like a rutting bull.

His lips curved into a rueful smile. Och, what was ailing him this night? After the way Lucy had behaved—kicking, slapping, swearing like a sailor—he had every right to horsewhip her and sell her off to Maryland. His smile deepened, and he realized Venetia could see the quick dimples bracketing his mouth. But he could never sell Lucy—or let her go. Life would be too boring without her. This thought unsettled him so badly he was almost grateful for Venetia's angry snort.

"Wipe that smile off your face and tell me why I should care for your weariness," she demanded. "You're the cad who promised to marry me, then slunk away after some English slut. Lud, the whore looks like a Gypsy—"

"I've had enough name-calling for one night."

Diarmid jerked open the front gate to Venetia's father's town house on Duke of Gloucester Street. Earlier in the evening, after casting black looks in Diarmid's direction, Harry and Patsy had taken Lucy home in their carriage, no doubt outraged by the wee trollop's exaggerated account of his perfidious behavior. The moment they left, Venetia had descended and publicly demanded that Diarmid see her home. As a gentleman, he hadn't been able to refuse.

He bit back a profanity. Tomorrow all of Williamsburg would be gossiping about the distraught Madam Maclean and poor, cast-off Venetia, whom heartless Diarmid Maclean had walked home through darkened streets.

Venetia swept through the gate, then turned, caught his hand, and held it to her cheek. "Oh, Diarmid, I can't help it.

You know how much I love you! Imagine the shock of finding you married after you promised yourself to me—"

"I never promised to marry you, Venetia."

"But Aunt Celia said—"

"I merely told Celia I would consider her little ultimatum." He arched a knowing brow at her tightly laced, lavender-damask waistline. "By the way, how did you convince Celia to support your little marriage campaign? She's no great admirer of yours."

Venetia lowered her lashes. "Can you not guess? I told her I'm carrying your child."

Diarmid threw back his head and laughed, a cynical sound that rang down the empty street. So that was what had set Lucy into such a fash. Och, he *did* deserve a kick in the balls if that was what she believed of him.

"My child?" he queried. "I'm glad you narrowed the field, considering how widely you've sown your favors."

"Don't you dare laugh." Venetia smiled a blatant invitation, then cupped his hand to her lush cleavage. "Your child grows within me and will one day suckle at my breast. You and I are meant to be together, Diarmid. You've never been able to resist my bed."

"Enough." He extricated his hand and quelled the disgust rippling down his spine. How had he ever found this scheming, overpainted creature desirable? Guttersnipe Lucy might well be, but compared to Venetia, she was as pure and desirable as spring water to the fevered. "I know there is no babe. Or if there is, 'tis not mine."

Venetia's ice-blue eyes narrowed. "How can you say that?"

"Because you were in your monthly flux the last time we lay together."

"I beg your pardon?"

"Madam, you forget I am well versed in human biology. 'Tis physically impossible for a woman to get with child during her menses. I haven't lain with you for a month. Therefore, I have had no opportunity to be with you when you could conceive."

He nonchalantly withdrew his pocket watch and glanced

at it with deliberate detachment. "Furthermore, if my calculations are correct, you should be in your flux right now." He pinned her with an icy glare, determined once and for all to be rid of this dreadful shrew. "Now, madam, if you don't want me hauling you before your Aunt Celia and Dr. Walker I suggest you retract your little story." He stalked back through the gate, then closed it soundly behind him. "Or at the very least, contrive to have a convenient 'accident.' "

Nine

Isaiah Ludlow slumped down in the wing chair by his bed-chamber hearth and listened to the mournful rattle of the rain against the black windows. The logs on the fire popped and crackled, and he stared into the flames, pensively stroking the chair's red damask upholstery. Two hundred barrels of tobacco the fabric had cost him, but it was the finest to be had. His London merchant had sworn it. The man even sent his own wife to purchase it, according to Isaiah's strict, written speci-fications.

Sighing, Isaiah took a sip of brandy and forced himself to relax. 'Twas late—gone ten of the clock—and time to rest, for tomorrow promised to be a tiring day. Moving two thou-sand barrels of contraband tobacco was no small task, espe-cially since that bleeding heart Diarmid Maclean had forbidden him the use of the Stanton's Grove dock. This cov-eted gem of planks and pilings was the last spot on the James where an ocean-going merchantman could anchor to load and unload cargo. Less felicitously situated planters—Ludlow in-cluded—had to float their hogsheads on flatboats down the James, then pay Celia Stanton Lee a fee for the right to ship their cargo from the Stanton's Grove dock.

Isaiah scowled, then snatched off his wig and raked a hand through the thinning bristles of his hair. For years Celia had allowed him to use the dock for a steep price and over Maclean's strenuous objections, for the arrogant overseer ada-mantly opposed the importation of Isaiah's most lucrative cargo: African slaves. Now it appeared the damned Jacobite had gained complete control of Celia, and of Stanton's Grove, for six months ago he had denied Isaiah use of the dock at any price.

"Curse it," Isaiah muttered. He hadn't been able to land a shipment of slaves in over a year, and his debts were mounting ominously, as were the fees he paid other downriver planters to ship from their docks. But that imperious troublemaker Maclean would not beat him. Smuggling had provided royally for Isaiah in the past, and it would again.

He leaned his head against the chair's ample padding and carefully reviewed his plans. He'd smuggled tobacco for nigh onto twenty years, and he hadn't been caught yet. He smiled coldly. That was because he anticipated every possible mistake, every conceivable misstep. A pessimist he might be, but such caution had served him well.

He gritted his teeth. Curse the English for their contemptible laws! King and Parliament had long decreed that Virginia tobacco must be shipped to England for sale through a Crown-controlled cadre of merchants. This vile monopoly allowed Britain to set the price it paid Virginia planters for their outrageously popular crop—a crop deemed more vital than food in Virginia's first years. Once, when the colonists had endeavored to build a church, the king's attorney general was reputed to have said, "Damn your souls! Plant tobacco."

Isaiah poured himself a splash of brandy from a Spanish cut-crystal decanter. No English laws would stand in his way. Indeed, circumventing those laws had made him a rich man. One day—*if* he could resume his slave trading—he would be the richest man in the colony. Only one person stood in his way: Diarmid Maclean.

Isaiah cursed and kicked at the black-and-white spaniel bitch sleeping at his feet. The creature yelped and scuttled from the room as Isaiah tossed back another swig of brandy. What was the wretched cur doing up here, anyway? He wasn't a sentimental man, but after he had found one of the spaniel pups with its neck broken, he'd told the house niggers never to let any of the dogs beyond the ground floor.

Isaiah's brows slammed together. Curse it all, but Fate was

a bastard. It had rewarded Isaiah's obsessive work and ruthless ingenuity with ample wealth, but personally it had punished him almost beyond bearing. He cocked his head and peered up at the ceiling, straining to hear any suspicious sounds over the rain and the fire. All silent tonight, thank heaven. Or more likely thank hell, for surely it was hell he lived in.

He struggled to his feet and snatched up his crimson silk dressing gown and matching tasseled nightcap. As his fingers slid over the shimmering fabric, he felt a rare spurt of pleasure. French, this ensemble was—straight from Paris, and the latest fashion. Ah, indeed, smuggling had its rewards. The French, Dutch, and Spanish were more than happy to double England's price for Virginia tobacco—for they, like Isaiah, held no love for the blood-sucking Brits.

He belted the robe around his thin waist, settled the cap on his head, and returned to his chair's lonely embrace. Then he caught his reflection in a gleaming black windowpane. He flinched. For a moment, minus the fashionable cap, he had looked just like his dead father. His scowl deepened. Did others see the resemblance? Curse it all, he hoped not.

Isaiah's father had been a no-account farmer whose years of toiling over useless dirt had garnered him nothing but debt and the dismissive scorn of the Virginia gentry. Floyd Ludlow and his sickly wife had been carried away by malaria when Isaiah was eighteen and his sister, Emmaline, was ten. A distant cousin had cared for poor, darling Emmie, and Isaiah had signed on with a Norfolk merchant ship engaged in a spot of illegal trade with Virginia's colonial neighbors. From Charleston to Boston, he had learned the finer points of smuggling and had discovered a prodigious talent for gambling—a talent that had helped dull his . . . darker cravings.

Years later, back in Norfolk for a consultation with Emmie's doom-spewing quack of a doctor, he had sat down at a card game with a young English gentleman and had risen four hours later in possession of the luckless sod's plantation. Isaiah chuckled. Fate had smiled that time.

A sharp creak sounded from the ceiling. He froze, straining his ears for further sounds. Nothing.

He stood and paced to the window. What would happen now? Would Fate reward his impulsive attempt at reparation, or would it punish his sentimental foolishness?

Shivering, he peered out through the black sheet of rain. It was too dark to see, yet it calmed him to look down on Resolute. The lackwit Englishman's long-neglected plantation had flourished under Isaiah's care, and his gambling winnings and earnings from quick runs of contraband to the West Indies had enabled him to increase its acreage and improve its tobacco. On Isaiah's second run to the Indies, he had avidly entered the slave trade, smuggling Africans into Virginia via Barbados. Although the House of Burgesses had for years been trying to outlaw the direct importation of slaves from Africa, everyone looked the other way when Ludlow's latest crop of black gold hit the market.

Sudden rage flashed through him, and he quelled the urge to smash his fist through the windowpane. His first fight with Diarmid Maclean had been over those bloody slaves. Maclean abhorred slavery, damned fool that he was. When he'd discovered Isaiah's illicit trade, he had dragged it before the Burgesses relentlessly until they had been forced to put a stop to it. Then he'd convinced Celia to cut off Isaiah's dock privileges. And now Isaiah drowned in debt, all because of that arrogant Jacobite.

Curse it all! Being a nigger-lover in Virginia was as low as a man could sink, yet no one batted an eyelash at Maclean's obsession over the supposed injustice of slavery. Governor Fauquier laughed and chalked it up to the peculiarity of Highland Scots—an outrageous stance for the king's governor, considering Maclean had fought with the Jacobites to overthrow George II.

Isaiah paced across the bedchamber, for once not taking pleasure in the thick Turkey carpet under his feet. It galled him beyond bearing that Maclean—a filthy convict guilty of treason—should be so adored by the colony's finest families. George Wythe had made him his closest protégé, and the Carters, Randolphs, and Byrds had invited him to dine and to court their daughters. Worst of all, it was rumored that

Celia Stanton Lee—whose heart could fail at any moment—
was on the verge of leaving Stanton's Grove to the bloody
bastard.

He paused in front of an elaborate gilt mirror. What *was*
it that made Maclean—an outsider if there ever was one—the
darling of the planter aristocracy? And why should he, Isaiah
Ludlow of Resolute, be merely tolerated?

He gazed at his reflection, taking critical stock of his sallow, pockmarked skin and thin, hard lips. Nay, he could not
be called a handsome man—the ravages of malaria and small-
pox had seen to that. Yet neither was he repulsive. If not quite
up to Maclean's much-touted-by-the-ladies six-foot-four
height, he at least was taller than the average fellow. And
several women preferred his wiry build to Maclean's chiseled
muscles. He brushed away the annoying thought that his few
admirers were white-trash desperate to get their claws into
the owner of Resolute.

Nay, if it weren't for Maclean, Isaiah Ludlow would have
taken his rightful place in Virginia society by now. Maclean's
proximity—Resolute bordered Stanton's Grove—threw them
together in people's estimation, and while the gentry could
tolerate one black sheep among its ranks, it wouldn't countenance two. His fellow planters could not ignore Isaiah because of Resolute, but they made it pointedly clear that they
preferred Maclean, the patrician Scottish laird.

"Mast' Ludlow, you best come quick."

Isaiah snapped from his reverie. Sally, his favorite house
nigger, stood hesitantly in the bedchamber doorway. Her deep
brown eyes were wide as a startled doe's, and she twisted her
neat calico apron between callused hands.

"What is it?" he snapped.

"Weren't my fault. I tol' her you wouldn't like it." Sally
stepped back, and her eyes grew wider in her smooth, mahog-
any-skinned face.

"What wasn't your fault? Speak up, girl."

Tears rolled down Sally's cheeks. *"Please* don't beat me,
Mast' Ludlow. I tried, honest I did, but she wouldn't listen."

Isaiah strode toward the cowering slave. "Cease slinging snot about and answer me. Is something wrong with Miss Emmaline?"

The girl pawed at her eyes, desperate to dry her face before he reached her. Suddenly he noted the fear in her expression, and a shaft of ice plunged down his spine. This didn't look like the usual darky hysterics at all. He snatched a candlestick from his bedside table and quickly bent to light it in the fire. As he straightened, a dull thud reverberated across the ceiling. His heart lurched and he hurried across the room. Sally stumbled after him, sobbing and sniveling the while.

"Where's Moses?" he demanded. Curse it all, that damned nigger better be upstairs. He was the strongest man on the place. Years ago Isaiah had released him from his duties in the field and brought him into the house to tackle a much more taxing job.

He entered the eerie darkness of the hall. The candle's slanting flame cast bizarre, writhing shadows on the bare, plastered walls. Sally scuttled up behind him, and he inhaled the pungent musk of her sweat.

"Moses be sick," she blurted. "I tol' you this mornin'. He down with the fever."

Isaiah increased his stride until he was practically sprinting for the stairs. The narrow, twisting flight lay at the back of the house, hidden from the wide front hall and the palatial guest chambers—chambers that remained empty, no matter how Isaiah longed to fill them with guests, or even with a wife and child.

A surge of jealousy churned his vitals. Maclean was married now, curse it all, and it was clear he was besotted with his charming bride. Indeed, Isaiah was a bit smitten himself, for he had never seen a lovelier, wittier creature than Madam Maclean. For an instant, he closed his eyes and savored a vision of her slim body and gamine face. She would be just the thing to banish the gloom from Resolute's echoing halls.

A sudden recollection jolted his panicked brain. He had something that Lucy Maclean wanted desperately, something she was more than willing to bargain for. Best of all, he had something he could dangle over Diarmid Maclean's arrogant head.

He halted and grabbed Sally's elbow. "Where's the boy?" he demanded. She squealed and froze like a rabbit before a rattler. He shook her, and her turbaned head whipped back and forth on her pliant black neck. "Answer me or I'll beat it out of you."

"I tol' her not to do it! But she too strong. I couldn't hold her."

A sharp cry tore down the twisting staircase. They froze; then Isaiah shot forward. The hair pricked on the back of his neck, and the candle guttered and died in his hand. Everything went black, as black as the heart of a tomb. Isaiah clutched the heavy candlestick to his chest and bolted up the stairs—up into utter darkness.

Ten

Lucy gazed out at the green, shade-dappled banks of College Creek and tried to recall every Romany curse she had ever known. There was the one involving a silver coin, a dead pig, and a piece of linen worn close to the body. 'Twas absolutely warranted to strike the cursed one with itchy boils in a most compromising spot. She smothered a grin. 'Twas just the affliction for a rutting bull like Diarmid. Then her smile died. Where in blue blazes would she get a dead pig, let alone a silver coin? His highness hadn't allowed her near anything silver since the night he'd caught her stealing Patsy's spoons.

The carriage lurched over a rut and Lucy clutched at the padded leather seat, determined not to brush against the vile Scot's broad shoulders. God's teeth, she had been a fool to make the trip to Stanton's Grove in a two-seated chaise—or shay, as Harry Cheney called it in his foppish Virginia drawl. 'Twas entirely too intimate.

Diarmid glanced down at her, then winked impudently. "Still avoiding me, my queen? I warn you, Celia won't take you for a moonstruck young bride if you persist in leaping away like a scalded cat every time I touch you."

He grinned, and his wolfish teeth flashed in the morning sunlight. Lucy jerked up her chin and glanced away. She would not let him bait her into speaking. She'd steadfastly given him the silent treatment since their wretchedly embarrassing encounter at the governor's ball last night, and no amount of dimpled smiles or teasing comments would make her forgive him, blast his plague-rotted heart.

Diarmid idly flicked the buggy whip an inch above the horse's back. Then he chuckled—a low, suggestive sound that sent shivers down her spine. She wrapped her shawl around her shoulders and stiffened into a prime imitation of a Puritan goodwife. From the corner of her eye she noted Diarmid lazily studying her face.

Suddenly he cracked the whip above the horse's ears and yelled, "Hyaaah!" The frightened nag leaped forward and bolted down the narrow dirt track. "Here. Drive," Diarmid said, nonchalantly tossing her the reins.

A hairpin turn materialized out of the trees ahead. The horse careened forward on thundering hooves, showing no intention of following the rutted road's precarious course. Lucy grabbed the reins, gathered them in her fists, and hauled back with all her strength. The horse didn't slow a whit.

"God's ribs, ye bloody Scottish bastard," she spat. "Are ye trying to kill us?"

The bend loomed. A low-hanging branch clawed her cheek. God's ankles, if she couldn't stop this headstrong nag, then she'd damn sure drive it around that turn. She rose off the carriage seat and hauled on the right rein with all her strength. The horse plunged forward. Then, forced by the steely tension on the rein, it began to turn. The axles squealed like tortured banshees and the carriage tilted up on two wheels.

The track straightened and the shay crashed down into its proper place. Lucy's teeth cracked together and caught her tongue in a painful bite. The lathered horse slowed to a trot. She yanked the creature to a halt and rounded on Diarmid.

"What was that all about, ye addled-brained cove? We could have been killed!"

Diarmid arched a devilish brow and reclaimed the reins. "My dear wife, you're forever touting your Gypsy origins, and are not Gypsies veritable wizards with horses?" His aquamarine eyes sparkled like elven jewels. "Besides, I could stand the silence no longer. I'm dismayed to admit I've grown accustomed to your mindless chatter."

"Mindless chatter, me arse." Lucy considered snatching up the buggy whip and applying it to her husband's broad back. Then she noticed the mischievous dimples hovering at the corners of his mouth. "A pox on ye, ye sly trickster. I reckon ye find this little stunt amusing. 'Twouldn't a been such a lark if ye'd broken your stiff neck." She pouted and reached for her shawl. "Oh, Diarmid—stop. I've dropped my wrap."

He chuckled, and her stomach fluttered like a thousand angels' wings. There was no mistaking the indulgent affection in the sound. She slanted him a glance from beneath lowered lashes. What *was* possessing him this morning? Last night she'd made it as clear as a nun's conscience that she despised the very air he breathed, yet here he was, deliberately disarming her with that rare, impish charm of his.

She twisted and glanced uneasily after her lost shawl. This morning, when she had woken alone in her canopy bed, she had sworn on her grandma's tarot deck to escape Diarmid once and for all. She couldn't hang about, tamely waiting for sick old Madam Lee to die—especially since she could no longer trust Diarmid's flimsy promise that their marriage would be chaste. Chaste, ha! Last night had proved just how chaste he considered her. But she had to be cunning—no mad dashing off with empty pockets and no freedom papers.

Last night, Old Dame Luck had been with her, and she had discovered Mick's purchaser. Over grits and eggs this morning, it suddenly occurred to her that she could use her position as Diarmid's wife to inveigle Isaiah Ludlow into selling Mick. Then—with her newly acquired polish and whatever she could purloin from her sham husband's pockets—she and Mick would escape and start a rum new life in Maryland colony.

The only snag to her plans were the freedom papers: She and Mick *must* have them to travel. Somehow, she'd have to keep Diarmid on the string until she could figure out a way to buy, forge, or steal the needed documents.

"Dinna worry about your shawl, lass." Diarmid's Virginia-gentleman drawl gave way to a disarming Highland burr.

"Fool Celia the way ye fooled the governor last night, and I'll buy ye a shipload o' the latest Paris fashions."

She swiveled around, then pinned him with a jaded look. Was the cove mad? She'd slapped him silly last night, had insulted him every way she knew how. Her stepfather Jocko—curse his ballocks to the hottest rings of hell—would have wrung her neck for such behavior. God knows he'd beaten her mother for lesser offenses—such as being too slow to pour his precious ale. She bit back a snort. That's what love got you: a broken heart and the bruises to prove it.

Her hand surreptitiously clutched her deck of tarot cards, which nestled in the muslin pocket beneath the folds of her skirt. The Ace of Swords lay in there somewhere, working its dark destiny. She thrust up her chin. By God, she *would* rescue her little brother, but from now on she'd put her trust in her own wits and in Old Dame Luck—not in Diarmid's empty promises. And certainly not in his black heart.

He arched a brow at her scowling silence. "What this then, lass? The light-fingered Lucia Gravesceu no' overcome with rapture at the prospect of new clothes? Och, lass, ye disappoint me. I've grown partial to the avaricious gleam in your eye."

Lucy sniffed. She was beginning to recognize the taunting tone in Diarmid's rolling *r*s. But she would not be baited. She'd misdirect the rake instead. "Why do you do that?" she queried demurely.

"What?"

"Sometimes ye cant like a Scottish rogue, other times you drawl like a born Virginian, and other times ye sound as puffed up as King George himself."

Diarmid gave a dramatic wince worthy of her da. "Och, lass, ye wound me. Dinna compare me to German George. 'Tis a rare insult, and likely to throw me into a towerin' Scots rage. As to my varying accent"—his beguiling burr gave way to a crisp, exquisitely educated British clip—"let us ascribe it to a life fraught with formidable change, not all of it welcome." He smiled down at her, and for once she detected no mockery on his impossibly handsome face. "You are acquainted with such a life, are you not, my queen? And as to accents, madam, yours is most changeable as well, so it seems we're cats of the same stripe."

Curiosity overcame her judgment. "Where did ye come from in Scotland?"

"The West Highland isles. The Isle of Mull, to be precise. It lies at the mouth of the sea loch of Linnhe, bounded by the Sound of Mull, the Firth of Lorn, and the open ocean."

This little geography lesson meant nothing to Lucy, but the fleeting expression of sorrow on Diarmid's face set alarm bells ringing in her memory. What had Patsy muttered about his history? Nothing specific, just that some dark mystery clouded his past, no doubt back in Scotland's mist-shrouded isles.

"You miss it?" she ventured.

"Aye, lass. It haunts me still. Scotland was me life, me heritage, me heart. Then 'twas all destroyed—destroyed by betrayal and greed and wretched, misplaced trust."

"But . . . but surely Stanton's Grove is your life now."

"Aye. 'Tis." Sorrow ghosted like fog across his granite face. "But when in my dreams, I dream of the Isles."

Lucy's heart contracted, and she laid a gloved hand on his wrist. Could this austere and icy Highlander perhaps have a heart after all? "You love it very much." She was startled to hear an echo of his sorrow in her own voice. "And what of your family there?"

Rage flared like emerald fire in his eyes. "I never speak of me family back in Scotland, so dinna ask again." He slapped the reins, and the horse broke into a trot. "But aye, lass, I do love the Highlands. Ye see, I learned long ago that land's the only thing 'tis safe to love."

Moments later they turned off the dirt road and passed through two tall, ivy-entwined brick gateposts. The right-hand post held a discreet brass sign engraved in simple Roman lettering with the words STANTON'S GROVE—1725. Lucy had expected Stanton's Grove—touted as the largest and loveliest plantation in Virginia—to be even more elaborate than the Governor's Palace in Williamsburg. Yet the gate's austerity bespoke a refined elegance that made the Palace seem vulgar by comparison.

Her stomach gave an odd little twist. God's ribs, what had she let herself in for? The thinness of her ladylike veneer had gone undetected by the chattering throng at Governor Fauquier's party, but could it survive the harsh scrutiny of Celia Stanton Lee?

They turned down a long avenue shaded by towering oaks, whose limbs laced overhead in a canopy of green, red, and gold. Sunlight filtered through the rustling branches and cast a shifting pattern of light and shadow on the broad graveled drive. Lucy shivered in the breeze, and Diarmid cast her a chill glance, his face frozen once again in the severe lines of the born aristocrat. He looked every inch the Scottish laird of blue blood, old money, and impeccable education. God's heels, what *had* she done?

"You're pale, madam. I trust you remember your lessons?" She nodded, relieved that fear hadn't paralyzed her neck. "Excellent. *Do not*"—his voice bit emphasis into the words— "disgrace me in any way whatsoever. I'm sure I have no need to remind you of our bargain. You must fool Mistress Lee into thinking we're blissfully in love. She said she wanted to see me happily married before I inherited Stanton's Grove, so happily married we shall endeavor to be." His lips twisted. "A difficult task, I know, but one for which you will be amply rewarded. *If* you are successful."

Lucy swallowed the rising hysteria in her throat. Somehow Diarmid's curt words had pierced the fog around her brain, bringing blessed, saving anger.

"Worry not, your majesty," she retorted. "Although pretending to love and honor you will be the greatest acting challenge of my entire life, I will persevere. Somehow."

She demurely smoothed her skirts. Oh, she'd succeed all right. If there was one thing the Rom understood, 'twas the importance of illusion and misdirection. Diarmid and Celia

Stanton Lee would believe her a veritable paragon of wifely devotion, right up to the moment they discovered her gone.

They crested a long, low rise, then broke out of the woods. Below them, seemingly endless acres of emerald parkland swept down to the great house of Stanton's Grove plantation. Sheep meandered across the tall grass, cropping placidly in the golden sun, and Lucy was startled to see two stately peacocks dragging their incredible, iridescent-blue tails along the white-gravel drive leading up to the mansion. To the left and right, the colony's famed tobacco fields rolled away to the horizon. The harvest had been completed, and the reddish-brown earth lay harrowed into long, gently curving rows that patiently awaited a cover crop.

Behind the house lay a formal sunken garden, complete with raised brick flowerbeds, rose arbors, and a boxwood maze. Beyond the garden, the land flattened like a dance floor, then grew marshy and ragged at the margins, as if gnawed by some bored and hungry sea monster. A long wooden dock extended from the foot of the gardens, across the yellowing wetlands, then far out into the mighty James.

Lucy gaped, astounded. All the way from Williamsburg they had followed a narrow, curving, heavily wooded creek barely navigable by flat-bottomed boat. Now, suddenly, the James stretched before them to the horizon, in one broad, endless, silver-gold plane of shimmering water, destined to join the sea.

Enthralled, Lucy turned her gaze back to the house. Deep inside her something went utterly still. She flattened a hand over her heart. God's ears, no wonder Diarmid was so obsessed with Stanton's Grove. In a lifetime spent careering around London—the London of St. James and Kensington palaces, of Westminster Abbey and St. Paul's Cathedral, of Pall Mall and Hyde Park and the palace of Westminster itself—Stanton's Grove was, in truth, the most beautiful thing she had ever seen.

It stood on a graceful bluff in the middle of the wide green lawns, facing down over the sunken flower gardens toward the bright liquid mirror of the James. No outbuildings marred the purity of the mansion's isolation, and the drive curved around it with an eggshell's oblique perfection. Like the Governor's Palace in Williamsburg, it possessed two stories crowned by an exquisitely proportioned roof and massive, twin brick chimneys. The walls were of rosy-toned brick set in a subtle Flemish-bond design, and they glowed with mellow dignity, even in the direct glare of noon. Tall, perfectly symmetrical windows flanked a gleaming mahogany door, and formal boxwood shrubbery adorned the gravel path that swept down to the gardens and dock.

Without a word, Diarmid drove the shay around to the front door, then jumped down and reached for Lucy. She caught his hand with her gloved fingers.

"Diarmid. 'Tis so serene, so breathtaking. Oh, God's ankles! I'm scared blue."

He whisked her down as if she were a child. His hands encircled her waist for a breathless moment, then he gently placed a finger to her lips and smiled. "A Romany queen, scared? Impossible. When we first met you told me the Rom were prouder, smarter, and luckier than the English." His drawl remained teasing, but his expression hardened. "Certainly you've proved yourself proud. So now it's time for brains—and luck. And you're no stranger to making—or should I say taking?—your own luck, aye?" He arched a brow and dropped his gaze to the low curve of her bodice. She blushed hotly, certain that he alluded to her foiled attempt to escape with Patsy's silver spoons. "Your talent for innovation should serve you well . . . or not."

Something in his tone raised the hair at her nape. Then, without warning, he swept her off her feet and up into his arms. She squealed in protest, but he strode up the steps, then carried her across the threshold of Stanton's Grove.

"Welcome home, my love." He chuckled at her shocked expression. Then he lowered his mouth and kissed her. His tongue slid across her lips, and he expertly teased until she opened to him. His taste was enticingly sweet, and she suddenly ached to feed on the slick curve of his lower lip, to lick and nibble the tiny, exquisite dent. His tongue plunged deeper, thrusting, foraging, firing her passion. Desire barreled through her. Her breath caught, her limbs melted, and she clung to his neck.

"So, you wretched Scottish rogue, is this how you repay my years of kindness?"

Lucy's heart leaped. That piercing, querulous tone could belong to none other than Celia Stanton Lee. To Lucy's amazement, Diarmid's lips curled into a smile against hers and a rumble of amusement vibrated through the sculpted muscles of his chest. Then his tongue swirled around hers.

"That will be enough," Celia commanded, pounding her walking stick against the polished wood floor. "You've more than demonstrated your manliness without this rude and wanton display—as Venetia can attest."

Diarmid set Lucy on her feet. Then he sauntered forward, took Celia's hand, and bowed with a nonchalant grace that was startling in such a large man. "My dear madam. As always, it is inexpressibly charming to see you."

Lucy straightened her wide-brimmed straw hat and stifled a nervous giggle. It seemed Diarmid's tendency to tease extended even to his tyrannical employer, for one peaked black brow was cocked and rakish dimples scored his lean cheeks. Then, to Lucy's astonishment, he tossed the old lady a roguish wink.

He released Celia's hand, turned to Lucy, and motioned her forward. "Mistress Lee, please allow me the honor of introducing—"

"I know who she is." Celia scowled and brandished her cane—a polished mahogany affair topped with an ivory monkey's head—and her bird-claw hands trembled violently. "Venetia's father was here bright and early this morning, sniveling about this . . . this *outrage* of yours. Oh, you arrogant, infuriating man! How could you?"

Lucy gaped. Celia's frustrated wail might have come from Lucy herself, for certainly Lucy felt the same helpless, maddening irritation whenever Diarmid bested her. Intrigued, she studied the formidable old dame more closely.

Diarmid had told her that Celia was seventy-five years old,

yet an aura of defiant beauty, long since vanished, still shone through the skull-like bones of her face. Scanty yellowish-white hair peeped from beneath her lace cap, and a suffocating quantity of rice powder caked the deep furrows at her brow and around her eyes. Two garish spots of rouge clung to the gaunt hollows of her cheeks, and rivulets of rouge bled into the myriad lines around her sunken lips. Her eyebrows had been plucked to oblivion, then penciled in with a bold hand.

Celia caught Lucy's eye and glowered, secure in her ability to intimidate. Lucy quelled a secret smile. She had instantly recognized the emotion behind the old dragon's wail: Celia had a soft spot for Diarmid the size of a Virginia ham.

"Nonetheless, madam," Diarmid purred, offering Celia another courtly bow, "I must insist on introducing my wife, Madam Lucy Maclean."

A tiny edge of Lucy's nervousness crumbled away. "How do you do, madam?" she murmured, curtsying demurely.

Celia ignored Lucy's greeting and dismissed her curtsy with a caustic glare. "I heard you're a cousin of that beribboned fop Harry Cheney," she snapped. *"And* that half the men in the colony have been throwing themselves at your feet. Hummmph. Men are all the same. Enticed to foolishness over a pretty face and a trim waist."

Lucy raised her chin a fraction. "I couldn't agree more, madam. It does seem that women fall in love with their hearts and that men fall in love with their, ahem . . . eyes."

"Ha! Women don't fall in love with their hearts. They fall in love with their pocketbooks." Celia snatched up the monocle pinned to her lilac-silk bodice, then scrutinized Lucy through the gold-rimmed lens.

Lucy rose to the challenge. "My dear, departed father would have agreed with you most heartily, madam. He used to aver he found the institution of marriage bankrupt—unless, of course, one married the Prince of Wales."

Celia blinked, then gave a snort that sounded suspiciously like a chuckle. "Saucy minx." She rounded on Diarmid. "Now, sir, march right straight into the drawing room. I have a bone to pick with you"—her tone dropped to an aggrieved sniff, no doubt intended for Lucy's benefit—"about my poor, dear Venetia."

Diarmid's shoulders tensed. "Madam, anything you have to say about Venetia—indeed, anything you have to say at all—you may say in front of my wife."

"Don't be ridiculous. I keenly doubt you want your new *bride*"—scathing disdain this time—"hearing what I have to say."

The pair scowled at each other. Arrogant pride blazed back and forth from eyes of black-lashed aquamarine to eyes of wrinkle-shrouded gray. Lucy felt as if she was looking at a mirror image.

"All right. You asked for it, you stubborn Scottish fool." Celia stumped down the hallway, peevishly bumping her cane against the gleaming floor. "Come along, then, the both of you."

As they followed Celia's erect, defiant figure, Lucy caught a fleeting impression of rich mahogany paneling, jewel-toned Turkey carpets, and a grand staircase wide enough to accommodate a coach and six. Two enormous oil portraits of grizzle-wigged old gentlemen hung halfway up the steps, majestically encased in heavily carved gilt frames. A painting of a stunning young woman in a sweeping pink-satin ball gown hung between them. Lucy grinned. Celia's imperious gray gaze hadn't changed one whit, although time had not been kind to what once must have been a great beauty.

That same gray gaze assessed Lucy with withering scorn as she and Diarmid trailed into Celia's drawing room. The bright, high-ceilinged chamber made a delightful contrast to the dark and overwhelming grandeur of the hall, and Lucy bit back a small, admiring gasp. The space was superbly decorated in the graceful Georgian style, complete with paneled walls painted robin's egg blue, gilded pier glasses, and a cheery fire crackling on the red sandstone hearth.

"Sit, Diarmind Maclean," Celia commanded, "and listen

to what I have to say. Then you'll pack up and leave my plantation forever."

Diarmid clenched his angular jaw. "Madam, by any chance has your fair niece met with . . . an unfortunate accident?"

Slowly, the meaning of his words dawned on Lucy: Poor Venetia must have lost their babe. Lucy cast Diarmid a sympathetic glance. To her astonishment, his sensual mouth had thinned into a chill, cynical smile. Her heart began a choking thud. God's ears, even though she despised Venetia, she couldn't smile at the death of an unborn child, though she would gladly visit a curse on the babe's cold-hearted father— blast his randy Scottish yard with the virulent French pox.

Celia's penciled brows shot skyward. "How did you know? It only happened this morning. Venetia's father's told no one but me."

Diarmid steepled his fingers and assumed the remote, patronizing air of a scholar. "I know because it was I who suggested the tale."

Celia and Lucy exchanged confused glances. "I . . . I don't understand," Lucy ventured. A sudden, horrible thought assailed her. "God's bodkins! Do you mean you told that blanket-jig tart to slip the babe?"

There was a moment of shocked silence, and Lucy felt a mortified blush crawl across her cheeks. She'd done it now. Celia and Diarmid gawked at her, Celia with jaw agape, clearly appalled that a new bride should know of her husband's scandalous behavior; Diarmid with an infuriating air of startled amusement, quickly replaced by stern disapproval.

She leaped up, suddenly sick to the gills with his cold-heartedness, and with her own unwitting involvement in his perfidious behavior. Clearly, the blackguard would stop at nothing to gain Stanton's Grove. "God's nigs!" she cried. "Must ye goggle like I'm an organ-grinder's monkey?"

Diarmid rose and grasped her wrist with steely fingers. Then he sat and pulled her onto his knee. "You must forgive my dear wife," he drawled in an insufferably patronizing tone. "Her . . . deep love and respect for me makes her jealous, alas." Lucy gave an outraged squirm and his fingers, unseen in the billow of her indigo sarcenet skirts, dug implacably into her thigh. Phantom dimples bracketed his mouth for a split second, then vanished. "Indeed, it seems I owe you both an explanation. Venetia let slip within Lucy's earshot that she was carrying my child. That, of course, was a fabrication designed to produce just the effect you see now—a young bride, deeply in love with her husband, maddened by jealousy into feminine foolishness."

He smiled ruefully, and Lucy nearly burst with the urge to throttle him. She tried to struggle to her feet, but he hooked his arm around her waist and pulled her closer. "Hush, my dear," he murmured against her cheek. "You're overcome with emotion. Let me sort this out." He dropped a kiss on her nose, then his fingers bit into her buttock.

"Stop this nonsense at once, Diarmid Niall Altan Maclean." Celia waved her cane and nearly knocked a silver candelabra to the floor. "Poor young Lucy may have fallen for your roguish ways, but you're dealing with me. Now what's all this about? I don't understand you at all."

" 'Tis elementary," he drawled. "Venetia was determined to marry me. She knew the only way to drag me to the altar was for you to force me, using the shame of ruining your niece's reputation as the whip and Stanton's Grove as the carrot, so to speak. So she lied about carrying my child. Venetia is not now nor ever has been *enciente.*"

Celia gasped. Her stick clattered to the floor.

Diarmid's grip loosened for an instant. Lucy lunged to her feet. "How can you lie about such a thing? Why, Venetia's own father said—"

"Barnabas Lee is an idiot"—Celia's voice knifed through Lucy's rant—"and unlike Venetia and Barnabas, Diarmid has never lied to me. Oh, lud, what an old fool I am. I should have known better than to believe my scheming niece. This isn't the first time she's tried to force my hand over Stanton's Grove." She glanced at Diarmid, her indomitable gaze suddenly lost and weary. "But why did she contrive an accident? Barnabas found her at the bottom of the steps—"

Diarmid rose, crossed the room, and sat beside Celia. Then

he picked up wrinkled old hands and gently folded them over her stick. "She had to make it convincing. She told others besides you, me, and her father, you know. Rebecca Burwell, for one. Perhaps someone else. An 'accident' allowed her to save face. Those who believed her to be with child will think 'tis lost, and I'll be the villain." He cast the old lady a tender smile, then bent and kissed her hand.

Lucy's throat caught. Sun breaking through clouds, that beguiling smile of his. Hope breaking through despair.

"You are a rogue," Celia said, quickly recovering her usual asperity. "I suppose you realize your reputation will be well and truly cooked this time. Barnabas is prepared to call you out. Oh, that man is a lackwit." She sighed, suddenly looking like the small, dried carapace of a once-fierce queen bee. "I'll explain things to him, so at least you won't be forced to kill him in a duel, as surely you would. The drunken fool can't shoot straight, let alone handle a saber. And of course he owes me money, so he'll go along with what I say. As for Venetia . . . oh, dear. I suppose I must do something to keep up appearances. Perhaps the ball and race for Jamie and his wife will do the trick—"

She snatched up her monocle and glared at Lucy, eyes glinting like a falcon's. "I was born and raised in London, missy, and I knew the town well. Where are you from?"

Lucy swallowed. She'd almost blown their little scheme moments before; now she had a chance to set things right. And redeem herself she'd better, or she could forget about rescuing Mick, and look forward to chopping sugar in Barbados instead. But she'd been so *sure* Diarmid was lying, so *positive* Venetia was telling the truth. She scanned her husband's face, searching for some clue that her negative assumptions were correct. Diarmid's jade eyes grew wintry, and there was no mistaking the warning in his glare. Resolve hardened like a diamond in the pit of her stomach. Diarmid's icy frown was all the clue she needed. Doddering old Celia might be taken in by his charm, but Lucy didn't believe his cozening lies one whit.

She slanted Celia her most winning smile. "Lud, madam,

though born there, I spent but little time in London. My dear papa traveled a great deal and my mother and I traveled with him."

"He was a diplomat?" Celia eyed Lucy dubiously, as if she was some exotic species of parrot.

"Nay. He was a poet and a scholar . . . rather like Diarmid."

Diarmid rose and stirred up the fire. "I think Lucy means—"

"Hush," Celia snapped. "Let her speak for herself. Tell me about your mother, missy."

"She grew up in Yorkshire, madam. I spent most of my childhood there. My grandpapa was vicar of St. Boltoph's, you know." Lucy feigned a pious look, then warmed to her tale. "We spent most of our time in good works, as befits a clergyman's family. We ministered to the sick—taking them broth and ointments and whatnot, always with a prayer and bit of scripture, of course. And we helped the poor—although my grandpapa did aver that the poor will be with us always."

Diarmid made a choking sound. Lucy tossed him an airy smile, gleeful at having the upper hand. Ha! She'd teach him to paw and pinch her like she was a draggle-tailed bawd. "Then there was our school—" she continued.

"What school?" Diarmid asked in a strangled tone.

"I've told you this before, my love. Surely you remember. But if you're so intent in interrupting, perhaps you'd like to continue my little tale? No?" Diarmid's blazing eyes promised swift punishment once they were alone, but she cared not. She turned back to Celia and batted her eyelashes. "Men. So forgetful, don't you find? Now, where was I? Oh, yes. We had a little school to teach unfortunate children to read."

Celia plucked a tiny box from a Chippendale table, dipped a pinch of snuff, and inhaled sharply. Minute specks of tobacco drifted into her powder-caked cleavage. "A school. How fine of you. Reading was my dearest diversion, but my eyesight no longer allows it." This was confessed in the tone of a queen conferring a boon. "Diarmid used to read to me, but other tasks"—a sharp look at Lucy's ripe bosom—"do

tend to drag him away. So, missy, now that you're here, you
will be my reader."

"Nay, Celia." Diarmid reached Lucy with one long stride.
"Lucy will find much else to occupy her time."

"Nonsense, my love." Lucy skittered out of his reach, then
sat next to Celia. Her gaze fell on a thin, leather-bound book
resting on a side table. She picked it up and flipped a few
pages, fully cognizant of Diarmid's searing gaze on her
flushed cheeks. Arrogant varlet! He had assumed she couldn't
read just because she was a thief from London's gutters. Despite his scholarly bent, he hadn't even bothered to try to
teach her, concluding that she was beyond hope of ever learning anything.

She smiled. "Ah! Here's one of my father's favorites. He
loved John Donne, you know." In a husky, musical voice she
read,

"Come live with me and be my love,
And we will some new pleasures prove,
Of golden sands and crystal brooks,
With silken lines and silver hooks."

"That was your father's favorite?" Diarmid inquired acidly.
His blazing jade eyes burned into hers. "Then he made you
memorize it, of course."

Fury—swift, silent, painful—lanced Lucy's heart. Why
could he never give her a moment's praise? Why must he
remain haughty and aloof to the bitter end? She gnawed her
lip and flipped a few more pages.

"Here's one by Sir Walter Raleigh," she exclaimed. "I
knew not that he was a poet. And I see 'tis most appropriate,
under the circumstances." She read,

"Farewell, false love, the oracle of lies,
A mortal foe and enemy to rest;
An envious boy from whom all cares arise,
A bastard vile, a beast with rage possessed;

A way of error, a temple full of treason,
In all effects contrary unto reason."

"Madam, that will be enough. You've more than made your point." Diarmid bowed curtly, then spun on his heel and stalked toward the door. Reaching it, he paused and stood, rigid back to them, for a long, strained moment. Then, without turning, he tossed off, "Since you're such an admirer of John Donne, madam, I suggest you read 'The Canonization.' Just the first line, of course."

He slammed out, leaving Lucy and Celia in startled silence. When Lucy didn't resume reading, Celia took up the book, found the poem in question, and laboriously read it to herself. Dropping her monocle, she began to cackle.

"What does it say?" Lucy asked. Getting only more laughter in response, she snatched up the book and read, " 'For God's sake, hold your tongue, and let me love.' "

Eleven

Diarmid stood alone at the end of the Stanton's Grove dock and stared out over the silent river. Evening was falling early now, and the sky had faded to tranquil lavender on the eastern horizon, shading to indigo high overhead. The first evening stars had winked on—tiny and distant on their blue-velvet field—and a soft breeze drifted in off the James, caressing his hair and toying gently with the lace at his throat. It etched intricate riffled patterns across the river's glassy surface, then whistled mournfully through the dry marsh grass. At this time of night, Stanton's Grove always reminded him of the Western Isles—though more in feeling than in physical resemblance. 'Twas so peaceful, yet so sad, as beauty often was.

He wished Lucy was beside him. Or better yet, in his arms.

Disconcerted by this sudden—and most unwelcome—thought, Diarmid turned and gazed toward the house. It stood serene and silent on its low green rise, and candlelight glowed from a second-story window. Lucy should be sleeping by now, or so he assumed. He walked toward the house with long, easy strides, his boots making hollow *thunks* on the dock's weathered planks. His lips twitched in a rueful smile. He was rapidly learning that making assumptions about Lucy could be a grave mistake.

Off to his left, a silver-bellied mullet leaped from the silent water, then flopped back with a wet plop. Diarmid paused and scanned the river's reedy margin. He'd have to send Mercury down in the morning with the fishnets. He doubted Lucy ever had enjoyed smoked mullet while growing up in the sewers of Alsatia. He shook his head and smiled. Mercury would be more than happy to catch Lucy a mess of fish, for she already had charmed most of the house servants. Even Royal, Celia's mulish housekeeper, had succumbed to Lucy's wiles when she had insisted on going to the Row after supper to meet all sixteen of Royal's grandchildren.

As if drawn by a lodestone, his eyes turned back to his bedchamber window. For an instant, he imagined himself slipping into bed beside his luscious bride—candlelight glowing on her smooth, naked belly; her full, glorious breasts jiggling with each aroused pant. Desire flared in his loins. Och, why did the wench persist in bedeviling him? He'd thought of nothing but her all afternoon, most often with irritation, now and then with grudging pride, always—*always*—with mind-numbing lust.

He clattered down the dock steps and strode along the shadowy yew walk, then slipped, scowling, through the great-house door. Nay, he couldn't afford to think of her. He couldn't think of her long, tawny legs, damp with womanly passion, wrapped around his waist, urging him inside her.

In truth, he'd never ached to bed a lass more. The temptation to ravish her thoroughly and often was driving him to drink, but no doubt she would shriek and faint in full Romany theatrics if he so much as tried to touch her. Och, Saint Iona! She'd stolen his wits and bewitched his cock.

But why did he yearn to bury himself between her thighs when she'd nearly ruined his plans? Again and again he had impressed on her the importance of winning Celia's approval, but nay, at the first sign of trouble she had resorted to gutter cant and had hurled accusations that no proper lady would even understand. And then there had been that little scene with the poetry book.

He hurried up the stairs, sharply quelling a tiny spurt of remorse. How was he to know Lucy could read? How many gutter-thieves could? Precious few, he'd wager.

He gained the second-floor landing and strode across the plush Turkey carpet. Nay, he would not apologize for hurting her feelings. The wee trollop would only twist his honorable intentions to her own advantage. Wasn't that the way of all women, scheming jilts that they were?

He was about to storm into the bedchamber and give Lucy a stern lecture, then demand his conjugal rights, when a tiny sound arrested him. He leaned forward and pressed his ear to the gleaming, *faux-bois* door.

Tears.

He stepped back a pace. Lucy crying? Och, this was a sight he had to see. Smiling sardonically, he turned the silver doorknob. The door was locked.

"Lucy, let me in, please." He kept his voice soft, loathe to alert Celia to the embattled state of his marriage. In truth, it was imperative the old dragon believe he was vigorously pursuing his marital rights at this very moment. He grinned wolfishly. And that was precisely what he had in mind.

The sniffling stopped, but there was no sound of a key turning in the lock. "Lucy, let me in." He rattled the doorknob. "Madam, I'll remind you that I'm your husband, and you will do as I tell you." He heard a muffled sound and pressed his ear to the door. "What did you say?"

"I said go to hell!"

This was shrieked loud enough to wake Celia's two dead husbands. Diarmid ground his teeth and imagined a thousand wickedly carnal ways to punish his defiant bride. "I'll say this just once," he hissed. "Let me in, or by Saint Iona, I'll kick down this door and tan your bonnie wee—"

She flung open the door. "Oh, ye'd like that, I doubt not—"

He spun her around, yanked her rigid back against his chest, and stepped into the chamber. She started to squeal and he clapped a hand over her mouth, then closed and locked the door behind them. She kicked at his shin, then sank her teeth into his palm.

He released her as if she were a rabid ferret. "Ye wee—"

"Go on, hit me! You bloody blackguards are all the same. All ye care for is drinking and rutting and slapping a lass when she doesn't bow to your whims. Well, I care not! You've insulted me all ye can."

With a dramatic sob, she threw herself facedown on the

bed. Her long hair streamed down her back in a tangle of ebony curls, and a voluminous brown-calico nightshift covered her from clenched jaw to stocking-clad toes. He had never seen any garment so modest, or so sure to put a man off. His lips twitched into a quick, barely suppressed smile. Lucy knew that tonight, at long last, they must share a bedchamber. 'Twas a necessity to prove themselves happily wed. No doubt this gruesome bed garb was designed to thwart his desire.

Chuckling, he lay down on the bed beside her, stretched out his long legs, then playfully patted one of her luscious little buttocks. His manhood stirred and hardened deliciously. "Hmmmm," he mused. "What do you think, my queen? Since you're such an expert on the beastliness of men, tell me— shall I give you the screwing I crave or the beating you deserve?"

There was a marked absence of smart retorts. All at once she was crying again; crying with deep, silent sobs that wracked her thin frame and vibrated through the goose-down featherbed straight into his heart. His brows contracted. He doubted even Lucy could fake such misery. Och, now what should he do?

"Shhhhhh. Dinna fash, lass." He seductively stroked the wee bumps along her spine. " 'Tis just the rutting bull in me bellowin' and makin' himself heard. Ye ken I'd never harm ye, aye? And ye ken how much I want ye—for I want ye somethin' fierce. So why must ye fight me? We *are* legally wed, lass."

Her sobs increased—long, low, animal sounds that tore at his heart and left him strangely helpless. He murmured a Gaelic endearment, then gathered her into his arms. She resisted him at first, her delicate body as stiff and cold as a marble statue, then she dissolved against him. He gently rubbed the tender skin at the nape of her neck and rocked her back and forth. "Why all the tears, *mo cridhe?* "

She sniffed mightily, then wiped her nose on her calico sleeve. "I despise you, Diarmid Niall Altan Maclean."

"Aye, I'm sure ye do," he remarked dryly. The skin on her

throat felt warm and alive to his touch, like a quivering fawn.
Och, all of her felt warm and alive. She burned in his arms
like flame incarnate and he longed to be consumed. "Tell
me, *mo cridhe,* is all of this high drama perhaps—just perhaps—resultin' from of a wee bit o' hurt pride?"

She faced him, eyes bloodshot, nose swollen, lashes beaded
with tears—tears like tiny glistening moonstones. He caught
his breath, then leaned forward and kissed them away. She
flinched, glared, pouted. She'd never looked so beautiful.

"Nay," she snapped, voice acid with sarcasm. "I crave being treated like a jibbering lackwit. I rejoice when ye assume
that I can't read. I relish ye canting on about your bedsport
with that bottle-blond harpy. I applaud ye breaking your
promises as if I were no more than a dog."

She began to sob again, so deeply and raggedly he feared
she might retch. He scanned the room, desperate to distract
her, and his gaze fell on an empty brandy bottle half hidden
under his tiger-maple highboy.

He grasped her chin and forced her to look in his eyes.
"Lucy, have you been drinking?" She scowled; then her head
fell forward against her chest. "If you dinna tell me the truth,"
he warned, "I'll figure it out myself."

Her head lolled back. Then, with consummate Gypsy defiance, she stuck out her tongue.

He lowered his head and kissed her. Boldly, seductively,
with slow, expert thoroughness, his tongue explored the warm,
honeyed recesses of her mouth. She'd been drinking, all right;
Celia's best cherry brandy, from the taste of it. He cupped
his hands over the taut swell of her buttocks and pressed her
body to his until his manhood strained with desire. His mind
whirled with strange, exotic emotions; he felt as if *he* were
intoxicated. Och, but what was he doing? Making love to this
bewitching Gypsy wench would ruin his plans. For—God
help him—he could no longer separate raw, primal lust from
the exquisite tenderness flaring inside him.

He released her and glared down his nose in his best
schoolmaster fashion. "Did I no' warn ye to keep your wits
about ye?" he asked. His voice sounded dangerously hoarse,

and his damned Highland burr had cropped up. "I'd scarce call guzzlin' Celia's brandy the best way to ensure the success of our wee wager. Stanton's Grove—"

"Damn Stanton's Grove and damn you!" Lucy struggled to her feet and wavered just beyond his reach. Fresh tears streamed down her cheeks. "I hate it here. I'm not good enough for your fancy plantation, and Celia knows it. She needled me all day, sniffing, snooping, and prying into my past. And you . . . you—"

"Yes?" He arched a brow, genuinely curious.

"You wouldn't even eat supper with me."

Her expression was so outraged, her voice so aggrieved, he couldn't help laughing. This definitely was the wrong response, for she flew at him, fists raised. Instinctively, he caught her wrists and bent her arms behind her back. As she squirmed and cursed, he lifted her off her feet and deposited her on the bed, then nonchalantly rolled on top of her. He sealed his hips to hers, then supported his weight on his elbows.

"Madam, you flatter me to so desire my companionship," he drawled with elaborate courtesy, as if they were being introduced at St. James rather than lying belly-to-belly in bed. "Indeed, if I had known the true state of your heart, I gladly would have abandoned the weighty responsibilities I've let slip since yoking myself to you."

Lucy inhaled, clearly preparing for another tirade. Determined to keep the upper hand, he gave his hips a suggestive thrust and settled his engorged erection tight against her pubic bone. She froze, mouth agape. Wanton feelings flooded to his manhood, and a tidal wave of lust crashed over him, storming through his loins like an Indies hurricane.

He lowered himself until his lips were inches from hers, then playfully tapped her jaw shut. "Close your mouth, *mo cridhe*. Ye dinna want flies getting in." Sweet, drugging heat lapped at his reason, and he seductively dragged his thumb along the slick curve of her lower lip. "As to your not fitting in at Stanton's Grove, nothing could be further from the truth."

"But—"

He shushed her with an open-mouthed kiss. "As long as you watch yourself, mind your manners, guard your temper, and curb your tongue, there's no reason you shouldn't succeed in fooling Celia." His voice grew husky. "Then Stanton's Grove will be mine."

If only he could be sure of success. So much—and so many—depended on it. His swirling thoughts came to rest on his younger brother Jamie, coming to visit in a few weeks' time. He and Jamie were united in their hatred of slavery, and Diarmid prayed that his plans to free the Stanton's Grove slaves might somehow make amends for his bitter past—and for all Jamie had lost because of him. He clenched his jaw, determined to keep his memories at bay, to crush emotions too torturous to bear.

But as Jamie's visit approached, forgetting became impossible.

He gazed into Lucy's glistening black eyes and drew a sharp breath. She was so beautiful, so spirited. He was shocked to realize how precious she had become to him. But thanks to Catriona's vicious betrayal, he had sworn never to trust—or love—a woman again. That wretched liaison had brought disastrous consequences to Diarmid, to innocent young Jamie, and to the entire Maclean clan.

Diarmid gritted his teeth, and ice glazed over his arousal. But not to Lachlan, eldest brother and laird of *Taig Samhraidh,* the Maclean estate on the Isle of Mull. Nay, vile Lachlan had survived. As far as Diarmid knew, he was alive and well back in the Highlands. But he was dead to Diarmid and Jamie—dead for betraying his brothers and his clan.

A fierce, suffocating pain gripped Diarmid's heart. Och, what a cruel trap he'd sprung the day he'd fallen in love with Catriona. Deep in the blackest recesses of his mind, he knew he never could fully atone for the sins of his past. But admitting it would destroy his last glimmer of hope.

Aye, he had to make amends. And to do that, he needed Stanton's Grove.

The plantation had become his life, a precious substitute

for *Taig Samhraidh.* The Maclean estate had been confiscated, of course; given to Catriona's brother as a reward for helping destroy the Jacobites. When Diarmid finally had crawled from the worst of his despair and had realized that God was not going to strike him dead, he had poured his tortured heart into Celia's plantation, hoping one day it would be his. Stanton's Grove might not be *Taig Samhraidh,* but by Saint Iona, he loved it with a single-mindedness bordering on obsession. He couldn't bear the thought of losing it.

Suddenly he realized Lucy was staring at him with the same desperately sad expression she had worn the day of their marriage. On that dreadful occasion she had fainted from hunger—hunger he had been too selfish to detect. Now she looked overwhelmed by something so awful she could hope for neither reprieve nor escape.

"What is it?" he queried, half expecting her to burst into tears.

"Nothing."

He considered kissing her or deviling her a bit more, but the mood was broken. Lucy's sad demeanor no longer made an enticing target for his teasing. She had withdrawn to some dark world he couldn't enter.

Diarmid rolled off her rigid body, then rose and prowled around the room. He stirred up the fire, pulled off his boots, shrugged out of his coat, and untied his cravat. As he soaped his hands in his blue-and-white china washbowl, he caught Lucy's reflection in his mirror. She hadn't moved. He snatched up a linen towel and turned.

"Time for bed, *mo cridhe.* Surely ye canna wait to sleep by me side for the verra first time, aye?" He had intended to keep his tone bantering, but to his acute dismay, his Scottish burr was thick as Highland heather. Damn his bloody accent. It insisted on asserting itself whenever his emotions ran high. Or rather—he gazed at Lucy's long legs and smiled ruefully—whenever they ran amok.

Slowly, she sat up. Her shoulders were slumped—something he'd never seen with proud Lucy—and her stockinged feet dangled inches from the floor, like a wee bairn's. Diarmid made a mental note to have the plantation carpenter build her a set of steps so she could climb into bed. He knelt in front of her, then gently grasped one tiny foot. Och, she was so suddenly, appealingly helpless. What could he do to assure her he meant her no harm, to make her see how much he—

How much he what?

Lightly, tenderly, as if touching a newborn foal, he stroked the aristocratic arch of her foot. Who would have thought a Gypsy guttersnipe would have such elegant feet? He trailed his fingers over her ankle and up the intoxicating swell of her calf. She caught her breath—a quick, startled sound—and his heart thundered to life.

He pushed the hideous nightshirt up to her waist and buried his head in her lap. The rough calico scratched his brow, and he inhaled hungrily. Her woman's scent intoxicated him. She was spice, musk, gilly flowers. Och, Saint Iona, he wanted her, wanted her more than any woman, ever. He wanted her in his bed, aye—but damn his foolish heart to the hottest rings of hell—he also wanted her at his table, on his arm, by his side. He *must* claim her as his own.

But others had claimed her first—many times.

This ugly thought forced his mind down a dark, vile alley he didn't want to tread. He bit his lip, then slid his hands over Lucy's legs and tugged at her garters. Nay, he wouldn't dwell on her sordid past. In truth, he couldn't face it. Pain gnawed at his gut at the mere thought of her lying beneath another man, spreading her thighs, welcoming some panting blackguard into her wetness. With a strangled groan, he ripped her stockings from her legs.

"Don't do this," Lucy gasped. She clamped her thighs together, then shrank away from him. "You promised our marriage would be chaste."

He reared to his feet. Frustrated rage shot through his blood. Instantly, it transmuted into a primitive lust that drove all thoughts from his mind—all thoughts but pinning Lucy down and plunging his aching erection into the tight, wet clasp of her womanhood. By Saint Iona, how dare she refuse

him! He was her legal husband, and he'd been patient long
enough. He'd be her plaything no longer!

Lucy scrambled across the bed and her nightshift tangled
about her thighs, offering him maddening glimpses of soft,
tawny flesh and crisp black curls. He caught her ankles and
halted her escape. With a low curse, he wrapped her legs
around his waist and pinned them there with one iron hand.
Lucy squirmed and writhed. Her resistance drove his passion
to a staggering peak.

"Cease this wriggling," he growled. He had a quick, per-
versely delicious thought: a sound spanking would calm her
defiance *and* heat his already raging desire. With grim determination, he released her legs, flipped her onto her belly, and
threw up her nightshift.

He froze.

On the day Diarmid had purchased Lucy from Obediah
Pratt, the good captain had made it plain the Gypsy wench
was a thief. "Branded, she be," Pratt had remarked, as if
pressing a white-hot iron into tender flesh was a normal, ev-
eryday occurrence. Diarmid had seen Lucy's brand—a purplish, blurred *T* high up on her arm—the day he had walked
in on her trying on her new clothes at Sugarplum.

But no one, least of all Lucy, had prepared him for what
he saw now: His wife's back was a mass of tiny pinkish scars,
overlaid here and there with fading yellow bruises.

Diarmid clenched his eyes shut, desperately trying to erase
the image—and the wretched memories it resurrected. Sixteen
years ago, he'd watched in horror as a Sassenach soldier had
beaten Jamie nearly to death. Diarmid had been reprieved
from flogging because of the severe wounds he had sustained
at Culloden. He winced. He'd rather carry the scars of a hundred musket shots and a thousand lashes than the lethal guilt
that haunted him to this day.

Lucy squirmed beneath him and he dragged his attention
back to the present. "What on earth happened to you?" he
ground out.

She yanked her calico shift down over her nakedness and

squirmed into a sitting position. "Save your pity for someone who needs it."

"It seems you do. Och, tell me who did this, *mo cridhe.*"

Lucy scanned his face, obviously catching the agitation in his tone. She snorted. " 'Twould be rum sport to have your fine sensibilities, milord. God's neck, you should catch your viz in the mirror. White about the gills, ye are." She smoothed her hair with shaky bravado. "Have ye never beaten your slaves?"

"You know damned well I haven't." Unaccountably, he longed to shake away her impudence and kiss away her hurts, all at the same time.

"Oh? Ye seemed pretty hot to smack me a moment ago."

"That was before I encountered this . . . this brutality." He gestured toward her stiff little back. Och, what was wrong with the wench? She was glaring at him as if *he'd* been the one who had beaten her black and blue. Didn't she recognize genuine concern when she saw it?

She arched a wicked brow, mimicking his all-too-often sardonic behavior. "Whence this sudden caring, your majesty? Surely ye're not surprised. Have I not hinted that my stepfather was less than civil?"

Diarmid's stomach roiled. "What type o' beast would harm a lass so? A beatin' like that could have killed ye—"

"Aye, and nearly did, many times. That's why I thieved and plotted and lied, all to get away from Jocko. I knew once he killed me, he'd turn on Mick." Her voice broke. Catching his pitying gaze, she thrust up her chin. "Oh, I could take it—'tis not bellyaching you're hearing. 'Twas Mick I feared for. And who's to say Isaiah Ludlow isn't just as bad? Royal told me he pierced the tongue of one of his slaves—"

She must have seen disgust flare in his eyes, for she leaned forward and caught his wrist in one supple hand. The curve of her breast brushed his shoulder, and he stilled a shudder of desire. "Oh, Diarmid, don't make me beg. I saw the horrified look on your face a moment ago. You know what it is to be beaten, don't you?"

He swallowed, unnerved by the intensity of her lustrous

eyes. "Nay, I don't, but me brother Jamie—" He halted, dismayed that he had given her a hint of his past. Och, what was wrong with him? Two minutes in the wench's presence and he forgot sixteen years of rigid training and spilled his guts like a callow lad. His jaw tightened.

"You have a brother?" Her dark brows flew up. "I thought you said you had no family."

"I said I never speak of me family, not that I dinna have any. Ye jumped to conclusions—one of your more endearin' habits, aye?"

She pouted prettily, then dawning understanding lit her piquant face. "Today Celia mentioned a ball for Jamie and his wife. He's your brother?"

"Aye." Diarmid found himself beguiled by her vibrant enthusiasm. "A charming rogue, is Jamie—much given to pranks and teasing. Ye should love him."

"A Maclean given to teasing and roguery? How unique."

"Dinna be sarcastic." He cast her a stern glare, but she pressed her advantage.

"Since you have a little brother—and 'tis easy to apprehend that you love him—you *must* understand how I feel about Mick. Please, Diarmid. You've *got* to help me get him away from Ludlow."

His glared down his nose and she scrambled up, then rummaged frantically in her portmanteau. She raced back to the bed, jumped up beside him, and leaned close. Once more he caught her luscious scent. He inhaled slowly and eased his arm around her waist, oblivious to the object she thrust toward him. Och, how he wanted to suckle her lush velvet breasts. . . .

"Pay attention," she demanded, not without a hint of coquetry. She flourished a tattered deck of cards, then scrabbled through them, unaware of his hungry gaze on the tempting swell of her breasts. "There!" She brandished a card under his nose. " 'Tis the Ace of Swords."

"So?" Blandly.

"So! 'Tis Mick's fortune, ye great daft booby. 'Tis an awful card, portending disaster, disruption, loss, sorrow, upheaval—"

"All that in one wee square o' leather?" He rolled his *r*s rakishly, knowing it provoked her. She hit his arm.

"Don't you *dare* tease me, Diarmid Maclean. This is serious. I read Mick's fortune the night before he was sold, and *this*"—she slapped the card down on his thigh, inches from the straining bulge in his breeches—"is Mick's future. The Ace of Swords is tied to the late autumn, signifying endings or even death. And we're coming up on late autumn now." Her voice wavered, but she rushed on. "The Swords are always used against a person in a cruel, tyrannical way. They're ruthless. Oh, don't you see?"

He studied her. Two hectic red spots rode high on her cheekbones and her eyes glittered like a fever patient's. "But, *mo cridhe,* surely you dinna believe this nonsense?"

Wrong response. With a tiny shriek of aggravation, she leaped from the bed and paced back and forth. "Of course I believe it! Oh, me da taught me how to *dukker* a fancy fortune to cozen moon-sick scullions, but a genuine reading is, well . . . genuine. There's no doubt that Mick is in trouble now, and 'twill only get worse as autumn progresses." She spun to face him, planting her fists on her hips. "I've *tried* to do things your way, milord. I believed your promises, I kept our bargain, I watched and questioned and finally had the stroke of good luck to find Isaiah Ludlow myself. But now you *must* step in. You've got to get Mick away from that man before 'tis too late."

The room fell silent except for the soft pop of the fire and the sound of Lucy's agitated breathing. Her gaze never left his face, and there was no mistaking the fear and worry on her exquisite features. Och, he wanted to tease her, to find the right combination of wit and devilry to cajole her out of her black mood, but it was useless. She believed her ridiculous Romany claptrap as surely as the vicar of Bruton Parish believed in the Holy Trinity. In Lucy's fervid mind, her little brother was in danger.

He stood and stepped around her, then turned his back to her pleading gaze. In truth, she had kept up her end of the bargain. Everyone had fallen for her charm, and everyone believed her to be a fine English lady.

Diarmid smiled, pleased with his creation. Och, even old dragon Celia seemed to have surrendered the wench a wee bit of grudging respect, as she recognized a kindred spirit. Kindred in willful hardheadedness, to be sure, but kindred nonetheless. And he *had* led the poor lass to believe he would help her sooner or later, even though he had had no real intention of finding her pickpocket brother. He turned, folded his arms, tilted his head, and lazily studied her from head to toe.

Och, there was no denying it. Even with a runny nose, wild hair, and the ugliest nightrail this side of Hades, Lucia Gravesceu Maclean was the most beautiful and desirable woman he'd ever met. Never had he known a lass with such spirit, such wit—and, aye, he would admit it—such sharp intelligence, except where this fortune-telling nonsense was concerned. Saint Iona, he could fall in love with such a wench.

Lines from the Raleigh poem Lucy had so scornfully read to him flashed through his mind:

False love, desire, and beauty frail, adieu!
Dead is the root whence all these fancies grew.

If only his past were dead, then perhaps he could be free. But that malformed, pernicious root lived on. The obsession that had brought him to ruin and despair entwined about him still. Och, he no longer wanted Catriona, but the blight of her love was beyond his power to kill.

As if echoing his thoughts, Lucy said, "I know you don't trust me, Diarmid. To tell ye truly, I trust you not at all. But I've sworn to never let anything part me from me poor, wee brother. He's all I've got." Her voice sounded genuinely humble, and she glided forward, then rested a hand on his folded arms. Diarmid felt his resolve start to slip. "Can't we trust each other in this one area?" she pleaded. "Just long enough to get Mick away from Ludlow?"

Diarmid steeled himself, then gazed down into her dark, seductive eyes. Curse her Gypsy wiles. She knew just where to find the chinks in his armor. He clenched his eyes shut, intent on blotting out her enchanting face. As if colluding with her, his mind filled stealthily with an even more enchanting vision: Lucy's naked buttocks, curved and ripe and firm, beckoning him enticingly from atop the longest legs he'd ever seen.

Saint Iona!

He cracked open a lid and caught the look of triumph that flashed across her scheming face. Och, the wee strumpet was no different from Catriona. Well then, if that was how she wanted to play. Fast as thought, he bent, scooped her into his arms, and tossed her on the bed. She squeaked and clutched her hands over her lap.

"Aye, Gypsy, I'll cut ye another deal," he purred. "I'll get your brother back, and in return, ye'll release me from me promise of a chaste marriage." Almost idly, he joined her on the bed, then loomed over her and straddled her hips. He cast her a look of elaborate innocence. "Since we dinna trust each other, and since ye're gettin' your brother, 'tis fair I should get something, too, aye?"

For several long minutes she scrutinized his face, intent on reading thoughts he was too guarded to reveal. Despite his attempt at lighthearted mockery, his body responded to her ripe curves with deadly seriousness. His pulse throbbed and his cock strained against his breeches.

At last, with lips pinched and eyes clenched shut, she gave a tiny, curt nod.

His breath rushed from his lungs in a sigh of triumph and he lowered himself over her. He cupped the heavy fullness of her breasts and gloried in the startled quiver of her flat belly beneath his aching manhood. He brushed his lips over hers, then deepened the kiss. His tongue flicked over the delectable, bow-shaped curve of her upper lip, and he sucked the slick fullness of her lower lip between his teeth, laying siege to her mouth with a bold seductiveness bound to drive away all resistance. Instead of yielding, she stiffened and jerked her head away.

Diarmid froze, then spat out a Gaelic curse. "I see ye still toy with me, Lucia. Well, two can play such games." He reared back onto his haunches, then caught her chin and glared into his eyes. "I'll not force ye—not even when ye've given your consent and me body's achin' for ye, for I've never had a reluctant bed partner, and I willna start now." He dragged his thumb over her moist, trembling pout and ruthlessly quelled a dizzying wave of desire. "Och, no, *mo cridhe*. When I finally do take ye, 'twill be after ye've begged me for it on bended knee."

He grasped her jaw and kissed her with practiced cunning, boldly thrusting his tongue between her lips and savoring the sweet, secret taste of her. After several wanton swirls, his tongue settled into an instinctive rhythm, mimicking the plunging motion of a man's cock deep in a woman's core. Lucy moaned and raked her nails down his back. At last her hips lifted a fraction, and she pressed her mound against his swollen shaft.

With a harsh laugh, he rolled off her, shot up, and stalked into his dressing room. He'd sleep in his dressing room until the scheming trollop begged him to relieve her of her false virtue. And beg she would. He'd personally see to it.

Twelve

Venetia dug a spur into her mare's sweat-darkened hide and trotted through the tall brick gates of Stanton's Grove. It was midafternoon on the first truly chilly day of autumn, and the towering hickories, oaks, and chestnuts blazed with a dozen jeweled tones of red and gold. Normally Venetia would have reveled in a gallop through this sun-dappled alley, but today held no room for speed—only for strength.

A gust of wind whipped up a swirling spiral of leaves, and her horse shied. Venetia cursed and cut at the troublesome beast with her riding crop. The nag deserved it. Besides, if Venetia suffered, then everything around her should suffer as well.

Suffering. Pish! Suffering had been foreign to her until that English slut had stolen Diarmid. Venetia could scarce believe only a week had passed since the governor's ball—for then, in one brief evening, her world had collapsed. Even now she couldn't believe Diarmid had married someone else. She had been so sure of him, so positive that her physical charms would bind him to her—though, in truth, she always had suspected that he didn't really love her. He had drifted into her arms like a boat without a rudder—just as most men did, the damn fools. They found themselves lonely and in need of physical release, so they moored themselves to the first wench to strike their fancy, then floated idly until something more enticing bobbed across their wake.

With a furious jerk of the reins, Venetia halted her mount on the rise above Stanton's Grove. She stared down at the plantation, then glanced at the small gold pocket watch pinned to her bodice. 'Twas three o'clock, and Royal and the other house niggers would be setting dinner on the gleaming mahogany table in the center of the vast dining room. Venetia smirked, pleased with her timing. She'd confront Diarmid here, with Celia and his simpering, scheming bride as witnesses. She'd demand her due as Diarmid's longtime lover; then she'd order him to divorce Lucy and marry her.

In truth, had they not been betrothed? Hadn't every soul within two days' ride long considered them bound to wed?

A simmering purplish rage engulfed her mind and a searing pain throbbed at her temple. Why should she be made to suffer? She loved Diarmid. She'd be his wife right now if it weren't for that conniving, black-eyed English bitch.

Suddenly, as it had for the tenth time that week, a shard of thought pierced her self-pity: There was something queer about Miss Lucy Graves.

Venetia, who refused to think of her rival by her married name, had spent the last few days at her father's home in Williamsburg, ostensibly recovering from a case of the vapors. She snorted. Lud, her lackwit papa had swallowed her story of falling down the stairs and losing Diarmid's child as if it were fresh peach brandy. Then he'd galloped off to whine to Aunt Celia in a belated and utterly ridiculous fit of fatherly concern. Concern, pish! Six days out of seven Barnabas Lee was too drunk to clothe himself or to gobble solid food. The death of Venetia's mother had given him the perfect excuse for his revolting love of liquor, and he'd never shown the least concern for Venetia during her childhood and youth, so why should he start now?

Venetia made a sound of disgust, then smoothed her gloved hand over the black broadcloth skirt of her riding habit. Aunt Celia had paid for the outfit, as she did for all Venetia's clothes. This fetching ensemble had cost the earth, but it had been worth every farthing, for the long, sweeping skirt and gentleman's frock coat were the latest London fashion. She doubted that dusky-skinned English bitch had anything to compare.

Venetia spurred her horse forward. Oh, yes, there was something queer about Lucy, all right. During Venetia's recuperation, all her female visitors had remarked on it.

"Where did that garrulous fop Harry Cheney get such a charming cousin?" Rebecca Burwell had wondered. "He never mentioned such a belle in his family, and he *certainly* never mentioned that he was expecting a visit from London kin." Such an event was so thrilling to most Virginians that it was discussed with eager anticipation for months.

"Harry and Madam Maclean do resemble each other," Rebecca had added. "But Madam Maclean seems almost too cultured. Her accent, her manners, and those racy quips of hers . . . well, they just seem too fine for a lady not of the peerage. After all, the Cheneys are merchants, not gentry."

Then there had been the matter of Lucy's clothes. Rebecca Burwell had noted it first, but Ann Randolph had voiced the same question: "My dears, why would a lady from London appear at the Governor's Palace in a gown sewn by Katherine Rathall?"

"I saw that self-same fabric in Mistress Rathall's shop not a fortnight ago," Rebecca had declared over a cup of sack posset. "Mistress Rathall wouldn't sell it to me. She vowed such a bold shade would turn me sallow. I was most put out, for I had my heart set on it. So rest assured when I tell you—Madam Maclean was wearing a frock sewn by our own humble little mantua maker."

The English bitch's gown had been stunning, although it pained Venetia to admit it. That vile knave Diarmid clearly had agreed, for all during the governor's ball he had ogled his bride as if he wanted to throw her skirts over her head and ravish her in the middle of the ballroom.

Venetia felt a sudden, overwhelming urge to vomit. She clapped a hand to her mouth and swallowed hard. Lud, she'd never forget the look on that cursed Highlander's face when Isaiah Ludlow had danced with Lucy. Diarmid practically ignited with jealousy. Venetia had known then that Lucy had stolen his heart.

She yanked her mare to a halt outside the plantation's front door, dismounted, then angrily beckoned to a wooly-headed pickaninny whose job it was to hold visitors' horses. "Take Pegasus to the stable," she snapped, grabbing the boy's spindly shoulder. "I'll be staying for some time."

She turned, then paused before the low flight of steps leading to the front door. What would she say? This morning, when her father finally had gotten drunk enough to relax his vigil over her fake convalescence, she had raced from Williamsburg with little thought other than storming in on Diarmid, demanding her rights, and forcing him to renounce his little whore. Fury had spurred her, but now, staring up at the imposing mahogany door, she suddenly realized that bullying would never work with Diarmid. He'd never responded to her strident demands in the past; why should he start now?

She caught a movement in one of the front windows. Was her aunt watching her, or was it a nosy darky? Lud, 'twas bad enough that every white person in Williamsburg was whispering behind her back and congratulating themselves on having the luck to never be that most wretched of creatures: a jilted woman. 'Twould be vexation beyond bearing to find herself the brunt of a nigger's pity.

Squaring her shoulders, she gathered her skirts and marched up the steps. Nay, she wouldn't storm in and make demands, for Diarmid would come back to her if she could get rid of that scheming trollop he'd married. Nay, Diarmid wasn't her enemy; Lucy was. Lucy had caused Venetia's broken heart, her wounded pride, her mortification at being an object of petty gossip. Aye, Lucy must pay. Somehow Venetia would drive the bitch off; then Diarmid would be hers once more. She doubted it not a whit.

The front door swung open, and Celia hobbled out onto the steps. "What are you doing here?" the old shrew demanded. "I heard you'd had an accident."

As usual, Celia was overdressed, even for dinner. Venetia wrinkled her nose and suppressed a disdainful laugh. Her aunt might be the richest woman in Virginia, but she had the taste of a rich man's whore. Today, Celia's ensemble was canary yellow satin drawn back over a periwinkle-blue petticoat lib-

erally embellished with love knots and Brussels lace. Worst
of all, Celia's plunging décolletage revealed a wrinkled, powder-caked cleavage ugly enough to turn the stomach of even
the most dedicated roué.

"How kind of you to inquire after my health," Venetia
purred, bending to kiss her aunt's shriveled cheek. "But I'm
feeling much better, thank you. Indeed, I'd rather not speak
of it. One's health is a private matter, don't you think?" Without waiting for a reply, she swept into the front hall. She'd
learned from long experience sparring with Celia that nothing
could be gained by meekness and ladylike manners. Lud, no.
Celia Stanton Lee respected only one thing: strength.

Celia hobbled in behind her, grumbling under her breath
and pounding the floor with her cane. Venetia quickly scanned
the palatial staircase and elegantly paneled hall. She'd rather
hoped to beard Lucy and Diarmid right here, on their very
doorstep, so to speak. Oh, well. A few moments' delay would
give her time to gather her wits.

"You've come for dinner—on purpose, no doubt," Celia
remarked. "I wondered when you'd scrape up the nerve to
show that pretty face of yours." She blocked Venetia's way,
standing as erect and as proud as a duchess. "Diarmid and
his lovely wife will be down in a moment. They *do* so dote
on one another"—her beady eyes gleamed maliciously—"that
'tis hard to get them out of the bedchamber and to the table."

Venetia shoved past her aunt and hurried down the hall to
the dining room. Lud, she couldn't stand this. She couldn't
watch Diarmid and Lucy billing and cooing in revolting marital bliss. She'd rather die. The pain in her temple grew worse,
and she nearly stumbled into the dining room. A wall of beautiful Palladian windows offered a breathtaking view of the
gardens and the James, but she could focus only on her rage.
With trembling hands, she stripped off her gloves and grasped
the back of a graceful Chippendale chair. Suddenly she felt
faint. Lud, could she be ill after all?

Anxiously, she slowed her breathing, then yanked off her
pert little beaver hat and tossed it onto a side chair. If she
fell ill, it would be Lucy's fault. She should kill the little

bitch. Venetia gave a self-pitying sniff and hoped for heart palpitations. Lud, even Celia had turned against her; she had heard it in the old cow's tone.

Her breath caught. Dear God, Celia couldn't disown her. She was the old shrew's heir. For years, Celia had hinted that Stanton's Grove would be Venetia's. Indeed, Venetia and her father had counted on the inheritance, and they had borrowed heavily against their expectations, for as Celia's only living relatives, the vast plantation surely would come to them one day. Williamsburg's merchants had been only too happy to oblige. They knew to the last farthing the value of Stanton Grove's rolling fields and excellent, deep-water dock.

Venetia jerked the chair away from the table, ignoring the *skreek* and scratch the legs made on the waxed floor. She slumped down, her heart thundering. Why, only a month ago Celia had fallen for Venetia's lie about carrying Diarmid's child, and Venetia had thought that at last, Diarmid—and Stanton's Grove—would be hers.

Royal shuffled into the room, carrying a platter of steaming boiled crabs. Venetia ignored the slave's soft greeting and stared blankly at the briny-smelling shellfish. Her stomach lurched. Oh, Lud. What if Celia had turned from her at last? They always had disliked each other, but Celia had indulged Venetia, perhaps pretending that she was the child Celia had never had. They'd had dozens of spats over the years, but Celia always had forgotten, if not forgiven.

"Miz Venetia?"

Venetia jumped and glared at Royal. "What?"

"I axed what you think o' Miz Lucy. We all set a powerful store by her. But I was wonderin' what *you* thought, now that the two you's sorta kin by marriage and all."

"That English wench and I are not kin in any shape, form, or fashion," Venetia snapped. She reached across the table, snatched up a sweet cucumber pickle, and popped it into her mouth. "And I'll thank you to keep your comments to yourself, or you'll feel the sting of my riding crop."

"Venetia!"

She jumped up and spun around. Diarmid loomed in the

doorway, with Lucy clinging to his arm. His face was rigid with anger. "Royal works for your aunt, not for you," he enunciated icily. "She will say and do as she pleases without your interference."

Venetia stood speechless, acutely aware of the half-chewed pickle lying like lead in her mouth. She swallowed and nearly choked. Lud, the English bitch looked more stunning than ever today. She wore a gown of midnight-blue silk over a cream-colored petticoat embroidered with an exotic pattern of scarlet, cobalt, emerald, and gold flowers. Deep froths of lace fell from the gown's tight, elbow-length sleeves, and a gold and emerald locket hung on a blue-silk ribbon around her slender throat, its sheen echoing her tawny skin and amber-flecked eyes. She looked a veritable Gypsy.

Venetia dragged her gaze back to Diarmid's granite-hard face. His aquamarine eyes blazed in his tanned skin and the muscles tightened in his jaw. He'd never looked more commanding or more desirable.

Celia stumped in behind Diarmid. "Lucy, my dear," she purred, prodding the wench's slim arm. "Have you been properly introduced to my niece Venetia?"

Venetia's throat filled with bile. There was no mistaking the doting gleam in Celia's rheumy eyes. Somehow, the English whore had wormed her way into the old cow's good graces.

"We have met," Lucy said coolly. Her voice was husky, almost as deep as a man's, and she swept into a graceful curtsy.

With easy intimacy, Diarmid held out a strong hand and helped his wife to her feet. Lucy blushed slightly at his touch and he flashed her that dazzling, dimpled smile of his—the smile once reserved for Venetia.

Venetia's fingers curled into talons. How she'd love to strangle that whore's swanlike neck. Lud, the bitch had ruined her life! She had stolen the only man Venetia had ever loved, she had bewitched crotchety old Celia—who was notorious for disliking everyone—and doubtless she had urged the old shrew to disinherit Venetia.

Panic seized her. Wildly, her gaze darted around the room, searching for escape. What was she doing here? Celia was laughing at her, Diarmid was sneering at her, and that cat-eyed Gypsy was staring at her with unconcealed pity. Pity!

Suddenly, Venetia's gaze fell on the long, highly polished serving board. The piece was in the new Hepplewhite style, with a rich, mahogany veneer inlaid with delicate blond wood. Venetia remembered Celia's excitement when it had arrived by ship from England just a few months earlier. Now it was piled with a basket of hot biscuits, silver bowls of steaming corn pudding, sweet potatoes, and fried apples, and, of course, the heap of bright red crabs. In the center of the sideboard a magnificent Virginia ham rested magisterially on a blue-and-white Cantonware platter. A carving knife protruded from the ham like a sharp, shiny tusk.

An odd calmness descended over her. She nodded at Lucy, then swept into the chair at Celia's right—the place of honor. All would be well. Lucy had stolen Diarmid and Lucy would pay. Venetia leaned forward and speared another pickle. She smiled slyly as her fork pierced its lumpy green flesh. After all, she had sworn to get Diarmid back, and she would succeed. Even if she had to kill to do so.

Lucy raced up the wide staircase, skirts swirling around her ankles, heart pounding in her throat. God's teeth! When was she going to learn not to trust Diarmid? She'd been a goggling lackwit to believe that he no longer desired Venetia. Oh, he'd claimed he'd broken with her, but if he *had* stopped flourishing with the shameless tart, why had she turned up like a starved cat outside the fishmongers'?

Lucy cracked a knuckle on the banister and spat a quick Romany curse. Aye, she was a fool to trust Diarmid, a fool to trust her own weak heart. She dashed across the upstairs landing, no longer awed by the ceiling cornices, intricately carved paneling, and mirrored silver sconces. When she reached the chamber she supposedly shared with Diarmid, she slammed the door behind her. Instantly, she regretted her rashness. What if Venetia had heard the noise? Then the trollop would know her little scheme to upset Lucy was working all too well.

She began stripping off her bodice. Her trembling hands caught on what seemed like a thousand laces, and she nearly stumbled and sprawled on her face as she kicked off her billowing skirts. She had to get out of here. She had to get away from Diarmid and Celia and that smirking blonde harpy who perched downstairs in the dining room, maliciously flirting with Diarmid as if Lucy didn't exist. And he—the knavish piss-vinegar—*he* was gobbling it up like Eccles cakes.

She jammed her feet into riding boots. Oddly, she almost admired Venetia's courage, for only a true brazen would sit down to dinner with her rival. Venetia had chattered and laughed with Diarmid, had cast him just-between-us glances, and had alluded to private, shared memories. Several times during the meal, her pale, beringed hand had rested on his forearm in an overt gesture of possession. Each time it had happened, she had glanced at Lucy with blatant triumph in her marble-pale eyes.

Desperate to play the role of secure, happy young matron, Lucy had tried to assume an air of nonchalance. But for the first time in her life, her acting ability had failed. When Venetia had announced that she would be staying at Stanton's Grove until the horse race and ball in Jamie Maclean's honor, Lucy had fled.

Now, uttering pungent Romany curses and fighting with an endless row of buttons, she struggled into her forest-green riding habit. She'd ride to Resolute and again try to rescue Mick. Then, with the help of Old Dame Luck, she and her brother would start their fine new life.

She snatched up her riding crop, then hurried down the backstairs toward the kitchen, desperate to get away before Diarmid, Celia, and Venetia finished their sour-cherry trifle. She heard Diarmid's deep voice drifting from the dining room, but couldn't make out the words. Was he planning an assignation with Venetia? Surely his virile masculinity must be craving a woman by now.

He certainly hadn't laid a hand on Lucy since their first night together at Stanton's Grove. As promised, he'd slept in his dressing room, on a pallet that Moses, his body servant, made up each morning. Moses had been sworn to secrecy about this marital irregularity, and as far as Lucy could tell after days of avid eavesdropping on the slaves' gossip, Moses had kept quiet.

The sound of singing floated from the kitchen, and Lucy paused halfway down the backstairs. Royal and Cook must be washing the dinner dishes. The door to the kitchen lay on the left at the bottom of the steps, and the door to the back garden lay straight ahead. Lucy bit her lip, undecided. She didn't want the servants to see her skulking off like a whipped dog, and she didn't dare slip into the front hall, where Diarmid and Venetia might appear at any moment.

Suddenly, Lucy had a mortifying vision of how she must look: a fashionably dressed woman with straggling hair, a furrowed brow, and hunted eyes. God's ears! Where was her pride? What would Da say if he saw her slinking about like a priest in a whorehouse?

She took a slow, wavering breath. So here she was, shorn of dignity and reduced to shrewish jealousy. Her belly clenched, weariness washed over her, and she sank down on the narrow step. Despite her best efforts to spurn Diarmid, her heart had succumbed. She had to face it: She loved that infuriating Scot, and she always would. He had made her his slave, just as her mother had been Jocko's slave.

The stair tread bit into her spine and she stifled a jaded laugh. The worst part was that Diarmid had intended for her to fall in love with him all along—curse his scheming mind to the hottest rings of hell. She had run willingly into his trap and had plunged its steel jaws into her heart. He had vowed to lure her into his arms and make her beg for his caresses, and all week he'd used every masculine weapon in his arsenal to ensure victory.

At first she had been suspicious when her aloof husband suddenly became a model of attentiveness. He'd squired her about the plantation and introduced her to the slaves as if she were his most prized possession. No romantic gesture dear to female dreams was forgotten. He filled her bed with the last autumn blossoms from Celia's rose garden and he ordered Cook to prepare her favorite meals, taking great delight in introducing her to Virginia delicacies such as turnip greens and spoon bread.

She realized she was being lured into captivity when he personally selected which horse from his renowned stables should be her mount—although this strategy had almost backfired when he'd led out an ancient piebald gelding capable of nothing more strenuous than an amble. She'd demanded a more spirited creature, reminding him that Gypsies were veritable wizards with horses. He merely laughed, showing a dazzling array of perfect white teeth, and lifted her onto the piebald.

Every evening he had taken her riding through the twilight fields and had spun fascinating tales from the Highlands about selkies and a sea monster that lived in one of the great lochs. This unsuspected flare for storytelling had charmed her, but when Diarmid adamantly had refused to discuss the Rising or his family, a warning had tolled in her mind. At bedtime, he would stroll into their bedchamber after she had donned her nightshift and was safely hidden under the eiderdown. As he bent to brush a good-night kiss across her lips, her heart would pound with a strange, thrilling excitement. Half of her longed for him to rip back the blankets and ravish her; half of her feared just that.

Now, after one short week, all fear was gone. Diarmid had triumphed.

Although he hadn't yet realized it, his final victory had come three days earlier. After breakfast that foggy morning, he'd escorted her to the stables, where his chestnut stallion and her lugubrious piebald stood saddled and waiting. Then, to her joy and astonishment, he had taken her to Resolute to buy Mick's indenture from Isaiah Ludlow.

When they had ridden up to Ludlow's brick house—a poorly executed copy of Stanton's Grove—his surly overseer had informed them that Ludlow was on a trading trip to

Charleston and that he hadn't left word as to when he would return. Diarmid had tried to brazen his way into the house, but the overseer summoned a rabble of slaves armed with scythes, pitchforks, and axes, and Diarmid and Lucy had had no choice but to ride away—Lucy in despair, Diarmid seeming almost sorry that their mission had failed.

That night Lucy had cried herself to sleep in Diarmid's strong, comforting arms. In the morning, she awoke alone in a cold bed. Diarmid had left her while she slept.

Celia's cane thumped down the front hall, and Lucy's attention flew back to her predicament. Crouching on the stairs like a trapped rat, she listened anxiously to Venetia's shrill laugh and Diarmid's low chuckle and prayed she wouldn't be discovered. The front door creaked open, then clicked shut. Lucy heaved a sigh. With any luck, Diarmid and Venetia would walk through the gardens or down to the dock, leaving the way clear for her dash to the stables.

Shivering with nervous energy, Lucy leaped up and darted to the back door. She'd ride to Resolute, cozen her way into the house, and rescue Mick. Then they'd escape to Maryland, just as she'd planned. After selling the emerald brooch Diarmid had given her, she and Mick would have more than enough chink for the journey.

She softly closed the back door and tore through the herb garden. Pulse pounding, she jumped a low sprawl of sage, and her boots crunched in the neatly raked gravel. Ahead lay an ivy-covered brick wall that separated the garden from the lawn. Beyond it, another graveled path curved down to the stables.

Lucy rounded the corner of the wall and skidded to a halt. Diarmid and Venetia stood less than a hundred yards away, at the top of the brick steps leading down to the sunken flower garden. Lucy was too distant to hear their words, but there was no mistaking their actions: Diarmid's hand rested possessively on Venetia's substantial bosom, and they gazed raptly into each other's eyes, clearly in the midst of a deeply emotional discussion. Venetia seemed near tears, though whether tears of joy or of sorrow Lucy couldn't tell.

Then Diarmid bent and kissed Venetia's pouting red lips.

Lucy's heart jolted as if a lightning bolt had struck her. Her skin flushed, her stomach clenched as if she had been punched, and a poisonous fire raced through her veins. With a tiny sob, she whirled and ran.

Oh, God's ears, she was such a *fool*. When would she learn? Diarmid was a low, vile, lying varlet. He lied at breakfast, lied at dinner, lied at supper. He was a coil of deceit with the conscience of a snake—nay, worse than a snake. At least a snake ate rats and vermin. All Diarmid did was feed his own monstrous craving for pleasure.

Lucy stumbled into the stables and brushed away hot, sticky tears. The usual gaggle of stableboys had vanished, and there was no one to saddle a horse. Although she could easily perform the chore herself, she couldn't spare the time. She had to get away. Now.

Then, as if in answer to her silent plea, she spotted a magnificent black mare tethered to a post outside one of the stalls. Immediately, Lucy recognized the curving neck, alert ears, and delicate muzzle of a horse with pure Araby blood; a horse fit for a Romany queen—and it was saddled and bridled.

Without a second thought, Lucy gathered her skirts and riding crop in one hand, jammed her left foot in the stirrup, and with a heave and a squirm, threw her right leg up and over the awkward sidesaddle. Clasping the reins in her left hand, she leaned forward, deftly untied the rope tethering the horse, then tapped its sides with her heels. They shot out of the stable. As she reined toward the woods, she heard a shout behind her. Could Diarmid have seen her?

She leaned low over the horse's neck and urged it on with a soft Romany command. The magnificent creature responded instantly; seconds later they thundered into the deep autumn woods. There was no path through the trees, but by the position of the lowering sun, Lucy could tell they were headed east, toward Resolute. Shade from the towering canopy of massive chestnuts and venerable oaks had long ago choked out the forest undergrowth, and Lucy's course lay relatively clear. She grazed the mare with her riding crop, and the animal plunged forward. A low-hanging branch raked Lucy's hat and a cobweb clung to her cheek.

Another shout echoed behind her, nearer this time. Lucy kicked the horse's sides. She'd never let him catch her. Suddenly the path narrowed dangerously. Lucy reined the horse around a massive silver maple and her heart stalled.

Less than ten feet ahead lay a huge fallen log. She couldn't swerve right, for the tree's wrenched-up roots were jammed against a boulder and blocked the way. To the left, the tree's sprawling branches tangled into a maze that was sure to catch and snap the Arab's delicate legs. Lucy's only choice was to jump.

She heard a third shout, close behind her. Breathing a prayer, Lucy crouched low and drove the horse straight toward the chest-high tree trunk. Her last thought as the mare's muscles gathered beneath her was that an obstacle this tall was bound to be as broad. Then she leaned forward and up, and as her body rose, the animal rose with her, as fluid and strong and powerful as a river of time. Wind whistled in her ears and she felt as if she and the horse were one, moving at a magical tempo that sped and slowed all at once. The surrounding trees were a silver blur. She was flying.

The horse gave a desperate lunge as it suddenly realized the stunning width of the tree trunk. Then they plunged down. The gnarled, granite-gray wood hurtled up. Lucy clenched her eyes tight. She heard the horrible thunking scrape of hooves hitting bark. There was a bone-snapping thud as the mare's front hooves hit the ground. Lucy lurched forward, nearly flying over the animal's lathered neck. Her hat flew off, the crop jolted from her grip, and her teeth cracked together. The horse hurtled forward, almost down on its knees. Lucy's mind cleared instantly. She *wouldn't* let them die.

Gathering the reins tight in her fists, she pulled up and leaned back, using her weight as a counterbalance to slow the Arab's plunge. For an eternal split second, the horse lurched forward. It scrabbled madly in the slippery fallen leaves, then regained its footing. With breathtaking courage, it staggered up and galloped on, determined to obey Lucy's every command.

Lucy slowed the animal to a canter. She could still hear thundering hooves, and she glanced over her shoulder, terrified for her pursuer. Diarmid was a matchless rider, but his stallion was huge, muscle-bound, and heavy. With Diarmid's added weight, the poor brute would never clear the tree trunk. It would be suicide to try.

She reined and spun her horse around. "Diarmid! Don't do it!"

Suddenly the pounding hooves no longer approached the tree, but galloped toward her from off to her left. A horse shot through the trees at the edge of her vision. Before she could wheel, animal and rider crashed into her, crushing her leg against her mare's ribs and knocking her breathless. Lucy smelled acrid sweat, heard the Arab's frightened squeal. A steely hand grabbed her arm and yanked down, trying to capture her reins. There was a *skrrrrrk* of renting cloth. Lucy twisted in the saddle and screamed.

Thirteen

Her pursuer was not Diarmid, but a young black man.

"Let go of me!" Lucy cried, wrenching her arm free.

Her sleeve came away in one long tatter from shoulder to wrist, and the Arab danced sideways, rolling its eyes, jerking its head, and whickering nervously. The black man's horse—a lanky, mean-eyed roan—lowered its rangy neck and snaked forward, yellow teeth bared. It bit the Arab on the wither, just missing Lucy's thigh. Her mare squealed, stiffened its front legs, and pronged sideways in a series of outraged bucks.

Lucy tightened the reins, pulled the animal's head up, settled herself firmly in the saddle, and snapped, "Stop that. Is that any way for an Arab queen to behave? Show some dignity." The horse calmed and she rounded on the slave. "Who are you? How dare you accost me like this?"

Far from looking repentant, the black man grinned, reminding her for one uncomfortable moment of Diarmid. "Oh, Miss Lucy," he said. "Mr. Diarmid was right about you. If anything, he undershot a bit. Mmm, mmm, mmm." He chuckled, a sound as low and rich as persimmon brandy. "Wheeew. I ain't never seen a lady ride like that. You must be half hoss yourself."

Lucy jerked up her chin. "You seem to know me. Who are you?"

The man bowed low in the saddle. "I'm Mercury—head groom of the Stanton's Grove stables."

Lucy eyed him narrowly. There was something vaguely familiar about Mercury, although she couldn't say what. His skin was a light, warm brown, like coffee with lots of cream. She supposed that meant he had white blood, although in what proportion 'twas impossible to tell. His jaw was square, his nose long and fine boned, and he wore his thick black hair clubbed back in a leather thong. His hair, too, bespoke white blood, for it was straighter and silkier than that she'd seen on the other servants. He wore a simple, unbleached muslin shirt, navy osnaburg knee breeches, knitted woolen socks, and black leather shoes with brass buckles.

"I've never heard of you," she retorted, "and I've ridden every day for a week. Diarmid—Mr. Maclean—has never mentioned you."

Mercury, who had been appraising her hot face rather boldly, suddenly dropped his gaze to her bare arm. His lips thinned slightly. "I been off on a business trip, you might say."

"What business?"

"Oh, just helpin' someone less fortunate." He continued to stare at her arm.

She glanced down. The ragged, purplish T that branded her a thief glared out from her tawny skin as if it were alive. She felt a blush sweep up her throat and hastily smoothed the ripped sleeve over her naked flesh.

Mercury met her eyes and smiled sympathetically. "Mr. Diarmid said you'd fallen on hard times. He sure is a sucker for folks in trouble, anyone who's hurt and needin' help." He spoke slowly, as if mulling a problem. "That's how he come to hire me, you know."

Lucy frowned. "You're not a slave?"

Mercury reached forward and deftly plucked the reins from her hands. "Come on, Miss Lucy. We'd best walk these critters 'til they cool off. You know it's bad to let a lathered hoss stand still in the cold. They catch their death."

To Lucy's surprise, the Araby mare clopped alongside Mercury's peevish roan as if it were a pet lamb on a pink silk ribbon. Mercury rode with an easy, nonchalant grace, and again Lucy was reminded of Diarmid. She scrutinized her friendly captor from beneath lowered lashes and decided that he was quite young, hardly out of his teens, despite his air of assurance.

Suddenly a horrible thought struck her. Mercury had white blood. He was quite handsome, with certain mannerisms and a mildly teasing air that all but shrieked Diarmid. God's ears, could Mercury be Diarmid's son?

A sick tightening began in her chest. In the kitchens at Sugarplum and Stanton's Grove she'd heard whispers of such things. While trying to gather information on Mick and Isaiah Ludlow, she'd spent plenty of time loitering about, listening to the slaves gossip, and they had informed her that 'twas common for white masters to bed their more comely slave wenches. Indeed, many did so for the express purpose of breeding free labor. Such behavior was illegal, of course, but the law was hardly enforced.

She knew that Diarmid's powerful sexual needs must have found an outlet—nay, many outlets—before he got involved with Venetia. What if he'd lain with a slave and Mercury was the by-blow?

Mercury glanced up and caught her wary appraisal. He offered her a shy half smile. "Aye, I be a free man, thanks to Mr. Diarmid."

Lucy swayed forward in the saddle, suddenly bone weary. She couldn't take any more; she just couldn't. First Venetia, now some nameless black wench. God's ribs, *why* had she fallen in love with that damned rutting he-goat? And why couldn't the randy cove keep his yard in his pants? He was worse than a thousand Jockos.

Mercury reined to a halt. "Miss Lucy? You're lookin' a mite peaked. You feelin' vaporish?"

Lucy sat straighter and glared at him, chin out, brows lowered. "Hardly. I'm not some namby-pamby miss who faints after a brisk ride. I'm just sick and tired of being cooped up at Stanton's Grove—and I'm sick of that black-hearted devil you work for. I'm tired of being tricked and lied to, and for once I want the truth."

Mercury looked taken aback, as if he'd picked up a fawn

only to have it turn into a tiger. "I'll tell you the truth. Just ask."

Lucy's heart pounded so wildly she thought it might burst from her throat. "Are you Diarmid's son?"

Mercury's eyebrows flew up, and for a long moment he looked genuinely shocked. Then he laughed, a low, helpless, almost pitying laughter accompanied by several unbelieving head shakes. "Oh, Miss Lucy," he managed at last. "You sure got spirit . . . *and* a powerful imagination. No wonder Mr. Diarmid be so crazy about you." Noting her stricken expression, he sobered. "No'm, I ain't Mr. Diarmid's son—though I don't reckon there's a better man in all the colonies, and I'd be proud if I was. But you're not too far off the mark. I do have a white pappy—Mr. Uriah Lee."

Lucy's startled mind swam frantically, searching for the name. "You mean Celia's second husband?"

"Yes'm. I don' think Miss Celia ever knew it, but Mr. Uriah sure did. When I was born, he sold me and my momma to Mr. Isaiah Ludlow. He wanted his fun but didn't want no mulatto pickaninnies runnin' around remindin' him of it."

Lucy leaned forward and yanked on the pair of reins clasped in Mercury's callused hand. Both horses stopped under a towering shag-bark hickory and immediately lowered their heads to rest. "Do you know Isaiah Ludlow well?"

Mercury snorted in disgust. "That man's the Devil himself. He's a slave trader, Miss Lucy. That's how he got most of his money."

"H-he bought my little brother," Lucy stammered. "He wouldn't hurt him?"

"Hard to say. He never beat his field hands himself, like some massas do. But he sure let his overseer wield the cat. I seen hands at Resolute half killed from whippin'. One boy, he got his two littlest toes chopped off so's he'd quit runnin' away." Mercury pondered a moment, avoiding Lucy's shocked eyes. "No'm, he never beat no one himself, but he sure liked to watch."

This statement carried an import Lucy didn't quite catch. "I beg your pardon?"

"He liked to watch the beatin's. Then he'd take a wench up to his room and we'd hear screams and cries all night long." Mercury shifted uneasily in the saddle; then he touched his heels to the roan and they ambled forward. "In the mornin' them little girls was a mess. Weren't no weals on 'em, but he'd done somethin' awful to 'em, just the same. One girl, Teal . . . well, she died from it. Slit her wrists with a butcher knife so he'd never get at her again."

Lucy pressed a hand to her bosom. "You said young girls?"

Mercury nodded glumly. "Yes'm. Some young as ten, the best I reckon. Odd though—he ain't never gone after grown women, white or black. Jus' little girls."

Lucy dropped her hands onto the saddle's pommel, too upset to express her deepest fear. Mercury must somehow have sensed the direction of her thoughts, for suddenly he blurted, "Mr. Isaiah never went after boys, though."

Lucy tried to feel relief but could only imagine Mick alone with a sadistic devil who gained gratification from some unspeakable form of torture. She clenched her eyes shut. The Ace of Swords danced through her mind, gleaming with a cold, malevolent light before transforming into Isaiah Ludlow's leering, pockmarked face.

Her eyes flew open, and Mercury appeared in Ludlow's place. His brow was wrinkled with an almost comic expression of concern. "When Mr. Diarmid came here seventeen years ago, I was just a tyke," he said, "already sold over to Resolute. Momma and I stayed there 'til I was about ten. I never did know my birthday," he explained with a chagrined smile. "Then one day Momma fell afoul of the new overseer, John Veasey. He wanted to bed her, but she'd got her a new hand and didn't want no white man. So Veasey raped her. Done a prime job of it, too. She couldn't walk for two days."

Mercury's easygoing countenance hardened. "So we run. Just lit off in the middle of the night. We was makin' for the Stanton's Grove dock and one of the little boats Miss Celia kept tied there. Had some half-witted plan of rowin' to freedom." He gave a snort of laughter. "I learned me a hard lesson that night—you can't run from trouble and you can't run to freedom. You got to abide and find freedom where you at, even if it's just inside you. Then folks can't never make you a slave."

"But you're free now," Lucy interrupted. "You must have escaped."

"No'm. The sheriff catched us with his bloodhounds. 'Bout bit my poor momma to death—the dogs, not the sheriff."

Lucy raked a strand of hair from her eyes. "I don't understand."

Mercury grinned, as if pleased with his riddle. "We got catched on Stanton's Grove land." He glanced around, then pointed to an enormous chestnut at the edge of a small clearing. " 'Twas right about here. I'll never forget it. The sheriff's men was hollerin', hounds was squealing and bayin' for blood, fat pine torches was gutterin' and blazin' through the trees. The sheriff ran Momma down, then dragged her onto his hoss. Blood was runnin' down her legs like black pitch. I was so scared I pissed my pants. But then somethin' odd happened."

Mercury turned and gazed at the majestic chestnut. Its orange-gold leaves rustled in the breeze and fell from its massive branches in shimmering, magical swirls. The wind caught a few of the leaves and tossed them about like elves in a sprightly dance. It was nearly sunset and the woods were bathed in low, slanting, golden light. The only sound was the tick of the bare branches and the creak and sigh of wind through the tall pines. Even the birds were silent.

"Yes'm. Somethin' happened that night that still makes my hairs prickle up." Mercury's voice was hushed, as if he, too, were caught in the woods' enchantment. " 'Twas black as the bottom o' Hades that night, 'cept 'round them torches. Dogs was barkin', men was hollerin'. Then all of a sudden we heard this strange sound."

"What was it?"

"A wailin'. Low and awful, full o' despair, like a soul in torture in the bowels of hell. It started soft at first, and seemed to come from behind us. A few of the men shushed

and tried to place it. It weren't a catamount, one declared.
Nor a wolf nor a savage. It grew louder, then shifted over
toward the river. Even the dogs had shushed by then. The
sheriff tried to rally his boys, but they were a bunch o' white
trash and mighty superstitious. One of 'em recollected 'twas
All Hallow's Eve—the night when spirits and demons snatch
men's souls. One of the posse was half-Cherokee, and he
started to run off, sayin' he'd not be dragged down into the
James by a river demon. This spooked the men somethin'
awful and they fell to arguin' and roundin' up the dogs. Some
even fired their guns into the dark. But that spectral wailin'
just kept on.

"I was near mad with fear. Suddenly two hands grabbed
me and yanked me behind that there chestnut. I was sure
'twas a river demon. I tried to scream, but the demon stifled
me, then swooped me up and crashed off through the trees
with me slung over its shoulder like a sack o' corn grits. The
sheriff heard the ruckus and fired his pistol, and something
whined over the top 'o' my butt, like a dragonfly on a light-
nin' bolt. The demon grunted and stumbled, almost droppin'
me into a possumhaw. Then we went on crashin' through the
trees. After awhile I felt somethin' warm and wet seepin'
through my breeches. 'Twasn't piss this time—excuse the language, miss—'twas blood." Mercury stopped and flashed an
impish smile at her confounded expression.

"But what was it?" she demanded, Romany imagination
wild with possibilities.

"Can't you guess?"

Lucy surveyed the scene. The chestnut was large enough
to hide an elephant, three horses, or a dozen men. If something had run directly away from the tree and the clearing
where the sheriff had stood, it would wind up at the Stanton's
Grove stables—not the most likely place for a river demon.
She tapped a gloved finger against her lips, envisioning a
ten-year-old boy slung over a man's shoulder. If a bullet had
whizzed over Mercury's bottom, it would likely have grazed
the man's ear—or the side of his lip.

His lip. She turned and grinned delightedly at Mercury. "I

know what it was. 'Twasn't a river demon—'twas a stubborn, prideful Scottish Highlander." She nodded in satisfaction. "So *that's* how Diarmid got the scar on his lip." With a triumphant laugh, she snatched the reins from Mercury and urged the Arab mare into a trot. God's nose—would there ever be an end to Diarmid's surprises? Imagine him risking his aloof, arrogant hide to rescue a slave.

She squirmed around in the saddle and addressed Mercury as he rode behind her. "But I thought you said you were caught."

"We was. Momma was dragged right back to Resolute. Mr. Diarmid squirreled me away in the Stanton's Grove stables. He told me I had to trust him. No matter how things turned out, he said, he'd see things right in the end.

" 'Course that sheriff weren't dumb, just trashy. Come mornin' he figured what you figured, then come after Mr. Diarmid." Mercury grinned, obviously fond of the memory. "Mr. Diarmid denied it o' course, but it weren't no secret that he hated slavery, and there was that fresh gouge on his lip. Coulda been made by a bullet. Then when they searched the stables and found his bagpipes—"

"Bagpipes?"

Mercury rolled his eyes. "What you think made that awful noise? He'd got Ol' Pete, the plantation carpenter, to creep around in the woods, blowin' on that dang instrument. 'Course bagpipes don't sound none too good in the best o' hands, let alone ol' drunk Pete's. Anyway, when the sheriff found them pipes, Mr. Diarmid's goose was well and truly cooked."

"What did they do to him? I thought helping a runaway slave was a crime."

"Yes'm, it is. And a lesser man'd been fined or tossed in jail for a spell. But Mr. Diarmid's got powerful friends, so it was all hushed up with the understandin' that I'd be returned to Resolute. When Mr. Diarmid agreed to send me back, it 'bout broke my heart. Here I'd gone and trusted him, and he'd played me dirty." Mercury's voice had taken on a tone of aggrieved disgust that Lucy understood all too well. "But a week later, when things had simmered down a bit, Mr. Diarmid rode over to Resolute and asked to buy me and Momma, even though he didn't' have a penny to his name."

"How did he plan to buy you?"

"He extended his indenture with Miss Celia. He was a freedman by then, you know, workin' for her for wages. He told her he'd work free another year if she'd give him the money to buy me and Momma. Miss Celia went along with it, but by the time he got to Resolute, Momma had died. I 'spect the beatin' the posse gave her broke some of her ribs. They splintered through her gullet and she bled to death inside."

"How awful," Lucy murmured, sickened.

At that moment, she and Mercury broke out of the darkening woods. The vast lawns, fields, and gardens of Stanton's Grove lay before them, in one golden sweep to the James. The sun had set behind the forest to their right, and its vermilion grandeur lay hidden by a garrison of black cedars. The sky above them was tinged with faintest rose and the air was diamond clear, as the mists of twilight had not yet crept in off the river. Lucy felt a tiny, exultant shiver down her spine. She'd never known such air in London's soot-choked alleys. There, one could cut the noisome fog with a butter knife. Here, she could almost reach out a forefinger and ting the air as if it were fine crystal.

Lucy reined in the Arab and gazed down at the plantation stables. Golden lamplight glowed from the open double doors and the small-paned window of the tack room. Beyond, on the low grass rise, candlelight flickered from the windows of Stanton's Grove. Lucy felt a bittersweet pang of longing. She never wanted to leave.

For the first time, she could almost understand why Diarmid was so obsessed with Stanton's Grove. The plantation was a world apart, like some ethereal dream; a dream that filled your sleep with pure joy, then evaporated like morning mist when you awoke.

When Lucy was a child, it had been her habit to walk the dark London streets and gaze in the glowing windows of the rich. She'd seen many things: laughing ladies playing the harpsichord, plump gentlemen puffing their pipes, rosy-cheeked children receiving a good-night kiss before being whisked by their nursemaids to a cozy, top-floor nursery. Lucy had longed for that security with all her heart.

Now, it all floated before her: security, serenity, and perhaps—just perhaps—love. All she had to do was reach out and take it. After all, hadn't Mercury said Diarmid was crazy about her? Perhaps that cunning Highlander's kindness over the past week hadn't been a ruse to get between her thighs after all. But then again, perhaps it had.

She found this thought so overwhelmingly depressing that she turned to Mercury, anxious for distraction. "We're almost home. Please finish your story."

"There ain't much more to tell. Mr. Ludlow was more'n happy to take three times my worth in payment for me. What did he want with an uppity nigger when he could have pounds sterlin'? Then, when the deal was struck, Mr. Diarmid thrashed Mr. Ludlow somethin' fierce—payin' him back for killin' Momma, I reckon. The pair of them's been enemies ever since."

Lucy relaxed the reins, and the Arab dropped its head, then placidly cropped at the grass. "You said you couldn't run away to freedom. What did you mean?"

Mercury gazed out over the James. "Well, I was mad a long time 'bout what'd happened to Momma. And it plain galled me when Mr. Diarmid didn't set me free. He kept me a slave for eight more years. Oh, he was mighty kind. He give me a fine education—even though educatin' a slave's against the law. And he gave me the job I hankered for most—workin' with his prize hosses. But I chafed and sulked and about festered my soul away.

"Then one night a few years back, Mr. Diarmid rode into the stable, blind drunk. He'd started courtin' Miss Venetia, and she was givin' him an awful time. He was so soused he 'bout fell off his hoss, then he staggered into a stall, fetched his flask from his pocket, took a swig of liquor and told me a tale of sufferin' that made my troubles seem like a Sunday picnic. Right then I saw it. Mr. Diarmid weren't my oppressor, he was just another slave like me. That man's chained to the past and a misery that'd break your poor sweet heart, Miss Lucy. All them years I'd figured him for proud and arrogant, when all along he was worse off than me."

Mercury shook his head sadly. "The worst part was, I *had* to be a slave. I couldn't never go free, no matter how I ached to. But Mr. Diarmid didn't have to be that way. He coulda let the past go and started a new life. But he wouldn't. He was punishin' himself, I reckon. I decided right then I'd never turn out like that—all bitter and festerin'. Them books Mr. Diarmid made me read, they taught me all about how a man can be free inside." He tapped his head. "Here." He tapped his heart. "And here."

Mercury smoothed the ends of the reins back and forth between his fingers. His voice sounded sheepish, as if he feared Lucy might think him uppity. "So I set myself free. I quit bein' all prickly and suspicious. I stopped pawin' over all my hurts and I decided to trust Mr. Diarmid, just like he'd asked me to eight years before."

"But how did you finally get free? I mean *really* free?"

"When I reckoned it must be about my eighteenth birthday, I went up to Mr. Diarmid's office in the big house and asked him to set me free. 'I'm mighty obliged for all you done for me, sir,' I said, 'but I cain't believe you'd rescue me, buy me, and educate me just to keep me a slave. I got me a fine education now, thanks to you, and a fine skill with hosses. I'm askin' for the chance to make my own way.'

"Mr. Diarmid . . . well, he just glared down that long, fox-straight nose of his—you know how he does. 'And if I don't set you free?' he asked.

" 'If'n you don't, I'll make my peace with it. Fact, I already have. But it'd sure be a wicked waste.'

"Mr. Diarmid just shook his head and laughs that roguish laugh o' his. A prime rake, is Mr. Diarmid. Then he strolls to this leather trunk, unlocks it, takes out a document, and tosses it at me. 'Twas my freedom paper, making me my own man." Mercury halted, and Lucy caught him surreptitiously brushing something from his eye. "He'd signed and dated it eight years back, on the very day he bought me. I'd been free all along. All I'd had to do was ask and he'd a let me go."

Lucy's jaw dropped. "But weren't you angry? I mean, all those years you could have been free—"

"But what good would it a done me? A boy can't light off on his own. Neither can a man, for that matter, less he got a way to support himself. Mr. Diarmid knew that. So he give me a fine education and a respectable trade, so when I was ready to leave, I'd be able to make my way."

"But you're still here," Lucy protested.

Mercury grinned, and his chocolate-brown eyes took on an impish gleam. "I sure am. See, there's another reason Mr. Diarmid wanted me to stay 'til I was growed—the self-same reason you ain't met me 'til today." His grin turned distinctly elven, and Lucy gaped at the eerie resemblance to Diarmid. "Care to guess again, Miss Lucy?"

"No. Tell me."

Mercury glanced down at the roan's sugar-sprinkled withers, then smoothed a hand over the animal's hide. "Mr. Diarmid's been helpin' slaves escape north for the past ten years. And I'm the one who takes 'em there."

Fourteen

Lucy touched her heels to the Arab mare's ribs, and the horse trotted forward, eager for the comfort of the stable and a bucket of grain. Mercury had ridden on ahead so Lucy could enjoy the twilight alone—and so she could mull over his startling disclosure.

It must be true, for Mercury had no reason to lie. But she could not imagine her arrogant, aloof husband risking his neck—and his precious Stanton's Grove—to help a passel of slaves. She shifted uneasily in the saddle. She couldn't ask Diarmid straight out if it were true. Mercury had told her to keep her knowledge secret, and she doubted Diarmid would answer truthfully even if she did confront him. Despite his attentiveness of late, he still refused to discuss anything about his past—or about their future.

Their future. Ha! She knew all too well what that entailed: They would fool batty old Celia, Diarmid would inherit the plantation, and she and Mick—*if* his highness deigned to purchase her little brother—would be abandoned like a sack of mongrel pups. Oh, no. She'd do well to forget the future, and to forget Mercury's passing remark that Diarmid was crazy about her.

The breeze had died, and the only sound was the muffled *chunk* of the mare's hooves and the swish of damp, knee-high grass against Lucy's long skirt. It was odd the grass should be so high here, for Diarmid was conscientious to a fault when it came to running Stanton's Grove. Perhaps he'd been distracted of late—because of her, no doubt. Her lips twitched into a smile. As a Gypsy, she knew just how to use distraction, mis-direction, and illusion. 'Twas a vital skill for a fortune-teller, and she hoped it would serve her well in her campaign to free Mick.

She raked a strand of hair from her eyes, disturbed by the memory of the Ace of Swords—Mick's fortune. If Mercury's assessment of Isaiah Ludlow was correct, her reading was coming true. Time was running out. But what could she do?

Suddenly, her da's voice echoed through her mind, as real as if he rode along beside her. Nikolas had taught her how to read the future with her grandmother's tarot cards, and he'd impressed a warning on her again and again. It was that warn-ing she heard now: "The cards show only what the future *holds*. A person has the power to change that future, *if* he has the courage and strength."

Well, she had seven centuries of Rom strength flowing in her veins. She'd change Mick's future and she'd change hers. She just had to figure out how.

Sighing, she gazed up at the night sky. Stars glimmered above her like fairy diamonds sprinkled across a blue-velvet cloak. She recognized Orion the Hunter with his broad belt and dangling sword, then she swiveled in the saddle and scanned the horizon for Cassiopeia's chair. When she found it, a tiny shiver of delight rippled over her skin. She patted the mare's warm, damp neck.

Her mother had taught her the constellations. Proud of her education, Agnes Gravesceu had spent the early years of Lucy's childhood imparting to her the myths and magic of the night sky.

Lucy smiled, remembering. Many times when she couldn't sleep, she had climbed out of the Gravesceus' brightly painted wooden caravan and snuggled between her parents around a Rom campfire. There always had been music: a fiddle, a three-stringed guitar, a round cow-hide drum that made a primitive beat. And there had been dancing: the wild, forbidden flamenco or simple folk jigs passed down from ancestors who had trav-eled from Hungary, France, and Spain. The men passed a bottle and laughed, their voices low and deep and dangerously masculine. Girls danced and flirted, and the wives of middle years and the dames with gray hair gossiped about herbs and babies and whose husband had strayed where he'd no business going.

Nikolas had encouraged her to stay up, but after a few minutes, Agnes would gather Lucy in her arms and carry her back to bed. Just before they climbed the caravan's rickety wooden steps, Agnes would point to the night sky and whisper, "See, my heart? There's Taurus the Bull—a great, snorting, stubborn beast, rather like your papa." Then she would chuckle to herself, her laugh the sound of a woman who loves and is loved in return. "And there's the Great Bear . . . and there—see? 'Tis the North Star. That one neither wavers nor varies. 'Tis fixed and unchanging, like your papa's love. Remember that star, my heart. You can navigate by it and will never be lost."

Now, years later and half a world away, Lucy gazed up at that same star. It wasn't the brightest in the sky, as some folk thought, and it could be hard to locate, requiring that one first find the tail of the Big Dipper and count down three stars. But her mama had been right: It neither disappeared nor varied.

Lucy's throat closed and tears blurred her vision. Oh, God's teeth, she missed Mama. For years Lucy had nursed a rage against Agnes, blaming her for being weak and foolish enough to fall in love with a varlet like Jocko. But Agnes hadn't always been weak. She'd taken Lucy on long rambles through the woods, pointing out shy primrose and glossy green yew, which always smelled like cat piss, and she'd taught Lucy to cook, adding English trifle and Maids of Honour to the Roms' exotic fare. But it had been during those moments alone under the vast, dazzling sky that Lucy had felt most loved.

The Arab mare broke into a trot, and Lucy realized they were almost to the stables. She sniffed, determined not to cry. She hadn't cried for her mother on the day Agnes died; and she wouldn't cry now. Taking care of poor, wee Mick had required all of Lucy's strength, and she needed that strength now more than ever.

Against her better judgment, she thought of Diarmid. He was so like her father: stubborn, teasing, proud, quick-tempered. A rueful smile curved her lips. If Diarmid were a star, he'd be Sirius, the brightest in the heavens. But Sirius moved with the seasons and couldn't be trusted.

Suddenly, loud, angry shouts rang from the stable. Startled, Lucy flicked the mare with her riding crop and they shot forward, covering the last few yards to the stable in a blur. Lantern light glowed from the open double doors, and Lucy ducked beneath the low beam lintel, then clattered across the worn plank floor. She reined the horse sharply; the animal reared. Less than a yard away, Venetia stood with her arm raised and her hand clutching a buggy whip. Before Lucy could speak, the whip slashed down, whining through the air with brutal force, then cutting across Mercury's shoulders with a loud crack.

"There, you stupid black varmint," Venetia snarled. Her teeth were clenched, her face a white mask of fury, and a look of perverse excitement glittered in her blue-marble eyes. "That'll teach you."

Lucy jumped down.

"Never"—Venetia snapped as her arm slashed down. Lucy darted across the wooden floor. "Let that English bitch"—the whip cracked like pistol fire across Mercury's back, and Lucy lunged. "Ride my horse again!" Venetia's arm flew back for another blow.

Lucy caught it. "Stop it, Venetia."

Venetia spun, powdered blond ringlets flying, black skirts swirling like ink through water. "You." Her eyes bulged and a tide of scarlet flowed across her sweating cheeks. "Let me go, you rotten English whore!"

She wrenched her arm free and raised the whip. Lucy dodged around her, mind racing. She was slim, delicate, half Venetia's size. She could never best Venetia in a fight. The whip slashed down and cracked into the plank floor inches from Lucy's booted foot. Straw and dust flew like birdshot.

Lucy spun, praying her long, trailing skirt wouldn't trip her. With the lithe speed of a ferret, she bent and grabbed the whip's rawhide thong, twisted her wrist, wrapped it around her gloved hand, and yanked. The whip snapped from Venetia's grasp and arced overhead. At the top of the arc, Lucy released the whip. It flew behind her, narrowly missing a whale-oil lantern that hung from a ceiling post. Then it landed in a pile of hay.

"You *bitch*. I'll kill you!" Venetia lunged forward, hands curled into claws.

Lucy caught a frightening glimpse of scarlet cheeks, sweating brow, and eyes as popped and glazed as a rotten fish's. Desperate to avoid injury, she hurtled backward and slammed into the ceiling post. Her breath rushed from her lungs and she doubled over, gasping. The lantern—jarred free from its beam—dropped into the pile of hay behind her. Her nose crinkled at the smell of spilled whale oil; then she saw a spurt of orange flame.

Mercury shouted a warning, but Lucy's mind was lost in a suffocating fog of pain. Venetia grabbed Lucy's wrist and yanked her upright. The dangling sleeve of her riding habit— torn from shoulder to elbow in her scuffle with Mercury— ripped free and came away in Venetia's hand. Venetia cursed and flung the sleeve to the stable floor, madness blazing from her eyes.

Still gasping, Lucy raised her arm to ward off her attacker. But no blow came.

"I was right!" Venetia crowed. Her gaze was riveted to the *T*-shaped brand on Lucy's upper arm. "I knew there was something odd about you. You're no more Harry Cheney's cousin than I am. Oh, wait 'til people hear about this. You're no great lady. You're nothing but a filthy, lying thief."

Lucy edged sideways. She had to get out of here. She couldn't stand the leering triumph in Venetia's expression, couldn't bear her hectoring tone.

Venetia shot forward until her face was inches from Lucy. "I wanted to kill you," she hissed, voice pitched low so Mercury couldn't hear. "But now I won't have to. When Celia finds out you're a thief and an imposter she'll kick you out on your scheming little arse. Then Diarmid will be mine."

Mercury shouted a warning, and Diarmid appeared in the stable doorway, his aquamarine eyes wide. His jaw hardened to granite and he bolted toward Lucy just as Venetia grabbed her arm and shoved her backward. Lucy heard crackling behind her. She smelled smoke, felt fierce warmth through her skirt. God's ears, the hay was on fire!

Then she was falling, hurtling back into ravenous tongues of flame. She hit the burning pile. Momentarily, her skirts seemed to smother the blaze, then flames *whoomped* up around her, and she caught the nauseating stench of singing hair. Sparks leaped onto her bodice, lap, skirt. She shrieked.

Diarmid's steely hands gripped her wrists and yanked her to her feet. Then he swept her up into his arms and dashed from the stables. Mercury shouted, Venetia cursed, and a horse screamed.

Lucy struggled in Diarmid's arms, half aware that her skirts were aflame, wholly uncaring. "Diarmid, stop, please. 'Tis the Araby mare. I've got to save her."

Diarmid spat a curse. He reached the damp grass outside the stable, fell to his knees, dropped Lucy on her back, then roughly rolled her over onto her belly, and beat at her flaming skirts with his bare hands. "Och, *mo cridhe,*" he rasped. "Ye wilna leave me like this. I wilna allow it."

Lucy opened her mouth to plead, to order Diarmid into the stable to save the horse. Suddenly, Diarmid lunged over her and smothered her burning clothes with his body. His weight knocked the breath from her lungs. Cold, wet grass ground into her open mouth. She felt the knotted muscles of his thighs press into the backs of her legs, felt his hips shove against her buttocks, felt his massive chest crush her shoulder blades.

His lips trembled against her ear. "Och, ye foolish, foolish lass. Do ye think I'll ever let ye go? Ye're mine, *mo cridhe.* Mine."

They lay still a long moment, his weight heavy on her, his warm, whiskey-scented breath caressing her ear. She could feel his heart pounding against her shoulder, thundering like stallions' hooves and overpowering the foolish flutter of her own weak vessel. His hands stroked her tangled hair.

"I'll kill her if she hurt ye," he ground out, *r*s rolling like a storm-tossed sea. "Och, your hair's singed. Och, *mo cridhe*—ye could have died."

He pressed his lean, stubble-covered cheek against hers, and she felt his body shudder. Could he be crying? *Diarmid?* Surely not.

His hands resumed their journey, sliding down over her ribs, cupping the curve of her waist, sculpting the flare of her hips. Her eyes fluttered shut and tears scalded her lids. Even now, with the barn burning and horses dying and Venetia out to kill her, her traitorous body cried out for Diarmid's touch. The sure passage of his hands lit a fire in her that no water could quench. Her heart blazed with love, and her body smoldered with desire. Diarmid murmured Gaelic endearments into her ear, and with each whisper, the tingling ache in her breasts migrated southward, where it pooled between her thighs and throbbed with a frightening urgency.

There was a confused babble of shouts. Running feet pounded around them; then she heard shrill neighs and the clatter of hooves. Desperate to save the horses, she squirmed and cursed. At last Diarmid seemed satisfied that she was no longer aflame. He rolled off her and stood. Instantly, she scrambled to her knees.

"Oh, Diarmid, we've got to save—"

"Hush," he ordered, his voice cracking like Venetia's whip. "Sit here out of the way." She opened her mouth to protest, and he clapped a sooty hand over it. He glared at her, aquamarine eyes glittering like gems in the firelight. "If I catch you going into that stable, I'll take a whip and give you a flogging the likes of which you've never seen."

Then he shot off. Lucy lurched to her feet, heeding Diarmid's warning not one moment. She started to run, then halted, stunned.

Flames engulfed the stable and leaped through the double doors like writhing demons clawing at the sky. Smoke billowed like white ghosts into the darkness, and shouting slaves ran into and out of the lurid shadows cast by the fire's glare. The women had formed a line down to the James, and they passed sloshing buckets hand-over-hand to the men. Those closest to the blaze tossed water in great gleaming arcs at the flames, but it seemed to Lucy like tossing daisies at a ravening lion. The fire was too far gone.

Mercury raced past. She grabbed at his arm, but he slipped from her grasp, paying her no more attention than a fly. He bolted around the side of the stable, and Lucy followed, then almost collapsed with relief. Mercury had had the presence of mind not to try to take the horses out through the blazing front doors. Instead, he and the grooms had led the panicked animals through the narrow, cluttered tack room and out the side door.

Frantically, she counted the skittish horses: her piebald, looking as lugubrious as ever; Celia's four gray carriage horses; the chestnut pony who drew the trap; the three glossy thoroughbreds who lost to Harry Cheney's Nimbus at every race; Mercury's ill-tempered roan; the ancient white gelding Celia had hunted with in sprier days; three placid mares used as mounts for visitors with more desire to ride than talent in the saddle; and Diarmid's blood-bay thoroughbred stallion, Braw.

Lucy grabbed Mercury's arm. He turned, eyes frantic, brow streaming sweat. "Where's the Arab?" she cried.

He shook his head, then mopped a hand down over his face. "Ain't no use, Miss Lucy. We can't get her out. She's smack in the middle of the stable, hitched in the stall next to that pile a hay. When Miss Venetia pushed you, I seed the hay was burnin'. I shoulda gotten that hoss out then, but I forgot all about her. All I could think about was savin' you. Then, when Mr. Diarmid hauled you off, I went for the other hosses."

Mercury bent, hands on knees, head hanging. His shoulders heaved and his shirt clung to his back. "Thank the good God all the hosses was loose in their stalls, all on this side of the fire. We led 'em through the tack room—"

"I know. I'm not blind. But we've got to get the Araby—"

There was a loud, rending *screeek*, followed by a crash so loud it vibrated through the ground into the soles of Lucy's feet. A shower of sparks shot into the sky. Flames leaped up to catch them.

"God's teeth," Lucy cried, dumbfounded. "The stable's falling in."

Mercury's shoulders slumped, and he seemed to age before Lucy's appalled eyes. "We got more to worry 'bout now than that damn hoss," he said. "Mr. Diarmid done gone in after her."

Fifteen

Lucy didn't think; her body moved of its own accord—fast, light, running straight toward the tack room door. As she ran, she fumbled with the ties of her skirt and petticoats. Her fingers shook and she couldn't work the knots. She tried to focus, then imagined someone giving her a million pounds the moment she opened the ties. The knots came loose just as she reached the tack room door. She pelted up the steps, then paused to kick off her skirts. Clad only in chemise, bodice, shoes, and stockings, she raced into the stable.

She halted, stunned. The fire had devoured the trail of hay and dust littering the plank floor, and flames gyred toward her down the left side of the passageway. In the middle of the stable, just inside the double doors, the pile of hay was now an impenetrable wall of flame, bisected by the massive support post that had held the lantern. Smoke billowed everywhere. For an instant, an air current flattened the flames and Lucy could see beyond the burning hay. Her heart gave such a jolt she thought it would burst.

Diarmid stood on the other side of the flames, inside the sturdy box stall where the Arab mare was tethered. In its attempts to bolt to freedom, the terrified horse had pulled its rope tight, and Diarmid worked frantically at the knot. The stall door stood open. It was merely a matter of untying the horse and—

And what? There was no way Diarmid or the Arab could

break through that wall of flame. They would instantly be immolated.

Mercury dashed up behind her. "Miss Lucy—"

"Hush. They're still alive," she snapped, voice low and fast. "They're inside the stall with the door open. The fire's in front of them. Diarmid can't get the horse untied."

"Sheeeit." Mercury slammed his hand against the door-jamb. "Why ain't he carryin' a knife? He always naggin' me 'bout carryin' one. . . ."

Mercury rattled on about Diarmid's tendency to nag—a tendency Lucy would greet with shouts of joy at this particular moment—while she stared in horror at the fire. A hot breeze tossed a flaming scrap of sacking onto a coil of rope, and the rope began to smolder. Lucy followed it with her eyes. In a moment, flames would travel up that rope to the maze of support beams overhead; then the entire roof would ignite.

She studied the beams. They ran parallel to the outside wall and the front of the stalls, with trusses crossing at right angles to the other side of the stable. Lucy's heart slowed. So far, the right side of the stable had escaped the flames, up to the point where the hay blocked the doors. Just beyond, Diarmid and the horse were trapped. She whirled and grabbed at Mercury's belt.

"What you doin'?" Mercury squalled, fending her off.

"I'm taking your knife." She pointed to the beams. "I can walk along them 'til I get close. I can toss Diarmid the knife—"

"Then what'll you do? You're mad, Miss Lucy. Plum stark ravin'—"

" 'Tis the only way!" She stamped her foot, then grabbed his arm and yanked him down to chin level. "Do you want Diarmid to die?"

Mercury's eye's widened. Flames writhed in them. "Let me do it, Miss Lucy."

"You'd never fit. You're too tall, and I've seen you ride. You're as graceful as a haunch of ham."

"But you're a lady," he protested.

"No, I'm not."

Purposefully, she slid Mercury's knife from its sheath, then yanked up the skirt of her chemise and cut it at knee level. She ripped the linen into two long pieces, then soaked the first in a puddle of water sloshed by a bucket-brigader with poor aim. Then she tied it over her nose and mouth like a highwayman's mask. Diarmid would love that.

"I'm not a lady," she repeated. "As Diarmid loves to point out, I'm a Gypsy thief, and I was raised in a rat's warren. After me da died, I shinnied up drain pipes, crawled through windows, and scampered along rooflines—all to nick plate and jewels from the nobs. Jocko needed chink for gin, Ma needed chink for medicine, and Mick needed chink for food. I stole to survive, and I was damn good at it—'til I grew boobs, and Jocko decided I could make better money on me back."

She bent at the waist, flung her long, tangled hair over her head, knotted it into a tight bun, then tied it with the second strip of linen. Carefully, she tucked the knife into her bodice, where her stays held it tight against her skin. She strode to the first stall on the right side of the stable.

"But I never became a whore—though Diarmid won't believe it." She paused and stared into the roaring fire. The smoke was thick as Thames fog. She blinked and fought the urge to cough. The Ace of Swords danced in the flames. The Ace of Swords. Death and destruction. Whose future did it foretell? Mick's—or hers?

"Give me a boost," she ordered, pinning Mercury with a glare worthy of Milord Maclean himself. Tears fogged her vision. By God, she was going to save Diarmid's arrogant Scottish arse, or die trying.

Shaking his head and mumbling, Mercury bent and made a stirrup of his hands. Lucy stepped up, Mercury lifted, and she scrambled onto the top of the stall door. She took a deep breath and teetered across it to the nearest post, then grasped the supporting Y beam and pulled herself up until her foot caught in the crotch of the Y.

For a moment she couldn't figure out how to maneuver

onto the cross beam. She breathed in shallow little gasps, like a panting mouse. There was no way to pull herself up; the cross beam jutted out over her like a shelf. The only option was to jump onto the parallel beam that was to be her cat-walk. If she fell, she'd break a leg or her neck, or perhaps crack her skull; nothing more.

She wriggled around until she crouched on the *Y* beam, like a squirrel on the limb of an oak. Her target was less than a foot away, above her and slightly to her left. God's ribs, even if she made it, was she strong enough to pull her-self up?

There was another burst of flame, and the Arab mare screamed. Lucy closed her eyes, took a breath, and leaped.

Her chest slammed into the beam, and her arms closed automatically around the rough wood, even as her mind and ribs shrieked with pain. She couldn't breathe, but in this thick smoke, that was a good thing. Scrabbling madly, she hooked a foot onto the beam, then hauled herself up. Mercury shouted mingled curses and encouragement, but she blocked him out. She had to focus.

She drew her feet beneath her and crouched, facing the flames. Then, with the slow, fluid grace of a flower unfold-ing, she stood. She closed her eyes. All she had to do was traverse this forty or fifty feet, toss Diarmid the knife, then scurry back. She straightened her shoulders and raised her chin. The trick was to keep moving—fast, light, quick, quick, quick.

She began to walk.

The fire roared in her ears like a dragon guarding the gates of hell. Sparks shot up, popping around her like firecrackers and stinging her bare feet. Heat billowed over her, and she felt her skin tighten, like the flesh of a pig roasted over coals. Her dampened mask dried instantly, and smoke singed her nostrils and burned her throat.

She kept her eyes fixed on the end of the beam. She'd made worse runs many a-time—usually over a London-roof ridgepole as narrow as a Puritan's mind, always with Jocko waiting below in the street, ready to beat her if she dropped her bag of plate, or just for the hell of it. Back then the air had been cool and thick and damp with fog, and the roof slates had been slippery as an eel's back beneath her bare feet.

Mick had come with her once. In the darkness he'd taken a misstep and slid down the roof without a peep. She had lunged, grabbing his wrist just before he plunged to the cobbled street below. When they reached the ground, she'd defied Jocko for the first time in her life—and she'd vowed she'd never steal again.

Jocko had beaten her so badly, she'd actually been sent to hospital: a charity ward—hell itself. The Raker had come regularly. She could still hear the rumble of his wagon wheels over the slimy cobbles, the thunk of his stick against the wagon bed, the dolorous lure of his chant: "Bring out your dead. Bring out your dead."

She halted.

She hadn't died. But her mother had.

The heat of the fire scorched her face and her lashes began to curl. She looked down through the smoke and caught a glimpse into the stall where the Arab was tethered. Diarmid still worked at the knot, whispering reassurances to the horse the while. Sweat streamed down his face and his skin was flushed.

"Diarmid." She spoke the name as if they sat side-by-side on the drawing room settee and she wished to call his attention to some charming snippet of poetry.

He froze. Then he dropped his forehead against the horse's sweating neck. In the guttering firelight, she could scarce tell where his gleaming ebony hair ended and the horses shiny ebon hide began.

"Diarmid," she called again, more urgently this time.

He sighed, a long, low sound of despair. "Och, Saint Iona." His lean, handsome face was slick with sweat, and his massive shoulders heaved. "I need to tell Lucy—"

A *skreeking* crack rang in Lucy's ears. The lantern post broke in two and crashed to the floor. A brilliant blur of sparks exploded up toward the beamed roof. As much as she wanted to hear Diarmid's deathbed secrets—*especially* what he needed to tell her—their time had run out.

"Great God Almighty's right front tooth!" she yelled. "I'm not Saint Iona, Diarmid Maclean, but I'm here to help. Now pay attention."

Diarmid's head snapped up. Instantly he saw her, poised on the beam on the opposite side of the stable, just beyond the choking smoke. "Good Christ!" he bellowed, face alabaster. "Get back. Are you insane? I didn't save you just to have you burn—"

"Listen." Her skin was blistering. She jerked the knife from her bodice. "Cut through the rope, then ride that horse the hell out of there." She tossed the knife. It arced end-over-end high above the smoldering remains of hay, and Diarmid caught it easily.

"Run," he ordered. "I'll not move an inch 'til you're gone."

She nodded and crept back a few yards, then turned to watch.

With one fluid motion, Diarmid spun and cut the coarse hemp line. The horse neighed and reared, eyes rolling white, hooves slicing through the smoky air toward Diarmid's head.

Lucy opened her mouth to scream, but Diarmid lunged back, then skinned out of his torn shirt. Murmuring in Gaelic, he caught the horse's leather halter and bound the sweat-soaked linen over the animal's eyes. The Arab tossed its head and whickered nervously but calmed enough for Diarmid to loop the rope through its halter straps in a semblance of reins.

Diarmid jumped onto the Arab's back. Lucy held her breath. There was every possibility the panicked creature would refuse to move, for its gleaming, sweat-streaked muscles were rigid with fear. Diarmid leaned low over the Arab's back, whispered something Lucy couldn't hear, and stroked a strong, reassuring hand down the horses' quivering neck. The mare danced sideways and crushed Diarmid's leg against the wall. It sank back on its haunches, then bolted through the stall door.

The Arab halted, overpowered by the smell of smoke. Diar-

mid chirruped encouragingly, then dug his heels into the
horse's ribs. The animal refused to budge.

Lucy clutched a knuckle to her lips, then tiptoed forward.
Thanks to the slaves' renewed barrage, the hay had burned
down to a reeking mass of licking flames, blackened debris,
and smoldering coals. The knee-high pile hissed and spat bil-
lows of choking smoke as each new bucketful of water sought
to quench it. There was no way the terrified horse would bolt
through such an obstacle.

She closed her eyes in despair. Smoke mushroomed up and
seared her lungs. She doubled over, gagging and coughing.
Suddenly, dizziness engulfed her, and she felt as if she were
pitching forward into a searing black maw. Her eyes flew
open and she caught her balance just in time, oddly thrilled
with the belly-lurching sensation of flying.

Flying. That was it.

"Diarmid," she cried over the flames' hiss. "You'll have
to jump."

Diarmid's rigid face took on a look of contemptuous dis-
missal at such a mad suggestion, but she was beyond caring.
Already the horse was skittering back into the tomb of gray
smoke at the far end of the stable. Smoke could kill quicker
than flame, her da had warned.

"She can make it, I swear," Lucy pleaded. "She's an Arab,
aye? Close kin to the Rom? All courage and heart? Oh, God's
teeth, listen to me!" Diarmid's shoulders heaved with great,
racking coughs. In a moment it would be too late. "Take a
firm hand and *make* her trust you!"

Diarmid's jaw set in those stubborn, adamantine lines she
had thought she hated. He tightened the rope and yanked up
the Arab's head. He cast Lucy a sardonic look, then yelled,
"Hyaah!" He whipped the horse with the end of the rope
and drove his booted heels into its ribs. The animal shot
straight toward the smoldering hay.

Hoofbeats pounded in Lucy's ears and she clenched her
eyes tight. She couldn't watch. What if she was wrong? If
the Arab planted its feet and refused the jump, speed and

force would carry Diarmid over the animal's head, straight into the flames.

She heard a *thunk,* a low, animal grunt, then a rousing cheer from the slaves. Her eyes flew open just in time to see the Arab's long black tail swish through double doors.

She whirled and darted back along the beam, no longer noticing the noxious smoke and voracious flames. She dropped to her belly, swung herself down to the top of the stable door, then jumped to the floor. Then she raced through the tack room, straight into Diarmid's arms.

He grunted as her body hit his, then they were down, tumbling in the wet grass. "Oh, thank God you're all right," she cried

"Aye, I'm all right," he growled. He rolled atop her, caught her wrists, and pinned them above her head. " 'Tis you who could have been killed, ye wee, troublesome—"

"But I wasn't. It'd take more than a fire to get the better of me."

"—wench," he finished, voice husky with smoke and emotion.

Lucy's heart contracted. His Highness Diarmid Niall Altan Maclean. Oh, God's heart, she loved him. She loved the way he blustered and stomped when he was angry. She loved the way he glared down that knife-straight nose of his. She loved the deep resonance of his voice, at times scholarly and condescending, at times roguish and thick with a Highland burr as intoxicating as Scotch whiskey. She loved everything about him, curse it all.

Diarmid lowered his soot-streaked face inches from hers and his aquamarine eyes darkened to jade. The corners of his mouth twitched as he attempted to smother a smile. "By Saint Iona, I'm ought to give you the whipping you deserve."

"Oh, you'd like that, I'm sure. Tell me"—she slanted her eyes and wriggled beneath him, no longer afraid of what further fires she might kindle—"are you always so heroic, or was this just an elaborate way of getting between my thighs?"

"Tell me"—he arched a rakish brow, then eased the rock-hard bulge of his manhood against her pubic bone—"were you trying to save me or kill me?" He gave a low, wicked chuckle. "I'm not a rich man, you know. You wouldn't have inherited much."

She caught her breath. Suddenly, every inch of her flesh felt alive with silvery excitement. Ecstasy raced in her veins, tingled her nipples, shimmered through her womanhood. "You trusted me," she murmured, meeting his unwavering jade gaze.

All amusement vanished from his eyes. "Aye, *mo cridhe*. Imagine that."

Then he pressed into her with the whole hard length of his body. His mouth captured hers and he kissed her with deep, searching thoroughness, with kisses of possession and dominance and, finally, with kisses of wicked, taunting enticement. Her body rose to his. Desire laved her nipples and pooled deep in her belly. She wanted him inside her. She needed him to be part of her. She needed to be part of him.

His hand closed over her breast and his fingers rolled the stiff point of her nipple through the gauzy fabric of her chemise. Excitement barreled through her, and she moaned and arched her back against the maddening expertise of his hands. She cared not a whit that they lay in full view, amid running slaves and sloshing water and whickering horses. She was his, and she needed him—now.

"Faith! The stable's burning flat and this is where I find my overseer?" The querulous tones of Celia Stanton Lee pierced the passionate haze of Lucy's mind.

Diarmid suppressed a frustrated groan, then rose to his feet and gave Lucy a hand up. She was somewhat relieved to see that Celia—in a white nightshift and a wooly red shawl—was clad no more modestly than she. Diarmid sketched a courtly bow, then smiled down at Celia with maddening nonchalance. Celia brandished her cane and opened her mouth.

"Miss Celia!" Mercury dashed up, eyes wide, shoulders heaving.

"What is it?" Celia snapped. "I can see the stable's burned—"

"No'm, that's not it. Word just came. Mr. Diarmid's brother—he's here. Mr. James Maclean and his wife done arrived in Williamsburg."

Sixteen

Isaiah Ludlow turned the key in the lock. The wavering yellow light from the candle clutched in his fist scarcely illumined the stifling blackness of the passageway, and he bit back a twinge of uneasiness. He gave the stout iron door handle a surreptitious rattle, then crossed to the top of the attic stairs and paused for a long moment, shoulders taut, eyes closed, ears straining for the slightest sound. Hearing nothing, he slowly descended the narrow, twisting staircase.

With each step, bitter resentment settled over him—resentment he'd hoped to assuage with a trip to Charleston, half business, half pleasure. But, as with everything in his life right now, the trip had been an utter waste. The slaver making the Middle Passage had come and gone already, and as to pleasure—well, he'd have to look closer to home for that. He smiled mirthlessly. Perhaps with Madam Lucy Maclean.

On the second-floor landing, he paused by an open window and ran his hand down the splintery wood casement. He appraised the window, then muttered a curse. Damned shoddy workmanship, this. He'd paid a hundred barrels of tobacco to the slick journeyman who'd promised him windows exactly like those at Stanton's Grove. The knave had lied, of course, and the windows had warped since day one. But Isaiah had gotten his own back. The journeyman wouldn't make any more false bargains.

A thin, high-pitched, barely perceptible sound drifted to his ears. He froze, hands curled like talons around the windowsill.

Was it a night bird's call? Some pickaninny down on the Row crying for its mammy? Or something worse?

After a long moment of silence, he dared to breathe once more. He shrugged his shoulders up and down, trying to release the iron bands of tension that ran down his neck. Curse it all, why must he be saddled with so much trouble? Why must he be punished for sins—if sins they were—that he had committed years ago? He'd tried everything to right the situation; he'd even bought that snot-nosed English bondservant. Of course Mick's presence hadn't helped. If anything, it had worsened the problem. Now Isaiah felt as if he lived atop a hogshead of gunpowder. The right spark, and all would be destroyed.

He looked up, startled. It seemed the very air was mimicking his thoughts, for he could swear he smelled smoke. He frowned into the darkness and sniffed at the elusive scent, then cocked his head and calculated. The wind was from the southeast. Could there be fire at Stanton's Grove?

For the first time in days, his lips curled into a genuine smile. God in heaven, he hoped so—just so long as the Stanton's Grove dock survived. If that old bitch Celia and her arrogant Jacobite overseer suddenly found themselves homeless, they might think twice about Isaiah's offer to buy that coveted riverfront jewel.

He shuffled down the empty hall toward his bedchamber. He'd arrived back from Charleston less than an hour ago, and fatigue weighted his flesh like iron chains. Only Sally had been awake to greet him, and she none too happy about it.

He turned the engraved silver door handle—imported from London and said to be the exact duplicate of those in St. James Palace—and entered his chamber. A single candle illuminated the cavernous space, and there was no fire on the hearth, no wine or meal to comfort him. Most of all, there was no one to warm his bed.

Curse it all! He craved sexual release tonight. His trips to Charleston usually afforded ample opportunities to indulge his appetite for untried young beauties, but a certain house there—a house that specialized in choice meat under thirteen years of age—had been closed by an unusually upstanding magistrate. Isaiah had returned home feeling both physically and emotionally frustrated.

He shrugged out of his coat and waistcoat, then stripped off his shirt. Curse it all, it was time he faced it: He needed a wife. Although his darkest cravings were for hairless flesh and unbudded breasts, he could attain release with an adult woman if the mood was on him. He closed his eyes, sank into the hearthside wing chair, and brushed his hand over the bulge in his breeches. Someone youthful and thin and supple would fit the bill nicely. He thought of Lucy McLean and his erection gave a longing throb.

Damn it to hell that Maclean had gotten to her first. Sally had told him that Maclean and his bride had ridden over to see him a few days back, and that Maclean had seemed most devoted to his enticing wife. It seemed the Jacobite nigger-lover had expressed some interest in young Mick—a most extreme interest, if Sally's tale was to be believed. Isaiah gave a jaded snort of laughter. Perhaps he wasn't alone in his desire for young flesh—although at least he stuck to girls.

A vision of Lucy Maclean's supple young body flashed through Isaiah's mind. He gave a low groan, slumped in the chair, stretched out his legs, and freed his straining cock. Lud, he couldn't help it. He had to. He closed his hand over his burning member and began a rhythmic, up-and-down motion. Instantly, pleasure flooded his body. He dropped his head back and gave himself over to his fantasies.

It had started years ago, when he was just a lad—right before malaria had felled his parents. He had been ashamed at first; sure the wetness on his thighs when he awoke was a disease or a curse. Then he had discovered the mind-boggling pleasure to be had at his own hand and had sneered at his idiotic innocence.

One night, when his father was dead drunk and his mother was away tending a sick darky, he had come across his little sister, Emmaline, just out of her bath. Emmie was alone, naked on the plank floor of the farmhouse, playing with her rag doll. His little sister loved him dearly, and it had been a simple matter, really.

Isaiah groaned loudly and increased the tempo of his fist. He'd had her often after that. Curse it all, how he missed it! Over the intervening years, he had tried again and again to recapture that first sharp, perverse pleasure. He'd used twelve-year-old beggars from the streets of Norfolk, ten-year-old whores in Charleston, and his own slaves at the perfect age of ten—the age Emmie had been before it had all gone wrong.

A delicious, hopeless feeling of wickedness surged through him, and he longed to punish Emmie for deserting him. Nay, he longed to *be* punished.

He had been, of course. His parents had died and Emmie had been lost to him. The last time he'd tried to approach her, she had come at him with a knife, eyes wild and vacant as a rabid dog's. But he would never let her go, and he would never let anyone know their secret. Never. Never. Never.

Suddenly he heard a high-pitched voice and the clatter of boots coming up the stairs. "You cain't go in there!" Sally hollered. "Mist' Ludlow be sleepin'."

Isaiah scrambled to his feet and forced his straining organ into his breeches. His bedroom door burst open and Venetia Lee stormed in.

She stopped, mouth agape, taking in his disheveled appearance with one raking glance. She arched her brows and tossed him a mocking grin; then her flat blue eyes grew shrewd and assessing. "Why, Mr. Ludlow," she cooed in her pampered, Virginia-gentry drawl, "I do believe I, ahem . . . *came* at the right time."

With the air of a mistress born to command, she snatched off her riding hat and skimmed it onto a side table, then shooed the gaping Sally from the room and locked the door behind her. Then she sauntered toward him and slowly drew something from behind her long, trailing skirt. 'Twas her riding crop. Isaiah's erection gave a throb that nearly sent him to his knees.

"Why on earth is a rich, powerful man like you tossing

himself off all alone?" Venetia purred. Her cheeks grew flushed and her eyes glittered like a snake's in the guttering candlelight.

"I . . . I don't know what you mean," he croaked.

She slashed the crop forward, stopping it inches from his bare chest. Then she teasingly trailed it down over one tingling nipple, across the jumping muscles of his stomach, and up over his other nipple. "Don't lie," she snapped. "We'll leave the lying to Madam Maclean." She reached out and twisted his hardened nub between her gloved fingers. He gasped. Raw lust mingled with ecstatic pain shot through his veins.

"Isaiah, we've known each other a long time." Her voice grew cold and businesslike. "So I've come to make you a proposition—to offer you a deal that will finally bring down that vile bastard Diarmid Maclean."

Curse it all, why must she talk? What could he do to get her to whip him with that devilish little crop? "I understand you must be jealous," he ventured.

"Jealous? Pish! Why should I be jealous over a treasonous bond slave foolish enough to marry a thieving Gypsy whore?" Venetia drew back the crop, then slashed it down across Isaiah's thighs. The blow barely missed his bulging cock, and he whimpered and bit his lip to keep from spilling his seed.

"Oh, no." Venetia backed away and rhythmically slapped the crop against her gloved hand. "The only thing I want now is to destroy Diarmid and that slut he's married. And for that I'll need you." She spun, brow arched, eyes wild. "Tell me, Isaiah—would you like to be master of Stanton's Grove? And would you like it if Diarmid Maclean could never, ever show his face in Virginia again?"

Isaiah sank to his knees, mesmerized by the cruel goddess before him. Venetia might be well into her twenties, but she understood a man of his ambition and appetites. As Celia Stanton Lee's heir, she was as rich and as high up the social ladder as one could climb. And he'd heard the gossip about her—discreet and hushed up, of course, but gossip nonetheless. Evidently Venetia had more than a few skeletons in her closet. She wouldn't put too fine a point on his predilections, and she might even share them. Best of all, if she found out about Emmie, she wouldn't be in any position to object.

He closed his hand over his burning member and slowly drew it from his breeches. A smile of triumphant understanding spread across Venetia's face.

"I can help you with that," she whispered, "if you help me, of course."

He nodded ever so slightly. She crossed to him in one long stride, grabbed his shoulder, and forced him onto his hands and knees, like a dog. Nearly panting with lust, he closed his eyes and gripped his fist around his straining cock. He heard the swish of the crop behind him, inches above his naked buttocks. It bit into his flesh like a thousand stinging hornets, and he could hold back no longer. He pumped and moaned and writhed his hips, and Venetia whipped him with relentless cruelty. He reached his crisis and cried out with wild, mindless lust.

She placed a booted foot on his backside, then pushed him down onto his belly. "My turn now," she hissed in his ear. "But first, do you swear to help me?"

He closed his eyes and humped his hips against the rug. "I swear."

Seventeen

Lucy stood at her bedchamber window, wrapped her arms around her ribs, and stared out over Stanton's Grove. It was just past noon on a glorious October day of sparkling azure skies, gossamer clouds, and blazing leaves, and the house party in honor of Jamie and Clemency Maclean was about to begin.

Lucy shivered, nearly giddy with excitement. The green swath of lawn below her was jammed with every sort of equipage: ponderous coaches with colorful coats-of-arms emblazoned on the doors, smart shays, yellow-wheeled gigs, stylish phaetons, diminutive pony carts. Ladies and gentlemen from neighboring plantations, from Williamsburg and from forty miles around, swarmed amid the vehicles, and their voices rose like bright, intoxicating bubbles in the champagne air.

Lucy spotted Patsy Cheney, who strolled across the dusty lawn on her husband's arm. She wore a gown of burnt orange sarcenet drawn back over a rust-colored petticoat, and a broad-brimmed straw hat shaded her freckles from the sun. Lucy laughed and waved. "God's eyeballs, what prime duds. It looks like Patsy is giving her husband Harry a run for his money."

Clemency Maclean joined Lucy at the window. She gravely appraised Harry's saffron velvet coat and pumpkin-colored plush breeches, then dimpled. "Hmmmm, the plumage of the male is always brighter, is it not? And is Harry Cheney the owner of the famous Nimbus?"

Lucy rolled her eyes. "Aye. Harry and Diarmid made some

manner of bet for the horse, and Diarmid won—much to Harry's theatrical and vocal dismay. Nimbus is supposed to be the fastest thoroughbred in Virginia, and Diarmid is practically drooling to win today's race, since Harry's beaten him every year before this."

"What was the bet?" Clemency asked.

"I don't know. Diarmid refused to tell me."

Lucy turned and critically appraised her reflection in Diarmid's mahogany cheval glass. Clemency Maclean had proven a delightful surprise in the two days since she had arrived from the Province of Maine, in Massachusetts Colony. Lucy wasn't exactly sure what she had expected Diarmid's sister-in-law to be like, but whatever her expectation might have been, Clemency Alexandra Cameron Maclean didn't fit it.

First off, she was English, not Scottish, as Lucy had assumed. She also was young—just a year or two Lucy's senior. Lucy glanced shyly at her companion, in awe of her stunning beauty. Old Dame Luck clearly had smiled the day Clemency was born, for she was blessed with gleaming black hair, the alabaster skin of the Celts, and wide-set eyes the color of newly mined emeralds. Lucy turned back to the mirror and scowled at her reflection, suddenly displeased with her own tawny skin and brown eyes. Why, she looked like an Arab peasant next to Clemency's aristocratic grace.

Clemency glided up beside her, and Lucy started. Aristocratic—that's what had surprised her about Clemency. The Englishwoman possessed the same elegant mien as Diarmid. Lucy smiled wryly. Clemency might share her brother-in-law's patrician features, but the resemblance ended there. Unpredictable Clemency chattered like a magpie and disregarded convention utterly. Already Lucy had found her down at the slave quarters discussing the merits of Southern medicinal herbs and the methods of African healing with Royal, Mercury, and the other servants.

Lucy caught Clemency's eye and grinned. She was delighted—nay, overjoyed—to discover an irrepressible kindred spirit beneath Clemency's lovely face.

"Share the joke?" Clemency asked.

"I was just thinking about how different Jamie and Diarmid are. One would hardly think they were brothers."

"Aye, but they're like enough under the skin—stubborn, mischievous, and full of Scottish pride."

Lucy snorted. "Mischievous? Diarmid? God's nose—the man was born to be a cleric or a scholar. His idea of mischief is to eat fried chicken instead of ham on Sundays. The worst thing I've ever seen him do is drink too much and play those wretched bagpipes of his when Celia is trying to nap." She wrinkled her nose. "Lud, the man might love music, but he's as tone deaf as a lump of coal."

Clemency winked. "Ah, but I've seen how he taunts you— and how he looks at you when you're not paying attention. He's got Jamie's teasing ways, all right."

Lucy nodded her head while her mind slogged through a quagmire of conflicting thoughts and feelings about her changeable husband. In truth, Diarmid was the very devil himself when it came to throwing her into confusion, and that was a mischief of sorts. Since the night of the stable fire, he had been a pillar of propriety toward her. He no longer courted her with roses and jewels and intimate sunset rides, and he no longer tried to seduce her with stolen kisses. Instead, he acted as if their marriage was a business contract binding together two strangers, not two lovers.

Lucy bit her lip. She was a fool to be dismayed by Diarmid's coldness. Their marriage was arranged, for heaven's sake. Worse, it was a sham—a sham they both had every intention of ending the moment poor old Celia died and Stanton's Grove passed into Diarmid's hands.

But *did* they intend to end it? Until the night of the fire, Lucy had begun to believe that Diarmid's feelings for her went beyond the thrill of the chase and the siren's call of plain old lust. When Diarmid had risked his life for her, she had been sure he cared. And when she had risked hers for him, then thrilled in his arms—on the ground in front of Celia, no less!—she had faced the truth.

She loved Diarmid Maclean, blast his arrogant Scottish hide, and she was prepared to take the consequences of her emotions. If he wanted her in his bed, she would surrender her long-protected virtue with a cry of joy. If he wanted her at his side for the rest of his life, she would fall down on her knees and thank God. And if he wanted to banish her to Maryland the moment Celia died, then she would use every Gypsy trick at her command to get him to change his mind.

She snatched up her kid gloves and pulled them onto her hands with decisive little yanks. She had grown sick to death of all their arguing and misunderstandings and cross-purposes. She and that taunting Highland rogue needed to stop playing games and start telling the truth. She jerked up her chin, resolved. She would confront Diarmid at the first opportunity. She'd tell him that she loved him, she'd offer to become his wife in every sense of the word, and then she would revel in sweet release from the maddening physical cravings he aroused in her flesh.

But a tiny worry nibbled at her, like a field mouse gnawing on a blade of grass: men could *not* be trusted. She squared her shoulders and pushed the thought away. Aye, she couldn't trust Diarmid, but if she forged ahead *knowing* she couldn't trust him and *expecting* to get hurt, then she ultimately would survive when he abandoned her. Lucy's hands curled into fists. That's where her mother had gone wrong: She'd given up her courage along with her heart. She'd trusted that sod Jocko with her children and her life, and she'd lacked the strength to turn and walk away when things had turned bad.

Lucy whisked her plumed hat from the dressing table, perched it at a rakish angle on her high-piled curls, then rammed a silver hatpin into the whole confection. Well, she did *not* lack courage or strength or the good sense to never trust a man. She would give Diarmid her body, with pleasure. She might even give him her heart, but she would never, *ever* give him her trust.

The bell to call the workers in from the field clanged through the crisp fall air. "That's the signal that they're starting the race," Lucy said.

Clemency clapped her hands and sped toward the door. "Oh, we'd better hurry. I promised Jamie he could wear my handkerchief in his pocket while he raced—just like a knight of old bearing his lady's standard."

Lucy followed Clemency's billowing, apple-green skirts down the wide front staircase. She gave a little sigh but resisted the urge to pout. Diarmid hadn't asked to wear *her* handkerchief.

Out on the lawn, people strolled toward the makeshift racecourse. The flat, grassy, mile-long track stretched from the Stanton's Grove dock to the edge of College Creek—a muddy, catfish-choked tributary that emptied into the James. Women laughed and gave tiny mock screams as horseflies buzzed about their heads; men called jokes and betting odds to one another; and children ran after a flurry of barking dogs that were chasing Celia's outraged white peacocks. Lucy curtsied to George Wythe, who offered her a courtly bow, and waved at young Tom Jefferson, who blushed to the very tips of his ears and scuttled off to join the men at the starting line.

"How many horses will race?" Clemency asked. She nodded politely to a group of elderly ladies who sat fanning themselves beneath the dappled golden shade of a shag-bark hickory.

"Eight." Lucy picked up her skirts and hurried toward the starting post, all the while scanning the crush of prancing horses, chattering grooms, and swaggering owners for a glimpse of Diarmid.

"However, my dearest ladies, only Sea Hero should give the glorious Nimbus any competition." Harry Cheney stepped up beside them and bowed, then doffed his beaver hat with an elaborate flourish. Satisfied that he had arrested their attention, he drew a carved malachite snuffbox from his voluminous sleeve, dipped a pinch of snuff, placed it on the back of his hand, and inhaled.

"Stab my vitals," he gasped. "Ah . . . choo!" He sneezed twice more, then bowed his apology. "Demme, but the Maclean men have all the luck. They wed the two loveliest ladies in creation—my own darling Patsy excepted, of course—and then that rogue Diarmid wins the incomparable Nimbus from me."

Lucy laughed at Harry's woebegone face. "Come now, Harry. Confess. What did Diarmid do to pry Nimbus away from you? Surely it took some nefarious dealings on his part to secure such a prize."

" 'Tis a secret, madam, although I will confess 'twas on a bet. Suffice to say, 'tis a bet I'd gladly make again, now that I've seen the felicitous outcome." Harry tossed her an impish wink and tugged on his pointed black beard. "And allow me to add that by rights Nimbus should belong to you, madam, not to that charming rogue you married."

Lucy opened her mouth to reply, but a happy little squeal from Clemency cut her off.

"Look! There's Jamie on Braw . . . and there's Diarmid beside him, riding Nimbus." Clemency joggled Lucy's arm, then gazed at her husband with palpable pride. "Holy Mary, Mother of God, have you ever seen two handsomer men?"

Lucy gazed at the two brothers. Jamie Maclean was handsome, all right. He shared Diarmid's towering height, warrior's shoulders, and long, dangerously muscled legs; and he definitely had inherited his older brother's high cheekbones and blade-straight, aristocratic nose. But the resemblance ended there, for Jamie gave the impression of elven wit and irrepressible jauntiness. His indigo eyes sparkled with devilry, his red-gold hair blew like a lion's mane in the breeze, and his generous mouth curled in an easy smile. Handsome, yes, but—

Suddenly, she heard Diarmid's voice in her ear—low and husky and intimate. Her gaze flew to his face. Oddly, he wasn't looking at her at all—and he was too far away for her to have heard him speak. He was leaning forward over Nimbus's withers, politely greeting George Wythe, and his soldier-straight spine bent gracefully at the waist to better offer the eminent scholar his full attention.

Lucy's toes curled with delight in her silver-buckled shoes. No, Diarmid could never be called jaunty. His angular, granite-hard jaw bespoke a warrior who would swear revenge—or love—and who would never turn from his vow,

not even in the face of death. His lean, deeply tanned
cheeks were stern, austere, *hard,* and his long, glossy black
hair was clubbed back and bound with a leather thong.
'Twas a severe style amid his neighbors' foppishly powdered
and curled wigs, and that severity hinted at raw savagery
kept in check by an iron will.

Lucy shivered. Suddenly she felt weak and gloriously helpless, as if she were melting in the heat of Diarmid's alarming
virility. She imagined her trembling lips tracing the wicked
peaks of his brows and brushing kisses on the ebon curve of
his lashes—lashes so long and thick that they cast tiny
shadow crescents on his cheekbones. Her gaze lowered to his
mouth, and for the millionth time since the day he had bought
up her indenture, she longed to trail her tongue over the tiny
dent in his lush lower lip.

Suddenly Diarmid glanced up, and his gaze seared into
hers with the heat of a thousand suns. He didn't sit erect in
the saddle or interrupt Mr. Wythe's rambling story; he just
stared at her, his eyes blazing an intimate challenge. Lucy's
heart jolted as if she had been struck by lightning, and her
mind whirled with vague, liquid emotions. Slowly, Diarmid's
eyes darkened from aquamarine to deepest jade. Then—simply, quickly—he broke into that dazzling smile of his, and it
was as if the very heavens had opened, pouring brilliant, joyous sunlight straight into her soul.

"Pierce my vitals," Harry drawled in Lucy's ear. "It appears Maclean has a heart after all. And you've stolen it."

The bell clanged again, startling Lucy so badly, she
couldn't make a pert reply. Instead, she let the crowd sweep
her along as they surged toward the ropes marking the edge
of the racetrack. Diarmid bowed to Wythe, wheeled Nimbus
about, and took his place at the starting post. As the skittish
horses danced into position, Jamie flourished Clemency's
handkerchief aloft and earned a chorus of sighs from half the
ladies in the audience.

Diarmid shot his little brother a wry look, then caught
Lucy's eye. He tapped the breast pocket of his black broadcloth coat and tossed her a rakish wink. Then, with a non-

chalant expertise that melted Lucy's bones, he stilled his shying mount and waited calmly for the starting gun.

"Demme!" Harry cried, theatrically clutching a hand to his chest.

Lucy glanced at him, annoyed at the interruption. To her astonishment, his olive cheeks had gone quite pale. "What is it?"

" 'Tis Sea Hero."

Lucy followed the direction of Harry's jutted chin. To her astonishment, Isaiah Ludlow sat astride an enormous black gelding, three places down from Diarmid. Lucy ran an admiring gaze along the animal's sleek, powerful muscles.

"Strike me blue," Harry breathed. "Sea Hero's the only horse in Virginia capable of beating Nimbus."

Ludlow caught Lucy's eye, and his lips parted in a slow, leering smile. At the same moment, he sawed on his reins, gouging the bit into Sea Hero's soft mouth. Lucy's stomach fluttered and her gaze flew to her husband. So far, Diarmid hadn't noticed Ludlow. Either that or his proud Scottish heart refused to show any emotion—even disdain—in front of his guests.

She gnawed at her cheek, for the first time in years unsure what to do. Diarmid had forbidden her to speak with Ludlow or to ride to Resolute. He had reassured her that the moment Ludlow returned from Charleston, he would handle the negotiations to buy Mick. She had protested at first, demanding that he storm the gates of Resolute and rescue her little brother by force if necessary, but Diarmid had soothed her with cool, unassailable logic and with overwhelming Scottish charm. She had been lulled.

Now Ludlow obviously had returned from Charleston, and Diarmid had made no mention of it. Did he know? Or did he hope Lucy wouldn't find out?

Clemency's brows drew together. "I don't understand. Why all the fuss?"

Harry rolled his eyes heavenward, as if appalled at such ignorance of Virginia social intrigue. "Sea Hero belongs to Isaiah Ludlow, who owns the neighboring plantation. Ludlow and my dear friend Maclean absolutely despise each other, although Diarmid has always tried to keep up an appearance of cordiality."

Lucy grabbed Harry's spindly arm. "Does Diarmid know Ludlow is back from Charleston?" God's knees, if he did know, she was going to break his stiff Scottish neck, then buy Mick herself. She doubted not at all that she could nick the jewels Celia kept under lock and key in a small mahogany casket in her bedchamber. Why, the emerald brooch alone should more than cover poor Mick's indenture.

Harry's bright black eyes appraised her, clearly probing for the source of her agitation. "Of course he knows Ludlow is back, my dear. Why, just this morning he rescinded Ludlow's invitation to join our little fete. Quite appalling manners, don't you know, but then, Maclean was provoked."

"How?" Lucy demanded.

"It seems Ludlow rode over at cock's crow in response to an urgent request from your husband. I don't know what was said at their little tête-à-tête, but Ludlow flew out of Maclean's office looking like all hell's furies. Maclean stormed out a moment later, positively *livid*. A roaring Scottish lion, I vow. Lud, my dears, he wouldn't even speak to me." Harry contrived to look wounded, then fluffed his lace cuffs.

Patsy Cheney dashed up, eyes sparkling and freckled cheeks flushed. "Oh, there you are! Are they about to start?" She spun to face the line of riders poised for the starting gun. George Wythe bowed to Diarmid, then raised a pistol high overhead.

The pistol thundered, and Lucy clapped her hands to her ears. The horses leaped forward, each rider crouched low over his mount's neck. Patsy squealed, Clemency and Harry clapped, and the crowd hollered like redskin savages.

"Go, Nimbus! I got two hundred barrels on you!"

"Run, you damned idiot!"

"Sea Hero's in front! Go, boy, go!"

Instinctively, Lucy tried to pick Diarmid from the riders, but they thundered past in a blur of flashing spurs and slashing crops. She gripped her ivory-boned fan until one of the sticks snapped. Had Diarmid made an offer for Mick and been refused? Or had he even bothered to try?

The crowd whooped and raced for the finish line like a mob bound for Tyburn on hanging day. Harry grabbed Patsy and Lucy around the waist, then dove forward, nearly yanking Lucy off her feet. Then she was running along with the others. Dust billowed up from the track, the overpowering aroma of sweat and manure and leather assaulted her nose, and raucous whoops roared in her ears.

"Nimbus is gaining!"

"They're neck and neck!"

"Sea Hero—move your bloody arse!"

"Holy mother," Clemency panted, close on Lucy's heels. *"Why* did I lace these darn stays so tight?"

Pain knifed Lucy's side and she gulped for breath. God's ribs, she *knew* she couldn't trust Diarmid, so why did it hurt so much to doubt him? Why did she hope she was wrong, when she knew she was right? Diarmid cared more about his precious plantation than about her and Mick and all the slaves combined. He'd never risk Stanton's Grove—certainly not for a light-fingered brat from the gutters of Alsatia and his Gypsy thief of a sister.

A horrified gasp tore through the crowd. "Man down!"

A woman screamed; a bolt of fear shot down Lucy's spine; then she was hurtling forward with the surging throng. She clenched her eyes shut and prayed, *Oh dear God,* please *don't let it be Diarmid.*

The hemp line roping off the racecourse bit into her stomach. Her fingers closed over it just as she heard a dreadful snapping, like the nauseating crack of a dozen necks being broken by the drop at Tyburn gallows. There was a thud and a horrible squeal. Her eyes flew open.

The horse lay ten feet away, crumpled in the dusty grass: eyes rolling white, nostrils flaring, lathered sides heaving with each tortured breath. One long, elegant, delicate leg crooked at a sickening angle beneath the animal's shuddering body.

Lucy watched in stunned horror as it valiantly struggled to rise. It groaned, then collapsed back in the dust.

Then Lucy moved. As the rest of the crowd lapsed into shocked silence, she ducked under the rope and shot forward. She gave a great, gasping sob and realized she'd been holding her breath. "Oh, dear God," she whimpered, hot tears flooding down her cheeks, "please, please, don't let him die."

Sea Hero stopped struggling. His large brown eyes stared blankly at a spot three feet away, where Isaiah Ludlow sprawled on his back in the grass. The crowd gave a warning shout and Lucy glanced up.

The other horses had thundered on down the track. Their riders hadn't been able to keep Ludlow from falling; they barely had been able to steer their own mounts around the deadly hazard. But now a rider *had* turned back.

Diarmid.

Her heart bounded with relief and her hands shook uncontrollably. Diarmid flung himself down from Nimbus's back and checked Ludlow's pulse. The crowd jolted to life and surged onto the racecourse.

"I saw it," George Wythe cried, stumping breathlessly at the head of the mob. "Ludlow tried to cut Nimbus as Diarmid closed. The scoundrel overbalanced and fell."

"I saw it, too," young Tom Jefferson concurred. Other men assented, their outraged tones making it clear such intolerable behavior would not go unpunished.

Slowly, Diarmid stood. "He'll live. The fall just knocked the wind out of him." He turned and gazed at Lucy. His ashen face was streaked with dirt and sweat, his expression was grim, and his grave jade eyes pleaded with her, asking . . . asking what?

She turned away and knelt beside Sea Hero. The horse's breaths came in shallow, ragged wheezes, and she gently stroked his lathered neck.

"Get back!" Diarmid shot toward her, black brows lowered. "He's in terrible pain. He could kick."

His hand bit into her arm and he jerked her to her feet. For one dizzying moment, he clasped her tight against his chest. She could feel the drugging warmth of his body through the sweat-soaked linen of his shirt, could hear the beat of his heart beneath the sculpted perfection of his muscles. He smelled of leather and cherry tobacco and his own intoxicating musk, and for one hysterical moment, she wished the noise and the crowd and the bitter regret in her heart would vanish, and that she could rest in his arms forever.

He released her and waved George Wythe forward. "Hand me your gun," he ordered. "I must put the poor beast down."

"No! You can't kill him. I won't let you." Suddenly all her rage and pain and betrayal burst forth in a wild torrent of tears. She flung herself against her husband and pounded her fists against his chest. "Is that what you do here in Virginia? Get rid of something when it's no longer of use to you?"

Diarmid gently shrugged her off and took the pistol from Wythe. Desperately, she tried to pry the gun from Diarmid's hand. "Don't, please! Clemency can save him. She's a healer."

"I'm sorry, *mo cridhe,*" Diarmid murmured. His voice was strained and hollow, his burr thick as Highland mist. "But I've no choice. 'Tis kinder this way, and he'll no' suffer, I promise ye."

"Promise!" Lucy gasped. "I've had enough of your bloody promises. You're heartless, wicked, cruel. I hate—"

"Hush." Diarmid's eyes hardened to burning jade ice. "I'm sorry, but 'tis all I can do. We can't always get what we want, *mo cridhe.* I'd save him if I could, but 'tis beyond me power. Ye'll have to accept that."

He spun on one booted heel and strode toward the horse's crumpled body. George Wythe hobbled forward and grasped Lucy's elbow.

"Come with me, my dear," he whispered, his gentle voice as soothing as the sound of rustling leaves. "Your husband is right. 'Tis the kindest thing." He steered her away from the hushed crowd toward the opposite side of the makeshift racetrack. "Diarmid loves horseflesh more than any man in Virginia. He's raised and trained a score of thoroughbreds—fine, spirited beauties, all—and he treats them like they were his own bairns. Sea Hero was his once, you know. Sold to Ludlow in exchange for a ten-year-old runaway slave."

Wythe shook his head and sadly patted her icy hand. "Some folk around here think Diarmid Maclean has no heart. They're most grievously wrong. His heart's been crippled by horrors I pray you could never imagine. Nay, my dear. What Diarmid does, he does for good reason. If you love him, as I feel you do, you must learn to trust him—and to forgive him."

Lucy heard the cold metallic click of a pistol being cocked. She froze, then slowly turned.

Diarmid's face had gone gray beneath his tan, and his jaw hardened to granite. Then, with the powerful grace of the Highland warrior he had been long ago, he knelt. He remained motionless for a long moment, staring down at the dead, matted grass. Then he slowly raised his hand and stroked Sea Hero's velvet nose. The horse's nostrils flared, and it inhaled the comforting scent of a beloved master for the very last time.

Diarmid's hand trembled, then he stilled it. He raised the pistol and gently placed the double-barreled muzzle above Sea Hero's glazed eye. He murmured a Gaelic blessing, closed his own eyes, and pulled the trigger.

Eighteen

Clemency Maclean flung open the door to Lucy's bedchamber. "Lucy? Lucy, my dear, the ball's starting and Madam Lee is asking for—Oh." She halted, jaw hanging, emerald eyes wide. "Holy Mary—Don't you hear the carriages?" She shot across the chamber's polished wood floor and gestured dramatically at the damask-curtained window. Outside, the jingle of harnesses and clop of hooves blended with the genteel murmurs of the arriving guests. "Why, you're not even dressed!"

Clemency's exquisite black brows contracted and she peered at Lucy through the black-and-gold shadows thrown by the crackling hearth fire. "My dear, whatever is the matter?" She crossed to the four-poster bed, where Lucy lay fully clothed except for the silk petticoat and overskirt of her elaborate ball gown.

Lucy stared dully into the fire's orange coals. She knew she was expected to greet guests downstairs in the foyer with Celia and Diarmid, but somehow she hadn't been able to finish the chore of dressing. Finally, in utter exhaustion, she had dismissed Royal and curled up on the bed's plump eiderdown.

Clemency sat beside her, stripped off an elbow-length kid glove, and placed a cool, smooth palm against Lucy's brow. "You're not hot," she said. "Do you feel ill?"

Lucy shook her head but couldn't work up the energy to reply. She sighed. God's nerves, it seemed all she'd done lately was rush about, worrying what would become of Mick, worrying about what Diarmid felt for her, worrying whether Celia was taken in by their little scheme.

"No, I'm not ill," she mumbled. "I'm exhausted."

Clemency scanned Lucy's face. "This wouldn't have anything to do with that tall, dark, and mysterious husband of yours, now would it?" When Lucy didn't reply, Clemency stood. "Here—get up. I'll help you dress."

Lucy groaned, then stood stiffly, as if she were a marble statue come to life. Clemency snatched up the lustrous emerald-stain petticoat of Lucy's gown. Deftly, she lifted it over Lucy's head, then settled it on her hips. "I know you're upset by what happened at the race. We all were—Diarmid most of all. Jamie told me he's been locked in his office gulping whisky most of the afternoon—"

Lucy snorted.

"I don't know what's going on between you and that handsome husband of yours," Clemency said, "but it's clear he loves you—"

"Loves me! Milord Maclean doesn't know the meaning of the word." Lucy jerked free and stalked across the room, then stretched trembling hands to the fire.

"How much do you know about Diarmid's life in Scotland?" Clemency asked.

Lucy tensed. Since her marriage to Diarmid, several people had hinted about something awful in her husband's past, but none had told her the whole story. Perhaps Clemency would. She turned and smiled ingenuously.

"In truth, I know precious little about Diarmid. Our, er . . . courtship was quite brief." She lowered her lashes and pouted prettily. "And you know how stubborn men can be. They think it marks them weaklings to speak about past troubles. Could"—she raised her eyes hopefully and caught Clemency's han—"could *you* tell me, please?"

Clemency's lips curved into a wry smile. "I can see why Diarmid married you so quickly. You can be quite persuasive." She helped Lucy into her peacock-blue overskirt, all the while seeming to mull over whether to speak or not. "Did you know Jamie and Diarmid have an older brother?" she inquired at last.

Lucy's jaw dropped. "God's teeth—no!" She whirled and strode toward her dressing table. "That bull-headed Highlander couldn't even tell me that." She snatched up a rabbit's foot, smacked it into a box of rice power, and angrily patted her face.

Clemency glided up behind her, then smoothed Lucy's tousled curls into an elegant upsweep. "Don't be angry. I only found out a few days after Jamie's and my son was born. They disowned him, you see—their brother, not my son."

"What?" Lucy dropped the rabbit's foot. "That's the worst thing I ever heard." God's ears, was there no end to Diarmid's villainy? First he refused to buy her little brother, then he shot a horse that could well have been saved, and now she found out he'd turned his back on his own flesh and blood. "Why, 'tis positively heartless," she added lamely, too wary of Clemency's sharp eyes to reel off her usual string of Romany curses.

Clemency pursed her lips. "To you or me, perhaps. But Jamie and Diarmid see things differently. It seems Lachlan—their older brother, the laird of Mull—betrayed them both. Indeed, he betrayed his own clan." Clemency stopped suddenly, then pinned several trimmed and artfully arranged peacock feathers into Lucy's hair.

"Go on—tell!"

Clemency bit her lip, then stepped back and motioned for Lucy to stand. "I can't. I don't know the whole story, and I don't think Jamie does, either. Suffice it to say that something terrible happened between Diarmid and Lachlan during the Rising. Something so awful, in fact, that it destroyed the entire family—nay, the entire clan."

Lucy grasped Clemency's wrist and stared into her eyes. "What are you saying?"

The English healer covered Lucy's hand with her own. "Do you love Diarmid?"

Lucy jerked back as if Clemency had bitten her. God's eyes, she and Clemency were practically strangers, yet Clemency had the ballocks to ask such a question! But perhaps she was the one person in whom Lucy could confide. After all, a woman who sat on the dirt floor of a slave cabin and shared a hunk of cornbread with a black child wasn't exactly a pillar of propriety, at least by Virginia standards. And 'twas clear Clemency and Jamie loved each other with a devotion that was nearly magical.

Lucy scanned her sister-in-law's face. What would Clemency say if she knew Lucy was a convicted thief? Would she draw back in horror if she knew Lucy was a Gypsy? Would she run crying to Celia if she knew Lucy and Diarmid's marriage was a sham? Nay—Lucy couldn't see it. Like as not Clemency would ask Lucy to tell her fortune, then demand to know what herbs the Rom used for healing.

Lucy drew a deep breath. "I . . . I do love him." She spun and gazed down into the fire, loathe for Clemency to see her burning cheeks.

"Then I'll tell you a little secret," Clemency replied. "Loving a man is the hardest thing you'll ever do—especially when that man's a proud, stubborn Maclean. The Rising scarred them terribly, and they all have secrets they'll carry to the grave. The trick is to love them, and to forget about the past. To love them even when you can't begin to fathom the things they do, and have done."

Clemency dimpled and slanted her a conspiratorial smile. "Women are the strong ones, after all. 'Tis up to us to forgive their flaws." She checked her appearance in the dressing-table mirror, then motioned for Lucy to follow. As they swept through the bedchamber door, Clemency whispered, "Diarmid will tell you everything someday. And that's the day when you'll *know* he loves you."

Oddly enough, Stanton's Grove had no ballroom. Instead, Celia's practical first husband had designed the house with a cavernous, low-ceilinged card room off the formal front parlor. There Richard Stanton—a man who preferred ombre and baccarat to minuets and reels—had entertained his friends at gambling parties notorious throughout Virginia for their drunken revelry and high-stakes betting. Celia had taken to calling this paneled, beamed, vaguely Tudor-looking chamber the Refusal Room, for it was there she had refused offers of marriage from five hopeful gentlemen after Richard's death. The Refusal Room never had seen a successful proposal, for Celia had stood in the garden when at last she settled on Uriah Lee—a man with more money than sense, but one who wanted her for her beauty and spirit, not for poor, dead Richard's vast estate.

Lucy descended the stairs toward the Refusal Room and tried to quell the despair welling up in her heart. Diarmid seemed more remote now than he had on the day when he had purchased her off Captain Pratt's auction block. She had thought she had begun to carve a place in his granite heart, but his attentiveness had been an act—mere illusion designed to seduce her into surrendering her virtue. Ha! It seemed her Gorgio husband was more the Gypsy than she—at least when it came to cozening lackwits like her.

She knotted her hands in her skirts, not caring if she wrinkled the expensive cloth. Trollop, he'd called her, and thief. God's ankles, *he* was the thief! He'd stolen everything from her: her independence, her self-respect, and her determination to save Mick. Worst of all, he'd stolen her heart. All he had to do was lower his voice to a seductive pitch, flatter her, charm her, give the cards a flourish, and she was his.

The candlelit foyer was empty. Clearly, Celia and Diarmid had tired of waiting for her. Clemency reached the bottom of the stairs, then tugged Lucy toward the Refusal Room. She smiled and whispered, "Courage!"

Courage. How often had Lucy reviled her mother for lack of that very virtue? God's nose, on the very day Agnes Graves had died, Lucy had shouted, "How can ye trust us with Jocko? How can ye leave your own blood with a piss-drunk varlet who beats us black and blue? I'll never forgive ye!"

Lucy halted just outside the Refusal Room. Already the vast chamber was thronged with guests. Pungent tobacco smoke hung like a gray pall beneath the corniced ceiling, laughter rippled through the air, and the musicians tuned up in the far corner, their instruments squawking and squealing like a hog at the slaughterhouse. Honey-scented candles guttered and flared in mirrored silver sconces, and the gaily clad guests floated about on a sea of rose and scarlet, lavender and teal, and amber and lemon. Tears filled Lucy's eyes and her vision blurred.

God's heart, had she truly said such things to her own mother? Aye, she had. And ever since Agnes's death, determined to spurn her mother's bad example, she had sworn never to trust anyone but herself. A cynical smile twisted her lips. That was the joke of it: despite all her vows to never trust Diarmid, she had trusted him, again and again. She had trusted his word that he would rescue Mick, even when the facts spoke otherwise. She had trusted his judgment over poor Sea Hero's fate, even when her heart wailed with grief and outrage. God's ribs, soon she would trust the devil himself!

Clemency prodded her forward, and Lucy trailed into the room, eyes downcast.

"Good evenin', lass. Will ye forgive a wee liberty if I tell ye how verra bonny ye are this evenin'?"

At the first sound of a Highland burr, Lucy's heart surged. Then it sank in disappointment. Diarmid's accent was never this thick, even at his most agitated. It could only be Jamie.

"Thank you for your flattery, sir," she mumbled, too glum to glance at her cavalier.

"I vow, madam," a deep, velvet voice replied in a cool, patrician drawl, "an acquaintance that begins with flattery is bound to end in bosom friendship."

There was no mistaking *that* aloof, haughty tone. Lucy's gaze flew from its intense scrutiny of the floor. Her jaw dropped.

Jamie and Diarmid stood before her, towering head and shoulders over the other men in the crowd. Jamie was dressed in the discreet and clearly expensive evening garb of a successful New England merchant, understated and very proper. But Diarmid—her stern, austere, aloof husband—*Diarmid* wore the full regalia of a Scottish laird.

He stepped forward, and his blue-and-green Maclean tartan kilt swung gracefully about his knees. It was belted to his narrow hips by a black leather strap, and a badger-fur sporran brushed his powerful thighs. The jeweled hilt of a *sgian dhu* glittered from the top of one white stocking, and his high-heeled black shoes were buckled with silver. A full plaid, pinned at the shoulder with an engraved, circular silver brooch, crossed his broad chest and fell in loose pleats to his knees. His wide shoulders strained under a black velvet jacket, and a cascade of lace accentuated his snowy linen shirt. His gleaming ebony hair fell loose to his shoulders, and two tiny braids hung at his temples, giving him the primitive air of a Highland savage.

"God's heart," she breathed.

Diarmid's mouth curled into a lazy smile; then he leaned forward and tapped her jaw shut with one long, tanned finger. "Best watch yourself, *mo cridhe*. Ye dinna want flies gettin' in." His Highland burr was as thick and as devilish as Jamie's, and there was more than a hint of Scotch whiskey on his breath. She swallowed, utterly speechless. The orchestra struck up a reel and she jumped.

Jamie chuckled at her discomfiture. "Dinna fluster the lass," he growled at Diarmid. Then he winked and offered Lucy a bow. "And dinna mind me roguish brother, Mistress Maclean. He always was a tease and a show-off."

Clemency laughed. "Why, Jamie Maclean—imagine *you* calling Diarmid a tease and a show-off."

Jamie looked elaborately hurt, even as an impish smile played over his lips. "Och, ye wound me, *mo druidh*—my witch," he added for Lucy's benefit. "Just for that I'll ask me sister-in-law to dance the first reel."

Before Lucy could protest, Jamie swept her into the Virginian's favorite dance, the Roger de Coverley. The sprightly reel, with its quick steps and frequent change of partner, offered little chance to converse, but Lucy grasped the first opportunity

"Jamie, is *mo cridhe* Gaelic?" she asked.

Jamie cocked a brow. "Aye. 'Tis what me *athair*—me fa-

ther—always called me mother." His indigo eyes grew soft.
"And 'tis what I call Clemency."

"But what does it mean?"

"Mo cridhe?" He winked. "Ye should be askin' your husband that, me bonny lass. *Mo cridhe* means 'My heart.' "

The Roger de Coverley ended with a flourish of fiddles and a swirl of skirts. The guests cheered, and Lucy pressed a hand to her side, winded.

"Do ye need to sit down?" Jamie asked.

She managed to toss him a chagrined smile. There was a very real possibility she might faint, though whether from her tight stays or the shock of Jamie's words she couldn't say. All at once, she got the distinct sensation that someone was watching her. She turned and was nearly scorched by Venetia's venomous blue glare. As Lucy watched, Venetia slipped her hand beneath Diarmid's arm, tugged him down to her level, and whispered something in his ear.

Dizziness and jealousy swirled through Lucy until she thought she truly would faint. She pressed a hand to her belly and tried to stop its sickening lurch into her throat.

Jamie grasped her elbow. "All ye all right, lass?"

She raised her chin. God's knees, why was everyone always asking if she was all right? She slanted Jamie a brilliant smile and said, "I'm fine, thank you." Her voice was much too loud, and several guests turned to gawk.

Lucy darted a quick glance toward her husband. Whatever Venetia had whispered in his ear did not meet with a positive response, for Diarmid's lips thinned and his eyes chilled to the color of the North Sea.

Celia waved her cane and called, "Mr. Maclean! A moment of your time, sir."

Diarmid disengaged himself from Venetia's clutches, bowed, and stalked toward Celia. They conferred for a moment, then Diarmid took the old lady's elbow, escorted her to the musician's dais, hushed the crowd, and began to speak.

"My dear friends and neighbors, I crave pardon for interrupting your festivities, but Madam Lee has informed me that she wishes to make an important announcement." Diarmid cast his employer a quizzical glance, then stepped aside.

Celia broke into the triumphant smile of a gloating vulture about to devour a rat. Then she planted her cane and began to speak in a shrill, querulous voice. "Friends and neighbors, I thank you for joining me this fine autumn evening. As you all know, my capable overseer Diarmid Maclean has been with me some sixteen years this October." She patted Diarmid's muscular arm and chuckled. "And to the chagrin of most of you, the pair of us have turned Stanton's Grove into the finest plantation in Virginia."

There were assenting cheers and a few good-natured boos. Lucy quelled a snort. She never had seen the old shrew enjoy herself more. "Celia missed her calling," she whispered to Jamie. "She should have trod the boards."

"But alas," Celia continued, "worldly success cannot take the place of a loving family, and despite Mr. Maclean's devoted work on my behalf, my life here has been lonely."

Lucy rolled her eyes. Celia, lonely? Aye, perhaps—except for her two rich, henpecked husbands and the overwhelmingly virile presence of the handsomest overseer a widow ever had the good fortune to bully.

Celia turned and waved an impatient hand at Royal. The enormously fat housekeeper, resplendent in shiny black chintz and a snow-white turban, lumbered forward. She carried a tray of crystal goblets filled with pale golden liquid, and Lucy noticed that the other house servants were offering similar glasses to the guests.

"That's why it gives me such pleasure to have you, my dear friends, here tonight," Celia said. "Now please join me in offering a warm Virginia welcome to my overseer's brother—Mr. James Maclean, of the Province of Maine, and his lovely wife, Clemency."

Diarmid and Celia raised their glasses in a toast. The guests followed suit, calling, "To the Macleans!"

Lucy snatched a goblet from a passing tray. She gulped the bubbly liquid, then grinned up at Jamie. "It tastes like stars."

"I couldna say," Jamie shot back. He straightened from a courtly bow in acknowledgment of the toast. "I canna bloody well drink to meself."

Celia brandished her cane and restored silence. "What I'm about to say is very difficult. Very difficult indeed." Celia sniffed and pressed a handkerchief to her rheumy eyes. "Dr. Walker tells me my heart is unsound, and 'tis unlikely I'll see another spring." The guests broke into murmurs of dismay, and Celia leaned on Diarmid's arm for support. The tall Highlander gazed down at her with deep and undisguised affection. Lucy's heart contracted. Would *she* ever see such tenderness in Diarmid's eyes?

Celia tugged him down to her level and whispered something in his ear. Diarmid's muscular frame went rigid; then the color drained from his lean, handsome face. Intently, he scanned the old lady's eyes, then murmured a question. Celia scowled, shook her head, and waved her cane in Lucy's direction. Diarmid stepped down from the dais and shouldered his way through the murmuring crowd. His eyes burned into Lucy's and the granite planes of his face were devoid of expression.

Lucy's heart thundered to life. God's ears—here it was at last. Somehow, Celia had found them out. She planned to denounce them, here, in public, before the whole of Virginia's gentry. Lucy spun and frantically looked for an escape route. Was fraud a crime in the colonies? Would she be thrown in prison, branded, hung?

She dove forward. Diarmid's steely hand grasped her elbow and brought her up short, and she spun and stumbled against his broad chest. The soft ruffled lace of his shirt brushed her cheek, and she clenched her eyes tight and dissolved into him, resting her whole weight against his heart for one split second. He smelled of Scotch whiskey, cherry tobacco, and his own intoxicating masculine scent. The warm, hard length of his body felt so solid, so *permanent* against hers.

Tears scalded her lids. Oh, she didn't want to lose him, didn't want him to abandon her. But 'twas too late. She had lost everyone she had ever loved—her mother, Da, Mick.

They were all transient, passing through her life, then vanishing. They were lesser stars. She needed Polaris.

Diarmid clasped her upper arms and firmly set her away from him. She blinked, determined not to cry, and his beloved face swam before her. He didn't seem angry, or even his usual austere self, but gazed down at her with the oddest expression she'd ever seen—an expression of startlement, disbelief, and . . . and what? Then he grasped her elbow and frog-marched her through the crowd toward Celia.

Lucy halted before the dais, and the old shrew grinned malevolently. "Many of you already have had the pleasure of meeting Diarmid's new bride," Celia said. "Madam Maclean is a Londoner, as I was before I arrived here in Virginia, and like me, she has proved herself *talented, resourceful,* and *clever.*" Celia bit special emphasis into her words; then she shot Lucy a look of utter, piercing comprehension.

Lucy sagged against Diarmid's tense arm. God's nerves, how had she ever thought she could fool the old bat? Celia had known she was a fake since day one, had sat like a patient spider in her web, luring Lucy in until she was stuck fast. Now she would deliver the coup de grâce.

"Madam Maclean's presence at Stanton's Grove and at Diarmid's side has finally forced me to reach a most painful decision." Celia's gray eyes sizzled into Lucy's. "Stanton's Grove cannot pass into untrustworthy hands—"

"Wait!"

The guests turned as one, murmuring, searching for the interruption. There was a flurry at the back of the room; then Venetia broke from the crowd and shot toward Lucy. A dark flush mottled her cheeks, and her bosom heaved with emotion. "I have something to say about Madam Maclean!"

Venetia halted before her rival, ice-blue eyes glittering with triumph. "She's not who she claims. She's no cousin of Harry Cheney's. She's nothing but a Gypsy whore, an indentured convict transported here as punishment for thievery."

Venetia's hand shot out like a striking snake and grasped the neckline of Lucy's bodice. Lucy gasped and lunged back. The thin silk gave a loud *rrrrrpt,* and her sleeve tore in one long tatter from shoulder to elbow. She heard the quick hiss of Diarmid's indrawn breath. The crowd gasped.

"There," Venetia crowed. "See the thief's brand on her Gypsy skin!"

Lucy bit her lip to keep from crying aloud. Coppery blood burst across her tongue; she clapped a hand over her naked, branded shoulder and plunged into the crowd.

"Lucy!" Diarmid's voice roared with all the power of an Old Testament prophet, but she slipped his grasp and pelted toward the foyer. The appalled guests fell back and gave her a clear field.

"Someone help Madam Lee," Jamie shouted.

The crowd surged toward the dais, suddenly not minding her at all. She ached to glance back, to see if Diarmid was following her, but pride wouldn't allow it. She skidded into the hall, grabbed the stairway banister, and paused for a split second, praying with all her heart that he would storm up behind her, sweep her into his arms, and free her from Stanton's Grove, and from her own hard heart, forever.

But he didn't come.

No longer caring who heard her, Lucy broke into gut-wrenching sobs, snatched up her skirts, and dashed up the stairs. She had to get out of here, away from Diarmid and away from Virginia for good. Mick was all that mattered now, all that had ever mattered. She never should have lost sight of him.

She raced across the second-floor landing, and her mind did a lightning-quick inventory: There was the emerald brooch, a gold hatpin, the ruby earbobs, a diamond bracelet, and a string of freshwater pearls. They were locked in the jewel box in Celia's bedchamber, but Lucy had nicked tougher prizes many a time. She jerked up her chin. One last theft; then she would be free.

Nineteen

"I knows you. Mercury done tol' me about you. He says you's a fine lady."

"Then, please, may I come in?" Lucy clutched her cloak at the throat and turned pleading eyes to the pretty young slave girl who blocked the doorway. The October night had turned frosty, and the helter-skelter ride through the black woods had chilled her bare fingers to the point where she scarce could feel the garment's soft red wool.

The servant stepped back, gesturing Lucy into the dim, apple-scented, firelit warmth of Resolute's kitchen. "I be Sally," she said, shyly dropping her gaze. "Mercury and me was raised together."

Lucy smiled brilliantly and clasped the slave's callused hand. "Please, Sally, you've got to help me. Does your master keep a young boy here—a white boy from England, who was a bond slave?"

Sally's large brown eyes grew wary. "I cain't be talkin' 'bout such."

"Please, Sally. I know he's here. He's my little brother. I love him very much, and I've come to take him away from here, so he can be free. So we both can be free."

The servant twined her hands in her homespun skirt and darted nervous glances everywhere but into Lucy's eyes. "You's married to Mast' Maclean?" she finally asked.

"Aye."

"Then I'll help you. Mast' Maclean a true gentleman, and

I's happy to 'sist his wife." Sally beckoned for Lucy to follow her into the main house.

Lucy scowled, in no mood to hear the sham virtues of that black-hearted knave she was chained to. God's knees, he'd married her out of sheer selfishness and nothing else; not even lust, it appeared, since he'd made no further attempts to bed her. She gritted her teeth. If he had cared for her at all, he would have come after her, but clearly Venetia's little scene had revealed Diarmid's true colors along with Lucy's brand.

They glided through the butler's pantry and the dining room, then turned and tiptoed toward the stairwell. The bare wooden treads spiraled up into impenetrable shadows, and Lucy shivered, suddenly afraid.

A faint cry drifted through the darkness. Lucy's breath caught.

"Be quiet as the grave," Sally whispered, turning. "Mast' Ludlow be sleepin' one off in his office. If he catches us, 'tis Barbados for me."

Lucy grimaced. For her, too—especially if he caught her with the jewels she had just stolen from Stanton's Grove.

They crept up the stairs, then gained the second floor. Sally glanced back at Lucy, all white-rimmed eyes and furrowed brow. Then she scuttled down the candlelit hallway and halted before a narrow staircase. It was set back in an alcove and turned sharply, so that Lucy could see only four steep risers of rough wood, then nothing.

Sally rooted in the pocket of her apron, then drew out a primitive-looking iron key. "Here," she hissed. "That room be locked all the time."

They stood in a dim shaft of moonlight that slanted in the window at the end of the hall. As Sally handed her the key, Lucy's pulse began to race. The slave's face was taut with fear.

Sally thrust the key into Lucy's palm. "Sneak in there, grab your li'l brother, then get out—and lock the door behind you. If you're lucky, she'll be sleepin'."

"Who'll be sleeping?"

"Never you mind. Now go on." Sally pushed Lucy up the first step, then scurried back down the hall.

Lucy took a deep breath and crept forward, feeling her way with trembling fingers along the rough plank wall. At the first sharp turn, she stubbed her toe and bit back a cry. The stairway turned again, and her heart slowed to a sluggish thud. God's teeth, what was up there? Mercury had told her Ludlow had a taste for young slave girls. Was this an attic torture chamber, hidden far away from prying eyes?

She ordered herself to stay calm. She was too imaginative—the curse of the Rom. Imagination had served her well when she had concocted outlandish fortunes for mooning maids and lovesick grooms, but now she needed a cool head.

She stumbled around the final turn and froze. A dim, blurred line of yellow light lay directly before her, on level with her eyes. She held her breath and strained her ears to catch any sound, however faint or terrible. All was silent. Then, after a long moment, she heard a barely perceptible soughing sound, as if something was brushing itself slowly and surreptitiously against the opposite side of the locked door.

Lucy leaned forward, rested her palms on the worn stair, and peered at the thin yellow line. She jerked back. Half the light had gone black. Was some massive, malevolent creature crouched on the other side of the door, waiting and listening as intently as she?

Then she heard another sound. An icy shaft of fear plunged down her spine. Something was breathing.

'Twas a low, labored sound—raspy and moist and ragged; the sound of a being unused to fresh air and exercise, or cursed with a dread disease.

Lucy's heart jolted to life. It pounded hysterically in her chest, racing faster and faster, like a terrified rabbit sprinting from the jaws of a wolf. She pressed a hand to her bosom, desperate to still the sound, for surely the unseen creature must hear the thunder of her blood—even through the locked door. Indeed, even through her very flesh.

Then she heard it: the slow, slithering, splintery rasp of

fingernails on wood. Lucy lurched back, frantically stifling
the cry that tore from her throat. Her unknown listener was
scratching on the door.

At the same moment, the door handle rattled and shook
violently, as if a wild beast was trying to break from its cage.
Lucy whirled and started to plunge down the black, twisting
staircase. A voice on the other side of the door stopped her.

"Oi, Em—what's amiss? Be someone there?"

Lucy froze. There was no mistaking that high, bright voice,
that lilting Cockney accent. "Mick!" She whirled and clawed
wildly at the dark wood until her hands found the door handle. It wouldn't turn. Her heart gave another lurch of fear.
Someone was holding it, determined to keep her from Mick.
Frantically, she rammed the key against the handle again and
again, trying to find the keyhole. It slipped and gouged her
finger; tears sprang to her eyes.

"Mick," she cried. " 'Tis Lucy. Oh, let me in, let me in!"

"Loose!" Mick's yelp of joy was cut short by a sharp slap
and a gasp of pain. Then Lucy's key slipped into the lock
and the handle turned. Lucy rammed her shoulder into the
door and tumbled into the room.

Instantly, she was blinded by brilliant light, for the entire
chamber blazed with the greasy, melting stubs of a dozen
tallow candles. She struggled upright, gasping for breath. The
room was tiny—no larger then a box stall in the Stanton's
Grove stable—and sparsely furnished. Her stunned gaze took
in a low pallet, a wooden table, two chairs, a basin and ewer
on a mirrorless washstand, and—in a pathetic attempt at gracious decor—an old, moth-eaten tapestry hanging to the right
of a single tiny window. The air was thick with the stench
of rancid tallow, boiled cabbage, and unemptied chamber pots.
'Twas Spartan, but Lucy had seen worse. Indeed, by Alsatia
standards, the room could have passed for St. James Palace.

She blinked, half turned, and froze. A dark figure hunched
in the corner, clutching poor Mick in a death grip. Instinctively, Lucy started toward her little brother, hands outstretched. Mick's captor snarled, and Lucy halted, appalled by
the vicious, guttural sound—the sound of a mad dog about

to tear out a throat. Her gaze flew to the creature's face and she gasped.

Mick's captor was a woman. She was young, ashen-faced, and almost pretty, in a mad, vacant way. She wore a loose, frayed black muslin gown, and a threadbare blue shawl covered her head in some bizarre imitation of the Madonna's mantle. Long, mouse-brown hair straggled over her pinched face; thin lips curled back in a ferocious grimace over her teeth; and bleary eyes rolled from Mick to Lucy and back again.

Then her arm closed around Mick's throat. Lucy opened her mouth to cry out, and she dragged him back against her body, then crouched, like a vulture protecting carrion from a jackal.

"Loose," Mick gasped, "back up. Don't scare her. She won't hurt me."

"Mick—"

"Listen to me. Oi knows her." Mick placed filthy, nail-bitten hands on the woman's bony arm and gently pried it away from his throat. To Lucy's astonishment, his captor loosened her grip. "She fancies me. She won't smack me if ye back off."

Lucy stood her ground. How could she back off and leave her poor, darling little brother to this monster? God's teeth, if she'd tried harder to find him, he wouldn't have suffered so already. Sweet Jesus, 'twas all her fault!

Her gaze darted over Mick's precious face. His cheekbones jutted like a skeleton's, and grime caked his freckles, but his indigo eyes still sparkled with mischief. He caught her eye and flashed her a gap-toothed grin. "Trust me, Loose."

Trust. Why did it always come down to that?

Frowning, trembling, desperately afraid, Lucy stepped back. Instantly, the madwoman released Mick and scuttled to her pallet; then she sat with her head down and rocked back and forth. A thin, high-pitched wail issued from her clenched lips.

To Lucy's astonishment, Mick perched beside his captor and patted her shoulder. "Nigs, Em—it be all roight. 'Tis just me sister. She be an orphan, too. Just like us."

Em raised her head and fixed Lucy with a wary gaze. "You won't take my baby," she croaked. Her voice rasped like rusted hinges. "He's mine. You won't hurt him."

Lucy glanced at Mick, uncertain how to respond.

Mick said, "This be Miss Emmaline Ludlow. She's been sick"—he rolled his eyes and twirled a finger around one ear—"and her little boy died—"

Footsteps thundered up the staircase, then Isaiah Ludlow staggered into the room. His eye had been blackened by his fall off Sea Hero, his skin was alarmingly flushed, and his cravat hung open at his throat. He gaped at Lucy for a long moment; then his pale eyes leered at her bosom. Disgust and shame crawled across Lucy's skin.

"Mistress Maclean, this is a surprise." Ludlow's words were slurred, and as he swayed closer, Lucy recognized the all-too-familiar signs of a drunk teetering on the edge of violence. "I had hoped we'd become better acquainted, but not like this. This is a problem, indeed."

Lucy sidestepped, weighing her chances of grabbing Mick and fleeing down the stairs to freedom. Ludlow grabbed her wrist and yanked her against him.

"Oh no you don't. If you think I'll let you go tearing out of here, tattling my little secret all over the county, you've got another think coming."

His gaze wavered toward Emmaline. "She's beautiful, isn't she? My little sister. I wanted to make a life with her, you know, but she's madder than a March hare." A regretful smile ghosted across his pocked face. "I've kept her up here for years. Oh, she wasn't violent at first. At first, she just talked. She rattled on and on about horrible things, things she said I'd done, things . . . well, I couldn't have sick lies like those floating about in polite society, now could I?"

Ludlow cast Lucy a skewed, questioning glance, as if genuinely seeking her approval. "Then she quit eating—nearly wasted away until Moses figured out how to force her. She quieted for awhile; then she began cuttin' on herself." He snapped over his shoulder, "Show her, Emmie."

Emmaline jumped as if she'd been shot. Then, with trembling fingers, she slowly peeled back her gown's frayed sleeve. Lucy shuddered. The woman's forearm was scored with white scars.

Ludlow shook his head dolefully. "I've done my best for her. I've tried to be a loving brother—" His voice broke and genuine anguish flashed through his eyes. "I wanted her to love me, but . . . Oh, curse it all!" Quick as a snake, he grasped Lucy's chin. His clammy fingers dug into her flesh. "All she ever cared about was that dead brat of hers—a boy, gone nine years now." Emmaline began to sob, and Ludlow stiffened. "That's why I bought your wretched brother. I . . . I thought perhaps he'd make her happy. And it was working, 'til now. Now what'll we do? I can't have my high-and-mighty neighbors knowing my sister is mad."

Lucy's jaw ached, but she refused to quail. She was used to bullies. She'd handled Jocko and she would handle Ludlow. She had to; he owned Mick. "Let go of me at once," she demanded.

"Tut, tut. You might have put on airs as Maclean's charming London bride, but I know better. You're a thief, a whore, and a bond slave."

"I don't know where you get your information, sir, but I'm no bondslave."

He gave a harsh laugh. "Oh, but you are. And if my dear Venetia has done her work, all the colony knows it by now."

White-hot anger shot through Lucy. She jerked back and broke Ludlow's hold. "Mayhap that painted harpy dragged me name through the mud, but I care not. I was a thief. What of it? *Ye* be a lyin' piss-pot who keeps his poor, addled sister locked in the attic. God's teeth!" Fury incinerated her fear and fueled her gutter accent. "Be there no end to this world's black-hearted knaves?"

She stalked toward Mick, no longer caring what Ludlow might do. She'd had it. Jocko had killed her mother, Diarmid had broken his promises, Ludlow had driven his own flesh and blood to madness. Men were pigs, and only a fool would waste her breath on a pig.

"Stop right there." Ludlow's voice cracked like musket

fire. "One more step and I wring that brat's neck like Sunday's chicken—and I'll take great delight in making you watch."

Lucy halted. Quick, hopeless exhaustion washed over her, and she sank down on the pallet beside Emmaline. The gaunt young woman stopped crying and stared at her with blank eyes.

Mick, who had been standing frozen and wide eyed since Ludlow's appearance, crept up and touched Lucy's shoulder. "Don't worry, Loose," he whispered. "Stay here with me. 'Taint as bad as life with Jocko, and we'd have each other. That's better'n anything ol' Virginny can dish up."

She gripped his sweaty little hand and cast him a teary smile. Dear, brave, loyal Mick. He'd said something just like that the night their ship had landed in Virginia—the night they had tied their wrists together and vowed never to part. Scalding tears threatened to spill over her lids. And she'd let him down. She hadn't kept her promise. She was as bad as Diarmid.

Worse. She was as bad as her mother.

Ludlow interrupted her thoughts. "You want young Mick here to be freed, do you not?"

She jumped up. "Oh, yes!"

"I believe we can come to terms, if you'd step downstairs with me."

Her heart leaped. Perhaps it wasn't too late. She had the jewels she'd purloined from that scheming Jacobite cad, and Ludlow was desperate to keep Emmaline's condition a secret. Mayhap if she swore silence . . .

Her conscience pricked her, but she brushed it aside. Emmie wasn't actually being abused. Besides, Lucy hadn't survived this long by splitting too many fine hairs. She glanced down at Ludlow's sister, then glanced at Mick's impish, freckled face. She had no choice. She couldn't let her brother down again.

She nodded at Ludlow, then offered him her arm. "Excellent," he hissed, grasping Mick's arm. "Your brother will be free in a matter of days."

"No!" Emmie scrambled up, lunged forward, and clawed at Lucy's face. "You'll not take him! He's mine!"

"Get downstairs—now," Ludlow snapped as Lucy raised an arm to ward off Emmie's blow. He wrestled Emmie's arms to her sides, then pushed her down on the pallet. "Go!"

Lucy hesitated at the doorway, then grabbed Mick's scrawny hand and plunged into the darkness. As she stumbled and groped her way down the twisting staircase, one thought surfaced in her churning mind: Emmaline Ludlow was insane. No matter how Lucy pitied her, she couldn't leave Mick in a madwoman's clutches.

Ludlow clattered down the stairs. Without meeting her eyes, he grasped her arm and hustled them through a doorway farther down the hall. Once inside, Lucy realized they stood in a candlelit bedchamber.

"Shouldn't we discuss business in your office?" she ventured.

Ludlow shrugged off his coat and tossed it onto a wing chair. "Don't act so naïve. False innocence doesn't become a Gypsy thief."

Lucy's brows slammed together. "I beg your pardon?"

"There's but one thing of yours I want in exchange for your brother's freedom, and prefer to take it in bed, not on a desk."

He tossed his waistcoat to the floor, then sat and pulled off his boots. Lucy and Mick exchanged anxious glances; then Lucy's eyes fluttered shut. This couldn't be happening again. God's heels, what did Diarmid and Ludlow find so enticing about her maidenhead?

In spite of the despair leaching into her bones, she bit back a snort. Bloody lackwits. Most coves slavered at the thought of deflowering a virgin, but Diarmid and Ludlow stubbornly persisted in believing she was a whore. They didn't even realize what a prize they had. She jerked up her chin and opened her eyes. Well, curse them all to the hottest rings of hell.

"I'll make you a better bargain." She slanted her eyes and called up all her Romany charm. Illusion, misdirection, and luck—that's what allowed the Rom to flourish. Great lady be damned; she'd rather be a Gypsy!

With a sloe-eyed glance and a graceful flourish, she drew her stolen jewels from the hidden pocket of her skirt. The emeralds flashed in the candlelight and conjured up a vision of Diarmid's eyes, dark with desire. She quelled a shaft of longing and flaunted the brooch under Ludlow's nose. "A prize of double value, milord. I nipped these from Stanton's Grove—aye, from Diarmid Maclean himself. I'm no expert"—she lifted the emerald brooch, held it up to the candlelight, and squinted at it with a practiced eye—"but I'd say this is worth nigh onto three hundred pounds."

"Why would I want stolen jewelry?"

"Because you're short of chink—and if you hawk these, you can buy the Stanton's Grove dock and best Diarmid once and for all." She relished the astonished look on Ludlow's greasy, pocked face. "You really ought to spend more time on the Row," she said airily. "One learns the most fascinating gossip in the slave quarters. Mercury told me you're nearly broke because Diarmid refuses to let you ship your tobacco off Celia's dock. You have to float your hogsheads to deep-water merchant ships, and it's costing you a fortune. Even worse"—she flashed a cunning smile, then batted her lashes—"you can't use Celia's dock to land your illegal African slaves."

Suddenly, she relived a wretched memory of her voyage aboard the *Eliza Pratt*. How much worse it must be for slaves! Mercury had told her that his mother had been torn from her family, chained head to ankle with a dying woman, then stacked like cordwood in a disease-ridden hold swarming with rats, awash with vomit and piss and shit.

She shuddered. No matter how vile Diarmid had been to her, at least he had done one good thing: He had stopped Ludlow from importing human beings as if they were barrels of sot-weed.

With this realization came another terrible thought. Her hands dropped to her sides, and the emerald brooch clunked to the floor. She couldn't trade Celia's jewels to Ludlow—

because she couldn't be party to his slave trading. If he bought the dock, untold numbers of Africans would suffer horribly, and all Diarmid's attempts to help them would be for naught.

She lowered her gaze, awash with confusion. Mick darted forward and snatched up the brooch, then staunchly stood beside her, ready as always to help with a scam. His black hair stood up in a cowlick, and his peaked little chin thrust out defiantly. He was her heart.

Mo cridhe. Diarmid's beguiling Highland burr whispered through her mind. My heart. Lucy bit her lip. Oh, God's teeth—she loved them both. No matter what Diarmid had done, she couldn't stop loving him. She would never trust him, she could never forgive him, 'twas likely she would never get over the hurt he had caused, but she loved him— almost as much as she loved Mick.

Ludlow's jaded chuckle broke through her thoughts. "I admire your attempt at horse trading, but 'twill do neither of us any good. There's nothing on earth that will induce Maclean to sell me that dock."

She snatched the brooch from Mick and thrust it back in her pocket. "How do you know?"

"Because he called me to Stanton's Grove this morning to discuss Mick's indenture." Ludlow clasped his hands behind his head, spread his legs, and leaned back in the wing chair. "It seems you've made quite a dent in that icy chunk of Scottish granite. He made several generous offers for your brother, including five hundred pounds sterling."

Mick gasped and tossed Lucy a look of unbelieving delight. Lucy's stomach heaved, then roiled; then she backed up until her knees hit the edge of Ludlow's bed. She sank down, stunned.

"You're pale, my dear. Who knew your heartless Highlander could be so generous? I'd always heard the Scots would pinch a farthing 'til it screamed." Ludlow smiled coldly. "But, alas, we couldn't come to terms."

"Why not?"

"I only wanted one thing—access to the Stanton's Grove

dock. I even offered to *rent* it, as I had before he came along. But he flat-out refused—"

Lucy waved a limp hand. "Stop. I don't want to hear another word." Giddily, she stared up at the crocheted canopy over Ludlow's bed as her heart seethed with emotion.

Ludlow stripped off his cravat and began to work the buttons at his shirt collar. His eyes never left her bosom. Lucy gave herself a mental shake and tried to regroup. Fine Rom she was. She was showing her hand, letting her opponent read her emotions, letting the stool pigeon get the upper hand—or wing, as the case may be. She bit back a smile. That was better. Illusion, misdirection, and luck. What would work here?

Mick slid up beside her and whispered, "Don't forget Em."

Another horse trade, then. "Governor Fauquier was at the ball this evening," Lucy said. Ludlow stopped his unbuttoning. "Before Venetia's little *announcement*"—she couldn't keep venom from her tone—"he and I spoke about you. He's quite keen on seeing the master of Resolute in the House of Burgesses." Anxiously, she searched her memory. Had she gotten the name of Virginia's governing assembly right? Evidently she had, for Ludlow sat up.

"Is this true, or more of your Gypsy tricks?"

She looked elaborately offended, then grinned. *"I'm* not the trickster here, Mr. Ludlow. I leave that to my husband." She stood and strolled around the room, as confident and nonchalant as Queen Charlotte at a garden party. "The governor averred that 'tis high time you took your proper place in the colony." She cast him an ingenuous glance. "A fine plantation and hundreds of acres are all well and good, but nothing ensures acceptance in the highest social circles like political power, don't you think?"

Ludlow looked intrigued, then crossed his arms and said, "Why do I feel there's a 'Part Two' to this tale?"

"My dear Mr. Ludlow, such cynicism is unbecoming. I was merely going to suggest that word of your poor, dear sister's unfortunate illness—and even more unfortunate incarceration—would be most harmful to your career with the Burgesses." She stood in front of him, then slanted him her most killing smile. "You know what a favorite of the governor I've become. A word from me and you'd be in the House by Christmastide. Or not."

"I'll not be blackmailed!" Ludlow shot up, grabbed her arm, and shook her. "You're in no position to bargain. You seem to forget that half the colony has seen the brand on your supple young arm. You're a convicted thief, and by now you've lost all status in the governor's eyes."

He wound a hand in her curls, jerked her head back, and leered. "And while you may belong to Diarmid Maclean now, he'll rid himself of you in a flash once he's learned that I've sampled your wares. In truth, whore though you are, I can scarce contain my glee at the thought of burying myself between your tawny thighs."

With all her strength, Lucy slapped Ludlow's sneering face. He recoiled, then snarled, "You little bitch!" He clutched a hand to his livid cheek and glared at Lucy as if she were a rabid wolf.

"No man owns me," Lucy ground through clenched teeth, "and you'll never bed me." She raked her tangled hair from her eyes and spun, intent on grabbing Mick and dashing for the door.

Ludlow reached Mick first. "You like violence, eh?" His hands closed like vulture's talons over her brother's thin shoulders. "Then perhaps watching me beat this sweet little boy will warm your blood." He shoved Mick against the bedstead, then snatched up an object propped behind the nightstand. Lucy's stomach lurched. 'Twas a cat-o'-nine-tails.

This cat was no ordinary buggy whip, but a brutal, heavy instrument designed to torture the most recalcitrant field hand. A few strokes could flay a man's back into a mass of bleeding, tattered pulp. It would kill poor, scrawny Mick with four blows.

"No!" She dove forward, determined to wrest the scourge from Ludlow's hand.

Ludlow stepped back and flourished the cat over his head. It sliced through the air with a lethal thrum. Lucy felt the draft of its passing on her cheek, felt a surge of pure terror through her veins.

"Wait!" She lunged in front of Mick and raised her hands to shield them both. "Don't. I'll . . . I'll lay with you. Just please don't hurt Mick!"

Instantly, Ludlow arrested the blow. Casting her an oily smile, he laid the cat back in its corner. "We may need that yet," he hissed. "Pain does so add to one's enjoyment, don't you find?"

He grabbed her arm in a steely grip, then shoved her onto the bed beside Mick. Lucy caught a quick impression of her brother's eyes—wide and blue in a stark white face. His expression said it all: This madman wasn't Jocko, to be cozened with quick wits and lulled with cheap gin. This cove would kill them both.

Lucy darted a glance at Ludlow. To her horror, he had stripped out of his breeches and wore only his wrinkled muslin shirt. The shirt poked out at his crotch, like a canvas tent thrust over a pole. His pale eyes glittered in the flickering candlelight, and he slowly advanced toward the bed. She nearly gagged at the stench of excited sweat, rotgut rum, and decayed teeth clinging to him.

"Wait," she blurted. She cast an eloquent glance at her brother. "You . . . aren't you going to send Mick out?"

Ludlow licked his lips. "On the contrary," he hissed, "I rather fancy you both."

A shudder tore through Lucy's frame. This couldn't happen. She wouldn't let it. Always in the past, when there was no one else to trust, she had protected Mick. Ludlow grasped her thighs through her satin skirt, and she started, stomach heaving, heart pounding. God's ribs—this couldn't happen. She hadn't protected her virtue all these years to have it savaged by some colonial pervert.

She opened her mouth and screamed—a scream to shatter the windowpanes, to rouse the slaves, to wake the dead, to call down the fury of God himself. Ludlow reared back and slammed the flat of his hand into her rib cage. She cried out and curled into a ball, arms clutched to her ribs. Her back muscles locked into wrenching spasms, searing pain shot through her side, her mind drifted in an aching fog, and she barely noticed Ludlow lift her skirts and part her thighs. He bunched the billowing satin up around her waist, then rolled her onto her back. She caught a bleary image of Mick, crouched against the bedpost, freckles standing in stark relief against his ashen skin.

"Run," she croaked. The effort cost her another wave of pain, but Mick leaped off the bed, narrowly missing Ludlow's lightning grasp. She heard her brother's light footsteps race across the room, then the desperate rattle of the door handle.

Ludlow grabbed her chin and forced her to look into his eyes. "It's locked," he murmured, as softly as if he were whispering an intimate endearment. "There's no escape." He smiled, casually grasped the front of her bodice, and ripped. The delicate fabric tore with a loud *rrrrrp*. Lucy clenched her eyes shut. She couldn't watch his mad, gloating expression.

"My, how the mighty are fallen." Ludlow traced a clammy hand between her breasts, from collarbone to navel.

Silently, Lucy began to pray. *Please God, don't let Mick see this. Please God, don't let me show fear. Please God . . .*

"Tell me you want it."

Lucy's eyes flew open. Ludlow gazed down at her, face calm and polite, as if he were asking the governor's wife for a glass of punch. He smiled at her confusion. "I want you to beg."

"Never."

"Oh, I think you will. If you don't, young Master Mick will feel the cat—will feel it 'til his blood soaks my prize Turkey carpet."

Lucy tried to look for Mick, but Ludlow's hunched shoulders blocked her view. Then she heard it: Mick was crying— soft, stifled sobs entirely bereft of hope. God's heart, what was the use? Pride couldn't help her now. A dull feeling of hopelessness settled over her like a chill fog and sapped what little strength she had left. There was only one way to help Mick now. "Please . . ."

"Louder," Ludlow ordered. He leaned forward, cupped her breasts in slithery snake hands, and thrust his erection against her hip. His breath came in fetid pants. "Say my name. Beg me to suck your titties."

"Please . . ." From somewhere far away, at the very edge of her consciousness, she heard a shout, then the thud of boots on the stairs. "Please, Isaiah, suck my—"

The bedchamber door exploded in with a splintering crash. Mick yelped. Ludlow reared back. His nails raked her breasts and she screeched in pain.

"Good Christ! Ye filthy, ruttin', perverted bastard!"

Lucy went limp. There was no mistaking that Highland burr—and Diarmid must be livid, for his outraged *r*s rolled like a storm-tossed sea.

Twenty

Diarmid crossed the room in one stride, caught Ludlow by his shirt collar, and jerked him to his feet. The shirt tore, and Ludlow rounded on his enemy, fists raised to commence a fight. Then he quailed, and his hands dropped to his sides.

Diarmid's icy austerity had vanished. The aquamarine eyes that so often chilled like killing frost now burned with a fierce, glittering rage. Vivid red flushed his tanned cheeks, and scorching rage contorted his elegant features.

"How dare ye?" he thundered. His fists clenched and he advanced on Ludlow with the measured tread of a stalking tiger. "Ye vile, besotted cur. She is my wife!"

Sally crept into the room behind Diarmid. Then she fell to her knees and reached supplicating hands toward him. "Oh, don' kill him, Mast' Maclean!"

Diarmid grabbed Ludlow by the throat, lifted him as if he were a boiled chicken, and shoved his back into the fireplace wall. Ludlow squealed in pain. His eyes seemed to pop from their sockets, then rolled wildly from side to side. "Don't . . . please—" he gasped, clawing wildly at Diarmid's steely hand.

Lucy struggled to her feet. She wriggled her torn bodice up over her breasts, and pain raced along her ribs. "Diarmid—stop. Don't kill him! He's not worth it."

But the Highlander was beyond hearing. The icy veneer over his savage warrior's soul had shattered. He tightened his grip on Ludlow, then slid him along the wall, closer and closer to the fire. Sally screeched and sobbed. Mick rushed to Lucy's side and tugged her toward the door.

"C'mon, Loose," he pleaded. "Here's our chance."

Lucy swayed. Three quick strides and she and Mick would be out of the chamber, then down the stairs. From there it was a brief sprint to the stable, where she had tethered her horse. She still had the jewels. If they rode with the swiftness of Romany princes, they would gain the port of Norfolk by dawn. Once there, if Dame Luck smiled, they could book passage to Maryland colony and to freedom.

Freedom. Her gaze flew to Diarmid's face. He stood in profile, towering over Ludlow and glaring down his chiseled, blade-straight nose with the righteous fury of an avenging angel—no, of an enraged demon. Diarmid could never be an angel. Mick tugged at her, nearly in a frenzy to escape. Diarmid inched Ludlow closer to the hearth flames, and a slow, wolfish smile curved his lips.

Lucy sniffed. Smoke.

She lurched forward and caught Diarmid's arm. "Stop! You're burning him—"

"Ooooh! Mast' Ludlow!"

Sally's scream nearly shattered Lucy's eardrums. She glanced over her shoulder. The slave girl huddled in the doorway. Confusion, fear, and desperation flashed through her rolling eyes, and she twisted her calico skirts with shaking hands.

"Fire!" Sally shrieked. "It ain't Mast' Ludlow burnin'. It's comin' from upstairs."

Lucy sniffed again. The smell of smoke grew stronger; then a dull thud reverberated across the ceiling. Ludlow ceased his squirming and looked up. A horrified understanding crossed his sweaty face.

"Emmie," he rasped. He struggled frantically, no longer cowed by Diarmid's rage.

Lucy spun. "Mick, go with Sally, quick. Emmie's locked in. If there's fire—"

She didn't need to finish the sentence. Mick shot forward with the fleetness of a born London pickpocket, Sally hard on his heels. Lucy turned and grasped the rigid muscle of Diarmid's upper arm. "Ludlow's sister is locked upstairs," she cried. "She's stark, starin' barmy, and there are candles all over her chamber. We've got to help her."

Diarmid cast her a livid glare, then tightened his hold on Ludlow's throat. Lucy instantly realized he didn't believe her.

"God's teeth, ye bloody, stubborn, arrogant Scot! I may be a thief and a guttersnipe, but I've never lied to ye. If ye want to snort and paw about like the ruttin' bull ye are, go ahead. Throttle that arsehole with my blessing. Then go straight to hell. *I'm* going to help."

She whirled and raced down the hall toward the hidden staircase. As she turned to dash up the stairs, her thin slippers skidded on the bare, polished floor. She crashed down and landed on her hip. Pain blasted through her and she groaned a Romany curse.

"You shock me, madam. Is that proper language for the mistress of Stanton's Grove?" The cool, cultured tones of the born aristocrat glided to her ear. Then two large, warm hands—at once both rough and tender—slipped beneath her thighs and under her shoulders. Before she could protest, Diarmid swept her up into his arms, then set her on her feet. He bent and kissed her open mouth. "Are ye all right?"

She closed her mouth and nodded giddily, concentrating hard on her wobbly knees.

He tossed her a look of wry amusement mingled with banked rage. "Then, madam, I'll deal with you later." He spun and charged up the stairs.

"Wait!" Lucy yelled.

She gathered her skirts and followed, tripping twice more as the stairs twisted up into smoke and darkness. She felt her way around the last, tight turn and stumbled against Diarmid's broad back. He reached a hand behind him, steadied her, and pulled her tight against the taut curve of his kilted buttocks without so much as turning his head.

"Where's the key?" he asked Sally in a grim voice.

"I tol' you. I done give it to Miss Lucy."

Lucy's mind stalled. Frantically, she tried to recall what had happened to the key. She'd turned it in the lock, burst into the room, then . . . what?

The smell of smoke was choking now, and red-gold light flickered from the crack beneath the door. She couldn't hear Emmie moving about. Suddenly a horrible thought assailed her: What if the poor creature had already succumbed to the smoke and flames?

"I don't have it," she murmured guiltily. For an instant, she pressed her cheek against the soft velvet of Diarmid's evening coat. It smelled of him—all leather and cherry tobacco and that delicious, indefinable male musk that was so uniquely his. She felt his muscles tense; then she stepped back and turned. "Ludlow must have it. I'll go down—"

"Nay." Diarmid's voice rang with the authority of the aristocratic warrior accustomed to command—and to submission. "Mick and Sally, get away from the door. Stand by Lucy. I'll break it down."

Sally and Mick stumbled around him, then groped through the darkness, following the rough plank walls. When they were a safe distance back, Diarmid took a deep breath and lunged forward. The door cracked on impact, and Lucy winced at Diarmid's stifled grunt of pain. Twice more he hurled himself against the door; at last it splintered along the hinges, then burst inward. Diarmid vaulted into the room.

To Lucy, it seemed as if Diarmid had stepped into the antechamber of hell. Voracious tongues of fire devoured the tabletop and licked up the legs of Emmie's low pallet. The stubby tallow candles had been flung like chaff across the floor, and they guttered wildly in a dozen spots, like individual bonfires on Guy Fawkes night. The calico curtains flapped in the draft, then brushed against the burning washstand and flared up like oil-soaked torches. Sparks leaped onto the moth-eaten tapestry hanging next to the window, and the old, dry wool burst into flame. Smoke billowed through the chamber door, stinging Lucy's eyes. Tears raced down her cheeks and she doubled over, coughing.

Emmaline crouched in the far corner of the room, sucking her thumb, staring blankly at the encroaching flames and slowly rocking back and forth. Diarmid started toward her, and she shrank back, then snarled like a cornered wolverine.

"Wait!" Mick cried. "She wants me." He darted past Lucy's clutching hands and tried to slip around Diarmid's long legs. At the sight of him, Emmaline's glazed eyes came to life. She hunched forward on her knees, arms outstretched, a smile of pure love transforming her gaunt and vacant face.

Diarmid grabbed Mick by the shirt collar, then bent close to his peaked little ear. "Go to her," he directed in a low, calm voice, "and distract her attention away from me. As soon as she's not looking, I'll grab her and carry her out." He looked up, met Lucy's horrified gaze, then slanted Mick a conspiratorial wink. "And ye'll follow me as quick as your sister's tongue, aye? There'll be no livin' with her if anything happens to you."

Mick glanced anxiously at the blazing tapestry. Then he quickly picked his way between the candles and allowed himself to be engulfed in Emmie's desperate embrace. Footsteps pounded up the stairs. Before Lucy could shout a warning, Ludlow hurtled past Lucy and Sally, lunged around Diarmid, and rushed toward Emmie. Startled, Emmie glanced up, saw her brother, and screamed.

Ludlow halted. He still wore only his thin linen shirt, and sweat had plastered it to his thin frame, leaving precious little to the imagination. He attempted a reassuring smile; in the lurid, gyrating firelight, it looked like a predatory leer.

Emmie's eyes widened; her pallid skin turned sickly gray; she began to tremble uncontrollably. "No," she whimpered. She crawled backward on her knees, dragging Mick with her. Ludlow inched forward, hands outstretched.

"It's all right," he said in a high, singsong voice. "I don't want to hurt you. Just give me your hand—"

"Monster! You'll never touch me again!" With blinding speed, Emmie surged to her feet. For a moment she wavered, inches from the burning tapestry. Then, as if freeing herself at last from a long, dreadful nightmare, she kissed Mick's cheek, wound her arms around his shoulders, smiled beatifically, and plunged backward. The tapestry broke from its fastenings, then crumpled over them in a roar of devouring flames.

"Diarmid! Oh, sweet Jesus—Diarmid, save my brother!"
Before the shriek left Lucy's throat, Diarmid lunged forward.
Lucy gouged her fingernails into her cheeks, paralyzed with
fear. 'Twas the Ace of Swords: separation, destruction, death
by fire.

Diarmid grabbed the burning tapestry with his bare hands,
flung it up, and grasped Mick's arm. Sparks exploded; flames
leaped wildly. For an instant smoke obscured Lucy's vision.
Then Diarmid roared a Gaelic battle cry and yanked the boy
from Emmie's arms. He staggered back, Mick caught to his
massive chest like a wee, newborn babe.

Lucy shrieked, "Sally, get help," then shot forward. The
slave whirled and ran. Lucy grabbed Diarmid's shoulder and
dragged him back with all her strength. At the same moment,
she heard an agonized wail. The tapestry had fallen back over
Emmaline.

Diarmid shoved Mick into Lucy's arms, then he and Ludlow dove toward the writhing mass of flame. Twice the heat
and fire drove them back; twice they renewed the assault.
Finally, Diarmid crouched down, face inches from the flames,
and stripped the burning wool from Emmie's body with his
bare hands.

It was too late.

Ludlow collapsed to his knees. Tears mingled with his
sweat and pooled in the scars on his face. Diarmid dragged
him out of harm's way just as Moses charged up the stairs
with a sloshing bucket. The enormous African dashed the
water on the flames, then other slaves surged up behind Lucy,
shouting and lugging various vessels of water. Somehow she
found herself back at the bottom of the stairs, in the relative
peace of the hallway, Mick still clasped in her arms.

She knelt and covered his filthy face with kisses. "Oh,
thank God you're all right."

Mick grinned. " 'Tis broken now, Loose. Me fortune. Ye
saved me after all."

Lucy closed her eyes. She hadn't been the one to save
Mick.

Quick, light steps descended the stairs behind her. Ever so slowly, she stood and opened her eyes.

Sparks still smoldered on Diarmid's velvet coat, the skin on his hands was blackened and bubbly, and the flames had singed away his long, beautiful lashes. Sorrow, pain, and exhaustion had sharpened the austerity of his features, but he managed a shaky half bow, then tossed her a rueful smile, teeth very white in his soot-streaked face.

"Madam . . ." He sighed, then coughed, hard. "Twice now I've waded through fire for you . . . so I do wish you'd stop stealing my valuables and bolting."

Then his jade eyes fluttered shut, his long, muscular legs folded beneath him, and he collapsed in a dead faint.

Twenty-one

Somewhere deep in the heart of the plantation mansion, a clock chimed the hour. Lucy glanced at the tall casement window and strained her eyes to catch the approaching dawn, but the shiny black glass merely reflected her own anxious image. Sighing, she rose from the hearthside wing chair and glided silently to the bed. Diarmid had been asleep for hours—a normal reaction to such severe burns, Clemency had said—and Lucy wished he would wake. She needed to thank him—and to ask his forgiveness.

She gazed down at his bandaged hands. Tears clogged her throat and she knotted her fingers in the soft, trailing gauze of her nightshift. How on earth had he managed to ride back to Stanton's Grove with such dreadful injuries? Sheer bullheadedness, no doubt—her lips curved in a tender smile—*and* sheer strength. She hated to admit it, even to herself, but she adored his stubborn Scottish strength. In truth, she had come to depend on it, just as poor, widowed Celia had depended on it down through the years.

Lucy's brows knit. Poor Celia. When Lucy, Mick, and Diarmid had returned from Resolute, Clemency had met them in the hall with dreadful news: Celia's heart was failing. The crotchety old dame had collapsed at the ball, moments after Venetia had denounced Lucy as a thief. Lucy bit her lip, suddenly ashamed. That was why Diarmid hadn't stormed after her: He'd been too busy carrying Celia's frail body to her chamber, then anxiously waiting for Dr. Walker's diagnosis.

Earlier in the evening the surgeon had entertained hopes

for Celia's recovery. Now it was clear that death approached. Stanton's Grove would slip from Celia's indomitable old claws, but it would not come to rest in Diarmid's sure hands, for Lucy had ruined everything. Even if she begged—which she most assuredly would not—she doubted Diarmid would ever forgive her.

Tentatively, she reached out and trailed her finger across his high, chiseled cheekbone. A few hours ago, while Clemency had cleaned and bandaged his burned hands, Lucy had tenderly sponged the soot from his face. He had grumbled and growled, of course, but his sensuous mouth had curled up at the corners in a complacent smile—rather like a lordly lion reveling in the ministrations of his devoted lioness.

She stifled a giggle, then stroked her finger over the wicked black peaks of his eyebrows. They were singed—

"Enjoying yourself, madam?"

Lucy jumped, then snatched her hand away. "Diarmid! You scared me to death."

A low chuckle rumbled from his bare chest; then his aquamarine eyes opened just enough to slant her an elven glance. "And what were ye grinnin' aboot, lassie?"

Her heart bounded with relief. Diarmid couldn't be too hurt—or too angry—if he had the energy to tease. "I was imagining you as a lazy, pampered lion."

"Hmmmm. King of the forest. So ye fancy me a beast, aye?" He arched a brow, then flashed his dazzling dimples. As always when he smiled, her eyes flew to the tiny dent in the middle of his lower lip. God's teeth, but she ached to suckle that luscious curve of flesh, to slide her tongue over that enthralling notch. . . .

His eyes darkened and his expression grew blatantly suggestive. "And what else are ye thinkin', lass?"

" 'Tis a shame you've singed off your eyelashes."

"I beg your pardon?"

Gathering all her courage, Lucy clambered onto the bed beside him and leaned close—so close she could feel the heat of his body and smell the warm, intoxicating, sleep scent of his skin. She caught her breath, then lightly brushed a kiss against the tanned, smile-crinkled skin around his eyes.

"I mean, milord, that I'm jealous of your lashes. They're longer than the law should allow on any man—least of all on a handsome rake like you." She slanted him a flirtatious smile—and was utterly taken aback by the intensity of his searing jade gaze.

"Don't toy with me, madam." His voice stung like a whip's lash.

"I wasn't. I mean, I . . ." Lucy flounced back against the pillows, huffed, and crossed her arms over her breasts. "God's ears, Diarmid Niall Altan Maclean. You needn't bite my head off. I just wanted to thank you. You risked your life for Mick tonight, and I want you to know I'm grateful. Also . . ." She risked a sidelong glance, and was further disconcerted by his cool and impenetrable expression. She gnawed at her lip. "I . . . I want to apologize for ruining your chance to inherit Stanton's Grove."

"What?"

"You heard me. God's ankles—is it so unbelievable that a guttersnipe like me could have the decency to apologize? After what happened tonight"—she glanced at the brand on her upper arm, just visible beneath her gauzy shift—"Celia will never accept me, and she'll never approve of our marriage. I'm sure by now she's figured out the whole thing was a scheme so you could sink your hooks into her plantation. I've ruined everything for you, and I just wanted you to know I'm sorry."

Diarmid was silent for a long time. Lucy tried to will the tension from her muscles, then watched anxiously as the sky outside the windows lightened to gray. The change was so imperceptible, she couldn't mark its progress; she could only appreciate the result.

Suddenly, Diarmid's bandaged hand closed over her arm. He jerked it back and flapped it in the air, a grimace of pain contorting his handsome face. "Good Christ!"

"Are you all right?" She scrambled to her knees and hovered over him.

"Aye. Sit down, *mo cridhe*. Ye're embarassin' me. Do ye no ken a Highland warrior canna abide a soul seein' him in pain?"

"Why . . . why did you touch me?"

He rolled his eyes and looked elaborately exasperated. "I'd have thought that would be obvious by now. Och—ye're the bonniest lass I've ever laid eyes on, and ye're lyin' in bed beside me, clad in a scrap o' silk so thin I could read the *Virginia Gazette* through it. There's not a pain in the world bad enough to keep me from touchin' ye."

"Oh."

He collapsed back against the pillows and stared up at the elegant, blue-brocade bed canopy. "And ye dinna need to apologize. Humility doesna become ye, *mo cridhe*." He scanned her face. "Besides, did ye no' hear me call ye the mistress of Stanton's Grove a few hours ago?"

"No."

"Och, weel—ye never have listened to me. Why should I expect it now?" He glared down his blade-straight nose, but his eyes were soft. "Ye havena failed, *mo cridhe*." He grinned at her startled expression, then sat up and sketched a courtly bow. "On the contrary, madam, you have succeeded quite beyond my wildest expectations."

"What?"

"Celia told me right before I made the toast to Jamie. She said she never had wanted to leave Stanton's Grove to Venetia, and now that I was happily married"—he arched a wry eyebrow—"she had decided to leave everything to me."

"Diarmid! That's wonderful!" Lucy flung her arms around his neck, knocking him back against the pillows.

"No need to strangle me." He loosened her grip but caught her to him when she tried to slide away. "Can you keep a secret?"

"Haven't I proved that by now? I fooled Celia, didn't I?"

Diarmid grinned. "I never said you fooled her, *mo cridhe*. On the contrary, Celia saw through you the first day she met you. It seems she recognized a fellow, ah . . . kindred spirit."

"What do you mean?" Lucy pouted at his elven expression. "Stop dragging it out and tell me."

"You're always nattering on about how bright the Rom are. Can't you guess? No? Well, here's our little secret. Celia Stanton Lee—the grand dame of Virginia society—came to the colony nearly sixty years ago . . . as a bond slave."

Lucy's jaw dropped. She tried to ignore Diarmid's unnervingly virile presence and processed his stunning news. "You mean she was a convict, too?" she managed at last.

"Aye—sent up for prostitution."

Lucy whooped and clapped her hands together. "Celia Stanton Lee—a lightskirt?"

Diarmid cast her a pointed glance, then winked lewdly. "How do you think she landed two rich husbands?"

Lucy nestled against his broad shoulder. "So, you're master of Stanton's Grove after all—or soon will be."

To her astonishment, sorrow drifted across his jade eyes. "Aye. But I guess in all me schemin', I never allowed myself to face the fact that Celia's truly goin' to die. She's always been the heart of Stanton's Grove, ye ken—proud, strong, indomitable. The more I fought her, the more she fought me—and the more I teased her, the more she loved it." He flashed Lucy his quick, dazzling, dimpled smile. "She reminds me of ye, *mo cridhe.*"

As always, the urge to kiss the dent in his lower lip shot like quicksilver through her veins. "I never said I loved your teasing, Diarmid Maclean." But God's knees—how she loved the man!

Then she did what she had longed to do since the day he had lifted her down from Captain Pratt's auction block: She leaned forward and tenderly closed her teeth around his lower lip, then slid her tongue up and down along the delicious little groove.

Diarmid inhaled so sharply, she thought she'd bitten him. He started back, and his eyes darkened from aquamarine to emerald. "Ye're playin' with fire, *mo cridhe.* Have ye no' had enough sparks for one night?" In a heartbeat, her mind rang with a thousand precious images of their odd life together, and each image tolled like a bell through her soul.

Diarmid, furiously whisking her away from lovesick Tom Jefferson. Diarmid, bowing and tenderly kissing Celia's trembling old hand. Diarmid, dimpling wickedly and telling Jamie a bawdy Gaelic tale. Diarmid, gently placing a pistol to poor Sea Hero's beloved head. Diarmid, valiantly dashing into the flames to rescue her little brother.

In another heartbeat, she made up her mind. She slipped her hand around his neck and twined her fingers in the glossy black waves of his hair. "Enough? I've just started gathering kindling, milord." She slid her tongue along his lip once more.

He gave a low groan and angled his jaw hard against hers. His tongue filled her mouth, then began a teasing, coaxing dance that melted her bones and ignited a fire sure to consume her. His flesh burned through the filmy gauze of her nightshift, and aching desire flared inside her.

With the languid, feline grace of a cat, she stretched out, leaned her weight against the hard length of his body, then slipped one leg over his. Her pubic bone pressed against the knotted muscle of his thigh. Instantly, sensual yearning blossomed inside her; her womanhood seemed to swell, to unfurl.

Diarmid's tongue danced and swirled around her own, moving in a rhythm as natural as breathing. Ecstasy shimmered over her skin and rippled down to her tingling nipples. They contracted deliciously, and she daringly brushed one hard little point against his shoulder. He groaned, then increased the tempo of his kisses. She responded, meeting his hunger, urging him on.

"Och, *mo cridhe*," he murmured against her lips, "come to me, lay with me, release me from me promise, for I would make ye truly me wife."

A rich, deep joy flushed through her veins and her heart took flight. She'd never let a man touch her in love; only Diarmid had opened her soul, seduced her body and stolen her heart. "Take me," she whispered. "I want you."

He reared up, grasped the curve of her buttock, and

reached for the hem of her shift. "Saint Iona!" he gasped. He yanked his bandaged hand away, then flapped it in the air. "Och, these bloody burns hurt like the devil."

Lucy's heart contracted. Hectic red suffused Diarmid's high cheekbones, his eyes blazed like emerald flame, his lips were swollen and moist with passion—and the most outraged expression she'd ever seen adorned his chiseled features. He looked like an aggrieved and furious satyr—a Gaelic satyr. She began to giggle.

He shot her a sizzling aquamarine glare. "What's so funny, ye saucy wench?"

Gently, she pushed him back against the pillows. "I just can't believe it. I finally decide to give in to your overwhelming masculine charms, and you can't even touch me."

The corners of his mouth quirked. "But we're no' goin' to let that stop us, aye?"

"Aye." She rose to her knees, raised her nightshift to midthigh, then straddled his narrow hips. He moved as if to grasp her waist and press her down against him. "Ah, ah," she warned. "Remember—no hands." Suddenly, a disconcerting thought gnawed its way through her desire. Her smile vanished.

"What is it, *mo cridhe?*"

The husky tenderness in his voice disarmed her. "I'm not sure what to do."

He chuckled devilishly and pushed his knees outward against her thighs, spreading her and lowering her toward the enormous bulge that tented the front of his nightshirt. Lucy closed her eyes, took a deep breath, and brushed her woman's core against him. A wave of passion crashed over her, so powerful she thought she might collapse. She swayed forward, then gently pushed Diarmid's arms over his head.

"Hold them there," she ordered, pressing his steely biceps into the pillow. An intense feeling of power shot through her, sharpening her desire to agonizing hunger, hardening her nipples to aching points, flooding her womanhood with slick wetness. Her breath caught and she gently pressed her mound against Diarmid's straining erection.

He closed his eyes and tipped his head back. "Give me your breasts, *mo cridhe.*"

"Keep your eyes closed," she murmured.

Frail with longing, she skinned out of her shift, then lowered herself to his waiting mouth. He captured her taut nipple between his lips, sighed ecstatically, and began a hard, rhythmic suckling. His teeth nibbled her flesh. Sensual fire exploded through her veins and seared its way to her belly, then trailed lower, until she burned in two places—two aching, yearning spots that demanded his mouth, his tongue, his stiff, jutting manhood.

He moved to her other breast, and the tip of his tongue licked her nipple with lightning-quick strokes, teasing until she thought she would melt into a pool of honeyed lust. In an agony of desire, she lifted her hips and tugged at his nightshirt. He opened his eyes and sat up. His gaze seared down over her swollen nipples and across her quivering belly to the neat black triangle between her thighs. He gave a low, frustrated groan.

"Och, lassie—ye're so lovely. I long to caress every inch of ye. *Damn* these hands." Fixing her with a frustrated jade glare, he raised his arms, and she wrestled the garment over his head. "Easy, *mo cridhe,*" he murmured, eyes crinkling rakishly. "Remember, I'm wounded."

She flung his shirt to the floor, then halted, overwhelmed by his masculine beauty. She'd seen him shirtless often enough, and hungrily had admired the powerful width of his shoulders, the curved muscles of his arms—hardened and defined in battle—and the sculpted perfection of his flat belly. But she'd never seen what lay below his belt. Her gaze drifted lower, and she gasped. He was stunning—boldly erect, pulsing with life.

"God's bones," she breathed. "Ye're hung like a prize bull."

Diarmid roared with laugher. "Aye, weel—ye always said I rutted about the hedgerows like such a beast." Chuckling, he lay back against the pillows, and his erection reared proudly from its glossy black thicket. Fascinated, she reached out, then stopped.

"Touch me," Diarmid urged. "Come, lass. Can ye no' see how I long for ye?"

Timidly, she closed her fingers around him. His quick intake of breath rasped through his teeth, and he lifted his hips a fraction. She was amazed by the size of him—fully as long as her forearm, and as thick around as her wrist. She stroked lightly, enthralled. Steel sheathed in velvet. Engorged veins bulged along the shaft, the beautiful head flushed a reddish purple, and a tiny jewel of moisture glistened at the tip.

"Take me in your mouth, lass," Diarmid murmured.

A week ago—nay, an hour ago—she'd never have dreamed of doing such. Now she longed to taste him. Unsure how to proceed, she eased her body between his legs, then lowered her head. Her long black hair curtained forward and brushed his belly, and his stomach muscles jumped and quivered. Looking up, she saw his nipples harden; then she parted her lips and took the tip of him into her mouth. Diarmid groaned and raised his hips. Encouraged, she ran her tongue along the shaft, then licked the salty-sweet crown of him with lightning strokes, mimicking the expert touch he had lavished on her nipples.

"Stop teasin', *mo cridhe*," he gasped. "Saint Iona—*take me.*"

She lowered her mouth over him, then began a slow, gentle, back-and-forth motion, swirling her tongue around his shaft with each upward stroke. Diarmid twisted his head against the pillow and bucked up to meet her. She caught his rhythm and increased the tempo; her hand caressed the warm, velvet skin of his naked buttocks.

"Och, lass—" he groaned "ye'll make me explode." He cupped his hands around her head to stop her movement. "I want to come in ye, *mo cridhe*. Ye'll no' believe how I've dreamed and ached and longed for that." He dimpled wickedly. "And I'll no' have ye deprivin' me of me fun."

He urged her to sit back on her heels, then smiled deep into her eyes. For an instant, pure, true emotion blazed from his luminous jade gaze. Her heart contracted, and she felt as if her soul had fused with his, leaving her shaken, broken open, washed clean. Oh, God's heart—she loved this man to the very bottom of her being.

And for one brief, blinding moment, she knew he loved her.

His lips crushed hers and his tongue darted deep into her mouth. He kissed her until her head whirled and her nipples throbbed and her womb ached to be filled. Then, with his tongue still twined around hers, Diarmid lay back, pulling her along with him. She sprawled against the musky slickness of his chest, belly to naked belly, half wild with raw desire. His lips roamed to her ear and his tongue encircled her intricate whorls of flesh, sending shudders of ecstasy across her skin.

"Make love to me, *mo cridhe,*" he whispered.

Her nipples itched for the demanding tug of his lips. The swollen nub between her thighs throbbed and keened for the tantalizing stroke of his fingers. Most of all, her womanhood longed for the thrust of his steely manhood deep in her very core.

"Take me in your hand," Diarmid entreated against her lips, expertly luring her from her passion-drugged torpor. "Guide me to ye, lass."

She slipped her hand down between their sweating bodies, reveling in the opposing sensations of smooth, damp skin and crisp, curling hair. The aroused jut of his penis pressed boldly into her hand; then he nudged her up until her knees straddled his thighs. She hovered over him for a languorous instant, then—panting, flushed, wide-eyed—she lowered her hips. The wet ripeness of her womanhood slid along his burning flesh, and a storm surge of desire crashed through her every nerve and sinew. She pressed harder, and the velvety head of him slipped inside. She froze, trembled, chewed her lip.

Diarmid placed a bandaged hand lightly on her hip. "Ye're me wife," he murmured hoarsely, "and me darlin', darlin' heart. Come to me, lass. Love me." He pressed gently and slipped deeper.

Lucy gasped and her heart thundered into her throat. Her nipples hardened to points of exquisite pain, and her swollen female nub ached for the press and stroke and glide of Diarmid's shaft. But she couldn't go farther. He was too large, and her cursed maidenhead blocked the way.

She whimpered with frustrated desire. Lightly cupping her buttocks, Diarmid sat up, his erection still lodged just inside the gates of paradise. "Wrap your legs around my waist," he breathed, pressing tender, nibbling kisses to her throat.

Awkwardly, she wriggled about until her thighs gripped his narrow waist. Then he eased back and his steely shaft rubbed against her passion-drenched flesh. That was all it took. Mad for release, Lucy rocked forward, then leaned back. With each movement, Diarmid sank a hairsbreadth deeper, whispering Gaelic endearments the while.

He clamped his hands to her buttocks, suddenly oblivious to pain. He rolled her onto her back and gasped, "Och, forgive me, lass. I canna wait. I've got to have ye—now." He planted his mouth to hers and gave a commanding thrust.

Lucy felt a blinding flash of pain, quickly followed by the delicious plunge of Diarmid's manhood deep into her womb. She shrieked, then cried out again as Diarmid drew back. He stared down at the juncture of their bodies, then unsheathed himself farther. In the pale gleam of dawn, Lucy saw dark traces of blood on his penis.

"Mo cridhe—are ye all right?" His tone was astounded, his eyes wide.

"Aye," she whimpered. "Please, Diarmid—don't stop now. It hurts, but I want you so much." She dug her nails into his shoulder, then clutched his taut buttocks.

Setting his jaw in a thrilling display of masculine control, Diarmid sank into her. He moved slowly and gently at first. Then his thrusts came harder, faster, deeper. Lucy lifted her hips to meet him, and all pain vanished, replaced by a searing, blinding lust. Gradually, her senses narrowed until she could no longer smell the luscious scent of his sex; she could no longer taste the delicious salt of his sweat; she could no longer feel the heat of his skin or the swell of his muscles. Her focus narrowed to one thing: the maddening glide of his penis as it thrust deep inside her. With each measured plunge, it dragged against her pleasure nub and sent her wild with desire. She cried Diarmid's name, clawed his back, bit his shoulder, bucked her hips.

Then—oh, then—she exploded; exploded into a thousand shards of shimmering ecstasy. Her womanhood spasmed around Diarmid's shaft. A great wail tore from her lungs, her spine arched, her muscles clenched, and her convulsing body drained each dazzling sensation from her first climax.

Diarmid ground into her, intensifying her sensation, prolonging her release. Suddenly he drove deep, and his thrusts grew lightning quick. "Och, *mo cridhe*. I'm coming." His jaw clenched, his belly jerked, then he plunged down into her, groaning to the very depths of his soul.

At last, when his labored gasps had slowed to the relaxed breathing of a man about to drift into sleep, he eased from her sated flesh and pillowed his head against her bosom. "Me darlin', darlin' heart," he murmured. Then he closed his eyes and rested his bandaged hand on her breast with a possessive tenderness that reduced her to tears.

The golden morning sun slanted between the dark trees and gleamed through the tall casement windows of Diarmid's bedchamber—*uncurtained* tall casement windows, Diarmid noted with a wry smile. Saint Iona, who had been thinking about pulling the draperies last night? Certainly not he.

He rolled onto his side and pressed his naked body to Lucy's sleeping form. Dawn's radiance suited her, and he sank into enchantment, watching dreamily as it limned the line of her neck, gilded the slope of her cheekbones, and lent a lustrous sheen to her tawny skin. Och, what wouldn't he give to be that light! He wanted to melt across her like molten gold, warm her with kisses, then wake her to the joy of a bright new day.

He slipped his arm around the curve of her waist and snuggled closer. The warmth of her thighs and buttocks intoxicated him, and he felt himself slipping into a voluptuous haze of lust. Och, how could he still be so hot for her after such a night? He brushed his stubbly cheek against her velvety one, then smiled tenderly. His Romany queen might be the proudest, strongest, cleverest person on God's earth, but surely he was the luckiest.

In truth, he scarce could believe the treasure he had purchased when he'd bought up her indenture—Saint Iona, had it really been six short weeks ago? Lucy was all he had ever hoped for in a woman—and all he had never found. He closed his eyes and wantonly recalled his pleasure of the night, when his defiant Gypsy bride had opened her body and loved him as if she were welcoming him home after a long, hard journey.

His eyes flew open and he bit back a groan of remorse. Och, how could he have been such a cad? He'd blithely assumed that because Lucy was a convict, a bond slave, and a thief, she must also be a whore. He had taunted her relentlessly, had sneered each time she had insisted that she was a maiden. He'd patronized her, disrespected her; used her. Chained to his dreams for the future—and fleeing the nightmares of the past—he haughtily had assumed that only a woman of his aristocratic background could be worthy of his love. Och, what a proud, arrogant fool he had been. And how incredibly wrong.

Lucy stirred in her sleep, and he arrested his hand's seductive stroking. He quelled another ripple of remorse, then grinned. Och, the poor, wee lass must be tired, for he'd loved her long and hard before they both collapsed into sleep.

Suddenly, a great, aching wave of emotion choked his throat. Saint Iona—he ought to be horsewhipped! When Lucy had kissed him, he had reveled in his triumph, had gloried that his luscious Romany prize had come begging at last. He'd all but rubbed his hands together in gleeful anticipation of the carnal pleasures awaiting. If he'd only realized—if he'd only known.

He clenched his eyes tight, reliving the moment of agonizing lust when his cock had slipped between the slick folds of her womanhood. He had ached to plunge into her—to thrust and pound and spend the thwarted desire that had tortured him since their wedding night. Never in his wildest dreams had he expected to feel the unmistakable impediment of her maidenhead.

Lucy muttered something, then twisted her head against the pillow. Her eyelids flickered, and for a moment he hoped she might wake. But what would he say to her? Part of him—a very large, very *hard* part—wanted to say nothing at all. It merely wanted to re-ignite the passion that had blazed between them. Lucy had come to him fully and he had found himself doing things with her that he'd never done—had never even imagined doing—with any other woman.

He raised a hand and smoothed a strand of hair from her cheek. She made a small, lost sound, and his pulse thundered to life so strongly, so suddenly, he thought his heart might burst. Saint Iona—what should he say to her? What *could* he say? He was in no position to pour out his heart.

Och, he'd built himself a fine snare, indeed. He'd made clear to Lucy the cold, calculated nature of their marriage, and he'd offered her no hope and no reason to trust him. In truth, he wouldn't blame her if she left him the moment she awoke, for he hadn't done the one thing she'd asked of him: He hadn't kept his promise to buy and free Mick.

His thoughts flew to the scrawny, freckle-faced boy he'd snatched from the flames. Although blue-eyed and fair-skinned—not dark like his sister—Mick's braw spirit and snapping, mischievous eyes clearly marked him as Lucy's half brother. Diarmid's lips twitched into a smile. The lad finally had succumbed to exhaustion when they had arrived at Stanton's Grove last night, and Diarmid somehow had found himself carrying Mick upstairs to bed. He still could feel the lad's painfully thin arms wound around his neck.

With a rueful, hushed sigh, Diarmid lifted the covers and

slipped out of bed. He longed to wake his tempting bride with kisses and caresses, but he couldn't face her.

Not until he'd made the hardest decision of his life.

Twenty-two

"C'mon, Loose, wake up." Lucy cracked open an eye. Dazzling sunlight lanced through it, and she groaned. "Loose." A determined hand joggled her arm. "There's biscuits and eggs and Virginny 'am for breakfast. So rattle yer pins. I'm 'ungry."

Both Lucy's eyes flew open, then she sat up and dragged her little brother against her. "Oh, Mick, it wasn't a dream after all!" She pressed a kiss on his wild, stand-up hair, then squeezed his scrawny arm. "God's teeth, I scarce can believe 'tis you."

Mick squirmed away, jumped off the bed, and raced to her dressing table. " 'Nigs, Loose. 'Tis a rum setup ye got 'ere." He snatched up her silver-backed hairbrush, ran the engraved surface reverently along his freckled cheek, then tossed it at her. " 'Ere. Yer 'air looks like a 'orse's tail after the knackers been at it."

Lucy wrinkled her nose and stuck out her tongue, then dreamily began brushing her snarled locks. She doubted not a whit that she looked the very devil—thanks to the attentions of one rakish and astonishingly passionate demon. Suddenly, worry unfurled like a noxious weed in her belly, and she dropped the brush and glanced around the room. Why wasn't Diarmid here? No tall leather riding boots lay beside the bed. No snowy muslin shirt lay slung across the hearthside wing chair. No wickedly tight breeches lay crumpled on the floor. Apprehension rooted itself in her heart.

"Mick, have you seen Mr. Maclean?" She tried to keep her voice nonchalant.

Mick had discovered Diarmid's razor and was mimicking the motions of a man shaving. "The cove 'oo saved me last night? I seen 'im ridin' off this mornin' on a strappin' fine nag. Scowlin' like Ol' Nick, 'ee was—the cove, not the 'orse." Mick shot Lucy a canny glance. "Why? Be 'ee the one who bought ye and set ye up prime?"

Lucy had been about to rise, but something in Mick's tone stopped her. He continued to make elaborate shaving motions, and his peaked little face seemed happy enough, but his shoulders stiffened with tension. She caught up her dressing gown, and her stomach lurched. God's knees, did Mick think she'd turned whore like their mother?

"He's my husband," she blurted.

Mick's azure eyes grew saucer-wide. "Blimey! 'Struth?"

Lucy strode to her dressing table and perched primly on the stool. "Aye. He bought me the same morning Mr. Ludlow bought you. And he freed me."

"Just like that?"

"Just like that." Lucy smiled at her reflection in the dressing table mirror. Her eyes gleamed like a complacent cat's, her lips looked swollen and slightly bruised, and a delightfully embarrassed flush spread across her cheeks.

Mick's reflection joined hers. "Why would a toff like that marry the likes of ye?"

Lucy scowled. Mick's tone sounded jaded and worldly wise far beyond his years. But why should that surprise her? He'd seen their mother trawling for customers through fetid dockside alleys at all hours of the night. He'd heard moans and panting from behind the ragged curtain that separated Jocko and Agnes's bed from prying eyes. To Mick, a cove's interest in a woman began and ended with one thing: her muff.

"Mayhap he was dazzled by me beauty," Lucy remarked tartly.

"Yer not that dazzlin', Loose."

She tied back her hair with a black-velvet ribbon, then rose and crossed to the tiger-maple wardrobe. She flung the doors wide, and Mick gaped at the rainbow of expensive silk gowns. "Yer cove gave ye all them duds?" His tone was gratifyingly astonished. "And he freed ye?"

"That's right."

"Stab me gizzards." Mick's expression grew pinched. "I wished 'eed bought me."

A shaft of worry contracted Lucy's brows. Last night, Diarmid hadn't hesitated a whit when it came to rescuing Mick from poor, crazy Emmaline and the devouring flames, but he'd said nothing about buying and freeing him. In truth, he'd said nothing at all except the most scandalous, intimate love talk.

But had it been love between them? Last night, in the dark intimacy of his embrace, she'd been certain Diarmid loved her. But now, in the glaring light of day, with Mick's skeptical gaze upon her, she swiftly, utterly doubted it. Never once had the word *love* crossed Diarmid's expert lips. He'd been too busy with other things to speak of love, or the future, or her poor little brother.

Lucy slammed the wardrobe door and paced to the window. God's ears, what if Diarmid couldn't face her, now that she'd surrendered her virtue? After all, he'd always called her a whore, had always made clear his contempt for loose and brazen women. She swallowed. And they didn't come any more brazen than she had been last night. The gnawing fear in her mind descended to her belly, where it clenched and roiled her innards. Nay, she couldn't let her imagination run wild. No man could have made love to a woman like Diarmid had made love to her and not be madly, crazily smitten.

But being smitten wasn't the same as being in love, now was it? Nay. Being smitten was just a polite mask for that selfish old bastard: lust.

She pressed her forehead against the cool windowpane and stared out over Stanton's Grove. Precious Stanton's Grove. God's teeth, how could she ever compare? Diarmid loved this damned plantation, not her. 'Twas his life. 'Twas all he had ever desired. Well, soon it would be his, and he would want a pure, unsullied, virginal wife—a wife of his own aristocratic background—to bear his sons and help him run it.

Lucy's heart contracted in a long, agonizing ache. Why had she believed for one little minute that a Scottish laird could love a Gypsy thief and her light-fingered brother? Her gaze flew to the Stanton's Grove dock, thrust far out into the choppy blue water of the James. Diarmid valued that wretched old hunk of wood more than her little brother's freedom. God's knees, why had he even bothered to rescue Mick?

She took a step toward Mick and felt a trickle of wetness on her thighs. 'Twas Diarmid's seed, spilling out of her. She balled her hands into fists. Aye—Diarmid had gotten what he wanted. And now that he had, would he still want her?

Lucy hovered outside the door to Celia's bedchamber, ears straining to catch any sound. The old lady's palatial boudoir was situated on the ground floor, as Dr. Walker had forbidden his richest patient to climb the stairs, and the tantalizing aroma of fried ham drifted from the dining room across the hall. She clutched the stolen pocketful of jewels and eased open the door. With any luck, she could replace the goods before Celia awoke.

"Just what do you think you're doing?"

Lucy gasped and whirled. "Venetia. I didn't expect to see you."

Venetia stepped through the dining room doorway and sauntered forward. A supercilious smile curled her full lips. "I'm sure you didn't. What's that in your hand?"

Swift as thought, Lucy slipped the bag of jewels into the hidden pocket of her skirt. She held her hands palms up and smiled innocently. "Nothing. Perhaps your eyes are succumbing to age." She closed Celia's door and blocked Venetia's way. "If you're looking for Diarmid, I'm afraid he's gone out for a morning ride."

Venetia snorted. "A ride, is it? Lud, I must say you're a genius at fooling yourself—if at nothing else. Diarmid hasn't gone for a ride. He's left until we can get rid of you."

Lucy felt a spark of fear, followed instantly by white-hot rage. "How dare you say such a thing to me? I'm Diarmid's wife—"

"Wife, pish! Your sham marriage was nothing but a ruse to trick my aunt into leaving Stanton's Grove to Diarmid. We've been planning to get rid of you since day one."

Lucy's mind began to whirl sickeningly. It couldn't be true . . . but Venetia looked so sure, so triumphant. "Why in heaven's name would you want Diarmid to get Stanton's Grove?" she demanded, trying desperately to keep her voice calm. "Correct me if I'm wrong, but haven't you been, ah . . . *banking* on inheriting this place?"

Venetia eyed Lucy as if she were a particularly loathsome sewer rat. "And to think Diarmid once told me you were intelligent," she scoffed. "You know what a vindictive old bitch Celia is. You've heard her rant about my useless, drunken father. And I'm sure you've heard her list my many faults." Venetia hunched over, waved an invisible cane, and mimicked Celia with a fiendish flair that would have delighted Nikolas Gravesceu. "Venetia is a liar, Venetia is a trollop, Venetia is a spendthrift."

She straightened. "Do you honestly think Celia would leave Stanton's Grove to me? Pish! She didn't want me to inherit her plantation—she wanted me to marry Isaiah Ludlow. Even when the whole county knew that Diarmid and I were lovers, she persisted in flinging me at Ludlow's greasy head. She'd never have allowed me to marry her darling Highlander." She sneered viciously. "Celia's a hopeless romantic, you know, beneath that leathery hide of hers. It seems she cherished a delusion that Diarmid would settle into a happy marriage before she kicked off. She couldn't abide his attachment to me—"

Lucy couldn't breathe, couldn't think. "But Celia wanted Diarmid to marry you. She demanded it. You tricked her with a false pregnancy—"

"Who said it was false?"

Nausea hit Lucy like a tidal wave. "You . . . you mean—"

"That's exactly what I mean. I truly was pregnant, and I truly did lose the babe." Venetia gave a harsh laugh that sent a shiver across Lucy's skin. "When Diarmid succeeded in getting me with child, we thought we'd found the answer to our problem. Celia was livid when I told her, but she refused to see the Lee family brought low. In Virginia, no one is appalled by a bit of discreet dalliance, but heaven forefend that a Lee should bear a convict's bastard! So she ordered Diarmid to marry me. He didn't want her figuring out that we'd planned the whole thing, so he feigned reluctance—"

"But why did you need me? You could have married, gotten Stanton's—"

"Lud, what a lackwit. Celia hates me. No matter how much she loves Diarmid, she couldn't stand to see me mistress of Stanton's Grove. So she altered her will. She directed that after her death, Stanton's Grove should be sold to Ludlow. Diarmid would inherit half the proceeds on the condition that he and I leave Stanton's Grove forever. The balance of the money would be given to William and Mary College.

"Diarmid found out quite by accident. That man has the devil's own luck. He was drinking and gaming in the Raleigh Tavern when the solicitor's clerk let the cat out of the bag. Diarmid knew he had to take drastic measures—immediately—or we would lose Stanton's Grove *and* Celia's fortune. Then you popped up, and Diarmid got his wild idea. He'd marry you, then trick Celia into thinking he'd escaped my loathsome clutches and fallen in love with an English lady. He'd be restored to favor, and to Celia's will. When the old bitch died, you'd suddenly return to England. Word would arrive that you'd died on the journey, and after a suitable mourning period, Diarmid and I would marry."

Lucy's knees started to buckle. "But I heard you in the garden at the Governor's Palace. You were jealous, furious—"

"Of course I was. Diarmid undertook his little plan without

telling me. I was so distressed the next day, I fell and lost our babe." Venetia's sorrowful tone rang as hollow as a beggar's cheeks. "Diarmid explained the whole charade the day I rode out here for dinner. He told me that we just had to bide our time until Celia died; then we'd get rid of you." Venetia's frigid gaze slid over Lucy's slender frame. "I'll admit I was jealous of you at first, even though Diarmid swore he'd never touch you. Then I realized he'd never want your skinny carcass—not when he could have me." She stretched like a malicious cat, making certain that Lucy's stricken gaze fell on her lush breasts.

"I don't believe you," Lucy repeated woodenly. She couldn't; not after Diarmid had taken her virtue and stolen her heart. Venetia was the liar here, not Diarmid. Hadn't George Wythe—sweet, honorable George Wythe—told her to trust her unfathomable husband? "Diarmid would never do such—"

Venetia reached tauntingly into the voluminous flowered-chintz folds of her skirt and drew out a folded paper. "On the contrary, lackwit. Your charming husband has well and truly duped you." Venetia threw the document at Lucy.

Lucy snatched it up, unrolled it, and read.

The entire house went utterly silent. In truth, the low rumble of Royal's laughter still echoed from the kitchen, and the scent of spoon bread and fried apples still drifted from the dining room, but Lucy experienced the oddest sensation—as if she had been sealed off in a tomb. She was dimly aware of a crushing ache in her heart, but for the life of her, she couldn't work up any emotion. She couldn't scream, or cry, or lash out. Venetia's revelation was too massive, too . . . *real*.

The document was a notarized copy of her indenture, made over to Diarmid Niall Altan Maclean, Esq., and dated September 25, 1763. It clearly and plainly set forth that Diarmid Maclean of Stanton's Grove Plantation owned one white, English, female bond servant by the name of Lucy Graves, bought at custom of the country from Captain Obediah Pratt, and legally bound to serve Mr. Maclean until September 25, 1770.

"He never freed you," Venetia hissed. "This is the only legal document on file. Diarmid forged the other one in order to trick you into trusting him."

"But . . . the vicar of Bruton Parish married us," Lucy croaked. "He never would have done so if I weren't free. 'Tis illegal for bond servants to marry."

Venetia shrugged. "Diarmid fooled him as well. But you're right on one point." Her marble-pale eyes glittered. "You and Diarmid were *never legally married.*"

Lucy whirled and fled down the hall. She didn't see Royal's astonished face peer from the dining room, nor hear Celia's weak voice calling her from the bedchamber. She gathered her skirts and tore up the stairs, and a clumsy weight bumped against her thigh. Slowly, her dazed brain formed a single coherent thought: She still had Celia's jewels.

She careened around the newel post and dashed across the upper hall. A near-paralyzing shaft of pain stabbed her heart and she furiously bit back a torrent of tears. God's nose! What a fool she'd been, what a mush-brained fool to think Diarmid possibly could love her. What a dunce she'd been, what a lackwitted ass, what a treacherous, self-deluded weakling to betray her own principles, to let down her guard, to willingly play victim to the first seductive rogue to touch her with tenderness.

She relived a sudden, feverish memory of her night in Diarmid's arms. She'd been swept away by the glory of their passion: by Diarmid's honeyed mouth plundering hers, by his burned hands stroking her aching breasts, by his maddening tongue coaxing her nipples to diamond hardness. She'd surrendered her maidenhead with a cry of joy. She'd reached the pinnacle of pleasure under his practiced ministrations, and she'd encouraged him to do things to her body that she'd never have imagined possible. God's heart, she had become his wife in every way!

She dug her fingernails into her palms. And to think she'd believed she was legally married! She'd behaved like a whore in Diarmid's arms, but at least she'd been a *married* whore. Now, to discover that lying cur had tricked her all along! She banged open the door and flung herself across the bed. A gut-wrenching sob tore from her throat.

" 'Cor, Loose—what's ailin' ye?"

Mick's astonished voice sliced through her maelstrom of rage and betrayal and heartbreak. She tried to answer but succeeded only in pounding her fists into the eiderdown. Oh, that Mick should see her like this—brought low, wailing like a jilted scullion, playing the *victim,* just like their mother!

She sat up and gulped for air. Mick's blue eyes widened, and his peaked brows knit in an anxious frown. He patted her shoulder. " 'Tis all right, Loose. Did 'ee hit ye?"

"Who?"

"Mr. Maclean."

Lucy shook her head wildly. "I wish that's all he'd d-done. He's tricked me, betrayed me, lied to me. I t-trusted him. And all the time he was playing me for a fool."

Mick cast her a jaded look far beyond his years. "Then what's the point of snivelin', Loose? A cove like that ain't worth the snot."

Despite the torment tearing at her heart, Lucy wiped her nose on the back of her sleeve and gave a harsh laugh. "Ye're right, luv. He's no better than Jocko—curse their yards to the hottest rings of hell." She jumped up. "Mick, what say ye to Maryland?"

"Never 'eard of it."

" 'Tis north of here. And it has a lovely sound—Maryland. Rolls off the tongue like almond comfits. We could go there and start our new life, just like I promised."

Mick's frown deepened. "But Oi can't go nowheres—Emmie said. A bond slave can't travel without 'is papers."

"I'm a great lady now, remember?" Lucy sniffed and nodded at the wardrobe full of elegant gowns. "Dressed like that and carrying these"—she drew the bag of jewels from her

ocket—"no one will stop us. If they do, I'm Madam Lucy
Maclean, traveling with her bond servant to visit her Mary-
and kin."

Twenty-three

Twenty-three

Diarmid reined Braw to a halt at the edge of the woods and gazed down over Stanton's Grove. Glowing red leaves lay scattered before him like jewels in the dust, and the afternoon sun gilded his mount's glossy coat with liquid amber.

Amber. 'Twas a lovely name. If he and Lucy ever had a daughter, perhaps they could christen her that, for the wee bairn was bound to inherit her mother's exotic beauty. He gripped the reins and clenched his eyes shut. He had longed for a bairn for years, but he hadn't been able to stomach the thought of creating a new life with a woman he didn't love. Now, perhaps his dream lay within his grasp.

He opened his eyes and nearly shuddered with a happiness so pure, he feared it would dissolve into the crystalline fall air. No man could go through life bearing such love for one woman and not ultimately be disappointed. Yet how could Lucy's spirit and virtuous, honest heart ever disappoint him?

He bit back a chagrined smile. He'd been wrong when he'd assumed Lucy was a whore, and for the first time in his life he wasn't ashamed to admit an error. Och, mayhap he was a wee bit ashamed, for he'd been a proud, stubborn fool. He'd been so obsessed with the past that he'd ignored the joyous future that lay right in front of him.

Or did it? He shifted uneasily in the saddle, then urged Braw forward. The time had come to tell Lucy the truth, but would she stay with him when he revealed the dreadful thing he'd done back in Scotland, or would she spurn him and bolt? His jaw tightened. He was a fool to take the risk, but he could deceive her no longer.

Och, perhaps he should have spoken up last night. He should have told her how her impish glances fired his blood, how her catlike step melted his heart, how her quick repartee filled him with delight. Saint Iona, he should have told her how much he loved her.

Tremors of pure delight raced down his spine as he envisioned her astonishment when he handed her Mick's freedom paper. Doubtless she would fling herself into his arms in jubilation, then kick him in the shins for taking so long about it.

He flicked a fly from Braw's neck and debated telling her what he'd traded for Mick. Nay—he'd never reveal the bargain. Now that he had conceded the dock to Ludlow, he feared that Jamie would believe that he condoned the slave trade. Of course, Ludlow had sworn in writing that he would never land or transport slaves from the property, but Diarmid put little stock in a madman's promises.

He shook his head. This morning he had been astonished to feel a wee stab of pity for Ludlow, for it seemed Emmie's horrible death had ripped his heart from his body. Diarmid even had wondered whether Emmie's tragic condition had accounted for Ludlow's perverse behavior down through the years. Abruptly, he reined Braw to a halt outside the great house and quelled all vestiges of sympathy. Nothing could excuse Ludlow's vile treatment of his sister, or his loathsome attempt to rape Lucy.

He barely had started up the steps when the front door flew open and his brother strode toward him. "Och, thank God you're back," Jamie said. "We were about to send a search party."

Diarmid frowned. "What's amiss?"

"I'm verra sorry to tell ye this, Diarmid, but Madam Lee is dead."

Diarmid froze. His hand rested on the polished wood

door and he bent forward, as if absorbing a blow. Och, Saint Iona—poor, wee, proud Celia. Och, Christ, she couldn't be dead. For sixteen years she'd been his harshest critic and staunchest ally. She'd bullied, teased, taunted, and raged. She'd laughed, tricked, commanded, and obeyed. She'd given him a reason to live when he'd longed to die, and she had held his best interests at heart to the very end— even when he'd been too stubborn to see it.

He clenched his eyes shut and breathed a silent prayer for her soul. She'd been a crusty, demanding old shrew, and his sixteen years with her had been a bed of thorns, softened by the occasional rose. He'd thought her selfish and spoiled, yet she'd given him the one thing he loved more than life: She'd given him Lucy.

He turned stricken eyes to Jamie. "Where's my wife?"

Jamie glanced down at his polished riding boots. "I'm sorry, but she's no' here—"

"The wretched thief killed Celia, and now she's bolted!"

Diarmid whirled and found himself inches from Venetia's flushed face. "I caught the scheming slut at it this morning!" Venetia cried. "She came slinking out of Aunt Celia's room holding a small bag. I told her to stop, but she raced upstairs. I thought she just didn't want to face me, so I went into the bedchamber to see how Auntie was faring." Venetia dabbed a handkerchief to her eyes. Diarmid noted the fine cambric was dry. "Then . . . lud, 'twas terrible. Auntie was lying there all gray, with a pillow over her face. That whore smothered her!" Venetia broke into hysterical sobs.

"This is preposterous," Diarmid snapped. "Lucy had no reason to kill Celia. Saint Iona—she loved the old crow."

"You besotted fool!" Venetia shrieked. "That Gypsy slut's been using you—scheming for weeks to get her hands on Celia's money. When I showed the colony she was a thief, she decided to cut her losses and run. But she didn't go empty-handed."

Diarmid cast Venetia a scathing glare. "What are you talking about?"

Venetia whirled and sailed down the echoing front hall. Diarmid and Jamie strode after her. At the door to Celia's bedchamber, Diarmid halted.

The yellow-damask curtains had been drawn across the tall windows, and the room lay in cool, gray shadow. Clemency stood beside Celia's canopied bed, gently smoothing a damp cloth over the old lady's shrunken face. Diarmid crossed the room in one long stride, then bent and grasped Celia's hand. 'Twas stiff and cold. He swallowed the tears clogging his throat, then choked back a cry of bitter grief. He'd touched dead bodies before, but never had he felt a greater emptiness. Celia's soul had departed long since.

Venetia grasped his arm and thrust an open jewel box under his nose. "Here," she hissed. "Here's your motive. Your gutter bride stole the Lee jewels. Aunt Celia must have woken and caught the slut red-handed, so she killed her." Diarmid flinched and Venetia gave a cruel bark of laughter. "Why so appalled, my love? Surely a genius like you would never be stupid enough to trust a Gypsy thief. But then, you've fallen for a schemer before, haven't you?" She stared straight into his eyes, and her shrill voice burned like acid across his heart: "At least this time the only victim was poor Celia."

Diarmid awoke, sniffed, and grimaced. He lay sprawled across the canopied bed in his chamber—his *empty* chamber, curse his traitorous wife to the hottest rings of hell—and he smelled like he'd spent the night in a dockside gutter, doused with rotgut rum. He heaved himself into a sitting position, then muzzily glanced about. Saint Iona, the room looked as if he'd hosted a Roman orgy. His coat and riding boots lay beside a heap of whiskey bottles, and the stale air stank of spirits and musky male flesh.

Groaning, he bent down to retrieve a dusty boot. His stomach heaved and he bit his lip, determined not to be sick. Och, he must be getting old. Any self-respecting Scot could handle his liquor better than this, although from the looks of things, he'd quaffed enough grog to fell an ox.

He struggled into his boots, then trailed to the window and twitched back the heavy drapery. The stars were beginning to fade from the pewter sky, and out across the mist-shrouded waters of the James a faint pink haze eased over the horizon. It must be near dawn. Sighing heavily, he let the drape fall back, then collapsed into the wing chair.

How long had he shut himself away in here? He tried to concentrate on the distorted images that fled through his mind: Royal waddling away from his enraged bellow, grumbling the while; Jamie bringing him a bottle of whiskey, disapproval shrouding his lean face. Suddenly, one horrible thought crystallized in his brain. He shook his head, oblivious to the pounding ache in his skull. Could Lucy—his beautiful, spirited, mischievous wife—truly have killed Celia, then fled with a fortune in jewels?

He lunged to his feet and paced across the bedchamber, kicking viciously at empty bottles with every long stride. Aye. Though it tore out his heart to admit it, Lucy was capable of such an act. Saint Iona, the wench was a convicted thief! She'd been defiantly proud of her wretched past, and never once had expressed remorse or regret. He'd seen the rage in her eyes whenever he'd brushed off her demand to rescue her pickpocket brother, and he'd seen her walk through smoke and flames to get what she wanted.

He gritted his teeth, then spat a stream of oaths, ignoring the thought that what she had wanted was to save his sorry arse. That didn't matter. What mattered was that Lucy was capable of anything. On their farcical wedding night, he'd admired her gritty determination. Now he saw it for what it was: clear evidence that once again he'd fallen in love with a scheming, selfish woman who would stop at nothing to gain her own ends.

He clenched a hand over his eyes, desperate to blot out

the foul images in his mind. Lucy's exotic face floated before him, but when she spoke, her voice was Catriona's.

"You're a fool," Lucy—or was it Catriona?—scoffed. "I never loved you. I loved what you could do for me. Now I've gotten what I want, so you can piss off."

Och, 'twas so real. Either the liquor was addling his wits, or he had gone mad.

Someone pounded on the bedchamber door. "Diarmid, open up," Jamie ordered. "Ye've wallowed in there long enough. Clemency needs ye to plan Celia's burial, and Venetia just took a strap to Royal for breakin' a china platter."

Diarmid felt a ripple of grief, followed by a wave of anger. Damn Venetia! He'd never have met that lying Gypsy thief if it weren't for her. He strode to the door, turned the key, and yanked it open.

Jamie entered, followed by Royal. His foot struck a whiskey bottle and his brow arched. "Saint Columba, 'tis like a tavern after a brawl in here." Despite his teasing tone, Jamie's eyes were distressed. He clapped a hand on Diarmid's back. "Are ye all right?"

"Aye, unless ye count my splitting head and heaving gut."

Jamie tossed Royal a conspiratorial smile. "Send up the hip bath and have Cook boil water. Mr. Maclean wishes to dress." He closed the door and raked an arch gaze over his brother's rumpled appearance. "Now then—are ye quite through sulkin'?"

Diarmid smoothed his baleful expression into an impenetrable mask. "Watch that smart tongue of yours, little brother. Remember, I'm older and wiser than ye. And I'm *not* sulking. I'm exhibiting an entirely proper grief for my late employer."

Jamie snorted. "Older ye may be, but ye're sure no' wiser. I ken ye loved Celia, and I offer ye all me sympathies on her passin', but ye canna keep hidin' up here, avoidin' the truth."

"And what truth is that? That I married a lying, thieving murderer?" Diarmid shoved his fist against Jamie's broad shoulder and knocked him off balance. "That I loved and trusted a woman who viciously betrayed me?" Another shove. "That once again I've let me heart bring ruin to me family?"

"Nay—that ye've got your head up your arse." Jamie grabbed Diarmid's arm. "And if you shove me one more time, I'll break your bloody neck."

Diarmid stared, then one corner of his mouth twitched. "Och, and how do ye reckon to do that, with me head so far up me arse?"

"Listen to me, Diarmid. We've been through hell and back, ye and I. I've never lied to ye nor played ye false—"

"Unlike Lachlan."

"This is no' about Lachlan!" Jamie thundered. " 'Tis about ye. For years I've seen ye eaten alive with bitterness and shame and remorse. Ye've blamed yourself for things that we all played a part in."

Diarmid braced his hands on the marble mantel, leaned forward, and slumped his head between his arms. Och, would he ever escape his past? Would he ever be free? "Ye didna betray your own clan, nor your own brothers. *I* did that. *I* told Catriona—"

" 'Tis over, Diarmid. Can ye no' let it go?"

"Nay, I canna." Diarmid whirled and stormed to the window. "Here—look." He flung open the draperies and flourished an arm at the plantation gardens and the James beyond. The sun had transformed the river to a gleaming gold mirror and sparkled like diamonds on the dew-spangled grass. "I've spent sixteen years breakin' me neck for this place. I lied and tricked a poor old lady who did naught but love me, just so I could get me hands on it. And now 'tis mine, for all the good it will do me—"

His voice broke and he tried to force his usual icy calmness over his fevered emotions. "I did it because I wanted to free the slaves, Jamie."

"Ye what?"

"I thought that would make up for the past. I thought ye'd forgive me if I—"

"Forgive ye?" Jamie's voice was incredulous, his indigo

eyes wide. "There's nothing to forgive, Diarmid, for I've never blamed ye."

"But we lost *Taig Samhraidh*. We lost our cousins and friends and . . . and Uncle Alexander." He buried his face in his hands, too ashamed to go on.

"Diarmid—did I ever tell ye how I met Clemency?" Jamie's voice was low and husky, tinged with affectionate amusement.

"Clemency? What's she to do with this?"

"Everything." Jamie strode over and rested a hand on Diarmid's tense shoulder. "One day I'll tell ye who she really is. For now, suffice it to say that I was a mess 'til I met her. I was eaten alive with hatred and bitterness. I lived for vengeance."

Something surged in Diarmid's blood, something black and burning and corrosive as quicklime. Lucy had played him for a fool. She'd lied and stolen and murdered. He balled his hands into fists so tight his skin tingled. Vengeance was just the thing.

Jamie tapped his arm. "Listen, Diarmid. One day I got my chance to take revenge, and I let it go. I forgave instead."

"I'll never forgive!" Diarmid snarled. "Not Catriona, not Lachlan, and not that Gypsy whore."

"That's not whom you need to forgive. You need to forgive yourself."

Diarmid's jaw twisted, and bands of tension screamed down his shoulders. He was about to bellow at Jamie to piss off when a knock sounded on the door.

"Jamie?" Clemency's English accent floated into the room. "Jamie—tell Diarmid he must come. Venetia's threatening to ride for the sheriff. She said if we don't accuse Lucy of murder, she will."

Jamie and Diarmid exchanged swift glances. "Lucy's your wife," Jamie said, low and urgent. "Somewhere inside that stubborn Scottish heart of yours, ye know she loves you. If she's run off, she had good reason. Ye must go after her."

"Go after her? Are ye mad?" Diarmid's pulse roared in his ears, and he felt as if his veins would burst. He stormed across the room, breath ragged through gritted teeth. His foot struck a bottle. Swift as lightning, he snatched it up and hurled it against the wall. It exploded in a shower of amber glass. "If I go for anyone, I go for the sheriff."

Twenty-four

Chill silver moonbeams slanted through barred windows and traced a distorted checkerboard pattern on the gaol's damp stone floor. Lucy huddled in the corner on a filthy ticking mattress and stared dully at her surroundings. Despite the slimy stone walls, the place wasn't so bad; not compared to Newgate.

The gaol was situated on a Williamsburg side street, and had seemed almost pleasant when she had arrived in shackles earlier in the day, with the sheriff as escort and a silent throng of townspeople as audience. The gaoler had ushered her into this dank, low-ceilinged cell, handed her a dipper of water and a stale biscuit, and then departed, locking the door behind him.

In the hours since, she had cursed her fate a million times, for Old Dame Luck had well and truly abandoned her. Lucy shook her head, still unable to fathom her spectacular fall. The catchpole had charged her not just with stealing Celia's jewels and fleeing with an indentured servant. He had charged her with murder.

She flung herself onto her back. A cloud of dust billowed from the mattress and she sneezed. God's toes, how had she gotten herself into this mess? She had been sure her brains and luck would carry her through anything; she had been positive it would be just a hop and skip to Maryland. Ha! What a fool she'd been.

She choked back a sob and pounded a fist into the mattress. She wasn't just a fool; she was a failure. She had sworn to protect Mick; now he'd been torn from her once more—returned, she presumed, to that madman Ludlow. She had vowed to become a great lady; now everyone in the colony knew she was a convicted thief, and assumed she was a scheming murderer. She had promised to keep her virtue; now she could well be pregnant by a ruthless, lying knave who had abused her heart and her trust.

And that hurt more than the cruelest physical blow Jocko had ever landed.

She raked a trembling hand through her hair, and hot, despairing tears raced down her cheeks. She had sworn she would be free—someday, somehow. Now she lay in this filthy hole, chained like one of Diarmid's field hands. Worst of all, it wasn't just her body that was chained—'twas her heart. No matter how Diarmid had used her, she couldn't run away from the truth: She still loved that aloof, arrogant, infuriating Scot.

The pale, slanting moonlight silvered the mattress, and Lucy listlessly watched it creep across her bare ankles. Her sobs subsided, drained away not by peace of mind but by sheer bodily exhaustion. It must be midnight by now—less than twelve hours until she must stand and face her enemies with her life in the balance. Her lips went dry. Surely they wouldn't hang her—would they? God's heart, she didn't want to die.

Sleep tugged her down into black nothingness, and she rolled on her stomach and buried her head in her arms. She might snivel about ill luck, but death was the worst enemy of all. No one escaped death.

She was dreaming—wasn't she? Oh, please God, let it be a dream. But she felt cold, slimy stones beneath her bare feet, smelled the dank, fetid tang of swirling Thames fog. She was running, running—

Then she heard it. Her guts heaved. The echoing clop, clop, clop of the nag's worn hooves; the thunk and rattle of the wagon wheels over cobblestones. She froze, shuddered, dashed

*forward. No other cart sounded like that. 'Twas the Raker,
come to drag away the dead.*

She was running, running. She had to get there before—

*She rounded the corner. The crumbling black building
seemed to recede, recede. Then she heard it. Her heart
stopped. "Bring out your dead. Bring out your dead."*

Too late. A trailing gray shroud, a pale, stiff hand.

She was running, running. Come back!

*The mist grew thicker, and the air grew cold. The cobble-
stones transmogrified into damp, spectral grass. Then she saw
it. All hope died.*

*Black hole, putrid stench, rotting corpses dumped in a
heap.*

*And her mother, her mother—falling, twisting, crumpling,
naked, cold, dead.*

*Dead. Too late. She screamed, "Give me another chance!"
Her mother's eyes opened. And the dream vanished.*

Lucy scrambled to her feet and clutched a hand to her
throat. Had she screamed? God's teeth, why had she dreamed
that, tonight of all nights? For years she'd buried the memory,
just as the Raker had buried her mother in the porthole. Was
it a sign—her destiny, like Mick's Ace of Swords?

She collapsed onto the mattress, then drew her knees up
to her chin and hid her face against them. Aye, she might be
no better than Agnes, but at last she realized that love didn't
always make a woman weak. She had surrendered to Diarmid
because she loved him—and love had made her strong.

Slowly, she raised her head and jerked up her chin. She
had never doubted that prison would be her end—although
she'd never imagined she'd die on some colonial gallows. She
just wished she'd had the chance to tell her mother she had
forgiven her.

The eerie screech of a fox caught Lucy's attention, and she
glanced out the barred window. The moon had set, and for
the first time all night, she could see the stars. A tremulous

smile touched her lips—for 'twas the North Star shining down on her, shining down with pure, lustrous light.

"Oyer, oyer, oyer! The Quarter Sessions court of the Royal Colony of Virginia is now in session. All be upstanding for Magistrate Lee." The bailiff thumped his truncheon on the courtroom floor, and the crowd rose like cornstalks rustling in the breeze. Lucy jerked up her chin. God's teeth, would she ever manage to stay out of trouble?

Barnabas Lee settled himself in the judge's box. Clearly, Venetia had not inherited her beauty from her father, for Barnabas Lee was short and slightly humpbacked, and although Lucy couldn't see his figure beneath his voluminous black robes, she guessed that he was spindly legged and hollow chested as well. Even his English judge's full-bottomed wig failed to intimidate her, sitting as it did above rabbity eyes and a red nose.

Lee rapped his gavel, and she forced herself to take slow, deep breaths. This little man might look like a fidgety hare, but he was Venetia's father and Celia's brother-in-law. He couldn't be charmed like the judge back in London.

Lee pinned her with a malevolent glare. "Bailiff, read the charges."

The hawk stood and unrolled a document. "Lucy Graves Maclean, you are accused of the following charges, sworn to by warrant and here so presented."

Lucy shifted from foot to foot and firmly blocked out the bailiff's droning voice. What did their accusations matter? They'd tried her and found her guilty the moment Venetia had ripped Lucy's sleeve and revealed the thief's brand on her upper arm. Oh, it wasn't so much that she was a transported convict; in truth, many of the colony's finest families had begun that way, the Lees being a prime example. What had turned Lucy's former friends against her was their embarrassment at being so thoroughly gulled by a thieving Gypsy guttersnipe. After all, if the cream of the Virginia gentry had believed her to be a fine English lady, what did that say about *their* social status?

"Mistress Maclean." Magistrate Lee looked singularly displeased at her inattention. "You have been charged with thievery and the most heinous crime of murder. Both crimes are felonies punishable by death. What say you to these charges?"

She tilted her chin defiantly. "Sir, I am innocent." Lee cast her a glare of disgust and her mind began to race. There was no hope of transport for her crimes, no ship to whisk her away to a new life, as the *Eliza Pratt* had had done less than six months before. All at once something clicked in her mind, and she blinked. There had been only two charges against her. What had happened to the charge for breaking her indenture and fleeing?

Suddenly, the courthouse doors burst open. Lucy spun and saw Jamie and Clemency Maclean standing on the threshold. She cast them a grateful smile; then her stomach lurched as Diarmid appeared behind them. His wintry jade eyes met hers, then slid past without so much as a flicker of recognition. His handsome face was as stiff as frozen granite, and although he stood but a few yards away, he might have been on a distant star, so remote was his expression.

He brushed past his brother and sister-in-law, then strode toward the judge's box. "Magistrate Lee, I must speak with you in private," he said, "for I have information crucial to the settlement of this case."

Lucy shivered. She'd never heard Diarmid's voice so utterly devoid of emotion.

The crowd broke into curious murmurs, and Lee seemed disconcerted. He peevishly pounded his gavel. "The charges against this woman are quite clear, sir—and quite appalling. There is evidence and there is an eyewitness. What can you say that will make a difference in the grievous events that have occurred at the hands of this woman?"

Diarmid reached her side. Lucy's heart gave a dizzying leap, but he stalked past without a glance in her direction, then towered in front of the judge. His broad shoulders tensed, and Lucy realized he wasn't devoid of feeling at all. He was ready to explode.

"What can I say, your honor?" Diarmid's aristocratic voice was glacial. "Simply the truth. This lady is innocent."

"Demme! Step lively, Madam Maclean. Unless you wish to be trampled by outraged ragamuffins, we'd best be off at once!" Harry Cheney all but threw Lucy into his carriage, then vaulted up beside her. Jamie and Clemency jumped in behind him.

Lucy stared at her friends' flushed cheeks and shining eyes. "God's toes," she snapped. "Ye look like sots let loose in a warehouse of ale. What's going on?"

The carriage lurched forward, and Lucy darted a glance at the passing buildings. Why her sudden change of fortune? And where was Diarmid? She bit her lip, and for one weak moment wished he would ride up beside them. Then she jutted her chin. If that cold-hearted Highlander indeed had arranged her release, then his motives were selfish, not chivalrous. And they certainly weren't based on any tender feelings toward her.

She envisioned Diarmid—all wintry eyes and adamantine jaw—storming into the courtroom. Once the crowd had quieted, he had disappeared behind closed doors with Magistrate Lee for what seemed like hours, but what in reality had been only fifteen minutes. When they returned, the magistrate's watery eyes avoided Lucy's, and the red flush on his nose spread like a flood tide across his narrow cheeks. He rapped his gavel.

"Order. Order I say! It appears there has been, um . . . a slight misunderstanding in the charges against Madam Maclean. New, ah . . . evidence has been given which compels me to dismiss this case. Madam Maclean is free to go." The gavel fell.

Before Lucy's brain could process this startling turn of events, Jamie and Clemency had whisked her out the courthouse doors and into Harry's waiting carriage.

Now Harry appraised her through his gold monocle, black eyes mischievous. "Strike me blue, my dear. You look positively ashen! Are you not pleased with your sudden change of luck?"

"Luck?" she said sourly. "Old Dame Luck has deserted me."

Clemency squeezed Lucy's cold hand. "My Granny Amais used to say we make our own luck. 'Faint heart never won the field' was her motto."

"Every fortune-teller believes we make our own destiny," Lucy replied, "but I have a feeling the three of you gave destiny a hand."

"Oh, it wasn't us," Clemency said. " 'Twas Diarmid."

Lucy gave a jaded laugh. "Diarmid—lift a lordly finger to help a Gypsy thief? Ha! With me gone, he and Venetia could marry. After all, he's loved her for years—"

"Where on earth did you get that mad idea?" Clemency paused, then slanted her husband and Harry a knowing glance. "Wait—let me guess. Venetia told you that, didn't she? Holy Mary, Mother of God! Is there no end to the trouble that witch—"

"Easy, *mo cridhe.*" Jamie patted his wife's knee. "The truth's out now."

"But she accused Lucy—"

"And Diarmid's set everything to rights—"

"Will ye both stop!" Lucy clapped her hands to her ears and squinted her eyes shut. "Ye're driving me to drink. Now will someone please tell me what's happened—*and* what they've done with Mick? *Please* tell me they didn't return him to Ludlow."

"My pleasure, madam. Rest assured your little brother is safe. He's at my house, cozening comfits from Patsy. Diarmid insisted the sheriff leave him in our care." Harry slapped his padded thigh. "Stab my vitals, but I wish I'd wagered on *this* little drama. I mean, who would have thought our icy Scottish laird would fall in love?" He threw up his hands and gave a dramatic shrug. "When we made our bet over Lucy here, he just wanted to escape Venetia and get the better of Celia. Of course, there *was* Nimbus—"

Lucy's eyes flew open. "What are you nattering about?"

"Demme, my dear. Didn't Maclean tell you? He married you on a wager with me! That's right—I bet him that even with his lah-dee-dah education, he couldn't turn you into a lady grand enough to win over Celia Stanton Lee. If he did, he'd get Nimbus. . . ."

Harry's drawl droned on like an irritating gnat, but Lucy's shrieking thoughts blocked him out. God's teeth, was there no end to Diarmid's schemes? Oh, curse his hide! And had he married her over a selfish bet, or as part of a vile plot hatched with Venetia?

She knotted her fingers in her skirt and prayed she wouldn't burst into a spate of Romany oaths—or a torrent of tears. Diarmid had lied to her, tricked her, seduced her, and left her. He'd gotten Stanton's Grove, her maidenhead, and—curse his bloody wager!—that damned Nimbus. She'd gotten nothing; not even her freedom.

She felt a strong, warm hand on her forearm and looked up into Jamie's indigo gaze. Her heart gave a tiny flutter. His eyes were so like Diarmid's: wide set and long lashed, with beguiling little laugh lines radiating out from the corners.

He drew a document from his pocket and pressed it into her palm. "Diarmid asked me to give ye this. And dinna listen to Harry's ramblin's, lass. Listen to your heart."

She unfolded the paper, scanned it listlessly, and gasped. Then she read it two more times, slowly and painstakingly. "Jamie . . . is this a joke?"

"Nay, lass. 'Tis real enough." With one tanned finger, he tapped down the corner of the document, then pointed to the bottom. "Pay special attention to the date."

Lucy's stomach heaved. For one horrible moment she thought she might vomit on the tall Highlander's silver-buckled shoes.

The document was her freedom paper, drawn up and witnessed by Captain Obediah Pratt and a justice of the peace, and signed by Diarmid Niall Altan Maclean, Esq. It stated unequivocally that Mistress Lucy Graves was a free woman. It was dated September 25, 1763—her wedding day. She had been free all along.

"Mistress Maclean, are you ill?" Harry's languid drawl had vanished. He snatched up her limp hands and chafed her skin.

"But Venetia showed me a paper just like this," she protested weakly. "She said I was still a bond slave—"

" 'Twas a forgery," Clemency snapped. "That conniving witch got Isaiah Ludlow to pay Captain Pratt for a false document saying that Diarmid still owned you. 'Twas never filed with the county, and Captain Pratt is prepared to swear 'tis worthless." She arched a brow at Jamie. "That took a bit of persuading on Jamie's part, but my charming husband has a way of getting what he wants."

"Then . . . then you mean Diarmid and I truly are married?"

"Aye, lass," Jamie declared. "Ye're every bit as married as Clemency and I."

Lucy turned and gazed out the window. Confusion drifted through her mind like a chill fog, and she shook her head numbly, still unsure what to believe. If the indenture Venetia had showed her was forged, then was Venetia's whole story a lie?

As if reading her thoughts, Jamie said, "I dinna ken what Venetia told ye, lass, but I'd place a wager with Harry that not a whit was true."

"But Venetia and Diarmid were lovers," Lucy said.

"Aye, weel, all men make mistakes." Jamie winked and tossed her a rueful smile. "I ken a bit about trouble-makin' lassies—"

"At least Lydia never accused you of murder," Clemency snapped.

Lucy whirled. "Do you mean to tell me Venetia accused me of killing Celia?"

"Aye, lass. Did ye no' ken?" Jamie seemed genuinely surprised.

"Of course I didn't know! That piss-pot catchpole barged into Harry's crib and dragged me off without so much as a by-your-leave. He said Celia was stiff, and that I'd done her. I tried to explain, but when he eyed the jewels . . . well"— Lucy felt a hot blush swarm over her cheeks—"I wasn't too believable." She curled her hands into fists. "God's teeth! I'll throttle that scheming harpy—"

Jamie chuckled. "Just be glad Diarmid didna believe her."

Lucy's jaw dropped. "He didn't?"

"Nay. Och, he got stone drunk and snorted about a wee bit. Nothin' like wounded pride to make a Scotsman pitch a fit, ye ken. After all, ye had left him, so I canna blame him for fashin'. But when I got done with the stubborn bastard, he saw 'twas his own pride blindin' him to the truth." Jamie gave her a smile of such kindness, she nearly broke into tears. "He kent ye didna do it, lass."

"Then why did that bloody catchpole arrest me?"

"Venetia," Clemency said. "She rode off and accused you before Diarmid could stop her. She claimed to be an eyewitness, so Diarmid needed evidence to prove that you were innocent." Clemency's lips thinned into a cynical smile. "But Miss High-and-Mighty got her comeuppance. It seems there was indeed an eyewitness—or at least an earwitness—who heard you argue with Venetia. This witness also heard you leave."

"Who was it?" Lucy asked.

"Royal. She was setting breakfast in the dining room, right across the hall from Celia's bedchamber. After you left, she heard Venetia talking to Celia. The poor old lady was alive and well then, and she and Venetia got into a huge fight."

Jamie took up the tale. "It seems Venetia didna ken that Celia already had altered her will, leavin' Stanton's Grove to Diarmid. She thought Celia still hadna decided. Since Diarmid had married a convicted thief"—he smiled an apology— "and had tried to trick Celia into belivin' ye were a fine lady, Venetia was sure Celia would cut Diarmid off."

The carriage hit a rut. The passengers clutched at the red-silk seat, then Clemency said, "The fight must have been too much for Celia's weak heart. Royal said the poor old thing suddenly stopped speaking. Venetia called her aunt's name

once or twice in a low, shocked tone, then hustled out of the
room and screamed for help. It took some time for the servants to find Jamie and me—"

Jamie winked. "We were, ah . . . sleepin' late."

"—And by the time we got to Celia's bedchamber, Venetia
must have decided to pin the death on you." Clemency's delicate black brows drew together. "Doubtless she saw the perfect way to be rid of you forever. Mayhap she hoped Diarmid
would come back to her, or mayhap she wanted revenge. Who
knows?"

Lucy wished the carriage would stop lurching. "Did
Venetia confess?"

"Nay," Jamie said. "Royal finally came forward. Seems
Venetia beat her for ruinin' breakfast the next mornin', and
she'd had enough. She said ye'd always been kind to her, and
Miss Venetia was worse than a snake."

Lucy pressed a hand to her flushed cheek. "But I still
don't understand. If Venetia didn't retract her story, why did
her father let me go?"

Harry's black eyes grew merry. "Lud, my dear—Barnabas
Lee may be county magistrate, but I vow he's a drunken fool,
hopelessly in debt. He's lived for years on his connection to
Celia—and on the assumption that his daughter would make
a brilliant marriage. Why, if word got 'round that she'd had
a hand in Madam Lee's death—"

Lucy read Harry's expressively arched brows and began to
smile. "You mean—"

"I do." Harry fluffed his lace cuffs with the preening air
of a peacock. "Your scholarly husband gave the good magistrate a choice. Lee would either dismiss all charges against
you, or Diarmid would accuse Venetia of murder. Oh"—
Harry airily waved a manicured hand—"Venetia would never
be convicted, or even arrested, on the word of a slave. But,
my dear, the rumors alone would ruin any hope of her marrying a rich planter—*and* they would ruin Barnabas's credit
with certain generous merchants."

Lucy's grin grew wider. "But that sounds like blackmail—"

"Demme!" Harry pressed a hand to his chest and dramatically fell back against the seat. "Let us not use such a harsh word, my dear. A tiny bit of leverage, perhaps."

Jamie chuckled. "Och, aye. And leave it to a Scot to draw a wee dram for himself out o' the jug." Harry and Jamie exchanged conspiratorial glances.

Lucy nudged Harry in the ribs. "What are you talking about?"

"My dear—that Highland rogue you married has just struck a blow for his precious cause of freedom." Harry's impish eyes shone with something suspiciously close to genuine admiration. "He's gotten legal consent to free all two hundred of his slaves."

Lucy's brows flew up just as the carriage halted outside the Cheney residence. Harry alighted and helped Clemency down. Jamie followed, then turned to assist Lucy.

He caught her hand in his. "Ye look surprised, lass."

"Aye," Lucy said softly. "I scarce can take it all in." She shot Jamie a questioning glance. "Are you proud of what Diarmid has done?"

"His freein' two hundred enslaved souls? Aye, lass. 'Tis a braw, noble thing. Are *ye* proud of him?"

Lucy couldn't answer. During the carriage ride, a throbbing ache had oozed from the pit of her stomach to her heart, then up into her throat. Now the ache was expanding, choking her until she scarce could breathe. Jamie placed a hand on her waist to help her down, and she clenched her eyes shut, certain that if she didn't, her brother-in-law would see straight into her tortured soul.

All at once, on the black-velvet field of her mind, Lucy saw Diarmid—as real as if it were he who lifted her from the carriage. Her gaze hungrily traced the granite angle of his jaw, and she longed to stroke his lean cheeks and kiss the beguiling little dent in his lower lip. Pure, overwhelming love shimmered through her, and she adored his high, chiseled cheekbones and devilish black brows. She drowned in his changeable eyes—now the gleaming aquamarine of the warm Caribbean, now the chill jade of the stormy North Sea—and yearned to stroke her finger down his elegant, blade-straight nose. God's teeth, how she loved his scholarly glares down that stern nose!

Then he smiled—his quick, dazzling, dimpled smile. Sunlight flashing through thunderclouds. Hope breaking through despair.

"Lucy. Ye're pale, lass. Are ye all right?"

The Highland burr was low and warm, the *r*s rolling like a breaking sea. But it wasn't Diarmid's voice: deep and resonant as an Old Testament prophet's, magical and intoxicating as honeyed Scotch whiskey, sardonic and teasing as a fallen black angel's.

She opened her eyes and met Jamie's gaze. "Listen, lass," he said. "Clemency and I are returnin' to Maine in a few days, and Diarmid asked me to give ye a few things before we go." He reached into the pocket of his elegantly tailored coat, then drew out a pocketbook and a second document.

Puzzled, she took them from him, then tucked the pocketbook under her arm and unrolled the document. 'Twas Mick's freedom paper, signed and dated two days earlier.

Jamie grinned at her gaping mouth. "Diarmid kept his bargain, lass. Your wee brother is free. Diarmid gave Ludlow the Stanton's Grove dock in exchange for him. That's where he went the mornin' poor Celia died. He was filin' the freedom paper with the county magistrate—Lee, as it turns out." Jamie smiled wryly.

The ache in Lucy's throat threatened to scorch through her flesh. She fought for breath, then opened the pocketbook with trembling hands. It was filled with gold coins.

She swayed, and Jamie caught her elbow. "Easy, lass. 'Twas all Diarmid could lay hands on on such short notice. But he wanted to give ye enough so ye could come to Maine with Clemency and me. Or . . . what was it he said, now?"

Clemency had glided up beside them without Lucy noticing. "He said he wanted to give her enough 'to start her fine new life in Maryland, since that's all she ever talks about.' " Clemency mimicked Diarmid's refined British clip with dead-on accuracy.

Lucy's knees buckled. With Jamie's arm guiding her, she

collapsed onto Harry's front steps, and the ache in her throat exploded into tears. Harry made clucking noises, then fled for Patsy. Clemency knelt beside her and patted her hand. Jamie paced back and forth, handsome face as stern as Diarmid's.

After sobbing wildly for several minutes, Lucy dragged in a deep breath and howled, "Damn that black-hearted piss-pot to the hottest rings of hell!"

Jamie halted in his tracks, aghast. Clemency began to chuckle.

"D-don't ye dare laugh!" Lucy cried. She wiped her runny nose on her sleeve, then sobbed louder. "I h-hate him."

Clemency tried to stop giggling. "Holy Mary, Mother of God. If I ever doubted that you love Diarmid, all doubt is now gone."

Lucy shot her a scathing glance, then stabbed a finger at the dropped pocketbook. "Does that varlet want to get r-rid of me this badly?" Suddenly she remembered what Thomas Jefferson had told her: Divorce was illegal in Virginia. "He can't divorce me—"

"Is that what ye think?" Jamie bellowed. Lucy and Clemency gaped at the furious, towering Scot. For one split second, despite his red-gold hair and indigo eyes, Jamie was the image of Diarmid. He planted his fists on his narrow hips and glared down his nose. "Saint Columba, ye bloody wee Sassenach! Me brother is mad in love with ye. He was livid the day ye ran, for he canna bear the thought o' losin' ye."

Lucy gathered her courage. "But he's never said he loves me—"

"Och, good Christ!" Jamie raked a hand through his hair. "I've only seen Diarmid this torn up once before—and that was the day our clan was slaughtered. Even Catriona—curse her bloody traitorous heart—even Catriona never hurt him this much."

Lucy stopped sniveling. "What happened back in Scotland? I know 'twas something awful, but no one will tell—"

"Never mind that," Jamie snapped. "That's for me brother to tell—if the pigheaded pair of ye ever quit squabblin'." He took Lucy's hands. "Believe me, lass. If Diarmid's never said he loves ye, 'tis because he's too stubborn and proud to admit it."

Clemency suddenly leaned forward and kissed her husband's flushed cheek. Jamie blinked owlishly; then they exchanged a smile of pure love.

" 'Tis a family trait," Clemency remarked. She shooed her husband away. "Leave this to me, James Alasdair Ian Maclean. You men just make things worse."

When Jamie had trailed over to stand beside the goggling coachman, Clemency took Lucy's hand and whispered, "I know how you feel, my dear. I tried to run away from Jamie once." She dimpled; then her smile grew distant, as if she was watching a harrowing drama far in the past. " 'Twas like trying to run away from my soul. I learned right then that you can't find happiness—or freedom—by running away. And you know what?" She lifted Lucy's hand to her cheek. "Another person can't give us happiness. We give it to ourselves."

"But how?"

"By forgiving others and by trusting our own heart."

They sat in silence a long moment. Cool blue shadows slanted across the quiet street, and the lowering sun gilded the village green with the glowing gold light peculiar to autumn sunsets. It burnished Jamie's hair to auburn, and Clemency smiled. "Do that, and it's like getting a second chance at life."

Lucy straightened her shoulders and slowly rose to her feet. Then she smiled down at her healer, and said, "Clemency, please take care of Mick 'til I send for him."

Then she caught up her skirts and dashed toward the carriage.

Twenty-five

The front hall of Stanton's Grove was empty, and Lucy's footsteps echoed through the silence as she hurried toward Diarmid's office. She reached the door, then slowly pushed it open and peered into the chamber. Her breath caught, and for one horrible moment she thought she was too late.

The office was a shambles. Books had been pulled from the simple, green-painted bookcases and lay strewn across the plank floor like the last dry leaves of autumn. Three packing crates and a leather trunk stood in the center of the room, the wing chair had been shoved close to the hearth with its high back to the door, and a whirlwind seemed to have struck the papers on Diarmid's desk.

The door creaked mournfully as Lucy stepped into the chaos. One of the tall, bare windows was open, and the evening breeze gusted through it, rustling the papers, then swinging the door shut with a swift, loud bang. Lucy jumped.

"Diarmid?" She crept forward, chilled and trembling, for the sunset had faded and the room was sinking into dismal gray shadows. Diarmid's enormous oak desk sat in front of the long windows, and although the light was dying, Lucy easily could discern the document lying on top of his jumbled papers. The script was elegant, slanted, and bold, but a splatter of ink had all but obliterated the signature.

"Diarmid?" she called again. She glanced down at the document. Suddenly the words leaped out at her. She snatched it up and read with lightning speed, then her breath left her body in a gasp. She slumped against the desk, the paper clutched in her hand.

"God's teeth, I can't believe it!" she cried. "After everything we went through. Oh, that bloody, secretive varlet!" Without thinking, she grabbed the inkbottle and hurled it against the hearth. It exploded in a shower of black glass.

A long, low whistle sounded from the wing chair. "Temper, temper, Lucia. Remember that Rom dignity of yours." Slowly, Diarmid rose from behind the chair's high back. His lean face was as austere as a monk's, his mouth was a stern slash, and only the sardonic arch of his black brows and the glitter of his jade eyes betrayed emotion.

Lucy gasped again, then flew forward. "What is this?" She waved the document under his aristocratic nose. "Why in bloody hell did you put me through this whole ordeal? Just to give Stanton's Grove away? Are you stark, starin' mad?"

Diarmid stepped around her, strolled to the window, and stared out at the darkening woods. "Why do you care, Lucia?" His tone was nonchalant, his accent that of the perfect British patrician. "You've made it clear you've no wish to remain here with me. You've got Mick, you've got your freedom, and you've got enough money to start your fine new life." He spun, and his eyes flashed like emerald fire through the gathering dusk. "So, I repeat, why the hell do you care?"

"I've had enough of this." She threw down the document, darted forward, and jabbed a finger into his broad chest. He wore wickedly snug breeches and tall black riding boots, and his linen shirt lay open to his waist. The dusting of black curls across his sculpted muscles distracted her momentarily, and she gulped, then gazed up into his eyes. A taunting, virile challenge flared in their depths, and she regained her resolve.

"I care because I love you, you arrogant, infuriating rogue! I care because I've spent the last seven weeks playing the lady—curtsying and simpering and even eating oysters!—all so you could get your paws on this bloody plantation. And now you go and deed it over to Jamie!"

She staggered backward and collapsed dramatically into the wing chair. "God Almighty's holy and righteous shinbone! Why would ye do such a thing?"

Diarmid gazed down at her. His handsome face was unfathomable and his wintry eyes studied her with a detachment that unnerved her more than all the thunderous Gaelic oaths the worst Scottish temper could muster. Without taking his eyes from hers, he sat on the floor with his back against the fireplace, then stretched out his wickedly long legs.

"Madam, you say you love me, and that may well be true." He arched a sardonic brow. "Although forgive me if I'm inclined to doubt your veracity. Still, I wonder—will you love me once you hear what happened back in Scotland? Will you love me once you hear what I did to my clan?" His tone was detached, and he seemed to speak to thin air, as if she weren't there at all and he was merely debating an interesting scholarly point.

He steepled his fingers. "Ye see, when I was a young man back on the Isle of Mull, I fell in love with a beautiful woman. Och, I was a dreamy lad then, always in me books, always imagining heroic deeds and courtly love with maidens fair—and me the gallant knight, of course." He gave a husky laugh, then slipped deeper into his beguiling Highland burr. "And when I met Catriona—och, I believed all me dreams had come true.

"Ye never saw a bonnier lass than Catriona Campbell. She could have stepped from an ancient tapestry—the one with the lady feedin' the unicorn. She was all silver-blond, with sapphire eyes and ivory skin and a voice like the murmur of the sea. Saint Iona—to a lad like me, she seemed an angel. But Catriona was no angel"—his jaw hardened and his eyes grew dark—"she was me eldest brother Lachlan's half-English wife."

Diarmid fell silent, and Lucy scarce dared to breath. Outside the windows, the breeze died and the shadows lengthened.

"She was a Campbell," Diarmid said at last. "And the Campbells always allied with the Sassenachs. In the Risin' of 1715, Catriona's family fought for the British. They didna want a Catholic rulin' the kingdom, ye see, even if James Stuart was their rightful sovereign. Lachlan should have remembered that, but I guess he was smitten, too.

"After their weddin', I grew to hate me brother." Diarmid's voice went deathly cold. "I couldna stand the thought of him layin' with the woman I loved—a woman I couldna so much as hope to touch. But their's wasna a happy union, and they were soon at each other's throat. Then word came that Bonnie Prince Charlie was returnin' to the Highlands to raise an army and regain his throne. Catriona's brother, Duncan, threw his support behind German George—ye'd ken him as George the Second. Duncan joined the British army led by the Duke of Cumberland, and he insisted Lachlan do the same. At first, me brother refused . . . and that's when Catriona turned to me."

Jealousy—sharp as daggers and twice as lethal—slashed at Lucy's gut. She wanted to leap up and shriek at Diarmid to stop; she couldn't stand to hear any more. But he had to confess. And she had to listen.

He dropped his head forward and clenched a hand over his brow. "What a fool I was. I was so flattered that me darlin' Cat loved me at last. Och, it started innocently enough. We'd flirt and try to be alone, but before I kent it, we were lovers. She was me first. She overwhelmed me with her passion, and I grew obsessed with pleasin' her.

"By this time, Jamie and I had declared for Charles Stuart, although Lachlan still straddled the fence. I scorned his wafflin'. No real man let his brother-in-law lead him around by the nose. Our Uncle Alexander was already marchin' with our clan chieftain, and Jamie and I pounced on every bit o' news about the prince's movements. And I . . . fool that I was, I unwittingly passed the information along to Catriona every time we made love." He raised haunted eyes, and Lucy was shocked to see tears in their tortured depths. "She was a spy. And I never kent 'til 'twas too late."

He swallowed, then hurried on. "Jamie and I joined up with the prince's army the night before Culloden. 'Twas the Duke o' Cumberland's birthday, ye ken, and the prince thought to surprise him durin' his drunken revelries. Jamie marched off to fight wi' the Maclean clan, while I . . . I lay with Catriona for the verra last time. Och, I imagined meself the conquerin' hero, takin' me love's last kiss into battle. Saint Iona, what a damned fool!"

He buried his face in his hands. "The moment I left to join the prince, Catriona sent a message to her brother. He rode through the sleet that April midnight and informed the Duke of Cumberland of Prince Charlie's plan. The prince ended up changin' his mind and holdin' his attack 'til dawn, but by then 'twas too late. The duke's full forces awaited us. We were doomed from the start. Och, Christ—they outnumbered us by more than four thousand men. 'Twas a slaughter. Jamie and I were wounded, and two thousand Highlanders died that day—includin' me Uncle Alexander and most o' me clan. And 'twas all my fault. Och, Christ. 'Twas all my fault!"

Lucy flew out of the chair and fell to her knees beside him. "But you didn't know. You couldn't have known she was a spy."

Diarmid raised his head, and tears flooded down his cheeks. "But she was me brother's wife. I committed adultery and betrayed me clan—"

"Nay—she betrayed the clan. Diarmid, you were just a lad, and you've more than paid for your unwitting sins. You were wounded, imprisoned, convicted, and banished. You've spent your life helping slaves to freedom. Isn't that enough?"

"Jamie lost his birthright because of me."

All at once, understanding dawned. Lucy leaned back and snatched up the deed. "Is that why you're giving Stanton's Grove to Jamie?"

"Aye. I swore I'd make up for what I'd done. I could think of only two ways to try to put things right—free the slaves and give them the opportunity to work the land for a share of the crop and profits, and give Jamie an estate to make up for what he lost."

Lucy sat back on her heels and studied her husband. His anguished expression quickly regained its usual austere composure, but his blazing eyes devoured her face, as if searching for some sign, some clue, that she still could love a man with such blood on his hands. She returned his gaze calmly, but her mind swirled with strange emotion.

Days ago—nay, hours ago—she would have turned away in scorn at Diarmid's confession. She would have taken it as proof that only the weak and foolish followed their hearts. After all, Agnes had done just that, and look where it had landed her. Lucy's eyes fluttered shut, and she forced herself to relive the memory of her mother's body tumbling into a putrid mass grave. But somehow she couldn't hold the image. It kept melting into a vision of the night sky—endless and velvet-black, strewn with a million diamond stars and a dozen mystical constellations.

All at once, Lucy could have sworn she heard her mother's voice: "See, Lucia—'tis the North Star. That one neither wavers nor varies. 'Tis fixed and unchanging, like Papa's love. Remember that, my heart. You can navigate by it and will never be lost."

Lucy frowned. Years later and half a world away, she still could gaze up at Polaris. It wasn't the brightest in the sky, as some folk thought, and it could be hard to find. But Agnes had been right: It neither varied nor disappeared.

She opened her eyes and found Diarmid's searching gaze still on her. His black brows slammed down in a fierce scowl, and she had to bite her tongue to keep from laughing. He looked every inch the stubborn Scottish bull, head lowered, ready to charge.

A sudden thought occurred to her. "What happened to Lachlan?" she asked.

It seemed impossible for Diarmid's baleful expression to grow blacker, but he managed it. "Forget Lachlan," he rasped. "He's no longer me brother, and ye'll never hear me speak of him again."

Lucy's lips twitched. Really, it was almost perverse how much she adored Diarmid when he was in one of his stormy moods. "Aren't you rather making an assumption that I'll be around to hear you speak at all?" she queried tartly.

His brows flew up; then hard, masculine dimples hovered at the corners of his mouth. "Weel, ye havena stolen me horse and run off to Maryland—at least not yet."

She tilted her chin. "If you think you can get rid of me with a bit of gold—"

Diarmid chuckled. "Och, nay. 'Twould take a lot more than that, I ken."

"Then why did you give it to me?"

"Money means nothing to me." He cast her a wintry smile. Then, for a second, raw, vulnerable need ghosted through his eyes. He blinked and it vanished. "Stanton's Grove means nothing to me."

Lucy brandished the deed and cried, "God's ears, you're driving me to drink! You're obsessed with Stanton's Grove. You've devoted sixteen years of your life to it. You've turned it into the greatest plantation in the colony. You plotted and schemed and made a damned silly bet"—she ground her teeth at the look of amused surprise on his face—"all so you could own the bloody place. 'Tis your life—"

Diarmid grabbed the deed, hurled it across the room, and dragged her against him. The feverish heat of his bare skin seared through the wool of her bodice, and his warm, whiskey-scented breath caressed her cheek, followed instantly by hungry, searching lips.

"You say Stanton's Grove is my life," he rasped. "But what good is my life without my heart?"

He bent her back over his arm, then trailed burning kisses down the angle of her jaw to the pulse that fluttered at the base of her throat. He nibbled at the maddening spot, teasing her until she closed her eyes and prayed for him to take her.

"Och, I love ye, *mo cridhe,*" he murmured, "and I canna live without ye. When ye left me, I went wild with pain.

I wanted to hunt ye down, bring ye to heel, destroy ye. Then I longed to bury meself in ye and beg ye to stay." He raised his head, and she gazed into his eyes—and in their gleaming emerald depths, she saw a love that surpassed even her own. "I gave ye the money and your freedom because I couldna bear to keep ye chained to me, if . . . if ye didna love me."

Lucy pressed a finger to his sensual lips, then struggled from his grasp and sat up. His brows contracted, but before his hurt expression could turn positively murderous, she plunged her hand into her bodice and drew out a folded paper.

"What's that?" he grumbled.

She tore the document in half. "My." *Tear.* "Freedom." *Tear.* "Paper." *Tear.* With a giddy surge of joy, she tossed the pieces aloft, and they fluttered down around their shoulders like swirling snow. "I don't need it, milord, because I'll never leave you."

Diarmid crushed her to his heart and his mouth captured hers. With a tiny cry, she opened to him, and their tongues swirled in a brazen surge of passion. Lucy's heart took flight, and she longed to slip her skin and merge with this man, merge until they were utterly free and completely one. She pressed against him, straining to push her emotions from her own wild heart deep into his.

He cradled her in his arms and eased her back onto the bare planks. The three packing cases shielded them like silent monoliths, and the last thing Lucy noticed before Diarmid's expert tongue melted her into a river of passion was the battered leather trunk.

"What's that?" she asked dreamily as Diarmid fumbled with the ties on her bodice.

"Hush, lass. Ye chatter too much." The ties came loose, and he peeled her bodice from her shoulders and bosom. He growled appreciatively, then lowered his mouth to her breast. Instantly, she gasped and arched against him. Goose bumps sizzled across her flesh, and her nipples peaked into tingling points. Sensing the urgency of her need, he cupped her breasts in skilled hands and began a deep, caressing motion.

She raked her hands down the rippling muscles of his back, then tugged his shirt over his head. He reared back and fumbled with the buckle of his wide leather belt, and she giggled at the sight of the huge bulge straining against his breeches. Her laughter ceased when he shoved the garment down and his lusty manhood jutted free. He leaned forward, biceps bulging, and kissed her until she was limp, breathless, and passion drugged. Then he skinned off his breeches and rucked her skirts up about her waist.

"Aren't ye going to undress me, your highness?"

He trailed teasing fingers up the inside of her thigh. "I said hush." His hand brushed over the crisp curls covering her womanhood, and she restively wriggled her hips. Then he rubbed down over her, palm tight and hard against her public bone. The pressure caressed her woman's nub and paralyzing arrows of ecstasy shot through her veins. She twisted her head and moaned. Then she wasn't paralyzed at all; her hips lifted and ground against Diarmid's hand, and her arms tugged his head toward her breasts.

"Please . . . please," she whimpered.

His mouth clamped over her aching nipple; then his deft fingers unfurled her, stroked her, and eased into her soaking heat. She cried aloud and raked her hands through his gleaming ebony hair—tugging, pulling, desperate to gain relief from the maddening sensations his hands and lips provoked. He eased a second finger into her. She moaned, whimpered, cried out. He angled his hand, concentrating his tantalizing friction on her woman's nub, then slowly thrust into her.

She teetered at the very brink of ecstasy; then he gently withdrew his fingers. "Don't stop," she pleaded frantically. Her hands caught the delicious taut curve of his buttocks and she urged him over her. He mounted her, then stared down into her eyes.

"Say ye'll never leave me again, *mo cridhe.*"

"Are you . . . mad?" Her breath came in desperate little pants. "Never."

His lips closed over hers—swift, savage, hungry. His tongue stabbed into her mouth, and she felt the velvety head of his erection slide into her womanhood. He groaned and hovered there until she begged for more.

Instead of plunging home and mercifully relieving her wanton need, he leaned forward, and with deep concentration, slid the burning length of his shaft between her clinging lips, never leaving her flesh, yet never entering her fully.

"Diarmid, now . . . please," she gasped.

He cupped his hands around her face, plunged his tongue into her mouth, and thrust home with one swift surge. Lucy cried out, half in delicious pain, half in savage lust. Diarmid bent and served her with intense concentration. He kissed her with melting sensuality and teased her with slow, languorous strokes. Waves of pleasure rippled through her womanhood, out through her boneless legs and into the tips of her toes.

"Now," she wailed, bucking her hips against him.

His thrusts deepened, then deepened again. She was so close, so close. Her nipples smoldered; she was burning alive, consumed with lust, yet unable to reach utter conflagration. Finally, crazed with lust, she wrenched her mouth from Diarmid's and sank her teeth into his shoulder. He gave a low groan, then hammered into her, all restraint vanished, all teasing gone. Her legs tensed, her back arched, and a shaft of liquid fire shot through her. Her body froze; then she convulsed on storm-tossed waves of ecstasy. Diarmid rode her, deep and hard, until she quieted.

"I love ye, *mo cridhe*," he moaned. The he lowered his head and thrust with the shallow, lightning strokes of approaching climax. He cried aloud, then shuddered and collapsed in her arms.

Hot, joyous tears coursed down Lucy's cheeks. She nuzzled Diarmid's angular jaw and reveled in the musky scent of his body, then pressed openmouthed kisses on his damp, salty shoulder. She had found her Polaris, and she would never be lost again.

Lucy shook off the wanton languor that had lulled her to sleep in Diarmid's powerful arms and realized with a jolt of panic that the office was completely black. Worse, Diarmid no longer lay beside her on the cold wood floor. She sat up. Her hips and shoulders ached like the devil, and her neck had stiffened into immobility. She rubbed it and glanced around the room, ears straining for any sound.

The door creaked open. Lucy's heart leaped into her throat, and she scrabbled in the darkness for her bodice and skirts, which Diarmid had flung over the top of a packing crate. A wavering shaft of yellow light slipped through the doorway, followed immediately by a single flickering candle clasped in Diarmid's tanned hand.

Even through the inky shadows, her panic must have shown on her face, for Diarmid flashed her his dimpled smile. "Did ye think I'd left ye, *mo cridhe?* Or were ye just plannin' to steal me silver spoons?" His Highland burr was gruff with affection.

Lucy took this as a good sign. She snatched up her shift and yanked it over her head. "God's ears, you scared me. I thought it might be one of the servants, barging in and catching me stark naked." Diarmid, she noted sourly, was completely dressed and looked as elegant and unruffled as ever.

He crossed to where she stood, then bent and kissed her. His lips were tender, expert, seductive, and she melted against him. "You did scare me," she confessed. She stepped back and gestured at the crates and trunk. "Obviously you were packing to leave, so I thought . . ." She didn't dare finish the sentence.

He nodded. "I am packing. When ye ran off I decided I'd do the same thing. If ye were goin' to start a fine new life in Maryland . . . weel, I made up my mind to disappear over the mountains into Kentucky."

She swallowed. "Did . . . do you want me to go with you? I don't know much about Kentucky, and I've never seen any mountains—"

Diarmid's tanned skin crinkled around his eyes. He set the candle on a crate and playfully pressed a finger to her lips. "Hush, lass. Have I not told ye ye chatter too much? Of course I wanted ye to go with me. The wilderness would be much too quiet—and safe, and dull—without ye."

Lucy frowned. "You just said you *wanted* me to go. Do you still want me to?

Diarmid sadly shook his head. "Nay, lass, I'm afraid ye canna go." He paused for a long, tense moment, then broke into a dazzling smile. "And I'm not goin' either. Me pigheaded brother refused to take Stanton's Grove. He said he'd more than enough to contend with, owning a fleet of ships and the biggest sawmill and the finest stand of timber in the Province of Maine. He said he's not the laird for Stanton's Grove—I am."

Diarmid grabbed her hands, twirled her around, and danced her in a circle. Then he swept her a courtly bow. "Madam Maclean, do allow me the honor of congratulating you on your splendid good fortune, for you are now the mistress of the greatest plantation on the James. You, my dear madam, are a very great lady." His Highland burr had softened to an aristocratic drawl, and he bent and kissed her hand. Suddenly, his elven expression grew solemn and bittersweet. "But then, you always have been."

Tears sprang to Lucy's eyes. She fanned herself weakly and cast Diarmid a tremulous smile. God's heart, how she loved this man! She'd traipse to the very ends of the earth with him and live among the naked savages if he wanted to. She grinned and wound her arms around his waist. But, thank God and Old Dame Luck, he didn't!

Diarmid stepped back, bent, and opened the leather trunk. He rummaged around for a moment, then drew out a small object and rubbed it against his shirt as if to polish it.

"What's that?" she asked. He held it up, and she caught the glint of candlelight on engraved silver. 'Twas a small, round brooch. "I've seen that before, haven't I?" She closed her eyes and tried to remember. " 'Twas the night of the ball. You wore it pinned to that swath of tartan over your chest."

He cast a dry look down his blade-straight nose. " 'Twas on me plaid, lass—not on 'that swath of tartan.' " Chuckling, he leaned forward and pinned the brooch to the gauzy fabric of her shift. His fingers felt like living fire against her skin. "There. Now ye're a real Maclean." Pensively, he traced the brooch's inscription.

She tried to read it in the flickering candlelight. "What does it say?"

"Virtue Mine Honor." His voice was grave, and he tenderly smiled deep into her eyes. "And I canna think of a motto more fittin' for ye, *mo cridhe.*"

She blinked rapidly, determined not to cry. A few tears slipped down her cheeks, and Diarmid crushed her to his chest, then smoothed his hand down over her tousled curls. "Och, me darlin', darlin' heart. Ye'll never ken how much I love ye."

They stood wrapped in each other's arms until Lucy gained control of her sniffling. Then she fixed Diarmid with a skeptical eye. "Tell me the truth, Diarmid Niall Altan Maclean. The *real* truth, not one of your beguilements. Are we really, truly married?"

Diarmid's lips quirked, but he kept his expression grave. "Aye, lass. We really, truly are. And ye ken somethin' else? Divorce is illegal in Virginia."

She smothered a smile, then conjured up a look of naïve surprise. "Is that right?"

"Aye." He cocked his head and half turned. "Do ye hear that sound, lass?"

She listened and heard drums: wild, primitive drums that set her blood surging and her feet aching to stamp and twirl in the forbidden *flamenco.* She slanted Diarmid a puzzled glance. "What could it be?"

He grabbed up her skirt and bodice. "Get dressed and I'll show ye."

Within minutes they were hurrying down the front steps of Stanton's Grove, with Lucy's hand tucked securely under Diarmid's strong arm. The night was as black as a raven's wing, but the stars offered a glimmering haze of light to guide them. The music grew louder, and Lucy shivered. She'd never heard such a primal sound, at least not since her childhood days with the Rom. They strode through the cold, damp grass, then threaded their way through the grove of oaks beyond the stables. Suddenly, Lucy realized they were hurrying toward the slave quarters. Light glowed ahead of them through the bare trees, then they broke into the clearing. Lucy halted.

A huge bonfire leaped and crackled on the packed dirt. Half a hundred of the freed Stanton's Grove slaves stood in a ring around the fire, and behind them, towering oaks spread their sheltering limbs over neat rows of weathered wooden cabins. The Africans saw Lucy and Diarmid. A great shout went up, and those closest to the fire began a strange, primitive dance.

Lucy watched, enthralled, as bare, callused feet stamped, jumped, and whirled. The drumbeats intensified, and the former slaves began to sing a low, rhythmic chant that sent shivers down her spine. Firelight gleamed on sweating black faces, and eerie orange-and-gold shadows writhed and gyred up into the trees.

Suddenly Mercury broke from the line of dancers and loped toward Lucy and Diarmid. He bowed, then broke into a grin.

"Mr. Diarmid—Miss Lucy. We got everything ready for you." He gestured toward the fire, where two field hands held a broom handle a few feet from the flames. "And we all wants to thank you. There's not a soul in the world woulda done what you did, Mr. Diarmid—freein' us and givin' us a chance to earn a livin' with some pride and dignity." Mercury halted, as if surprised at his impromptu speech, then gestured them forward. "That's all. Jus' thank you, and please accept our best wishes for your weddin'."

Lucy wheeled on Diarmid. "I thought you said we already were married!"

Diarmid hooked an arm around her waist and ushered her toward the fire. "We are. But ye seemed so anxious on the point that I decided to arrange a wee surprise."

By now the Africans were clapping and singing loudly and jubilantly. Women grinned and winked at Lucy, men rolled their eyes and laughed, and dozens of squealing children darted about, enchanted by the flames and the music and the excitement in the air. The two field hands lowered the broom until it was about two feet off the ground.

"We be ready, Mr. Diarmid," Mercury called.

Lucy scanned Diarmid's mischievous face. "God's feet, what's going on?"

He laughed, then bent and kissed her deeply. The Africans clapped and cheered. "We're jumping the broom, *mo cridhe*. 'Tis the slave wedding ceremony. 'Tis illegal for slaves to marry, ye ken, so this is the ritual they perform for themselves. 'Tis based on ancient African traditions. Knowing your penchant for wild, forbidden dances"—his aquamarine eyes sparkled like elven jewels in the firelight—"I thought ye might like it."

"Like it?" She whirled and stared at the crackling fire, the dancing Africans, the laughing children. She felt the chill night breeze trail through her hair like spirit fingers, and she heard the tree branches creak and sigh, as if they suddenly had come to life. Excitement surged in her veins, savage and free, like the wild leaping shadows and the endless black night. She ran to the fire, flung her hands high above her head, then whirled in a circle. "Like it? Diarmid Niall Altan Maclean—I *love* it."

Laughing aloud, white teeth glinting like a seductive demon's, Diarmid strode toward her. He caught her hand, spun her to face the broom, and flashed a wicked grin. "That jump looks a wee mite high, Lucia."

"I can make it."

"Last chance to be free, my queen."

"I am free, milord."

Their eyes met and locked. Then Diarmid nodded, and they dashed forward. Lucy felt as if she were flying—hurtling through air and space and time on endless wings of joy. Then she jumped. Her heart gave a wild lunge and she felt herself rising up in one long surge of strength and love and passion.

They landed together, inches from the fire, still laughing like prime lunatics. Diarmid swept her into his arms and whisked her off her feet. As the dancing, clapping Africans cheered their approval, he kissed her, long and hard. Then he brushed his lips against her ear and whispered: "Now, Madam Lucia Gravesceu Maclean—*now* we can start that fine new life. Together."

If you liked AUTUMN'S FLAME, be sure to look for Lynne Hayworth's next release in the Clan Maclean series, WINTER FIRE, available in October 2001 wherever books are sold.

His brothers banished to the Colonies, his own clan turned against him, Lachlan Maclean paid a devastating price for his wife's madness when she blackmailed him into fighting for the English. Now he is laird in name only—and a man haunted by the ghosts of his past. Then Fiona Fraser Maclean returns from France on a secret mission that could alter his life forever, and for the first time in years, Lachlan feels the flame of passion. . . .

Put a Little Romance in Your Life With
Hannah Howell

Put a Little Romance in Your Life With
Betina Krahn

Celebrate Romance With Two of Today's Hottest Authors

Meagan McKinney

__In the Dark	$6.99US/$8.99CAN	0-8217-6341-5
__The Fortune Hunter	$6.50US/$8.00CAN	0-8217-6037-8
__Gentle from the Night	$5.99US/$7.50CAN	0-8217-5803-9
__A Man to Slay Dragons	$5.99US/$6.99CAN	0-8217-5345-2
__My Wicked Enchantress	$5.99US/$7.50CAN	0-8217-5661-3
__No Choice But Surrender	$5.99US/$7.50CAN	0-8217-5859-4

Meryl Sawyer

__Thunder Island	$6.99US/$8.99CAN	0-8217-6378-4
__Half Moon Bay	$6.50US/$8.00CAN	0-8217-6144-7
__The Hideaway	$5.99US/$7.50CAN	0-8217-5780-6
__Tempting Fate	$6.50US/$8.00CAN	0-8217-5858-6
__Unforgettable	$6.50US/$8.00CAN	0-8217-5564-1

Call toll free **1-888-345-BOOK** to order by phone, use this coupon to order by mail, or order online at www.kensingtonbooks.com.

Name _____

Address _____

City _____ State _____ Zip _____

Please send me the books I have checked above.

I am enclosing	$_____
Plus postage and handling*	$_____
Sales tax (in New York and Tennessee only)	$_____
Total amount enclosed	$_____

*Add $2.50 for the first book and $.50 for each additional book.

Send check or money order (no cash or CODs) to:

Kensington Publishing Corp., Dept. C.O., 850 Third Avenue, New York, NY 10022

Prices and numbers subject to change without notice.

All orders subject to availability.

Visit our website at **www.kensingtonbooks.com**.